D0887518

FINCH MERLIN AND THE FOUNT OF YOUTH

Harley Merlin 10

BELLA FORREST

Copyright © 2019

Nightlight Press

All rights reserved.

No part of this book may be reproduced in any form or by any electronic or mechanical means, including information storage and retrieval systems, without written permission from the author, except for the use of brief quotations in a book review.

ONE

Finch

—————

Well, *wearing black was a bad choice.* I'd been going for ninja vibes and now I was paying the price—baking in the Cuban sun, my T-shirt sticking to me like a slug on a window.

Smearing my sweat even further across my face with the back of my forearm, I paused beside the edge of a nearby wall and peered around it. This was my version of incognito sneaking, though I did have some cloaking magic at my disposal to make it easier.

Morro Castle was beautiful, all sandstone and cannons and fortifications that looked like they'd come right out of a George R.R. Martin novel. No dragons, though, unfortunately. Even though I'd seen an impressive array of creatures in Tobe the Beast Master's massive Bestiary, I still hadn't seen a dragon. Disappointing didn't even cover it.

Catching my breath, I looked over the nearest wall. The ocean crashed against the rock promontory below, on which this whole fortress had been built. Taking a dip in the chilly water would've been a mercy right about now—I didn't understand how there could be any sweat left in my body.

"Morro" sounded so very mystical and exotic to dumb foreigners like me, but the funny thing was, it just meant "rock." Rock Castle. Not very inventive, really. Still, it was crazy beautiful, standing alone on this outcrop where it had defended Havana against the British. Not that it had done a very good job. Those sneaky Brits had slipped in anyway.

I know of another slippery Brit I could mention. Davin Doncaster, the Necromancer and slime-ball extraordinaire who'd been a major pain in our asses during the Katherine campaign. He was still off the radar.

But that wasn't why I was here. And this place was just a tourist destination now, diminished to nothing more than an opportunity for vacation photos in front of a cannon.

Why did I never get to just enjoy these exotic places? Why didn't I ever get to pause and take selfies? Nope, this was no vacation, and sneaking through the narrow, boiling-hot paths of this fortress wasn't exactly my idea of a lazy Sunday.

I'd spent the past year doing insane errands for Erebus, the Prince of Darkness—my constant, irritating shadow. It was the price I'd paid for killing Katherine, but the debt was starting to wear thin.

I mean, how many more errands could Erebus possibly have left? Sometimes, I got the feeling he was just messing with me. Asking me to fetch the Easter Bunny had definitely been a joke at my expense. As it turned out, when I'd reached Easter Island, what he'd actually meant was a sacred jade rabbit that had been hidden there by Chinese magicals way back when. *What's next—the Tooth Fairy? Santa Claus? Meryl Streep?*

I had to keep telling myself that it was actually a pretty small price to pay. He could've asked for my life, or my sister's life, or one of my friends' lives. He liked death deals more than anything, and he had a weird fetish for making exchanges. So I supposed I should've been thanking my lucky stars, but there was only so much thanking a guy could do when he was hightailing it around the globe in search of a million bizarre wish-list items.

At least the magical world had recovered pretty well after my mother's demise, so I couldn't complain there. We had good leaders and a decent new setup, which seemed to be lasting. Our world was definitely in a better state than it had been pre-Katherine. That was how we defined time now—post-Katherine and pre-Katherine.

Magicals were still a secret to humans, which meant the biggest danger had been averted. If the humans had found out, it would've just caused more unrest, and nobody wanted that. In their eyes, we would have become a powerful threat that would need to be stopped, and they would've come up with some military tool to detect us all, like in the *X-Men* comics. Nukes, advanced weaponry, special cells, the whole shebang. I've said it before and I'll say it again—folks could learn a lot from comic books.

Seeing that the coast was clear, I hurried along the narrow path leading toward the lighthouse—the tip of the fortress, so to speak. Since I was armed with my cloaking magic and a bunch of knockout powders, this was finally going to go my way.

After a year's worth of in-depth research, and a whole bunch of antihistamines to stop my allergies from going crazy while digging through all those dusty tomes, I'd found out that this fortress was the resting place of Ponce de León's spirit. Now, most people thought he had been buried in San Juan Bautista Cathedral in San Juan, Puerto Rico, but those people hadn't endured sneezing fits and watering eyes after devouring book after book on the subject. They also hadn't endured going to San Juan and finding out they were wrong, the hard way. It was just one of many lies surrounding the conquistador's life and death.

"Conquistador" is a great word. Finch the Conquistador. Maybe one day, when I'd conquistador-ed my way out of my deal with Erebus.

This wasn't the first time I'd broken into a famous monument. San Juan Bautista Cathedral hadn't even been my first, and this wasn't the first time I'd broken into Morro Castle, either. I'd tried it five times. That's right, *five.* But I'd only gotten myself arrested once, so I was going to chalk that up as a win.

Those previous attempts hadn't been failures, though—they'd given me the opportunity to fully understand the layout of this labyrinth. How the British had done it on their first try, I wished I'd known. I supposed I had to give them props for that.

After my last attempt, now broke thanks to paying my bail, I'd realized there was one place I hadn't checked out—the very lighthouse I was edging toward, slow and steady, like the proverbial tortoise. It was the only place left to search through, which meant it had to be hiding what I was looking for.

Mr. Conquistador himself.

I rounded another corner, where the path opened out. Sand covered the ground, leading to a wall on my left and a Spanish-style chunk of the castle to my right. The lighthouse rose up ahead, like a proud…well, lighthouse. Now, why wasn't I doing this in the dark? A good question. I'd tried that, and it hadn't worked. This way, if anyone caught me creeping around, I could just pretend I was an idiotic tourist who'd somehow gone somewhere they weren't supposed to. But I hoped the cloaking magic would spare me that embarrassment.

I needed to get past the security guards to reach the lighthouse. The cloaking magic covered me visually, but if I touched anyone, they would feel it.

Heading back the way I'd come, I almost barreled into a pair of guards doing their rounds. I pressed against the wall again and waited for them to pass. They were almost clear when one brushed a hand right across my abdomen. I froze. He paused, too, looking around.

"Did you hear something?" he asked.

Crap.

I darted along the wall behind them until I reached an open expanse of path with no tourists or guards in sight. Turning, I sketched a doorway on the wall and whispered, *"Aperi Si Ostium."* The edges of the door fizzed and cracked, causing way too much of a scene. However, I'd started the process now, and no guards had caught up with me yet. As soon as the lines sank into the wall, forming a three-dimensional indent, I pushed it open and rushed through, slamming the door shut behind me.

Unfortunately, I'd misjudged the location of the far side of the lighthouse. I stepped through the doorway into air. The ocean crashed below, waves frothing up like jaws ready to devour me.

Dammit! I went into freefall, plummeting to a watery landing. Could I have been cool about it? Sure. Was I? No. I flailed frantically as the water rushed up to meet me.

Fortunately, I hadn't just spent the past year traipsing around completing Erebus's whims and fancies. Oh no. I'd also spent it sprucing up my newfound Elemental abilities, which had been in full force since Erebus had snapped my Dempsey Suppressor to smithereens. So I guess he had some uses.

Sending out a wave of Air with my hands, I created a cushion beneath me. It caught me like a pillowy cloud when I was just shy of hitting the water. *Ah, this is what it must feel like to be an angel.* I recovered quickly, forging another pillow of Air that I could jump to in order to get myself back to the edge of the promontory.

There, I ducked behind the fortification. I was crouched on the roof of what had once been part of the fort—a little house-like building that had now been reduced to a toilet for seagulls. And almost for me, after that little shocker. As my pulse returned to normal, I peered over the lip of the wall. The guards were standing right in front of the lighthouse door, chattering to each other in Spanish. I rolled my eyes. Couldn't they have picked a better place?

I sat down on the roof and tried to unstick my shirt from my skin as I waited for the guards to move. After all, I couldn't mess this up again. There was a pesky proviso in the deal I had with Erebus: no failures. I could die attempting a mission, sure—Erebus didn't give a hoot about that. But failure? Nope, not acceptable.

Still, I'd been using my time wisely. Since my end of the bargain showed no signs of arriving, I'd realized about six months in that I needed to start looking into ways of freeing myself. Loopholes, spells, hexes, even the viability of faking my own death. I hadn't found anything useful yet, though I'd read a *lot* of good stuff about the scammers of this world. Devious wives, spiteful husbands, psychotic parents—all the juicy, true-crime before-bedtime sort of stuff. I'd thought I'd known everything there was to know about psychotic mothers, but the Internet had proven me wrong.

Anyway, nothing useful had turned up. I wasn't trying to get away with murder or an insurance payout. I just wanted to be free of these shackles. I'd thought about asking Lux if she could help me, but I was still working up the courage. She and Erebus came as a pair. A bad pair, like two sour grapes on a vine. They made Antony and Cleopatra look like pussycats, and the War of the Roses look like a petty squabble. Love and hate times a million.

The frustrating thing was, you never knew which one was going to come out when they were together. I'd lost count of the times I'd had to duck as one chucked half a mountain at the other. I'd also lost count of the times I'd had to cough in an oh-so-over-the-top way to stop them from tonguing each other's faces off while I was standing right there! This was all the more impressive considering they didn't have real tongues. At first, it'd been a hell of a shock to see that side of things, since I'd presumed they were siblings. But, apparently, it wasn't literal. They were Chaos's kiddos, yes, but not actually related.

Pushing away the horrible memory, I looked back over the wall. *Yes!* The guards had moved on, giving me a direct line to the door of the lighthouse. I vaulted myself over the wall, checked to make sure nobody was watching, and sidled up to the wooden door. I smirked at a man standing in front of a nearby cannon while his girlfriend snapped a photo. *Attaboy.*

Pressing my hand to the lock, I fed a blast of Air through it. My new quartet of Elemental abilities definitely had some benefits. Well, my powers weren't so new anymore, but I was still getting used to them. It was hard to break the habits I'd learned over a lifetime.

The door lock mechanism clicked as Air pushed the teeth upward. Slipping into the lighthouse, I ran up the winding staircase.

Halfway up, I paused to drag in a breath. I might've been running around the world for a year, but I really needed to hit the treadmill. Using the spare moment, I took out the amulet I'd brought with me. The cops had given me a thorough pat-down during my last attempt at this, and even they hadn't found it. *Though nobody needs to know why.* Fortunately, I was back to using a conventional pocket to stow this thing away.

The amulet was a legitimate Eye of Horus, stolen about a month ago from Luxor by a tomb raider. That tomb raider had been me, minus the leg straps, pistols, tiny shorts, and curve-hugging tank top of the video game version. I only went after this amulet because Erebus had told me I'd have to actually speak to the Ponce. Naturally, that was all he'd given me. I'd asked for a little help in learning to use it, and he'd shrugged and told me to figure it out. Sweet of him to be so caring.

An amber bead lay where the Eye's pupil should've been. It was supposed to glow yellow in the presence of a spirit. I'd tested the theory in a couple of cemeteries with the help of Tatyana—the San Diego Coven's resident spirit whisperer—but whether Ponce de León would bite or not was yet to be seen.

I needed the amulet to speak with his spirit about the location of the Fountain of Youth. No idea what Erebus wanted that for, since the dude was already immortal.

Also, apparently this meant the Fountain of Youth was a real thing. Who knew, right? I was still wrapping my head around it. Next, he'd be sending me on a wild goose chase to the Isle of Avalon to have a chat with King Arthur, then sending me swimming in some lake to bring back Excalibur. Just to really bring that Merlin dynasty home.

I froze as I heard voices drifting down from a platform above my head. They didn't sound like spirits. No, it sounded like two jackasses egging each other on.

"Go on, I dare you," one guard said. My Spanish was muddy at best, but Santana had given me a crash course prior to this little jaunt.

"You go, if you're that worried," the second replied.

"No way, man! Everyone knows there's a spirit up there."

"So? It's daylight. Spirits don't come out in daylight."

"Who says? My mother saw one once, at, like, two o'clock in the afternoon."

"You sure she wasn't drunk?"

"Hey, you watch your mouth!"

"You brought it up. And I'm not going up there, so stuff it."

I glanced back down at the amulet. It was flashing yellow.

TWO

Finch

The amulet's glow intensified as I moved up the stairs. I paused on the platform where the guards were still egging each other on. It was too narrow for me to just slip past them. I watched for a moment, and then an idea popped into my head.

Edging forward, I held my breath and reached up. My fingertips tickled the back of the first guard's neck. He whirled around, and I ducked out of the way.

"Stop messing around," he muttered to his colleague.

"What are you talking about?" the other answered, looking annoyed.

"You're trying to freak me out, just because I said you weren't brave enough to go up there." He pointed to the top of the lighthouse.

My end goal.

"I didn't do anything," the other guard protested. I crept forward again and poked the nearest guy in the spine. He spun around again.

"Quit it!" he yelped.

"Quit what?" the second dude replied.

"Okay, that's it. I'm getting out of here. I don't care if you think I'm a coward. I'm not staying in this place."

He didn't wait for his colleague to answer. Brushing right by me, he jogged down the stairs, leaving the other guard with no choice but to follow. I pressed myself against the curved wall as he went by. I waited a few moments longer until I heard the light-house door open and close.

Nothing a little haunting can't fix. I chuckled, giving myself a moment to enjoy my triumph. Getting rid of the guards had been surprisingly easy, but the rest of my task wasn't going to be. Craning my neck to look at the top of the lighthouse, I shuddered. The amulet was glowing like a beacon and getting hot in my hand. That couldn't be good.

Why couldn't it have been an artifact-finding mission? Artifacts were easy. Some digging here and there, maybe a bit of thievery, and the job was done. Spirits were crafty, and I didn't like them one bit.

Steeling myself, I made my way up the rickety stairs. With every step, the amulet glowed brighter. I wished I could've been back at the SDC, learning more about the ins and outs of my newfound abilities. Things were pretty much peaceful there. No dramas, no ghosts, no missions... just plain old coven life. Even when jobs came up, they were nothing compared to Erebus's endless list of tasks. Man, I envied Harley and the Muppet Babies.

This was the price. You know that. Right on time, my brain swept in with a sharp reminder. I'd taken my pills that morning, but sometimes my brain liked to chatter away of its own accord.

I reached the last landing, where a wooden ladder disappeared into a dark hole above. *What could possibly go wrong?* Crumbly ladder, pitch-black trapdoor, a twenty-foot drop to the ground below, and Ponce de León shivering everyone's timbers at the top.

Bad, good, scary, angry—it was anyone's guess what kind of spirit I'd be facing.

Taking a deep breath, I gripped the middle rung of the ladder and started to climb.

Eventually, I emerged from the trapdoor, grateful not to have plummeted to my death. The lantern room curved around me, with uninterrupted windows on all sides and a huge bulb in the center. As it was daylight, the lantern wasn't lit to warn ships, but the room gave one hell of an ocean view.

The waves churned and seagulls wheeled, and I could see ships in the distance, big ones, small ones, all kinds. I was about to step forward to get a better look when a shadow made me freeze. Someone stood on the other side of the lantern, looking out at the sea.

The figure wore a cloaked hood of some kind. They seemed to suck all the light out of the room. It should have been glaringly bright, with the sun shining down. But it wasn't.

I looked down at the amulet. It was so bright now that I couldn't look at it without risking my retinas. *Yep, I'm definitely dealing with a spirit.* I lifted the amulet toward the hooded figure, and the amber stone vibrated in my hand.

I cleared my throat. "Am I in the presence of Juan Ponce de León?" At least I didn't have to worry about trying to speak in broken Spanish to this guy. From my research, spirits were beyond the limits of languages—they could understand and converse in any tongue.

I figured it was best to get straight to the point. This had to be a super-powerful kind of spirit if I, a meager non-Kolduny, could see it with my bare eyes.

"Hello? Mr. Ponce de León?" I spoke again, since the shadow didn't seem very chatty. "Or do you prefer Juan? Mr. Juan? How about 'Conquistador?' Just so I know." I took a step closer and saw a waxy sheen of gray skin underneath the hood. The fabric covered half of his face, but I could make out a pale mouth. *Suitably ghoulish.*

I waited, but he didn't say a word. "See, the thing is, I was hoping you could help me out with something. I'm looking for the Fountain of Youth. I bet you're tired of hearing that, huh?"

I gave a nervous laugh. "I mean, that's quite a legacy, right? The man who found the Fountain of Youth. It's better than 'Pie-Eating Champion 2010,' anyway. Sorry, I babble when I'm excited. You're a legend, sir. You pretty much invented Florida, you explored the Caribbean, you governed Puerto Rico, and you're one of the most famous explorers of all time. You're a heck of a guy, Mr. Ponce de León, even without the Fountain of Youth stuff. But, unfortunately, I *am* here for the Fountain of Youth stuff. Erebus sent me to speak to you. He wants to gain some intel from you, via me."

I stopped again. The spirit had to be ready to answer me now that I'd just jabbered my way through an introduction like Mr. Bean on steroids... right? Plus, I'd dropped the big name, and that usually got folks talking. But the shadowy figure just stood there, staring out at the sea.

A spark of anxiety shot through me. I was getting a *very* bad feeling about this. Had I missed something important? Was I supposed to collect something else before I came here? A gift, or an offering, or something? Erebus hadn't said anything about it, but then, he wouldn't have. I tried to think back just in case, but the only thing on my to-get list had been this amulet.

"Can you hear me, Mr. Ponce de León?"

I held my breath as he turned. A ghastly face appeared under the hood—skeletal and drawn, with sunken cheeks and hollowed eyes. He opened his mouth, as if he was finally going to say something, only his mouth kept getting wider and wider, unnaturally wide, as if he were made of putty. The long sleeves of the cloak billowed out.

His entire being expanded like a swelling cloud. I stared as his gray skin morphed into a tempest of black tendrils with a vaguely skull-like head hovering in the middle.

"*GET OUT!*" it roared.

I staggered backward, dropping the amulet into my pocket—and forgetting about the trapdoor in the floor. My legs fell right through it, and my hands snapped out to stop the rest of me from following suit. I gripped the side of the trapdoor with every ounce of strength I had and hauled myself back up into the lantern room. I needed to slow down on the Wile E. Coyote mistakes, otherwise this would be the last mission I ever went on for Erebus.

Don't speak too soon. Judging by the seething mass of shadows dead ahead, it still could be.

"I'm here on behalf of Erebus!" I shouted, my voice snatched away by the wind that howled around the room.

"Leave this place!" the spirit boomed.

"I can't leave yet! You need to tell me where the Fountain is!" I ducked as a chair whizzed over my head and smashed against the back wall.

Ah. Poltergeist. It made sense now. I'd been able to see the spirit, which shouldn't have been possible. That meant it was another type of spirit—a pissed-off poltergeist.

A table came at me, full force. I dove out of the way, slamming into the lantern. Chunks of wood and steel and stone hurtled at me next, the poltergeist seizing whatever was handy and chucking it my way. I rolled and ducked and dove, but the attack just kept coming. Putting up my hands, I shot a blast of Telekinesis at the spirit, but it passed straight through him.

Okay, that's not good. How was I supposed to fight a spirit?

I hid behind the lantern, trying to catch my breath. A chunk of the ceiling fell away above me, giving me a split second to lunge forward before it crashed into the ground. It landed right where I'd been crouched. It would've brained me if it had hit its mark.

I stole a glance around the lantern to see the poltergeist shudder strangely. Its skull face disappeared. Long, black claws extended from its wrists. Before I could dart away, it charged at me. Those long claws raked right across my chest as my body was halfway turned.

Pain like no other erupted inside me. White-hot and searing, it spread out across my chest and up my throat.

I need to get out... I need to leave before it kills me. A sixth attempt might have to be my lucky charm. I scrambled toward the trapdoor. I needed more information about poltergeists before I went up against this creep. He was out of control, howling and raging, claws primed and ready to slash again.

My face twisted in agony as I ran, trying to reach the trapdoor before the poltergeist launched a second attack. But no matter where I went, the shadow appeared in front of me, like the worst kind of Whack-A-Mole. It was blocking my exit out of here.

I sent out a wave of Fire followed by a gust of Air to knock the thing back. It barely flinched, and I was starting to feel lightheaded. I hurled another barrage of Fire. Finally, the poltergeist reeled back for a moment, giving me a direct line to the trapdoor. My knees almost gave way as I ran for my life.

Man, I should not feel this weak... this... tired.

Something weird was definitely going on here. I was weakening way too fast for it to be natural.

Tumbling over the edge of the trapdoor, I caught one of the rungs with my foot and scampered down as quick as I could. Another chair followed me through. It careened right past me and plummeted the twenty feet to the ground. I heard it shatter on impact, though I didn't dare look. Vertigo wouldn't have been too helpful, when I already felt dizzy as hell.

"Get out! *Get out!*" The poltergeist's voice thundered through the lighthouse, shaking the walls. I sprinted down the spiral staircase, feeling the whole thing shudder underneath me.

So much for conversation. The poltergeist really didn't want to talk, and a deal was definitely off the table. I just had to hope I didn't die before I made it out of here.

Ponce de León's rage followed me all the way down, deafening me. Glancing over my shoulder, I saw darkness descending. *He* was following me down, his claws eager for another bite.

But he couldn't follow me out of the lighthouse, surely. Spirits like Ponce were supposed to be tied to a location.

I barreled out of the building, my thighs burning and my muscles aching. The searing pain across my chest made it hard to breathe. It was working its way higher up my throat. My ankle hurt, too, from landing awkwardly on the ladder rung. Fortunately, there were no tourists around to see me burst through the door. In fact, the fortress had become eerily empty and silent since I'd entered the lighthouse, the sky overhead now dark and ominous.

But that was the least of my concerns.

A powerful gust of wind exploded out of the door and smacked me in the back. I toppled forward, landing in the dirt, right on the ragged cut. And, inside my head, I heard the most terrifying scream:

"Never return here!"

Dragging myself to my feet, I staggered away from the lighthouse, my body barely able to hold me up as I lunged for the nearest wall. I needed to get away. All that screaming was too much, making it feel like my head was about to blow, as well as my chest.

I was almost at the castle wall when a shadow appeared in front of me, blocking my path. *What the—? How is this even possible?*

Gasping for breath and fighting to stay on my feet, I gave it one last burst of energy. I ran for the wall, getting a second scrape across the chest as I tore past the poltergeist. The pain as he raked the already-raw flesh was indescribable. A howl escaped my throat, every vein in my body ablaze with agony.

Struggling to stay upright, I fumbled for my trusty charmed chalk, then scraped the shaky lines of a doorway into the wall and choked out the *Aperi Si Ostium* spell. I looked over my shoulder to see the spirit surging toward me. I lifted my palms one last time and sent out a blast of Fire and Telekinesis.

Yanking at the handle, I pushed it open and lunged through. I got a final glimpse of the seething shadow mass as it zoomed toward me, missing me by a millisecond. I took a moment to assess my surroundings, to make sure not even a wisp of that thing had managed to get through.

I'd escaped it… just barely.

"Finch?"

Krieger was staring at me from his workbench. He held a screwdriver poised mid-air, frozen like a substandard mime. Jacob sat beside him, similarly stunned. What could I say? I knew how to make an entrance. A natural gift from my dearly departed mother.

I looked around and saw that they were working on a bronze device. Presumably, the one they'd been tinkering away at before I left for Cuba. It was supposed to be another magical detector to replace the one Katherine had stolen, just souped up a bit. An enhanced version based on Krieger's memories of the last one, complete with a fingerprint scanner so only vetted magicals could use it.

O'Halloran had been the one to suggest it. As the new and improved SDC director, it made sense that he'd want new and improved things. He thought we could use the device to find rogue magicals and keep them safe, especially after the Katherine debacle.

Or "the Blip of Eris," as I liked to call it. No more cults, thank you very much.

"Yep... sorry about the rough entry," I said. The strip lighting of Krieger's office stung my eyes as I braced my hands against my thighs. I tried to pull in a decent breath. Had the air here turned to slime while I'd been gone? It felt like it.

"Are you okay?" Krieger scraped back his stool. The sound splintered through my skull, as if I'd spent last night downing shots of tequila. I kept trying to breathe, but the pain in my chest was overwhelming.

Exhausted, I couldn't stay upright any longer. My knees buckled, and I crumpled to the floor, panting like a dog.

Jacob leapt up and ran with Krieger to my side.

I winced as they hauled me up by my pits and carried me through to the infirmary. They settled me down on a gurney, buzzing around me like flies. Krieger was tearing things out of a drawer, pulling out reams and reams of bandages as if he were a magician at a kid's party.

"We need to stop the bleeding," he said, glancing worriedly at me.

Okay, so maybe I lost more blood than I thought. That was another problem with black clothes—it was hard to tell if you were gushing your lifeblood all over the place.

"Come on, how bad can it be?" I croaked.

"Very bad," Krieger replied. "What on earth did you go up against, to get injuries like this?"

I smiled. "Tobe Hooper, 1982."

"What?" Krieger frowned. "What has this got to do with Tobe?"

"Not Tobe. Tobe *Hooper.*"

Jacob gasped. "*Poltergeist?*"

"See, and you said making you watch all those old movies was pointless," I wheezed.

"Are you saying a poltergeist did this?" Krieger paled.

"In my usual roundabout way… yeah." I sucked air through my teeth as Krieger pressed a wad of gauze against my wound. "You want to go easy there, Krieger? I'd like to keep my ribs intact, if that's okay with you?"

"Jacob, get Marianne Gracelyn here immediately." Krieger ignored me, giving Jacob a pointed look.

"What's she going to do?" I muttered, trying to stop my head from spinning.

"As the preceptor of Wicca and Herbalism, she'll know far more about poltergeist injuries than I do," Krieger replied. "They're not regular injuries and require special concoctions and herbal treatments to temper the wounds. If not treated correctly, you may…" He trailed off, visibly uncomfortable.

"You can say it, Doc." I smiled weakly. "I might die, right?"

He sighed gravely. "Yes, you might. A poltergeist's attacks are infused with dead-men's poison, otherwise referred to as 'concentrated death.' It's lethal if left untreated."

"And here I was, thinking you were going to say it was something serious." I stared up at the ceiling, trying to hide my gathering fear. I could put on a good show in front of most people, but this wasn't something I could laugh off. This was scary… genuinely scary. And I couldn't help thinking:

What the hell had I gotten myself into?

THREE

Finch

It took Marianne an hour to finish patching me up. She threw all kinds of poultices and potions at me in the hopes of drawing out the dead-men's poison. The stench from the goo she pounded up in a mortar and pestle was almost worse than the idea of dying from this wound—something like the bottom of a dumpster. But, apparently, it was good for me. Vile medicine for a vile injury.

She bandaged up the rest of me, too, where I'd gotten a few scrapes and cuts that I hadn't even noticed. The poltergeist had hurt me more than I'd thought, landing a few surprise blows. An Egyptian mummy had nothing on me right now. My ankle, thigh, hip, chest, and shoulders were neatly bound and stinking to high heaven.

"You'll have to wear these for the next twenty-four hours," Marianne instructed in her odd, musical voice. It was hard to feel negative when she was around. She buzzed with positivity. *Stick some of that in a drip for me, would you?*

"No showers, no water, and no exerting yourself. Take it easy over the next couple of days," she continued.

As preceptors went, Marianne was an emblem of the new order, young and beautiful and insanely smart, even though she'd been at the SDC pre-Katherine. She had long, red hair that was fastened in a braid to her waist, with feathers flowing down as if they were part of her locks. Not like my sister's red, and not like my real shade of ginger, which I kept permanently under a strawberry blond façade. It was more of a true red, like it had come out of a box instead of nature. She looked like she had old Woodstock photos on her walls and listened to Bob Dylan on repeat. Right now, she wore bright yellow bell-bottom cords, a tie-dyed T-shirt, and more beads than New Orleans at Mardi Gras.

"How easy?" I replied.

Taking it easy wasn't exactly an option for me. I had work to do, and Erebus didn't accept delays. And this definitely wasn't the first time I'd had to get on with a task while recovering from a plethora of injuries. As it turned out, being Erebus's messenger boy was a bigger risk to my health than being Katherine's sidekick.

"Basically, you need to stay on your back and rest." Marianne smiled as she stowed her many herbs and potions back into a big leather bag. A veritable hippie Mary Poppins.

I rolled my eyes. "I was worried you'd say that."

"She means it, Finch," Krieger interjected. "You must rest, or you won't get better."

"Okay, okay, I heard you the first time." I tried not to sulk.

"I wouldn't have taken you for a troublesome patient." Krieger chuckled, clearly relieved that he'd been able to help me out. For a doctor, there were some definite holes in his expertise. Then again, I supposed poltergeist attacks were fairly niche in his line of work.

"Where were you when this happened?" Jacob distracted me from my sulking. He sat to my left, in one of those ancient vinyl chairs that all hospitals seemed to have. "Which poltergeist was it? Do you know?"

I smiled. "How about you mind your beeswax and get back to tinkering with the shiny new magical detector?"

"Actually, he makes a valid point." Krieger folded his arms across his chest. "Where were you, and what on earth were you doing?"

"Will it make a difference to my healing?" I replied.

"Well, no, but—"

"Then it's none of your beeswax, either." I grinned. "No offense."

Krieger frowned. "I really think you should tell us."

"And I really think Marianne told me not to exert myself. Talking is making me so very weak." I closed my eyes as if I was going to sleep, only for them to fly open as the door to the infirmary burst inward and Harley came crashing through. Wade ran alongside her.

"Oh yeah, I might have called them," Jacob whispered.

"Snitch," I hissed back.

He gave me an oh-so-innocent shrug. "I thought she should know. She's your sister."

"Yeah, I don't need reminding." I sighed.

Harley hurried straight for me and threw her arms around me. I rolled my eyes.

"Ouch! Wounded invalid over here." It did hurt, but I was secretly glad to hug her again after my brush with death.

She drew back. "Are you okay? What happened?"

"It's nothing, I'm fine. You didn't have to come all the way down here to worry over me," I replied. "It was just a work accident. Stuff happens, but it's all good now."

"Stuff happens?" Wade asked. Harley arched a disapproving eyebrow at me. They were tag-teaming this in annoying couple fashion.

Krieger glanced between the three of us. "On that note, there's something I need to talk to you about. Marianne, Jacob, if you could join me in my office?" He led the way, with the other two following. Jacob was a little more reluctant, but Krieger was his adoptive dad now, so he had to do as he was told.

At least the good doctor still knew how to take a hint. It was considerate of him to leave me alone with my sister and Wonderboy Wade so she could whip my ass in relative privacy.

"How's everything in paradise?" I dove in first, before the questions could start again.

Harley shook her head. "Stop deflecting, Finch."

"Who's deflecting?" I smiled sweetly.

Paradise entailed Wade and Harley being at the top of their game and still nauseatingly in love. They'd moved into a shared, bigger office in the coven to run their taskforce. They'd also moved into a shared, bigger room in the living quarters, but the less said about that, the better. I was still her brother. I'd already had a few choice, brotherly words with Wade about their living arrangements, but he'd just laughed.

As part of their ongoing duties within the SDC, Harley and Wade had been appointed as Special Coven Agents. They had sparkly new uniforms and everything. Which meant, while I was out hunting down all of Erebus's whims and fancies, they were out hunting down rogue Cult of Eris members still at large, among other things. Frankly, I would've given anything to have their job.

As for the rest of the Muppet Babies, they had the easy, stress-free task of bringing new, undiscovered magicals into the coven.

"Finch!" Harley said sternly.

"Harley!" I mimicked. I knew it irked her when I did that.

"What happened to you?" Her tone softened. "When Jacob called, I was so worried."

Wade nodded. "We both were."

"Which is why he shouldn't have called you. Like I said, there's nothing to worry about. Hazard of the job, that's all." I grinned up at Wade. "Although, I'm touched. Wonderboy was worried about me—there's something you don't hear every day."

"Be serious, Finch," Wade replied. "Come on, just let us know what happened. You got injured by a *poltergeist*. That's not some simple occupational hazard. You could've died today."

I shrugged. "But I didn't, and I can't tell you. So it'll be easier for all of us if you both just let it go."

I wanted to tell them more, I really did, but I didn't want their pity. Or their self-pity, for that matter, particularly Harley's. She'd beaten herself up enough about Katherine's demise and the way things had gone down. I wasn't going to drag them into my troubles. I'd chosen this. I could do it on my own, the way I was supposed to. And, if there came a time when I couldn't anymore, then I'd reach out for help.

"We already know it's because of Erebus, Finch." Harley perched on the edge of the bed and held my hand.

I didn't pull away. Just because I wouldn't ask for their help didn't mean I didn't appreciate some sisterly comfort. I liked having her nearby. Maybe it was because of some residual abandonment issues, or maybe it was just because I finally had family, but it made me calmer when she was here.

Wade nodded. "You're always so secretive about the jobs you do for him, but sometimes it's best to ask for help before things get too dangerous."

"Are we forgetting how Harley tried to end Katherine on her own?" I regretted the words as soon as they slipped out, but I wanted them off my case. Not for me, but for their own sakes.

"And what did you do about that, huh?" Wade replied. "You

followed her around like a puppy until she gave in. I'm glad you did, don't get me wrong, but you might need a better example."

I narrowed my eyes at him. "Touché, Crowley... touché."

"You've been going at this by yourself for a year, Finch. Surely, it's time you let us take some of the weight?" Harley paused. "Or, if not me or Wade, then someone else you trust? You almost got snuffed out by a poltergeist today. We almost lost you. Please, just ask for freaking help."

"It's not that simple—" I started to protest, but she cut me off.

"My guess is, you needed something from that spirit—something Erebus wants—and you clearly can't get it on your own. I'm not saying you aren't capable, because I know you're capable of just about anything, but this may be biting off more than one person can chew." She gave my hand a squeeze.

Wade smirked. "I wouldn't say he's capable of just about anything. He still has trouble keeping his hair the same color."

"Pfft, says you. You've got enough product in your hair to baste a duck," I shot back.

"Don't say 'baste.'" Wade shuddered.

"Why not? Baste, baste, baste."

Harley rolled her eyes, though a smile tugged the corners of her lips. "Can you not do this now?"

"I wasn't doing anything," I replied, though I felt better. Making fun of Wade always made me feel better. "I know you're concerned, but I really do have this covered. I'm fine, honestly."

"Why don't I believe you?" She gave me a long look and sighed. I squeezed her hand back in response.

"You know I'm always here if you need support, and I know you've got some demons to work through, on top of this creepy servitude." Harley's eyes and voice were solemn and kind. "But I just want you to let me help you, if you ever need it. I know what you sacrificed to finish Katherine, and I hope that, one day, you might let us share that responsibility."

"As soon as my ass needs saving, you'll be the first to know."

I looked down at Harley's hand holding mine, my eyes drifting up to the leather cuff on her forearm, which covered her golden apple tattoo. She never went without her cuff. I wore a similar cuff whenever I didn't feel like shifting over my two apples—the first one that I'd willingly gotten, and the second one which I'd had poured onto me while gussied up as Pieter Mazinov. The cuffs served as a constant reminder for both of us of what we'd been through. We'd never have made it to the bitter end if we hadn't worked together.

So maybe she was right. Maybe I did need some help for this task, if I ever wanted to finish it. This wasn't Katherine-Shipton-level evil, but it left me with the same sick sense of dread.

A job shared... right? The sooner I got this over with, the better. And I had just the person in mind, someone who didn't share my sister's savior complex.

FOUR

Finch

The next morning, my eyes opened to daylight nagging me to wake up. I groaned and shoved my head back in the pillow. *My sweet, squishy love...* I'd deliberately refused to set an alarm, but the sun had transformed into a stressed-out mom ready to kick my ass if I didn't get up and ready, pronto. I dragged my second pillow over my head like a sandwich to block out the glare.

My body felt like it had been hit by an eighteen-wheeler, or like I'd downed a bottle of Diarmuid's secret brew, which could kill a grown man but, apparently, not a leprechaun. Everything hurt. No exaggeration. My skull throbbed, my limbs felt heavy, my wounds stung, and, man, did I stink. Those poultices should have come with a biohazard warning. I'd dragged myself to bed, not wanting to spend the night in the infirmary. Now, I wished I had. My sheets would never be the same.

Coffee... My delicious, caffeinated mistress will fix this. That and a hefty dose of painkillers, which Marianne had packed me off with. A stack of them sat on my desk. Grumbling a number of choice expletives under my breath, I removed the upper layer of my pillow sandwich and hauled myself out of bed. Every step took effort.

Padding over to the mirror, I took a long, hard look at myself. My skin was pale, and my hair was sticking up at all angles. My body hadn't fared much better. Bruises were blooming all over the visible parts of my chest and stomach, and the bandages that were keeping my dignity had turned a rank brown color thanks to the poultices.

It was weird how quickly I'd settled into life at the coven. This bedroom brought me that homey kind of comfort that people loved to harp on about—home is where the heart is and whatnot. I guessed my heart was in the SDC now. Plus, I'd done a killer job of decorating, if I did say so myself.

I had a red feature wall with framed comic books hanging on it. Rare copies, of course—first appearances, key issues, all the good stuff. There was a packed bookshelf on one side with all my favorite reads, from the classics to contemporary and everything in between. Harley liked to mock me for my copy of *Wuthering Heights* and my Austen collection, but I called her a philistine and that shut her up. A guy could enjoy whatever he wanted, and I liked to think of myself as a bit of a Heathcliff.

I had the rest of the usual suspects—a desk, a chair, a few knick-knacks. There was a collection of still-boxed figurines on the shelves and a wardrobe with my meager selection of clothes. Yeah, this was home. Well, when I actually got to spend some time here. I'd lost count of the countries I'd been to in the last year, thanks to Erebus.

Walking to said wardrobe, I took out jeans, a T-shirt, and some fresh boxers. My daily uniform. As I got dressed, wincing every time I bent the wrong way or brushed one of my many new injuries, I looked at the pictures on the desk. There was one of me and the Muppet Babies, all together, outside the Fleet Science

Center. It had been Jacob's idea, during his brief foray into photography. We were all smiling in the photo. Yes, even me.

Santana wasn't looking at the camera and appeared to be laughing at something Raffe had said. Dylan had scooped Tatyana into his arms and hoisted her in a fireman's lift. The shock in her eyes was captured for eternity.

Wade and Harley were standing as if they were trying to take a nice photo for prom, Wade's arms around her waist. Astrid and Garrett bookended them with strained smiles, as far apart as it was possible to be. As for me, I was crouched in the middle, giving it the rap-star vs. no whiff of a lover in sight. Well, not really.

I sat cross-legged in front of the mirror and dragged a comb through my hair. Staring at my reflection, I sighed. It was nice to see people happy, sure, but I would've liked to have someone, too. You know, someone I could vent to at night, or relax with when I was tired of missions and magic and all that malarkey.

Yeah, but you had yours. My brain came in with a sharp reminder. And maybe one was all a person got. I'd loved Adley more than I'd known, and it had taken my stupid head too long to realize it. I ruined it with her, so maybe I didn't get to have a second chance with someone else.

Just someone *else, eh?* I reached up to the top drawer of my desk and took out a packet of my special pills. My brain was being a little too chatty right now, and it was time to put those pesky gremlins to sleep for a bit. It had a point, though. Every morning, I woke up thinking about a certain woman, and every night, I went to sleep thinking of her.

Why did it have to be her? Harley would feed me to Murray if she found out I was crushing on her adoptive sister. And the psychological implications were borderline Ancient Grecian.

Not that it mattered. Between my mind gremlins and my servitude to Erebus, I wasn't exactly a catch. And I wasn't about to drag someone else into my world. Especially not Ryann Smith. Plus, whenever we met, I morphed into Finch the Jackass or Finch the Deathly Silent. Whichever my mind preferred that day. Oh, and I could never resist the urge to make fun of her towering Canuck moose of a boyfriend, Adam, which didn't exactly make her warm up to me.

But I couldn't help it. That guy riled me up, giving me all sorts of inferiority complexes. He looked like he spent all day at the gym, he'd gone to Harvard, he was interning as a pediatrician. *I mean, come on!* And it definitely didn't help that he was so damn nice. Like *too* nice. Like serial killer nice. And I'd never be like that.

I threw down the comb and lay back on the carpet, staring up at the ceiling. I blamed the Smiths for this—Mr. and Mrs. Smith, to be precise. They'd smothered me with love after the Blip of Eris was over. Mrs. Smith, the mother hen, had truly scooped me under her wing. I had an open invitation to their house, and Harley had hauled me along at every possible opportunity.

With all the cakes and homecooked food and watching Mr. and Mrs. Smith canoodling constantly, how could I not have fallen for Ryann? They'd set the mood, being all loved-up all the time! I didn't go over there as much anymore, but I was invited to the occasional Sunday barbecue. Which Captain Serial Killer was always at, too.

Okay, enough wallowing. I rolled over and stiffly got to my feet. Dispensing with all thoughts of Ryann, I hobbled into the bathroom to wash that girl right out of my... face. I couldn't shower. Marianne's orders.

Running the faucet, I splashed the cool water on my skin, along with some soap, and started to brush my teeth. After sticking my head under the faucet to rinse my mouth out, I straightened to take another look at myself.

A scream nearly squeaked out of my throat as I stared at the words that had appeared on the mirror. Bloody writing spelled out the ominous message:

"I summon thee."

"Oh yeah? Well, I summon you to stick your summons up your butt," I muttered, breathing sharply and bracing myself against the sink to stop myself from having an all-out heart attack. Why couldn't he just text me, or call, or send a letter? Even a carrier pigeon would've been better for my nerves than this.

It pissed me off… and scared me, a little bit. I was in no condition to face Erebus right now, especially after my colossal failure with Ponce de León.

You'll have to wait, sunshine. I needed a breather. And, anyway, what was the worst that could happen?

FIVE

Finch

An hour later, fresh as a daisy, I sat in the Banquet Hall for breakfast. I had coffee. I had pastries. Life was good. I always appreciated the spread they put on here. No matter what time of day it was, you could always swipe something tasty from the kitchens.

The Muppet Babies were assembled, looking annoyingly chirpy. Then again, they hadn't gone twelve rounds with a poltergeist.

"How are you feeling?" Tatyana asked, sipping delicately at some herbal nonsense.

"Ah, I see the news spread quickly," I replied. "I'm fine. I'm going to have some super-manly scars, but I'll live."

"Poltergeists are very dangerous, Finch." She eyed me sternly.

I smiled back. "So everyone keeps telling me."

"Did they get all the poison out?"

I nodded. "Apparently. Turns out, Preceptor Gracelyn is pretty nifty with her Wiccan mumbo-jumbo."

"It's not mumbo-jumbo. Wiccan magic is very powerful, and

very legitimate," Santana said pointedly. She and I were still not quite in the realm of friendship. We'd been making progress, but then I'd doused her and her feather boa. Accidental, of course, but she had a big wet chip on her shoulder about it.

"Nothing wrong with a few scars, buddy," Dylan chimed in, as positive as ever. Honestly, I'd gotten used to his eternal optimism.

"At least you're not possessed or anything," Raffe added through a mouthful. *Charming.*

"And what's that supposed to mean?" Kadar rose to the surface for a moment.

Raffe rolled his eyes as he shifted back. "I didn't mean anything by it. Like Tatyana said, poltergeists are dangerous business. I was concerned for his welfare, that's all. You don't have to take everything so personally."

"Can poltergeists possess someone?" Jacob looked up from his bowl of technicolor puffs of cereal. He might've liked to pretend otherwise, but he was still a kid.

"They can if they're pushed to it, or they have a reason for it," Tatyana replied.

"I can think of a few reasons it'd want to possess Finch." A new voice in our group spoke, casting me a terrifyingly girlish smirk. Saskia Vasilis, Tatyana's sixteen-year-old sister, who'd have given Regina George a run for her money. I blamed Ryann and Harley for me even knowing who that was. They'd made me sit through *Mean Girls* on one of our evenings at the Smiths'.

Tatyana shot her a look. "Saskia!"

"What? I'm just saying." She pretended to pout, while fluttering her eyelashes at me.

Not in a million years, jailbait. I really hated teenagers, with the exception of Jacob, for the most part. Tatyana wasn't too happy about this teenager, either. Saskia had been sent here on the student exchange program, and Tatyana was trying to be sisterly about it. But Saskia was proving to be a heck of a nuisance. She'd already spent part of the morning poking Garrett, who had buried his head in a newspaper to avoid her.

I jumped as something brushed against my leg, and I slammed my knee into the underside of the table. I hissed through my teeth and ducked down to see what it had been. I half expected to see Saskia's leg trying to play footsie with me. Instead, I came eyeball-to-eyeball with that friggin' Purge beast of Santana's, Slinky.

"Do you have to bring your feather boa to breakfast, Santana? It's trying to cop a feel." I tucked my legs right under the bench so it couldn't have another lick of me with its hissy little tongue.

"I imagine he smelled you and wanted to figure out what had died," she shot back.

I smirked. "Well, can you call it back? I'm trying to eat, and having a reptile wrap itself around my legs isn't good for my digestion."

I'd seen that slithery pet way too much for my liking of late. Wherever Santana went, it went. Apparently, she was trying to train it to be a Familiar of sorts, although I got the feeling she liked bringing it everywhere just to freak me out. That thing had gotten *big* since Elysium. It was about the size of a mature boa, with a bright ruff of feathers around its neck. Not the same color as Quetzi, and not quite as massive, but he'd get there one day.

"You afraid he might bite?" Santana grinned.

"Actually, yes." As if to prove my point, Slinky lunged upward, nearly making me fall back off my seat.

"Aww, he just wants to say hello."

Santana knew that *wasn't* what he was doing, but the creepy creature decided to stroke its head against my cheek anyway. A snaky joke. I shuddered. I wasn't a big fan of snakes in general, but Slinky and I had a mutual dislike of each other.

"Yeah, well, if it could slink away from my face, that'd be great."

I shoved the Purge beast in the side of the head to get it to move and received a loud hiss for my pains.

"Hey, don't touch him!" Santana snapped.

"Then stop letting it sneak around under the tables, or I'll have to report it for inappropriate behavior," I replied.

Saskia batted her eyelashes. "I think Slinky has the right idea."

Save me, someone. Right now, I was fodder between Saskia, who delighted in making innocent folks like me as uncomfortable as possible, and Santana's beastie.

"Saskia! I'm not going to tell you again," Tatyana chided.

"Tell me what?" she replied sweetly.

"I mean it."

"Mean what?"

A muscle twitched in Tatyana's jaw. "Just... behave yourself."

"Killjoy," Saskia murmured under her breath.

"So, how did you end up toe-to-toe with a poltergeist?" Dylan asked, evidently eager to draw the attention away from his nightmarish potential sister-in-law.

I shrugged. "How does anyone end up dealing with a poltergeist?"

"No, seriously, what were you doing when it happened?" Raffe pressed.

"Oh, this and that," I replied. The King of Nonchalance.

"What does that mean?" Garrett finally spoke. "What have you been up to?"

"You know, just keeping busy." They weren't going to get anything out of me.

Garrett pulled a disgruntled face. "Clearly you were up to something. People don't just bump into poltergeists by accident."

"Maybe I'm the first." I smiled stiffly.

"If you're having some kind of trouble, I'd be happy to answer a few questions," Tatyana said. "I know a lot about poltergeists, after all. We studied them in depth while training to become a Kolduny."

That got my attention. "You did?"

"Yeah, a whole month on them," Saskia interjected. "I nearly broke my jaw in half, yawning through the lectures. It wasn't like they were teaching me anything new. I'd read all about poltergeists by the time I was five."

Tatyana gripped her mug until her knuckles whitened.

"Careful, you might smash it," I teased.

Her expression relaxed slightly. "What my sister is trying to say is, we're well-versed in poltergeist lore. We know a thing or two that other people don't. So, if you do—"

"If you need some help, I'd love to volunteer." Saskia cut her off again.

Tatyana stared at her sister, and even I was a bit frightened. These Kolduny women were scary, but for very different reasons. "You're not getting involved in anything that is tied to Erebus! Nothing. I mean it. If I hear so much as a whisper that you've disobeyed, I'll have words with O'Halloran."

Saskia glared back. "Ooh, you'll go running to the teacher?"

"I. Mean. It." Tatyana held her sister's gaze until Saskia sank back in her seat, admitting defeat with a petulant scowl on her face.

Just then, Ryann rushed over with a croissant and a coffee. How had I missed her coming in? That wasn't like me. My Ryann radar was usually primed and precise. All this poltergeist business must have been knocking me off my very poor game.

"Morning, all," she chirped, sliding onto the bench beside Harley. "I don't have much time, but thought I'd say hi before I dart off again."

"Ryann? What are you doing here?"

The words came out colder than I'd intended. She'd surprised me, that was all. Last time I was here, she wasn't. Her internship with Astrid in the shiny new department of human relations had finished, and she hadn't said anything about applying for another position. So I'd presumed that was the last of that.

She didn't seem to notice my brusqueness. "I've just started a summer internship with Miss Miranda Bontemps."

I nodded. "I bet you'll have a Bontemps with that."

She gave a pity laugh that made my insides curl up. "Hah. Good one."

"Yeah, good one, Finch." Wade smirked at me.

Does he know? No, he couldn't. I'd been so suave and discreet in my nonexistent displays of admiration.

"I'm focusing on human rights in the magical world," she continued.

Her face positively radiated with pride and enthusiasm. *Come on, Finch, say something cool and encouraging.* "So, how will you explain this to Ted Bundy?"

The Muppet Babies stared at me like I'd grown a second head.

"He means my boyfriend, Adam." Ryann chuckled, and the entire group relaxed. "Such a joker, isn't he?"

"He sure is." Garrett snorted.

"And Adam is wonderful," Harley added pointedly. "Definitely not a serial killer."

"That we know of," I said in an undertone. "Anyway, what are you going to tell him? I'm guessing he doesn't know about your toe-dip into the magical world. Or the magical world at all, for that matter."

Ryann smiled. "I'm still getting used to that word—magical. Although, some folks seem more magical than others."

The Muppet Babies snickered. *Does she mean me?* Pfft, I was plenty magical. More magical than everyone at this table, Harley excluded. I wanted to peacock a little, but Adam wouldn't have done that. He was modest, on top of everything else. Ugh, I hated him. Still, it stopped me from boasting about my magical prowess.

"Have they made you sign an NDA?" I asked, recovering.

"They have, but it's okay. I'm just grateful to have this opportunity, and O'Halloran gave me some pointers about how to keep things quiet without jeopardizing a relationship."

She had an answer for everything. That was one of things I liked most about her. She kept me on my toes. Sometimes so much so I felt like she had me en pointe.

"Hey, what happened to you? Did I miss something?"

I looked up as Ryann's expression softened and she gazed at me with concern.

I shrugged, cool as a cucumber. "It's nothing. Took a tumble, that's all."

"You don't look good. Should you be up and about?"

"It looks worse than it is," I replied.

"I could ask Adam to look at you on Sunday." She paused. "Although, I suppose Dr. Krieger has you covered. I keep forgetting you guys have everything you need right here."

I frowned. "Sunday?"

"Yeah—don't tell me you forgot! Mom invited you to Sunday dinner, remember?"

"Oh… yeah. I'll see how I feel." If Jack the Ripper touched me, I'd roast *him* on the barbecue.

Ryann nodded, looking a little disappointed. "Of course. If you're not feeling up to it, that's fine, but I know Mom and Dad are looking forward to it. They've been missing their adopted third child." She gave me a small smile that made my throat close, and I tried to think about Jacob to distract myself. Harley had tried to encourage him to reconnect with the Smiths, even if they couldn't remember those days. But he'd refused, coming up with countless excuses. The real truth, however, was much simpler. It hurt too much.

Harley put her hand on Ryann's forearm. "I'll make sure he comes along."

"Okay. Well, I need to be going. I'll see you all later." Ryann slid from the bench and got up, coffee and croissant still in hand. I tried to think of something to say that would make her stay longer. I wanted to ask her what she'd been up to, and just shoot the oh-so-casual breeze. I guessed it would have to wait until Sunday.

She turned, and my heart leapt. *She's going to stay, after all.* "Oh, and Finch?"

"Yes?" My pulse was raging.

"You know I think the world of you, but can you please leave Adam out of our conversations? I know you think it's funny to call him all those things, but there's really nothing funny about serial killers. It's beneath you."

I withered like a shrub in an arid desert. "Sure. No serial killer jokes. Got it."

"Wish me luck!" She smiled again.

A ripple of "good lucks" passed around the table as she turned and left, leaving me to stew.

"It's not like you to pass up the chance for a witty comeback," Santana said.

"She got you good!" Dylan laughed.

I tried not to meet anyone's gaze. "I didn't want to be rude."

"Did that poltergeist lobotomize you, as well?" Wade grinned.

"Are you sure you didn't meet a changeling instead?" Garrett added. "Where's the real Finch? Come on, where are you hiding him?"

"How's that for sympathy, huh?" I replied. "*You* try being Class A hilarious after having your chest gouged by a psycho spirit."

"Poltergeist," Tatyana corrected. "There's a big distinction between spirits and poltergeists. You see, a spirit is a—"

Saskia rolled her eyes. "Geez, Taty, don't bore him. He just escaped one near-death experience."

As the sisters scowled at each other, I glanced at Harley. I was waiting for a dig, but it didn't come. Instead, she offered a sympathetic smile. A comforting barnacle in a sea of ridicule. *Does she know?* Had she and Wade been gossiping in secret? See, this was why I needed someone. Everyone else had a person they could spill their secrets to, but I had to keep mine locked up for the gremlins to feed on.

I stared down into my coffee, only to jolt back. There was no coffee in this cup anymore. It had filled up with blood. Scarlet trickles sloshed over the sides. I looked around frantically, but nobody else seemed to have noticed.

Erebus. Another one of his hallucinatory tricks to put me on edge. A sign because I was keeping him waiting. Man, that guy sure was persistent. I guessed I couldn't put him off anymore, not unless I wanted a nasty surprise in my bed. Or something worse.

"I should get going, too." I clambered over the bench.

"Can't handle the heat, huh?" Santana grinned. "You can give it but can't take it?"

"It's got nothing to do with... never mind. I'm just tired." I balled my hands into fists. "Garrett, do you want to meet up later?"

He nodded. "We can swing by the burn unit, if you like."

I scrunched my face into a sarcastic smile. "I'll text you the details."

"Call me if you need anything," Harley said, saving me again. "And get some rest. Sister's orders."

I gave her a small nod before exiting the Banquet Hall, leaving the laughter and stinging puns behind. They hadn't meant anything by it, but their jabs made me feel like I was being pushed to the edges of the group again. Sometimes I wished I could be more a part of their group. But all of this Erebus stuff made me feel like an outsider, anyway. Until I was free again, I couldn't be part of their world... *Geez, am I going to start singing Under the Sea, next?* All I needed was a shell bra.

I trudged back to my room and went straight over to my desk, taking out an antique ring that Erebus had given me. It was a chunky gold monstrosity with a fat ruby in the center and strange etchings in the metal band—sigils and charms specific to the Lord of Darkness himself. But it wasn't just a gaudy accessory. Oh no. This was a modified portal opener with a direct line to Tartarus, crafted by an ancient servant of Erebus.

Wishing I didn't have to, I slid the ring on the middle finger of my right hand. The moment it was on, the world swirled around me in a dizzying vortex. The walls, the ground, everything all fell away.

The next moment, I landed in the darkest depths of Tartarus. As soon as I set foot in the shadowy otherworld, unable to see my own hand in front of my face, the noises started. Soft at first, they grew into a crescendo of growls and snarls and snapping jaws.

I formed a ball of Fire in my palms to light my way through the pitch black. I only had minutes to get to Erebus before the night-crawlers came a-hunting.

SIX

Finch

I broke into a sprint, the ball of Fire bobbing in my hands. Twisted faces and glinting fangs flickered in the glow.

Every damn time. I was tired of running this gauntlet. It was why I hated coming here, hated always rushing through the darkness as fast as possible. Why Erebus had crafted a grim underworld for an otherworld, I'd never know, but he really needed to hire someone to fix this place up. Maybe an interior designer. A few vases, a tree or two, maybe a water feature—that kind of thing.

At least I knew the route now. To the untrained eye, Tartarus looked like an endless vacuum of black, but there was more to this otherworld than simply darkness. Keeping the flame ahead of me, I followed the faint path that marked the black soil below. It was similar to emergency lights on a plane—a single trail of biolumi-nescence you had to really look for. Except if you strayed from the path, you got munched.

Suddenly, the path rose. The Sisyphean Mountain. I couldn't see it, but I knew what it was as I darted up the incline. *I really need to hit the gym.*

As I climbed, I understood Sisyphus's pains. Rolling a stone up this bad boy for eternity wasn't my idea of a good time. My lungs straining, I lifted one hand and cast Telekinesis to keep the monsters at bay. I didn't plan on giving them any Finch Mignon today. They whimpered and whined as my Telekinesis pressed them up against the mountainside.

Wheezing and feeling like I'd aged fifty years, I reached the mountaintop. A shimmer of silvery light shone down, though it was never clear where it came from. There was no moon or stars. The glow just seemed to come from nowhere, casting a spotlight on the "safe zone."

Where monsters feared to tread. This was Erebus's pad, and he didn't let his pets roam here.

Speak of the devil. Erebus, in his humanoid form, floated in the center of an ancient ruin just outside the circle of light. He drifted between broken pillars and traced smoky fingers across limbless nude statues. He'd been waiting for me.

He looked at me as I approached, all black smoke and dark red eyes. Emphasis on the dark. I supposed that was why he'd bothered to illuminate this place. Otherwise, he'd mostly be a scary voice in a sea of camouflage, and that wasn't his jam. No, Erebus liked to be seen *and* heard.

"I thought you'd be better at this by now." Captain Evil chuckled as I stood before him, panting and exhausted and not too happy about it. "I suppose that is one benefit of not having lungs—I never tire."

"Yeah, well, we can't all flit from place to place. Some of us have to run." I stooped to catch my breath. "You know, this would be easier if I didn't have to worry about getting chewed up when I came. You could let me portal right here and save me a cardiac arrest."

"Where would be the fun in that?" He scoffed. "Besides, I wouldn't want to rob you of valuable training. This is part of it, remember?"

"What if I promised to get a gym membership?"

"Do they have Purge beasts?"

"No, but—"

"Then I am doing you a great favor, giving you a chance to utilize your newfound abilities. You need to stay sharp, and Tartarus is your grindstone. You should be grateful for the challenge and the opportunity to flex your magical muscles. After all, you would still be weak and oblivious had I not broken your Dempsey Suppressor."

I rolled my eyes. "You're never going to change that track, are you?"

"Probably not. It is polite to show gratitude, though you always prefer impudence, to my perpetual disappointment. It's a good thing I find you amusing; otherwise, I'd toss you from this mountain and gift you to the beasts."

Yeah, then you'd have one less person to do your bidding, so shut your trap. I didn't say it out loud. I knew enough to tread carefully. I called Erebus out when necessary, and when I thought I wouldn't lose a much-loved appendage for it, but I also knew when to hold back. I'd been dangled over that swarm of Purge beasts before, and it wasn't something I fancied going through again. I hadn't brought any clean pants with me.

"I'm grateful that you broke the Suppressor," I said. *I'm just not grateful for the whole enslavement thing.* Again, I held my tongue. Since I had to tell Erebus about my failure with Ponce, I figured it was best not to make things worse. At the end of the day, he was still an extremely powerful Child of Chaos, and that would never fail to send shivers up my spine.

"Now then, about the spirit of Ponce de León. Did you find the information I asked for? Can we proceed to the final stage, where you will go to make sure it is where you've been told?" Erebus draped his wispy form against a pillar, his smoky tendrils trickling down the stone. He had a flair for the dramatic.

Why do I attract drama queens? From being my mother's slave to Erebus's—wasn't I just the luckiest boy in the world?

"It didn't go according to plan," I replied. That was putting it mildly. "You've probably noticed the bandages. Let me tell you, I'm not wearing them as a fashion statement, and they're definitely not as appealing to the ladies as you'd think." I felt the heat of his gaze on me. "In a nutshell, Ponce de León turned on me before I could get him to negotiate, and I barely escaped with my life."

Erebus snorted. "You think I don't already know that? I have eyes on you at all times, Finch, through various means."

Then why don't you send one of your other minions after all this stuff? I knew he had people bound to his service all over the world. Erebus might have been a crazy-powerful Child of Chaos, but that came at a cost. He was resigned to his existence in an otherworld, unable to cross into the mortal world unless summoned.

Even then, he couldn't just do whatever he wanted. That had been Katherine's biggest headache, and the cause of her ultimate demise—needing a human body to bridge that cosmic gap. Despite how formidable they were, Children of Chaos needed humans to do their earthly bidding. And I seemed to be Erebus's favorite. Or, at least, his most amusing plaything.

"Then why did you ask?" I tried not to show my irritation.

"I wanted to see if you would try to weasel your way out of the truth with excuses. You passed the test, congratulations to you, but that still leaves me without the information I asked for." His tone grew sharp. "Why did you go to the lighthouse so poorly prepared? You should have known what you would be up against."

I clenched my jaw. "Well, you didn't exactly give me details, Erebus. You just said I'd be dealing with a spirit. I didn't know it was going to be a friggin' poltergeist!"

"What did you expect?" Erebus laughed coldly. "The spirit of Ponce de León has been bound to this earth for hundreds of years, unable to cross over. Of course he degenerated into a poltergeist! He died a frustrated man, with unfinished business. Had he the courage to drink from the Fountain of Youth, he might have escaped such a fate, but he was cowardly, and this is his eternal punishment."

"A heads-up would've been nice," I muttered.

"You will be prepared *this* time." He swept closer to me. "Find a way to tame or compel the poltergeist. You must force Ponce de León to reveal the location of the Fountain of Youth. I will not accept another failure. My Purge beasts grow hungrier by the day."

"Why do you want the Fountain of Youth, anyway?" I blurted out. It'd bugged me ever since he set me on this task. He wasn't human. He couldn't use it himself. So what the hell was he up to? It wasn't the first time I'd been baffled by one of Erebus's errands, but this one seemed particularly weird.

"You are under my servitude to obey my orders, not to ask irrelevant questions."

I frowned. "Maybe if I knew why you wanted it, I could use that as leverage with Ponce de León. I tried to name-drop, but that didn't work."

Erebus chuckled. "Nice try, Finch. I can tell you're dying to know why, but it's none of your business. Since Gaia is intent on keeping her secrets, this is the only way I will get the information I want. If you'd rather quit, a quicker punishment can be arranged."

"Let me guess, you'll feed me to your beasties?" I would detach my retinas if he mentioned that one more time. You'd think after existing for so long, he would have better threats. He could at least spice them up now and then.

"Careful, Finch," Erebus warned.

"What do you mean about Gaia? What secrets?"

His smoky wisps prickled for a moment. "She knows the whereabouts of the Fountain, but she refuses to tell me. I've tried to trick her into aiding me, but she's always been a smart one. Even in her juvenile state, she can't be fooled."

I shuddered at the memory of seeing her by the lake in Mexico. That image was seared into my brain forever. She'd taken on Harley's teenage form and had emerged all naked, with strategically draped hair covering all the stuff I *never* wanted to see. Horrifying.

"So, I must rely on you," Erebus continued. "I really can't be bothered to explain everything to someone new and see them stumble through the same pitfalls you have. Besides, you are my most powerful asset. I doubt I'd be fortunate enough to happen upon another like you, with all your rich abilities, who'd willingly walk into a deal with me."

"Does that mean you're going to give me some pointers this time?"

He smiled through his smoky mouth. "I suppose I should, if I am ever going to get what I want. First and foremost, you must—"

He stopped mid-sentence, his eyes lifting skyward. A streak of light splintered across the darkness like lightning. From the moody energy bristling off the Prince of Darkness, I guessed he wasn't making this happen. A silver glow pooled downward. Like molten metal, it poured in a swirling torrent and hit the ground with a sparkling splash.

From within the weird substance, limbs stretched and a head began to form. The shape was definitely feminine. I'd seen this once before, back in Elysium. Lux had come to join the party, bringing her light to the dark realm of Tartarus. And Erebus didn't look happy to see her.

However, his manner changed as soon as she manifested properly. He carried himself like a husband who'd been caught looking at something forbidden and was trying to cover it by being overly affectionate.

"My radiant beauty, what an unexpected surprise," he purred. "Is heaven missing an angel? Because I think I have found her. Is there anything so divine as you, my beloved wife? My star, my moon, my world, my universe."

Erebus moved toward Lux, smoky arms outstretched. I resisted the urge to hurl. If I tried that on Ryann, she'd laugh me out of the country. Hell, I'd laugh myself out of the country. *Hmm, what's that I smell? Eau de fromage?* And man, was it ripe.

"What are you up to?" Lux swatted her lover's wispy hands away.

Ooh, someone's in trouble. I stifled a smirk, not wanting to attract Lux's ire. She might have been made of pure light, but there was a cold side to her. A no-nonsense, I'll-beat-the-crap-out-of-you kind of vibe. Erebus clearly agreed, or he wouldn't have been fawning so desperately.

"Me? Nothing at all, darling. Just a few errands. A bit of business that requires a magical. Nothing too complicated or worthy of your concern." He reached out for her again, only to be rebuffed.

Lux turned to me instead. "Is that true?"

"Uh…" I wanted to tell her everything, just to see what she'd do to her dearly beloved husband. But I couldn't. Erebus had already promised death to everyone I loved, including me, if I let anything slip to his hard-as-nails wifey. A Child of Chaos was not someone to mess with, no matter how much I hated Erebus. "That's about the gist of it."

Coward. Yeah, cheers, brain.

Lux's stare burned into me. "I hope you *are* telling the truth, Finch. For your sake. If Erebus is up to something, I want to know. I don't like his involvement with humans. Those plots of his never end well." Her tone softened at the end, but only slightly.

"Yep, no lies here." I couldn't look at her, but I hoped that wouldn't give me away. Her warning struck an ominous chord. *Will this end well?* Only time would tell.

I wasn't sure which of them was scarier right now. Probably Lux. But she hadn't threatened the people I cared about, so I was sticking with the program, being an obedient little slave. And Lux was actually showing me a bit of empathy, in her blunt and mildly threatening way, which was a nice change.

This wasn't the first time Erebus had kept secrets from her. She didn't burst into our meetings often, but he was always shifty when she was around. They had a dysfunctional relationship that made me second-guess the whole romance thing. Love and hate, in perfect harmony.

"You shouldn't be using him for your so-called errands," Lux said suddenly. "Look at the state of him."

Uh... thanks?

"He is obviously wounded, yet you don't give him time to rest. He agreed to your deal, but that doesn't mean you can take advantage. Mortals are not like us, Erebus. They can't keep going indefinitely, and you can't work them into the ground, or they'll die," she chided. "And why you won't let him come directly to the mountain is beyond me. You won't be laughing about watching him fight your monsters just to reach you when one of them snags him."

Erebus pouted. "Lux, I've asked you not to involve yourself in my affairs."

"And I have asked you to find something else to amuse yourself with. Everyone else manages it, so why can't you? You don't see

Eros or Uranus wandering around forcing humans to do their bidding!"

Ha. Uranus. If I'd been beholden to Uranus, I wouldn't have been able to control myself. He'd have killed me ages ago for giggling.

"It is necessary, my love," Erebus managed through gritted teeth.

"It's so necessary that you can't give a weak mortal a few days to recuperate? No doubt he was injured on one of these errands of yours. Where is your compassion? Sometimes I think you were created without it."

Erebus smiled. "But I have passion. That must count for something."

"You are intolerable!" She threw her glowing arms into the air. "This can't continue, Erebus. It's not your place to keep venturing vicariously into the mortal world, doing so through these poor souls. You are a Child of Chaos. Start acting like one."

"What does that even mean?" Erebus shot back, his humor turning sour.

"It means you're supposed to stay in your otherworld and observe, not meddle. Hasn't Katherine done enough to last us a lifetime? Or are you taking up her ideas now?"

Erebus bristled. "I'm nothing like her."

"You're using magicals for your own benefit, so please tell me what the difference is." Lux started to spark, little flecks of light spraying off her.

I felt totally caught in the middle of their domestic spat. It was nice that she was standing up for me, but I knew Erebus wouldn't listen. As soon as Lux was gone, he'd be back on the enslavement trail.

I raised a nervous hand. "Thanks for your concern, Lux, but

there's really nothing for you to worry about. I'm good, honestly. A few scrapes, nothing I can't handle. It looks worse than it is. I'll be fine. I mean, I *am* fine."

Lux clicked her tongue. "You don't have to defend him, Finch."

"He isn't," Erebus replied. "He understands the nature of our deal, and he knows what is expected of him. He doesn't need *your* protection. Do you think it was easy for me to end Katherine? I exerted a lot of energy, and I am still feeling the aftereffects. He made the agreement, which had nothing to do with you, so why don't you keep your nose out of it?"

"What did you just say?" Lux spun toward him.

"I just want you to understand that everything is fine," he said, softening his tone. He clearly knew he'd crossed a line.

This was better than a soap opera. I couldn't help watching with curiosity, wondering where all the bitterness was coming from. Maybe that was what happened when you were stuck with someone for millennia. All their little quirks became thorns. And these two loved a fight. They were always at it, whenever I saw them together.

"Fine, then understand *me*. Do not abuse this mortal, and do not do anything to upset the natural balance of Chaos. We have had quite enough of that," she replied. "If things are the way they are, it is because Chaos wants it so. Nothing more, nothing less. Don't mess with it."

What's that supposed to mean? What did she think Erebus was up to? That didn't sit well with me, considering he wouldn't breathe a word about why he wanted the Fountain of Youth.

Erebus raised his wispy hands in surrender. "I'm not messing around, and I'm not abusing anyone. Everything is in order."

"Make sure that's true, or I won't be so nice next time I come to you." Lux began to glow more brightly. "I mean it, Erebus. Do not play with nature. I have some of my own business to attend to, but I will be back."

"I look forward to it, my angel." Erebus gave a strained smile.

"I'm sure you do." Lux snorted as she twisted into a spiral of molten silver. The blinding light shot into the sky, blasting across like a shooting star and disappearing into the endless night.

I was left with questions—a lot of them. Not that I was going to get answers from Mr. Tight-Lipped.

"You admire her, don't you?" Erebus's voice distracted me.

I shrugged. "I like that she believes in mortal rights, if that counts."

"Don't be fooled by her, Finch. She may seem innocent and righteous, but she is as devious as I am, if not worse. There is a reason we fell for one another. We are kindred spirits, even if we appear to be opposites. But she plays her role very well. It is part of her charm."

Whatever you say, pal. There was no way that Lux was worse than Erebus. She was the perpetual mediator between him and everything he wanted to wreck. This was just another one of Erebus's games, something to stop me from spilling the beans to his wife and getting him in more trouble. I knew a trickster when I saw one, and Erebus was king of them all, always covering his own ass.

"Well, at least she gave a crap about my injuries. You should listen to her about the rest thing," I replied.

"You and I both know that isn't going to happen." He smirked. "Now, where was I before she interrupted?"

"Pointers."

"Ah, yes. You are to do whatever you must to get your hands on Ponce de León and force him to reveal the Fountain's location."

My jaw dropped. "Wait, that's it? That's your pointer?"

"What were you expecting, a map and a list of detailed instructions?"

"I guess that'd be asking too much, huh?" I folded my arms across my chest, irritated.

"Fine, I suppose I could give you one more. You need more power to bend one of these beings to your will. More than just the power that you alone possess. You need to be accompanied by someone who, perhaps, has experience with strange negotiations, and someone who isn't afraid of such scenarios."

"Now *that* I can work with." There was a slight problem with regards to *who* I could ask, if I wanted to keep the minutiae of this servitude business quiet, but I'd deal with that when I got back to the SDC.

"There is one more thing, however." Erebus dropped a dramatic pause.

"Yes?" I sighed. This was getting to be too much.

"Oh, I think you will like this one." He chuckled. "If you succeed in this, you will be rewarded for your efforts in the way you most desire. You don't want to be stuck with me forever, do you?"

I stared at him in disbelief. "Is this a trick?"

"No trick, merely an incentive to ensure you succeed. I may be known for my deceptive actions, but I am a Child of my word. I promise you, here and now, that you will receive your reward if you complete this mission and discover the Fount—making sure that it really is where you have been told it is, and that you can access it."

"Seriously?"

He opened out his arms. "With the Purge beasts and Tartarus as my witnesses, I make this vow to you."

My heart grew about three sizes. Grinch Merlin, in the flesh. This was the moment I'd been waiting for. But despite my excitement, a nagging doubt lingered in the back of my head, a loud and obnoxious skepticism.

Erebus had said it himself: he wasn't known for his honesty. He was Darkness incarnate. I couldn't trust him as far as I could throw him, which would've been hard considering he was made of fog. But if there was the slightest hope of escape, I had to seize it with both hands. I hoped he really was a Child of his word.

SEVEN

Garrett

I left the Banquet Hall with the taste of coffee still in my mouth —bitter and stale. I had a meeting with O'Halloran, and I was late. I hadn't intended to have breakfast with everyone there. Usually, I got up early so I could eat alone. Being at the table with Astrid was just too hard.

Not that I didn't like seeing her. I'd have done anything to be close to her again. But she couldn't look at me without sadness creeping into her eyes. Sometimes she'd laugh and catch herself, as if she wasn't supposed to be happy. That hurt the most. Those moments when she almost forgot, and almost allowed herself to smile without guilt.

We'd had a few moments in the year since Alton passed. I'd bring her coffee when I knew she'd been working all hours in her command center. She'd brought me the Avenging Angel to hang on my wall. I'd ask the chef to put her favorite dessert aside, because I knew she'd be hungry. She'd ask me questions that she could've asked anyone. But it was always awkward, like there was a wall between us and we were looking at each other through a tiny gap.

I understood why. If Alton hadn't brought me back, he might've had another year on this earth. He'd given that up for me. His intentions had been good, but he hadn't thought about the hit Astrid would take. How could she look at me, knowing what had been sacrificed so I could stand here? It was the elephant in every room the two of us were in. I was a living reminder of her father's last breath. Nobody could just get over that.

Truth be told, I didn't know if I deserved to be here in his place. He could've done more in that year than I could do in a lifetime. Every step felt borrowed. Every breath felt stolen. Every action felt insufficient. How could I ever pay back what Alton had given me? I was supposed to be taking care of his daughter, but she wouldn't let me near. And I couldn't blame her.

I couldn't be close to Astrid, but I couldn't stay away, either. All I could do was watch from afar and do whatever I could to make sure she was okay.

As I turned the corner toward O'Halloran's office, I felt relief. At least this would be a distraction. I needed all the distractions I could get my hands on these days. I approached the door, lifted the knocker, and let it drop.

"Come in," O'Halloran's voice echoed from inside.

Pushing open the large door, I stepped into the now-familiar room. It had changed a lot from previous regimes. O'Halloran was a man of simple tastes. The hefty desk had been replaced with a curved pine workspace and a computer. A smaller desk sat in one corner for Diarmuid. Diarmuid wasn't here, fortunately, but O'Halloran was at the larger desk, sifting through paperwork.

The leather wing-back armchairs were gone. I sat in a simple office chair with wheels. A small couch stood by the fireplace, plain and black, and the walls had been painted an inoffensive shade of magnolia. No art hung on the walls, only framed certificates of merit and a few old photos from O'Halloran's security service days.

Pictures of people I didn't know, whom O'Halloran didn't talk about.

At first glance it seemed as if Alton had never been there. However, looking closer, his presence lingered in small ways: the carriage clock on the mantelpiece, the green glass lampshade that covered the central light, and the books that lined the shelves. I always focused on these when I set foot in this room. The cumulative effect was nostalgic and sad and peppered with remorse.

That said, the SDC wasn't suffering under O'Halloran's leadership. He was doing a stellar job as director, bringing a military eye to improvements and making sure everything ran with precision. He made sure everyone had a role, even if that role was just guard duty or helping the cleanup operation in the kitchens.

It was because of O'Halloran that we had special agents now, including Harley and Wade, who went out to track down stubborn cultists. The special agents also protected the coven and the Bestiary to avoid any future mishaps. The SDC's reputation had skyrocketed because of our part in killing Katherine, and O'Halloran was determined to keep us riding that high.

"I just sent Diarmuid to fetch you," O'Halloran said with a smile. "I figured you'd get distracted at breakfast after Finch's unexpected injuries. Gossip travels fast, despite my efforts. How's he doing?"

I shrugged. "He's being very… Finch about it. He seems fine, but he probably wouldn't say if he wasn't. Looks like Marianne did a good job patching him up, though."

"It's fortunate we had her around. Poltergeists are a nasty business from what I hear, though I've never come across one myself." He gestured for me to sit, so I did. "But, as long as he's recovering, that's all that matters. I'm hoping to make it through the year without losing someone." An awkward silence stretched between us, as if he knew what he'd said and didn't know how to cover it up.

"What did you want to talk to me about?" I prompted.

This was the worst part about my situation—even after a year, nobody quite knew how to talk to me. It was like they were constantly terrified of saying the wrong thing. *Alton gave up his life for you; how does that feel?* It was the shadow to everyone's words, even though nobody actually came out and said it. If they had, they might've gotten a few answers. It felt like crap. And I hadn't asked for it. I was grateful, of course, but it wasn't as if I could say that to anyone.

"Ah, yes." O'Halloran reached for a folder on his desk and flipped it open. "I wanted to ask you to consider becoming the next preceptor of Physical Magic."

My eyes widened in surprise as O'Halloran continued.

"We've got a hole to fill, as you know, and options are thin on the ground. Not that you're a last resort. You're actually the best candidate we've got, internally and externally. It'd be a substitute position, for now, but the California Mage Council is starting to nag me about having a threadbare faculty. We can't teach properly if we don't have enough instructors, and you're experienced and capable. Plus, I know you'd do a bang-up job." He looked up at me. "So, what do you say?"

"You want *me* as a preceptor?" I spoke slowly, hardly believing what I'd just heard.

"Yes, lad, you. That's why you're here." He gave a quiet laugh.

"But... me?" I gaped at him. "Aren't I too young?" I'd never even thought about holding one of those positions. I was in my twenties. Most preceptors were in their thirties, or older, with a lot more experience. Except for Astrid, who was in charge of Human Relations these days. But she'd always been smarter than the rest of us, which I guess made her an exception.

"You complimented Marianne's skill before—she's not so much older than you. Anyway, I've found that students respond better to people they can relate to. Your youth is your advantage. I wish I still had that advantage. I'm getting grayer by the day. Personally, I blame this job." He ran a hand through his hair to emphasize the point.

I frowned. "But why me? Why not Wade, or Finch, or Santana, or someone like that?"

"Are you any different?" He cocked his head to one side. "You're just as competent. Besides, Santana's skillset is more niche, and Wade prefers fieldwork. And Finch... well, Finch is Finch. He might have the advantage of youth, but he has the disadvantage of a checkered record. So you're the ideal candidate, at least as a back-stop until I can get a decent permanent preceptor."

"You haven't had any luck hiring outside the coven?"

O'Halloran shook his head. "Who'd have thought people would be so unwilling to come and work here? Not a single bite in twelve months. The moment they hear 'SDC' they go running, even though our rep is on the rise. It's not as if Katherine is still hovering in the hallways, pretending to be Imogene." He shrugged. "The magical world has a long memory, and I can't force them to see past it."

"I... I don't know, O'Halloran." I fidgeted in my seat.

"I know things have been rough on you, Garrett. Anyone would feel strange after what happened to you in Elysium. It's not some-thing you can just reverse or erase, right? So, here's a chance for you to get back into the swing of things. I picked you because you use logic over emotions, you've got versatile fighting methods, and your go-to is to mess with your opponents using basic physical magic. No frills. That's what makes you perfect for this. Even if I weren't desperate, I'd be calling on you—if that's what you're worried about."

I shook my head. "It's not that. I'm worried I'll walk into a classroom and everything will go quiet. And then the whispers will start. I died, remember? Like you said, people don't forget easily."

"What's your point?" He gave me a sympathetic yet determined stare. "You died, but you died a hero, and you came back a hero and a man. That's all there is to it. It's easy to get in your own head, but I think this will prove a good distraction for you. It'll remind you what you're here for."

I squirmed in my chair, not knowing what to say to that.

"I won't be miffed if you say no, but I'd rather give the role to someone worthy—someone I know, who's full of promise and potential." O'Halloran flashed a smile. "I don't want to see you wasting yourself."

I nodded slowly. "Actually, I was hoping you'd assign me to a mission or two outside the SDC, for a change of scenery. I've been in the field before, for LA, and I was good at that." I'd been wanting to get away from the coven, just to distance myself from Astrid so I could clear my head. But nothing had come up.

"And that's got nothing to do with Astrid?" O'Halloran arched a knowing eyebrow.

I lowered my gaze. "Not specifically."

"Aye, and I'm the Queen of Sheba." He smiled. "Look, take it from an old fella—the more you run from what's bothering you, the heavier it'll weigh you down. One day, it'll get so heavy you can't run anymore. So, face your demons while the load is lighter, and don't keep hiding from them. That gives them power."

"Does that mean you won't assign me to a mission?" I grumbled.

"Aye, that's what I'm saying. I get why, lad, believe me, but it won't do you any good in the long run." He paused. "Just think about this preceptor position. I'm not in a rush for an answer, and don't worry about disappointing me, because it's up to you. This is your life, Garrett. You won't be putting me out. I just think it'll do you a world of good."

I sank back in the chair. "I'll think about it."

"Glad to hear it. But, like I said, take all the time you need."

Despite what he'd said, I really hoped I wouldn't disappoint him. O'Halloran had his moments of putting his foot in his mouth, but he was one of the only people at the SDC who didn't step on eggshells around me. He was a straight shooter.

Right now, the only way I knew to push all this confusion and pain out of my head was to get as far from the SDC as possible. But even then, it might not be far enough.

At the end of the day, how could anyone truly escape themselves?

EIGHT

Garrett

I left O'Halloran's office. It still felt weird calling it O'Halloran's office. It had always been Alton's, even when Levi and Imogene had taken over. I supposed it would always belong to Alton, in a way.

Alton had been the one to get the ball rolling on changing up the SDC and making it less of a laughingstock. I hadn't appreciated his efforts at the time, but that was the problem with things like that—you didn't know something was good until it was gone. It was the same with Astrid.

We'd only been on a few dates, still getting to know one another, when her resurrection after the Asphodel Meadows changed everything. Even then, with part of her soul missing, there'd been an unspoken bond between us—like we might've been able to get things back on track once the rest of her soul returned. That had been the first hurdle. Alton's death just raised that bar too high to jump over.

I kept my head down, thinking about O'Halloran's proposition as I turned toward the main network of hallways. I almost crashed into someone coming in the opposite direction. When I lifted my head, my heart jolted. Astrid stood in front of me, looking just as shocked. In a romantic movie, this would've been where the cutesy music started to play. For us, it was the start of another bout of anxiety and unspoken pain.

"Sorry, Astrid. Wasn't looking where I was going." I stared down at my sneakers, not wanting to see that familiar sadness in her eyes. It stung every time.

"Me, neither," she replied. "Have you just come from O'Halloran's office?"

I nodded. "Yeah."

"Are you in trouble?"

"No, no trouble. It was just... uh... he had a business proposal for me. I'm thinking about it, but I don't know if I'll take it."

She frowned. "What sort of business proposal?"

"One of the preceptor positions. I told him I was way too young for that. Preceptors are stuffy, bookish types, right?"

"Like me, you mean?" She gave a faint hint of a smile, but it didn't reach her eyes. It never did. I could tell she was trying to be funny, but the gesture fell flat without the real humor to go with it.

"I'm sure you would've been top of the list if you... uh... weren't already preceptor of Technology and Human Relations. Two positions would be hard to juggle, right? Plus, you know, it's a magical position and you're not... um... a magical." When had simple conversation become so difficult? Seriously, I sounded like an idiot. "I still find it hard to think of... uh... you as a preceptor. That's what I mean about the young thing; it's so hard to visualize someone our age teaching kids. How's that going? Students good?"

Dumbass, dumbass, dumbass...

She shrugged. "It's a lot of work, but I like keeping busy. Especially... well, it's good to have a purpose. Everything was so up in the air after Katherine. It's nice that there's some normality to focus on."

I knew she'd mention Alton. His memory dangled between us like a pendulum.

"Right…" I couldn't think of anything else to say. This always happened. We'd start off okay, and then it just descended into lengthy silences and agonizing small talk. If I wasn't careful, I'd start chatting with her about the weather.

"It was nice to see you at breakfast, even if Saskia was being a nuisance." Astrid broke the tension first. "It's been ages since you've been at the table with the rest of us."

I nodded. "Yeah, I've been busy. Early bird and all that."

"Good. That's good." She laughed nervously. "For a moment there, I thought you were avoiding me."

Avoiding you? If only it were that simple. Even now, I wanted to blurt out the truth, to tell her that I still had feelings for her—that I wanted to do what Alton had put me here to do. That I wanted to look after her, and to explore those feelings if she'd let me. But, as ever, I kept my mouth shut. I couldn't say it out loud.

"Ha… of course not. Just busy," I replied, my tongue in knots. "What are you doing in this neck of the woods, anyway?"

"O'Halloran wants to rename the Luis Paoletti Room after my dad." Her gaze dropped like a stone. "He needs my approval, since I'm… I'm his next of kin."

The tension between us came hurtling back, worse than before. Any mention of Alton and I lost her again to the grief. It was like a heavy metal shutter coming down, closing her off. On a good day, I could almost reach her. On a bad day, I might as well have been a hundred miles away. Perhaps it would've been easier if I had been.

"Okay, well, I'll… let you get on with that," I said awkwardly. She didn't say anything as I stepped past her, but I could feel her eyes on me. They were like hot pokers on my skin. Keeping my gaze fixed on the hallway ahead, I fought the urge to look back. To have her watch me and not be able to say a word was almost too much to bear. And it got harder each day.

But I'm not giving up on you. I swore it to myself as I kept walking. Alton had brought me back for a reason, but I needed to follow my own compass, too. I wanted to see her smile again, not just for Alton but for *me*. I wanted her to look at me like there were no ghosts lurking between us. I didn't want us to be haunted anymore. I didn't want us to share small talk and tiptoe around each other as if we were strangers. If it took another year, and another, and another, I'd keep trying.

Next time I see you, I'll try again. I was still human—I just needed to start acting like it in front of her.

I was halfway to the living quarters, hoping peace and quiet would help me put my head in order, when a voice called out and brought me to a halt.

"Garrett! Wait!" Finch barreled out of a nearby hallway. He still looked like a mess, but if he was running, he couldn't be that bad anymore. "Have you got a minute? I need to talk to you about something." He put his hands on his ribs and heaved in a breath. "I really need to start going to the gym."

"Is that what you wanted to talk to me about? Dylan's probably your guy for that."

He shook his head. "No, that's not it. I need your help." He pointed to my pocket. "Don't you check your phone anymore? I sent you a text about meeting up."

I patted it to check it was still there. "Ah, sorry about that. I was in a meeting, and then I saw Astrid. But sure… I guess it's about time we caught up."

"That's the spirit!" He clapped me on the back and urged me to follow him. I supposed this was as good a way as any to forget about Astrid, if only for a short while.

An hour later, Finch and I sat in a booth in Moll Dyer's Bar in Waterfront Park. Jazz music drifted from the speakers. It wasn't very busy, as it was early afternoon on a weekday, but I didn't mind. There was something about the mahogany and gloom that was comforting.

Finch dug into a bowl of peanuts as we talked. It reminded me of old times, when Finch and I would come here to relax after a day at the SDC, before I'd had a clue about Katherine, and before Harley ever came into our lives. Finch had obviously known about Katherine, but that hatchet had been buried.

"Garrett Kyteler, faculty member. It's got a ring to it," Finch said. I'd just told him about O'Halloran's job offer. "Should I be offended that O'Halloran didn't bother to ask me?"

I smirked. "Can you imagine yourself as a preceptor?"

"Hey, I look good in tweed."

"You don't have to wear tweed to be a preceptor, Finch. If you did, I'd have turned O'Halloran down on the spot." I took a sip of my drink, feeling more relaxed than I had an hour ago.

"Man, if he'd offered me the job, just think about the scheduling nightmare."

"Yeah, you'd have to keep darting out on your Erebus errands."

He laughed. "I can picture it now. 'Keep looking at section four, everyone, I just need to run out for a week. You can teach your-selves, right?' You're the more reliable choice, even if I didn't have Erebus to deal with." He washed his peanuts down with a mouthful of his drink. "My life's on hold until this contract is over with. I know it, you know it, O'Halloran knows it. No use making plans until there's an end in sight." He stared at the bar for a moment, as though he were thinking about something else.

"Everything okay?"

"Huh? Oh, yeah... Still feeling a bit weird after the poltergeist poison, but otherwise peachy."

"The Erebus stuff getting to you?"

He shrugged. "Nothing I can do about it, so there's no use crying over spilt Chaos. Speaking of crying, how are things with you and Astrid? I didn't expect to see you at breakfast, since you've spent most mornings avoiding her like the plague." Finch threw me a knowing glance, then grimaced. "Although, I was grateful to have someone take the heat from Saskia. I keep thinking about writing to immigration to get her deported, but I'm still coming up with a good excuse. I doubt 'She's a kid and she keeps flirting with me' will fly."

"She's a nightmare," I agreed. "I don't think I've ever seen Tatyana lose her cool, except with that sister of hers."

"It's a good thing Dylan is a Herculean—he might have to physically keep them from scratching each other's eyes out." Finch chuckled.

"It's only supposed to be temporary, so hopefully she'll be on her way soon," I said.

He nodded, before shooting me a curious glance. "So... Astrid? Any progress? I know I haven't been around much lately, but things didn't look warm and fuzzy this morning."

I tapped my fingers against my glass. "I know we weren't the romance of the century, but I cared about her. Still do. We only put a stop to things because part of her soul was missing, but I guess I always hoped she'd get it back and we'd try again. But it's hard, man. Seriously, it's impossible. I think we're making progress, then we end up back at square one. Every time she looks at me, she sees *him*."

"Not exactly sexy, right?" He was trying to keep things light, and I was grateful for that.

"No, not sexy at all, and definitely not helpful." I sighed. "I want her back, Finch, but I've got no idea how to do this. I can't even talk to her properly anymore. I get all stuttery and stupid, like I'm going to say the wrong thing. Even when we're talking, and it's going smoothly, there's always a moment—it's like a switch being flipped, and I can see her remembering. Then it gets weird again."

I didn't know why I was telling this to Finch, of all people, but I really needed someone to vent to. And we'd been close once. Maybe this was me confiding in him for old times' sake. Or maybe it was purely selfish. Either way, it felt good to shift some of that weight, just as O'Halloran had said.

"You're right, it's a mess," Finch replied, in his blunt way. "It's more complicated than time travel, which is ironic, since time travel would solve everything. Anyway, I digress—yeah, it's hard, and it's painful, and it's difficult as ass, but Alton sacrificed himself so the two of you could be happy together. You were metaphorically pushing up daisies when he said it, but he did say it. She heard him. If you stay apart, even though you both obviously care about each other, then you're going against Alton's wishes. You *have* to make it work. It'd be rude not to."

I'd had similar thoughts, but hearing it said aloud hammered the idea home. Finch was good at that. There was an advantage to his bluntness.

We have *to make it work.* That was why Alton had done what he did—well, that and bringing the missing part of Astrid's soul back so she could feel again. The two were intertwined. *We* were intertwined. And if we didn't try, then Alton died for nothing. I realized suddenly that the last part was exactly why things had felt so painfully sad. It was like we were letting something important slip away. It was the emptiness of not fulfilling a purpose.

"Finch, you're a genius," I said.

"Well, I know *that*." He grinned back.

I breathed a sigh of renewed confidence. This gave me the boost

I needed to try again with Astrid, as soon as I got another chance. I wouldn't lay it on thick, like, "Your dad said we should be together, so we should be together." But it would strengthen my resolve.

"What about *your* love life?" I turned the tables on Finch. "You're pretty tongue-tied around Ryann, which isn't something we see every day. You were practically drooling into your coffee at breakfast. Something I should know about?"

His expression changed in a millisecond. Cheerful to distant. *Distraction: success.* "Nope, nothing to know about or talk about. Ryann's a cool girl, but she's not my cup of tea. Too high maintenance. And also, taken."

I snorted. "I know you like her. It's obvious. I've never seen anyone able to throw you off your game. When she enters a room, it's like someone replaced you with a babbling idiot. If you like her, go get her."

"Did you not hear the part about Mr. Perfect?" Finch replied.

"You'd let that stop you?"

He took a sullen sip from his drink. "Hey, I've got morals. Loose ones, sure, but I have them. She's happy with Adam the serial killer. He's in pediatric care, for Pete's sake. I might be a magical, but I don't go around saving babies. Anyway, she's human, which is plain wrong. It makes her vulnerable, considering my Erebus issue. It's just not going to happen, even if I wanted it to." He looked up nervously. "Which I don't, by the way."

I smiled. "Never say never."

"All right, Justin Bieber," he muttered. "Anyway, I didn't bring you here to gossip about girls."

"Then why did you bring me here?"

"I'm getting to it." He leaned closer. "Up until now, working for Erebus has been relatively simple: tracking down ancient artifacts, a spell or two, a couple of rare Ephemeras, some one-of-a-kind herbs and flowers, that sort of jam. This one is giving me more of a headache than usual—and a couple of nasty wounds to go with it. I can't fail, or Erebus will have my head on a platter."

I frowned. "Does this have to do with the poltergeist?"

Finch rolled his eyes. "Keep up, snail. Erebus had me go on the hunt for the spirit of Ponce de León—a.k.a. our friendly neighborhood poltergeist—and, by proxy, the Fountain of Youth. It's okay, I'll pause while you gasp."

I hate to say it, but I did gasp. "What? That thing is actually real?"

"Very real, by all accounts, and I need your help if I'm going to survive this."

I nodded slowly. "Okay… I'm listening."

NINE

Finch

I gave Garrett the rundown on what had been going on, from the purpose behind Erebus's mission to my adventures in Cuba, and finished off with the pièce de résistance of Ponce de León's unexpected poltergeistness and the gory tale behind the gash across my chest.

"So you were trying to get him to tell you the location of the Fountain of Youth?" Garrett asked.

"Exactly."

"And I'm guessing Erebus isn't going to take too kindly to you not turning up with the goods?" Garrett was staring at me like he wished he hadn't agreed to talk.

"Bingo. Which, as luck would have it, is where you come in." I smiled. "I need some more brains on this case. I don't know what Imogene/Katherine had you doing, but you've got experience in the arena of dealing with the weird and wonderful. And you've got negotiation skills under your belt. I know those skills aren't specific to ghosts and spirits, but I'm thinking two against one might be the way to take him down. I'd ask Harley, but I don't want her getting involved. Erebus already has a thing for her, and it'd be too risky to dangle the carrot of making a deal with Harley in front of him. He just wouldn't pass up that opportunity." I paused for breath, realizing I'd been rambling. "Basically, I need to convince Ponce's poltergeist to tell me where that Fountain is, or I'll be getting anything but eternal life. To do that, I need more manpower. You're a man, and you have power. And you're the lowest risk option, no offence, since you're not likely to tell Harley about any of this—bro-code and whatnot."

Garrett frowned. "None taken. But can't you ask someone else about the Fountain's location?"

I looked at him as if he were an idiot. "You think I wouldn't be on my way, right now, if there was someone else I could ask? The spirit of Ponce de León is the only one who knows where it is. There's no other way to find the Fountain."

I paused to take a much-needed swig of water. I was good at keeping up appearances, but this injury was kicking my ass. Marianne might have gotten all the dead-men's poison out, but there were some lingering effects making me feel dozy and on-edge at the same time. My brain was already a little messed up, and this was making it ten times worse. My heart was constantly racing while my limbs felt like lead weights.

"I've already been to a few potential sites from my extensive research. Turns out, the location of the Fountain of Youth is the most frequently speculated place on the planet, with the exception of Atlantis and maybe Area 51. A lot of desperate people try to find it and sip its sweet, sweet nectar. Anyway, I searched Bimini from top to bottom, no stone unturned... literally. But it didn't pan out, and neither did the other places. I must have covered half of the Caribbean trying to find it, or someone who would know where it was. No luck. So, the only one with the 411 is my poltergeist pal."

Garrett said nothing for a moment. I didn't blame him. It was a lot to take in. Finally, he leaned forward in his seat, his expression businesslike.

"Sounds like you've had a hell of a time."

I nodded. "That's putting it mildly. The Caribbean is supposed to be a place for drinks with umbrellas and lounging about on the beach. All I've seen are mangroves and forests and endless caves filled with all sorts of critters you don't even want to know about. *Everything* scuttles or flaps down there. Not a cocktail in sight."

"Why does Erebus want this?"

It was the most obvious question, echoing my own curiosity. But Erebus's words boomed in my skull. I was his minion, bound to obey meekly and not ask questions like why a Child of Chaos would need something so very human.

"He won't say." I sighed anxiously. "I'd take more time with it and try to delve deeper if I could, but there's something else."

"Oh?" Garrett arched an eyebrow.

"He's offered my freedom in exchange for the Fountain's location." That's what he'd promised me—the thing I wanted most. That could only mean my freedom.

Every time I thought about it, I could feel it moving closer to my grasp. I didn't know if I had it in me to keep doing these errands for Erebus. It wasn't just the danger. Every time I left on one of his missions, the effort I had to put in was an enormous strain on my mind, my body, and my soul. I wanted a real life, without Erebus hanging over my every move, making me wonder when I would next see blood on the mirror.

I continued. "I keep thinking he might have made that offer because he doesn't expect me to survive, but he wants the location. He needs me to live so I can deliver it to him. Which means it's real. This could all end, if I just get him what he's after."

"It concerns me—the reason Erebus wants it. But since you're bound to him by that contract, and he's not giving you any answers, we'll put that aside for now," Garrett said. "What's important is getting the location and getting you out of the deal."

I nodded with a grateful sigh of relief. "Right."

"Can I make a suggestion?"

"Go ahead."

"I'd say we need a Kolduny's help on this. I might be decent at negotiations, and I might've dealt with some odd things, but if the poltergeist didn't listen to you, he's not going to listen to me. Manpower may not be enough, from what you've told me. Tatyana already said she knows about poltergeists, so we need to know what she knows."

I raised a hand. "I've been thinking about that. Tatyana has the experience, sure, but she's got a history of getting possessed by powerful spirits. She said poltergeists don't typically possess people, but she's like a magnet for spiritual danger. I think it's her power in this field that makes her a risk. I really don't want her getting possessed by Ponce de León on my conscience."

Garrett tapped the side of his glass. "Poltergeists are powerful. Far worse than the likes of Oberon Marx, though maybe not as bad as Marie Laveau. That's a tough call." His brow furrowed. "I hate to say it, but what about Saskia? She's younger than Tatyana, which means she's got less of that addictive power, but she still underwent rigorous Kolduny training with her parents. She might be the best of both worlds."

"Or a gigantic pain in our asses." I rolled my eyes, remembering her onslaught at breakfast.

"Hear me out. She's remarkably powerful and self-controlled, especially given her age, but she doesn't have the raw essence that Tatyana has—the magnetic spark that keeps getting her in trouble. Tatyana told me so herself, when I asked about Saskia. She might be strong enough to coax the intel out of the poltergeist, without being a target for possession."

I snorted. "Here I was, worrying about Erebus tossing me to his beasties. Tatyana would hang me by my entrails if I took her sister anywhere near that poltergeist, even if there is less risk. And I happen to like my innards where they are. I don't want them becoming my outtards. Although, I suppose she could just harass Ponce into submission."

Garrett smiled. "Fine, let's forget about getting her close to the poltergeist for now. We can at least ask Saskia for advice. We don't know how these things work yet. We might be able to pull it off without a Kolduny, as long as we understand what's needed to tame a poltergeist."

"What about Tatyana?"

"Do you want her to know?"

I swirled my drink, thinking. If Tatyana got involved, she would go running to Harley with intel on everything we were doing. Harley would worry. Harley always worried. It was her default setting. And then my sister would try and help me—or do what I'd done to her and creep around after me. She'd think she was doing me a favor, but it'd just make the whole thing more dangerous.

Yep, that's how that would play out. I'd be trying to save her, she'd be trying to save me, and the whole thing would be a distraction I didn't need. But I wasn't keen on dragging a teenage girl into that lighthouse, either, no matter how tough she was.

But it wouldn't hurt to get some info out of her, and keep her at arm's length. She'd be less likely to see through the BS than Tatyana, which made her the better intel source.

"No, I guess not," I replied.

"Then it has to be Saskia. She's already made it clear she's willing to help, which might make it easier to keep her quiet about this. To be honest, she'd do just about anything to get one over on her sister, which is useful for us. She gets to defy Taty, behind her back—she's not going to turn that down."

"Fine," I relented. "Saskia it is. Honestly, I'd have thought you'd be against this."

He chuckled. "Why? You know I'm all about logic, and she's the obvious choice if Tatyana is out."

"Yeah, but she's a pain in the ass." I smiled at him, my mind jittering. Another effect of the dead-men's poison, most likely. *Stupid poltergeist.* I just hoped these little aftershocks would disappear sooner rather than later, or this was going to be a whole lot harder. I needed my mind in good shape, with my gremlins safely tucked away.

"If it's just this one time, I'm sure we'll be fine. Anyway, we're just going to Saskia for information. We're not putting her in harm's way." He glanced at me. "Can I ask one other thing?"

I shrugged. "Shoot."

"Does the Fountain of Youth do what the legends say it does?"

"My gut says yes, based on the side-quests and interviews I've conducted so far. Everyone I've spoken to believes in it, and all the books are pretty definite. Plus, Erebus's desire for it would suggest it does exactly what it says on the package."

"Would you drink from it, then, to gain immortality?"

I gave a low whistle. "Now there's a question. I haven't really thought about it. It won't seem real until I see it, you know? But... I don't know. An eternity in solitude, watching everyone I love grow old and die, until I'm the only one left... that isn't exactly how I'd like to live my life. How about you?"

He frowned. "I don't know either. Everyone always says if something seems too good to be true, it probably is. Immortality can't be all it's cracked up to be. The Children of Chaos don't always seem so happy, and they've got it, so it's probably not perfect."

"Exactly. We don't know what effect it might have—downsides, provisos, that sort of thing. I've learned enough from Erebus to know that to gain something you have to give something." I paused, feeling a shiver creep up my spine. "And I don't know what the price for eternal life would be."

My guess? Astronomical.

TEN

Finch

W e headed straight back from Waterfront Park and found
Saskia where you'd find any good Kolduny—in the SDC
Crypt, chatting with ghosts who hadn't crossed over. I didn't like to
come here if I could help it. There were too many good people
buried here: Alton, Isadora, Nomura, Jacintha, and the majority of
the SDC allies who'd fallen in Elysium.

Saskia didn't seem to mind, though. Her laughter bubbled up as
we walked along the precipice, which looked over the vast cavern
below. The tombs and mausoleums made up a patchwork of
memorials on the far wall, rising up through level after level, with
only the façades visible. The main bodies of the structures were
embedded into the rock. There'd been more visitors in the aftermath of Katherine's demise, but today Saskia was the only one.

"Have you seen those pants she wears? I just wonder what she's
hiding up those flares. You could carry just about anything." Saskia
burst into another bout of hysterics. "I wouldn't be seen dead in
them, no offense. She's one of the youngest preceptors here—she

should be using that, not smothering herself in tie-dye. There are so many good-looking guys here. Way more than in Moscow."

Marianne seemed to be the topic of her teenage mockery. Not that we could hear what the spirits had to say in return. All we could see was Saskia, sitting in the dirt, howling to herself.

And they say I'm the mad one.

She didn't seem to notice as we made our way down the stairs, the temperature plummeting as we descended into the coven's underbelly. It felt a little disrespectful for Saskia to be here, making fun of folks, but if the spirits were enjoying it, who was I to ruin their fun?

"Dylan? No way. I like my men a bit more intellectual, though my sister doesn't seem to care," Saskia said to the empty air. "Lincoln Mont-Noir? Why should I stay away from him? He seems harmless enough... ah, I see. Never been kissed. Yeah, that's not for me. I prefer a man with experience."

It sounded like she was getting a rundown on all the guys at the SDC—who to date, who to avoid, who was top of the hot list—and she was clearly enjoying every minute. She was so engrossed in her conversation that she still hadn't noticed our approach.

"Jacob? Haven't you been listening? I like *much* older guys," she shrieked, startling me. I had to laugh. *Oh, Jacob... the spirits should be telling you to stay away from this one.* Saskia would eat that poor boy alive, judging by her terrifyingly intense display this morning. He'd be better off sticking to his inventions.

I cleared my throat. "Saskia?"

She finally turned, her face lighting up in a disturbing way. "Is it my birthday? Shouldn't the two of you have bows on, or something?"

Garrett shot me a this-was-a-bad-idea look, even though he was the one to suggest it. "This isn't a social call, and you really shouldn't speak to us like that."

"Why not? You don't strike me as a killjoy, Garrett." She flashed a kilowatt grin that made me feel nauseous. "I'm not causing any harm, just having a bit of fun. There's not much else to do around here. You don't mind, do you, Finch?"

I gave her a deadpan look. "Why don't you ask your spirit friends?"

"Oh, you don't want to hear what they've got to say about you." Saskia snorted. "There's a spirit here who would still be alive if it wasn't for you. I don't know if Lindsey Parrish rings a bell? She's told me *all* about you—said you were always odd, and that she knew there was something wrong about you. She was eaten alive by gargoyles, in case you were curious. Apparently, that was your fault."

I froze. "Is she standing near you right now?"

"Right here." Saskia gestured to her right. "It's a good thing I like a bad boy."

I faced the spirit. Guilt twisted in my stomach. I'd come a long way since I released those gargoyles, but I couldn't change the past, no matter how much I tried to better myself. It took moments like this to remind me of all the terrible things that I would never be able to make amends for. My gremlins were chomping at the bit, starting to scratch their claws against the inside of my brain.

She knew there was something wrong about me? Was there still something wrong with me?

"I... I'm sorry, Lindsey. I know there's nothing I can say or do to make it better, but I want you to know that I'm sorry. I wasn't me, then. I was someone else, under Katherine's thumb." I paused. "I won't ask for your forgiveness, because I don't deserve it, but I hope you can find a way to cross over. Don't be stuck here forever because of me."

"She says she's not giving you the satisfaction," Saskia replied. "Maybe you're not as exciting as I thought. You're not the person she described at all. She said you were this big, evil monster, but you seem like a pussycat to me. All trembling and apologetic. I suppose it's good to have both sides—the bad boy and the sweet guy, all rolled into one."

"Can you stop? I'm trying to apologize here," I shot back.

She laughed. "Why bother? It's not like you can resurrect her. She's pissed, so let her be. You owe her that much."

Suddenly, Saskia went still, a white glow piercing the center of her eyes. "There's someone else who wants to send you their best wishes."

"Who?" Garrett stepped in.

Saskia grinned. "Does the name Jacintha Parks mean anything to you?"

This was getting too *America's Most Haunted* for me.

"Yes," I replied.

"She says you were never her best students, but you made up for it with your pretty faces—two delicious snacks for her eyes to feast on." Saskia's eyes glowed brighter.

So she's the one who's coaching you on the sexiness of the coven's guys? Seriously, we weren't pieces of meat. We were human beings, with actual feelings. Still, I couldn't help but laugh at her trying to be oh so grown up. She probably had one of those Marilyn Monroe posters that said, "If you can't handle me at my worst, then you sure as hell don't deserve me at my best."

As my chuckle reverberated around the Crypt, she glared at me. "What are you laughing at?"

"Nothing." I tried to stifle my grin.

"No, come on, share the joke." She continued to glare at me, which only made it funnier. I started cracking up. Garrett nudged me in the ribs, trying to get me to knock it off.

"Just don't try to grow up so fast, that's all," I replied, stifling a snort. "Dating at your age isn't worth the trouble, believe me. And you definitely don't want to listen to Jacintha. She was legal, you're not. Plus, she really shouldn't have been eyeing up her students, no matter how irresistible we were."

She pouted, clearly not taking kindly to being laughed at. *If you can't take it, don't give it.*

"You weren't really speaking to Jacintha, were you?" Garrett said pointedly.

"No... but so what? Like I said, I'm just having a little fun. I'm not hurting anyone." Her gaze hardened, though she clearly felt uncomfortable about being called out. "Anyway, you're literally the last person on Earth who's got the right to join the morality police here. I might summon Adley's spirit right now, just to remind you that you used to date well above your age, once upon a time. But that would be beneath me."

She smiled sweetly as bitter anger spiked in my chest. It hurt just to hear her name, mentioned like that, like she was just some tool that could be used for Saskia's amusement. As if it was so friggin' easy to just bring her back.

"You don't get to talk about her," I warned.

"Isn't she another one who'd be alive if it weren't for you?"

Saskia was seconds away from crossing a line. I took a measured breath. "You couldn't summon her spirit even if you wanted to."

"Oh, couldn't I?"

"No, you couldn't."

She flicked her hair. "And why is that? Because you think I'm some dumb kid who doesn't know anything? I can call her here right now if you like and show you just what I'm capable of."

"She isn't buried here, Saskia, so you'd have a hard time." I landed the blow to shut her up. Adley was buried in the LA Coven, not here. If her spirit was still around, I'd beg Tatyana to speak with her every day. But Saskia clearly hadn't realized that little fact.

And besides, Adley's spirit had crossed over a long time ago, shortly after her murder. It was the reason nobody had been able to do anything to resurrect her.

She said nothing, and her eyes slowly lost their glow.

If I'd gained anything from Katherine's torment throughout my adolescence, it was the idea that lessons needed to be learned. Making Saskia feel foolish about her idle threats would go some way toward that, since this kid had clearly lived a charmed life so far. I could already see the embarrassment at being caught in a lie on her face. It was probably a bad idea to take parenting tips from a psychopath who'd crushed me beyond recognition for so many years and saddled me with a Suppressor from birth without telling me, but it was the only strategy I had.

In the end, Garrett broke the tension. "We need your help with a poltergeist," he said.

Saskia smirked. "Is it the same one who handed you your ass yesterday, Finch?"

I gave a sullen nod.

She snapped her fingers, and the air felt clearer. I hadn't realized until that moment, but the atmosphere had been so heavy with the presence of spirits that all the hairs on the back of my neck had been standing on end. The air had been thick and crackling, like before a storm. All of that went away at the click of Saskia's fingers, and I could suddenly breathe properly again.

"What did you do?" Garrett whispered, as if we were in a church or a library.

"I sent the spirits away, obviously." She gave him a withering look. "It's just me now. So, come on, I'm listening. Don't keep a girl in suspense."

I shrugged off my anger over Adley and focused. "We need to extract information from a poltergeist. We're going to need some way to subdue the spirit first."

"What information?" she replied.

Ha, no way, sunshine. "That's not important."

She stood and folded her arms across her chest. "That won't work for me, Finch. You probably thought I'd be easier than my sister, huh? Sorry to be the bearer of bad news, but you've got things twisted. If you wanted easy, you should've gone to Tatyana."

"Look, we just need help figuring out how to subdue this thing," I said.

Saskia put on that sickeningly sweet smile again. "Either you tell me everything about this poltergeist and what you're looking for, or I'll go right to my sister and tell her you wanted to involve me. I'll add some tears and everything, just to amp up the effect. She might think I'm a brat, but we're blood—she'll do everything in her power to protect me. And I'm pretty sure that includes ripping both your heads off and feeding them to that death horse she loves so much."

I put my hands up. "But we're not asking you to get involved in this. We just want advice."

"Do you think Taty will care about the nuances?" She chuckled, providing me with a firm reminder of why I hated teenagers so much. They were a law unto themselves. I hadn't even liked myself when I was one.

"Your choice, boys. Tell me everything or end up a Kelpie's dinner."

I really hadn't expected her to do a 180 on us like this. Then again, she was a Vasilis. We should've known. Tatyana was like a watered-down version of the Russian oligarchs she belonged to. It was easy to forget where she came from, and the types of people she called family. They were businesspeople, used to getting whatever they wanted by any means necessary. Looked like Little Miss Vasilis had picked up a thing or two along the way.

I cast a worried glance at Garrett. His face reflected mine.

Saskia had us by the balls. She knew we wanted Tatyana out of this, which was why we'd come to Saskia in the first place. And the devious little wretch was using it against us. I could only imagine the drama she'd cause if we didn't do what she asked.

"We have to tell her," Garrett said reluctantly.

I nodded. "Having Tatyana know doesn't seem so bad now."

"Tough luck," Saskia chimed in. "If you're thinking of changing your minds, you won't make it out of here. I can call those spirits back any time and give them enough clout to knock you both out. So don't even think about it."

The girl was clearly thrilled to have all the power over two grown men. *Ugh.*

I pulled a sour face. "The poltergeist is the spirit of Ponce de León, and we need him to tell us the whereabouts of the Fountain of Youth. That's pretty much it. Would you like a bow on that, too?"

"No, seeing the look on your faces is better than any bow." She smirked. "However, you'll be pleased to know that I can help you… on one condition."

"And what might that be?" I replied. *Seriously, what now?*

"I'm tagging along." It wasn't a question. "If I'm going to help you, then I'm going to be part of this, from start to finish."

Garrett sucked in a sharp breath. "No, absolutely not. You think your sister will forgive us if you get hurt? Nope, not happening."

"You got any other ways to say 'no' over there?" Saskia giggled.

"We're serious, Saskia," I cut in. "We just came to ask for advice. You're not getting involved in this, in any other way. No chance. You've seen what happened to me. You're not getting *close* to that thing, do you understand?"

Saskia examined her nails. "But you don't know what you're doing. I do. And, if you don't let me come with you, you will definitely end up dead. A poltergeist like this needs a Kolduny's presence. And, would you look at that, I'm right here."

"No!" Garrett pressed.

"Fine, you can try it on your own if you really want to, but can you truly afford to lose this fight... or worse, die?" She waited for an answer.

"If we survive it, and Tatyana finds out, we may as well have stayed and let the poltergeist get us," I retorted. "I know you hate hearing this, Saskia, but you're a kid. We're not putting you in danger."

She shrugged. "You'll be in more danger without me. I might be young, but I know what I'm capable of, and I know how to deal with poltergeists. I could go in there alone and come out alive, but I can't say the same for you two. You were almost killed once, Finch. Do you feel like getting the dead-men's poison sucked out of you again? Because, let me tell you, the more you're exposed to it, the harder it is to fix. Even Preceptor Woodstock might not be able to do anything for you."

"It's not happening, Saskia," Garrett insisted. "If we're trying to protect you and trying to subdue this poltergeist, we're splitting our focus. Your presence is only going to make things riskier. So, just tell us what we have to do, and we'll get on with it."

"Protect me?" She snorted. "Don't make me laugh. It'll be me protecting the two of you. Last I checked, neither of you had any spiritual skill whatsoever. If you're going to the spirit of Ponce de León without a Kolduny, you might as well not bother. You won't get what you want, and you'll both wind up in the infirmary, if you're lucky."

Conflict raged in my head. On the one hand, I didn't want to get Tatyana's kid sister tangled up in this. On the other hand, if I didn't get what Erebus wanted, then I could kiss my freedom—and possibly my life—goodbye. She made a compelling argument, but it just didn't feel right to have someone so young involved.

"How old were you when Katherine forced you into your first dangerous situation?" Saskia caught me off guard.

I frowned. "Sixteen."

"Exactly!" she said triumphantly. "And this isn't my first. I've been doing dangerous things since I was five years old. Do you think a Kolduny becomes a Kolduny by reading books and studying hard? No, we go through training like you wouldn't believe. We start encountering malevolent spirits as soon as we're able to wipe our own asses."

"Yeah, you really don't want to be following my mother's example," I retorted.

"Why not? She almost got what she wanted, didn't she? Even if she didn't reach her end goal, she got her way ninety-nine percent of the time. Seems like a pretty good example to me, even if she was a stone-cold bitch." Saskia shot me a sly glance. "And you were definitely tougher under her influence, from what I've been hearing, so it couldn't have been all bad."

"Saskia, it's not—" Garrett interjected, only for her to cut him off.

"I'm not idolizing Katherine Shipton, if that's what you're going to freak out about. I'm just saying, you don't have to worry about me. I've been doing things like this for years—longer than you were your mother's sidekick, Finch. So, when I say you'll die if you don't take me, you should know that I'm serious."

I turned to Garrett. "What do you think?"

"What choice do we have?"

"Ah… so that's it." Saskia smiled to herself.

"What's it?" Garrett replied.

"That's why you're not interested in girls." She pointed to Garrett. "You ignore Astrid completely, even though she's clearly in love with you. And you, Finch, act as if you hate Ryann, who definitely has a thing for you. Now it all makes sense. You two love each other, right?"

I rolled my eyes at her. "Very good. Hilarious. You get a slap on the back. No, we don't love each other. We're... we're friends. And Ryann does *not* have a thing for me. She's got a six-foot-something Canadian Adonis for a boyfriend. We're just friends, too."

I hadn't said that about Garrett in a long time, and I didn't even know if it was true. But I'd said it, which maybe lent it some weight.

"Sounds to me like you're in denial about *something*, but, hey, I won't press." She flashed me a mischievous smile. "So, what's it going to be? Life or death, you decide."

"You can come with us, but if Tatyana ever hears about this, you've got to stop her from murdering us," I replied.

"Deal." She gave an excited little chirp.

"Okay, how do we do this?" Garrett jumped in.

She smiled. "First off, I won't be able to capture a poltergeist all by myself. A job like this requires tools. So, I'm going to need an Ivan the Terrible Trap. It's an ancient mechanism created to trap and subdue a poltergeist."

"Let me guess, it's named after Ivan the Terrible—the ancient magical and scary-as-hell conqueror?" I smirked.

"Ten points to you, Finch. He used these devices to terrify his enemies, by setting poltergeists loose in their camps and cities, before invading them. The short name is an Ivan Trap. They're extremely—"

"Rare?" I guessed. Why did these items always have to be rare? One of these days, I'd be able to walk into a magical store and just buy a necessary artifact, instead of having to run around trying to locate it. Erebus had jaded me. *You happy now, oh Prince of Darkness?*

She nodded. "Yep, they're rare and expensive."

"So where do we get one?" Garrett asked.

"There are these Dark Tourist gatherings that go on in the nice parts of LA. I figure we can probably find one there, if we're lucky. They have all sorts of weird and awesome things, and they go crazy for anything from historical psychos and baddies." Her eyes were shining as she spoke. Worrying. Very worrying. The Kolduny was strong with this one.

"How do you know so much about this stuff?" I asked.

She grinned back. "I'm more of a social butterfly than my sister has ever been. I know my way around magical society, and I know a few back doors and shady alleys in said society. When Taty moved here, my parents focused all their attention on me. And, unlike Taty, I actually listened to our father's advice, including the importance of building and establishing a network of friends from all circles."

"All circles, huh?" I said dryly.

She laughed. "These days, you never know when you might need a rich Council Mage to bail you out without your parents knowing about it, or a Shapeshifting smuggler to get you a rare artifact."

Garrett and I exchanged baffled looks. Saskia, despite appearances, was turning out to be the savvy third wheel we needed for this mission. Whether we liked it or not. I imagined Mr. and Mrs. Vasilis didn't know half the stuff their youngest got up to. Clever, devious, and strong-willed—every parent's nightmare. But, perhaps, our ideal associate. I just hoped Tatyana wouldn't have our necks for this. I liked my neck, especially attached to the rest of me and not down in a Kelpie's stomach.

"So, how do we go about finding the Dark Tourist gathering that sells one of these Ivan Traps?" I looked to Saskia, who grinned back like the Cheshire Cat but twice as creepy.

Yeah, I had a really bad feeling about this.

ELEVEN

Garrett

"Are you nuts?!" Finch blurted out, before I could.

Saskia shrugged. "Miranda Bontemps is the only one who personally knows about these Dark Tourist gatherings. She goes to them."

"Yeah, Earth to Saskia—she's a preceptor!" Finch shook his head. He probably wished we hadn't come. I was starting to, as well.

Saskia had proven she had the alpha streak to be a useful accomplice, but there just seemed to be issue after issue, clause after clause. This wasn't exactly keeping things on the down-low. Telling a preceptor what we were up to, even vaguely, wasn't much better than letting Tatyana in on the secret.

"What are you afraid of?" Saskia said. "Miranda won't go spreading our names around, since these gatherings are kept quiet."

"Does that mean this Dark Tourist stuff is kind of... illegal?" I asked.

"They're frowned on, but no one is actually breaking any laws. Sure, *sometimes* black-market items get sold, but the majority is legal collectibles." Saskia sighed in frustration. "Miranda isn't going to tell anyone. You think she'd risk anyone finding out what she gets up to in her free time? She might as well confess she plays *Dungeons and Dragons*."

"Hey, there's nothing wrong with a bit of *D&D*," Finch replied defensively. Ever the nerd. Even back in the day, when I first met him, he'd been obsessed with all things geek. Finch looked up at me. "Wait, does Ryann know about this Dark Tourist stuff?"

Saskia smiled. "Maybe I was wrong about you, Finchy. Does someone have a little crush on his sister's adoptive sister after all? Bit too Ancient Greek for my taste, especially considering you could have your pick. There are plenty of fish in the sea. Prettier fish."

She batted her eyelashes at him, which made him go pale. I couldn't help laughing a bit, watching him squirm.

"Leave Ryann out of this, and keep your schnoz out of other people's business," Finch said. "People like the fish they like, okay? And that's got nothing to do with you."

"Did I hit a nerve?" Saskia chuckled. "Anyway, we can't leave Ryann out of this. She's our way in."

"Excuse me?" I cut in. "Ryann's a human. It's not safe for her to be involved."

The fewer people involved, the better. Especially where humans were concerned. Call it a residual effect of caring for Astrid. I had a soft, protective spot for the magically challenged.

Saskia rolled her eyes. "You two have one heck of a hero complex. I'm not suggesting we take her along to this lighthouse and make her face the poltergeist. We just need her to get us into the Dark Tourist party."

"Why?" Finch pressed.

"I can't just go ask Miranda directly, can I? Word would get out to my parents, and probably Harley and the Rag Team, too, which would lead to unpleasant complications for all of us. We need Ryann, and that's the end of it. She's Miranda's intern, so she's got the knowledge and ability to wangle us three invites to an upcoming Dark Tourist party. That's where we'll find an Ivan Trap. There are always rare and dangerous things offered at these auctions."

I wondered what else they sold. I wasn't familiar with Dark Tourism, or what it actually entailed. Was it just a bunch of weirdos getting together to look at creepy stuff from magical history? I imagined a convention for twisted individuals who enjoyed historical blood and gore. But that didn't fit my knowledge of Miranda Bontemps at all. *You never really know a person, though, do you?* Everyone had quirks. Maybe this was hers.

"And Miranda likes this crap?" I had to ask. It didn't make much sense to me right now.

Saskia shrugged. "Miranda likes what she likes, but I don't think she goes to these things out of real interest in Dark Tourism. It's more that there are a lot of people who go to these gatherings who have power in the magical world. It's their guilty secret, and she can worm her way in if she pretends she shares it. Building bonds and networking, like my dad always says."

"But she doesn't give off that vibe," Finch said. "I don't know her well, but didn't she set up a bunch of charities? Wouldn't that be a better way to gain the trust of the higher-ups? Rich people love to be seen giving away money, and Miranda is giving them ample opportunity."

"There's more than one way to skin a cat. She's using every means in her arsenal," Saskia explained. "That's why she's turned her focus to human rights in the magical world. Bontemps couldn't give two hoots about humans, but she likes the admiration and attention it gets her while she pretends to care." Saskia scoffed. "It's the same with her pretend interest in Dark Tourism. She fakes it until she makes it and uses the gatherings to her private advantage."

"And you're saying *Ryann* is in on this?" Finch looked gobsmacked. I felt a bit sorry for him. It wasn't easy to find out secrets about the person you cared about. And he did care about Ryann, no matter what he said to the contrary.

If Saskia was to be believed, I was shocked to hear about Miranda. She'd always seemed like a nice, decent woman full of good intentions. Then again, the last time we'd encountered one of those, she'd turned out to be Katherine. Some people were too good to be true.

"Ryann is the perfect match for Bontemps," Saskia shot back. "She's the self-righteous goody-two-shoes that Bontemps needs to pass as a genuinely charitable person. Ryann is prissy and naïve enough to believe whatever Bontemps feeds her, as long as it's phrased right. She's almost as bad as my sister—they're both so dull. I guess that's where the younger sisters come in, am I right? Me and Harley, making up for everything they lack."

I smirked. "Harley is only a couple of months younger than Ryann, so I wouldn't put her in the same boat as you. And Tatyana was the Ice Queen long before you came along."

"Yeah, until Dylan melted her into a mushy sap," Saskia retorted. "I'd never let a boy make me soft."

"That's because he'd probably be eaten alive before he had the chance," Finch said.

"So what does that make you, Saskia? The Queen of Mean?" I replied dryly. "Maybe 'Queen' is a bit generous. How about the Princess of Mean?"

"Ooh, that hurt." She made a show of clutching her heart. "And it doesn't quite have the same ring to it. You've got to make these things rhyme or have a bit of zing. Otherwise, you just sound like a dumb boy trying to hurl an insult at a teenage girl."

I had to agree—Saskia was more stone-cold than Tatyana had ever been. It must be something in the Russian water. Or something in the Vasilis blood. Tatyana softened up over time, for sure, but I doubted anything could do the same for Saskia.

"Nothing to say?" She smirked.

I shrugged. "Something will come to me."

"Well, you take your time there, old man, while I tell you what's going to happen." She took a hair tie and twisted her long, blonde hair into a bun on top of her head. Was this Saskia's business mode?

"We need Ryann's help and intel. That's where you come in, Finch. You can try and cover it up if it makes you feel more comfortable, but I know what a crush looks like. And I know the feeling is mutual. You think she just *happened* to run into you at breakfast, even though her schedule's packed? I don't. Boys are so stupid. They wouldn't see that a girl likes them even if it smacked them in the face."

Finch frowned. "But... she needs to eat. And Harley was there."

She'd hit him where he was vulnerable. And I knew he'd be even more uncomfortable that Saskia picked up on his feelings. I'd sensed he had a crush on Ryann, but I knew him. I could tell when something was off. Saskia was just a vague acquaintance. The poor guy was probably second-guessing everything he'd done that morning. Every word, every gesture, trying to figure out what gave him away.

"Yeah, and so were you. She could've grabbed coffee and something quick and headed back out again. But she didn't. She came over to the table, knowing she'd draw attention. Girls don't do that without a reason, and it had nothing to do with Harley." She laughed, her tone carrying a little envy. "So you're going to be the persuasive one. Once we get the Ivan Trap, I'll tell you what comes next with your poltergeist problem."

Finch sagged. "I have to talk to Ryann?"

"Yes, you do," she replied. "Even if you weren't in looove with her, you know her better than Garrett or I. So, wipe that kicked-dog look off your face and get your head in the game."

He nodded slowly. "If there's no getting around this, then I think I know the perfect time to speak to her."

"Good, glad someone else is finally doing some of the work." She grinned, her eyes glinting with excitement.

I stifled a deep sigh and closed my eyes. Speaking with Ryann and getting what we needed wouldn't be easy for Finch. There'd been a time when I thought he'd never like anyone again. He'd been hung up on Adley for so long, and their story had ended so tragically. That wasn't something that anyone could just get over. He probably felt guilty for even having a crush on Ryann.

But Finch wouldn't be able to say anything to her about Erebus or the Fountain of Youth, because that would mean involving her in what he'd been through over the past year. With most of the facts missing, it was going to be a big-ass mountain to climb to convince her to assist us.

And the worst part was, he was going to have to do it on his own… leaving me to deal with Ice Queen: The Sequel.

TWELVE

Finch

After dragging my heels, I set off to find Harley. This Saskia and Miranda thing had my head in knots, and the threat of a Kelpie stomping the life out of me if Tatyana got wind of this wasn't too tantalizing either. Still, I couldn't do this alone. I'd been there, tried that, and gotten nothing but a hole in my T-shirt.

The spirit of Ponce de León was beyond my skillset, broken Suppressor or no broken Suppressor. Mimicry was good and everything, and I was happy to have all the Elemental powers at my beck and call, but Necromancy or spirit-yakking would've been a tad more useful right about now.

I couldn't stop thinking about what Saskia had said about Ryann. I'd never asked for a girl's perspective, and I'd resigned myself to the fact that she was head over heels for Mr. Perfect. But what if Saskia was right? *She's not... she was manipulating you into speaking to Ryann.* That felt more like Saskia's MO. I really couldn't allow myself to hope that she felt anything more than friendship for me. This was complicated enough, being unrequited. I had no idea what I'd do if it wasn't.

Once I reached Wade's office, I knocked loudly. I could usually guarantee I'd find Harley here. Those two lovebirds were never far apart. Glued to each other… sometimes more literally than I'd have liked.

I waited for the familiar sound of furniture being scraped back and various decorations and things being shoved into place, but it didn't come. Instead, Wade's voice called out immediately.

"Come in!"

I turned the handle with closed eyes, just in case. "Everyone decent?"

"What's that supposed to mean?" Harley replied. I opened my eyes to find her cheeks reddening.

"You know exactly what that's supposed to mean. I learned my lesson. No more traumatic memories for me, thank you very—"

I froze as I saw a third figure in the room. One I wasn't expecting. Kenzie sat in one of the wing-backed armchairs Wade had definitely pilfered from Alton's office. She sprawled across it like a cat. *I guess part of that furball stayed with you, huh?* She'd managed to Morph back out of her cat form after Chaos was restored, but since then there'd always been something a bit feline and sneaky about her.

She smiled. "Finch. Long time, no see."

"Yeah, it's been a while." She'd been so busy dealing with her mom that she'd pretty much fallen off the face of the Earth. But I had to say, it was good to see her again. *She knows where to get rare items.* My brain kicked in, and I could have facepalmed myself. Once upon a time, before all this Erebus lark, I used to get all my valuable items from her. She might be able to get her paws on an Ivan Trap for us, with no need to involve Ryann. The trouble was, I had to find a way to ask her about it without Harley and Wade's bat ears listening in.

"You okay over there?" Kenzie smirked. "Do you need someone to come and press the factory reset?"

I frowned. "Huh?"

"You went all quiet."

"Sorry. It's these new meds; they're killing me," I replied. "Anyway, how's your mom? Any better?"

Kenzie sagged. "Still the same."

"Oh, that sucks, man. I'm so sorry to hear that." I offered a sympathetic look. "I thought maybe Marie might've pulled something else out of the bag for you."

"Nope, nothing left in that voodoo bag," she replied. She'd gone to Marie Laveau soon after the Battle of Elysium to see if anything could be done to remove the Voodoo curse on her mom. Marie had tried a few things, but nothing had worked. The Voodoo Queen had promised to keep thinking, to see if she could come up with anything else. Evidently, that had been a dead-end, too.

"So, what brings you to darken our hallways?" I tried to lighten the mood.

"She's considering joining the SDC," Harley replied when Kenzie didn't say anything. "She's yet to make a formal decision, but she's giving it serious thought."

"I thought you said you'd rather drink rat poison than join a coven," I commented, unsuccessfully trying to meet Kenzie's eye. Harley glared at me.

Kenzie shrugged. "Like she said, I haven't made a decision."

"How've you been, aside from the obvious?" I swallowed the lump in my throat. I might not have seen her in a while, but family and friends had become more important to me than anything, and I hated seeing them in pain. Even the ones who weren't around anymore. Especially those ones, in a weird way.

"How do you think?" She gave a tired grin.

I chuckled. "It's hard to tell. You've always had a good poker face."

"I've got all these coven drones on my back, and most of them aren't as easy to deal with as Wade and Harley. That's why I've refused to speak to anyone but them about the whole joining thing. Who knew trying to be a rogue magical could be so stressful?" She did look a little frazzled.

"They're not buying the Neutral vibe?" I asked.

She exhaled. "Nope. You should see the number of letters that come through my door, trying to pressure me into making a decision. Apparently, since I was part of the Elysium squad, I'm too important to be left to my own devices. Who knew I was important, right?"

"It's more that the SDC wants to be able to take care of you and your family," Harley cut in, though she looked sheepish. "I'd let you go on being a Neutral, but O'Halloran is pulling rank."

"More like the power's gone to his head, or he's getting hassle from the bigwigs," Kenzie muttered. "Anyway, that's why I finally gave up and agreed to a meeting." She shook her head, annoyed. "How come you haven't been by lately? Inez has been asking after you."

"I've... been busy." It was a lame excuse, but it was the only one I had. I didn't want to talk about Erebus and my contract anymore. Just thinking about it gave me a headache, though that might have been the last of the dead-men's poison having a party in my brain.

"Pfft, you call that an excuse? You can do better than that, Finch." Kenzie smirked. "At least you don't look too good. Someone finally had enough of you?"

I chuckled tightly. "Something like that."

"Okay, well, I'm heading out." Kenzie jumped up from her chair and prowled toward the door. I stepped aside to let her out, only for Wade to call her back.

"You will think about it, won't you?"

She nodded. "Yeah, I'll think about it."

"Take all the time you need, and just know that you can call us anytime, if you have any questions or you need anything," Wade told her.

"Thanks," she replied and slunk out of the room.

I quickly stepped out after her and pulled her to a stop before she'd made it ten feet outside the office. "Actually, I was wondering if I could have a word?" I asked softly.

She rolled her eyes. "Not you, too?"

"It's not about the SDC." I lowered my voice to a whisper. "I don't suppose you'd know where I could get my hands on an Ivan Trap?"

She paused for a moment, then shook her head. "Never heard of one."

"Ah… do you have anyone you could ask?" I was clutching at every straw I could reach.

"I don't really do that anymore, sorry. I'm more about the phones and merchandise these days, rather than the weird magical stuff. I didn't mind the risks before, but it's different now. My mom takes up most of my time, and Inez worries. Plus, I lost a lot of my contacts over this past year. I wouldn't even know where to start."

I nodded slowly. "Okay. Well, thanks anyway."

"Are you in some kind of trouble?"

"Me? Always." I forced a grin.

"Seriously, Finch. Are you in trouble?"

"No," I lied. "Nothing I can't handle; I was just hoping you might know where I could get one of those things. But I've got other avenues, so don't worry. You go back to your mom and Inez and give them both my love." She already looked stressed enough without me sending her on a wild goose chase for some rare object.

Old Finch wouldn't have cared, but New Finch had sprouted a heart.

"You'll come by sometime?" she asked.

I smiled. "When I've got a moment, I promise."

"You better." She reached out and pulled me into a hug. "I've missed you, man, but don't tell anyone I said that."

"I won't. Wouldn't want anyone thinking you'd gone soft." I hugged her back, before letting her go. I was disappointed, but I'd just have to find an Ivan Trap some other way.

Shooting me one last glance, Kenzie turned and headed down the hallway, disappearing into the labyrinth of the SDC.

"Things all good between the two of you?" Harley asked, as I returned to the room.

"Why wouldn't they be?"

She shrugged. "I don't know. I wasn't sure if there was something you wanted to say to her, since you rushed out of the room like that."

"Yeah. What was that about?" Wade chimed in.

I padded across the room and flopped down in the armchair Kenzie had vacated. "She's clearly stressed about all this coven stuff, and I wanted to offer some friendly, objective advice. It can't be easy having all this hassle while her mom is sick."

"You're right, it isn't," Harley replied. "I don't know why admin keeps sending her letters. I've asked them not to, but they're pretty insistent. She's a hero as far as the UCA is concerned, and they don't want her to be a Neutral." She gave a sigh that suggested she wasn't as down with all this authority as she appeared.

I shrugged. "Who knows, maybe she'll join the SDC just to get everyone off her case, then everyone can go home happy. She might find out she likes it when she's actually a part of it, though I can't promise that'll happen. Covens aren't really her jam, as you've probably guessed."

"I suppose we'll cross that bridge if we come to it." Harley sank down on the edge of the desk as Wade made his way over to her, drawn like a drunk moth to my sister's flame. He held her face in his hands and kissed her. They looked so synchronized in their matching uniforms, like heroes in a dystopian fantasy, fighting against all odds for their forbidden love.

I really need to lay off the books for a bit. But I did miss the jeans and leather jacket that Harley used to wear. That was more her style, not these stiff outfits. She was so busy with her special agent duties that I almost never saw her in normal clothes anymore.

I still had to resist the urge to throw Wade off her whenever he went in for a smooch, but I couldn't deny it was nice that they were still crazy in love. Even though I could only look for a couple of seconds without risking the contents of my stomach, I was envious, in a way. I wanted what they had, but I didn't know if it was possible. I came with built-in gremlins who ran amok from time to time—not to mention the Erebus contract.

"Hey! Brother over here! I don't want to see the lovey-dovey stuff, if you can keep your hands off each other for a moment?"

I forced down the twisty, sad feeling that gripped my chest. I didn't want them to try to act ambivalent around each other because I didn't have what they had. It'd taken Wade months to finally act like a boyfriend in public. I didn't want to set him back, but a bit of reining in wouldn't hurt. He'd gone from prude to romantic extrovert in the space of a year, surprising Harley with gifts and flowers, putting his arm around her, and stealing kisses. They acted as if they couldn't exist without each other.

"Sorry." Wade grinned as he released Harley.

"I'm going to have to start wearing eye patches whenever I see the two of you." I smiled wryly at them.

"What brings you here?" Harley sank down in the armchair

opposite me, with Wade perching on the armrest. "Aren't you supposed to be resting? Marianne's orders?"

"Pfft, me? Resting? I don't know the word." I shifted in my chair, suddenly more aware of my injuries. "Actually, I wanted to swing by and have a word about Sunday."

"Don't tell me you're not coming."

"No, I'm coming. I just wanted to make sure Ryann will definitely be there. I know she said she would and everything, and, yes, I know she was the one making sure *I* was coming, but she's got a heavy workload at the moment, and I just wanted to double-check that it wasn't going to interfere with Sunday." My cheeks started to burn while I tried to keep myself from sounding flustered. Finch Merlin did not blush! "It's a work-related thing."

Harley chuckled. "Oh, Finch."

"Oh, Harley." I narrowed my eyes at her.

"Hey, I'm thrilled you're finally putting yourself out there, but Ryann has a boyfriend. She's happy with Adam, and he's a really good guy, if you'd just get to know him better and stop comparing him to serial killers." She paused, her expression softening. "It's sweet that you care about her, but it won't end well if you let your feelings for her develop. A crush is fine—no harm there. But it has to stay a crush."

They know?! This was beyond mortifying. I wanted to bolt from the room and lock myself in a Bestiary box until all these feelings went away.

"But we don't choose who we love," Wade interjected, to my surprise. He took Harley's hand and kissed it.

I pulled a face. "Having second thoughts about my sister, Wonderboy? If you are, you can kiss your stones goodbye. I'll make them into a lovely pair of earrings and give them to Santana as a peace offering."

He laughed. "If I ever stopped loving your sister, I'd lose a part of myself."

"Pass the barf bucket, someone? Have you been rehearsing that —just waiting for an excuse?"

I shook my head as he kissed Harley's hand again, her giggle pretty much the last straw. Okay, so maybe I didn't want to see them being all sappy. Maybe I did want to pretend that everyone was as alone and romantically stunted as I was. How did they make it look so friggin' easy? Even with Adley, I'd constantly second-guessed myself: is this right, is this what she wants, is it okay to kiss her, am I saying the right things? And that was when I'd actually bothered to focus on her, instead of always thinking about Katherine's missions. *Man, did I screw that up...* The memories got consistently worse the more I thought about them.

"It's how she makes me feel," Wade replied.

"Anyway, before he starts on the sonnets, me asking about Ryann has no romantic subtext whatsoever," I said. "I just want to talk to her about something."

"What do you want to talk to her about?" Harley frowned.

"Just... something. Important business," I replied, my cheeks getting warm again. If it was like this talking to Harley, I was going to be a quivering wreck come Sunday.

"What business?" Her voice was tinged with suspicion. "Is this about Erebus?"

I waited too long to reply.

"Don't drag Ryann into it, please!" she cried, suddenly panicked.

"I'm not involving Ryann in anything regarding Erebus," I replied evenly. When had I gotten so rusty at lying? Not that it was a complete lie. More of a half-truth. The part involving Ryann was minimal. No Erebus involvement required.

"Finch, if you're in trouble, you can ask for my help." She leaned forward and put her hand on mine. "Seriously, whatever you need. Just say the word."

I took a breath. "You don't need to worry, honestly. I've got everything under control. Ryann isn't going to be dragged into my problems; I really do just need to talk to her. And I'm not professing my undying love, either, because it's not like that. Just make sure she's there on Sunday."

"Promise me you're not putting her in danger," Harley pressed.

"I promise." *It's not a lie, it's not a lie, it's not a lie...* I repeated the mantra in my head. The last thing I wanted was to put Ryann in harm's way. It was just going to be a quick chat about those invitations, nothing more. And then she'd be out of it and there'd be nothing to worry about. Well, except the nightmare of Saskia.

Harley sighed. "Fine, well, she's definitely going. Like she said she was. She knows it's good to have a break from work, and I doubt Miranda would have her running errands on a weekend. If I hear anything otherwise, I'll let you know."

"Thank you."

I might not have been able to compete with Mr. Perfect for Ryann's love—that was out of my hands. I could, however, get this job done and win my freedom. Maybe then I'd be able to find someone and achieve the happiness I craved. Maybe she was out there right now, just waiting for a Finch who didn't have a deal with the devil taking up all of his time.

I took a deep breath to strengthen my resolve. Even if I couldn't have that happiness, at least I wouldn't have the threat of death hanging over the people I cared about. Maybe that was the best I could hope for.

THIRTEEN

Finch

S unday arrived like a bullet train, hurtling into the metaphorical station before I could blink. I'd barely gotten back a sense of normality, and now this.

My body didn't ache so much anymore, which was a plus, but my head was still playing tricks. I blamed the hefty painkillers Marianne had me on. Or maybe it was just whatever was left of this poison taking its sweet time to leave my system. Sometimes, I'd catch shadows moving in the corner of my eye, but there was never anything there.

I'd had to stop my relaxation technique of watching old horror movies, too. The screams from my ensuing nightmares were starting to draw attention. Twice, Wade had burst into my room, thinking I was in trouble. Once, he'd been in nothing but his boxers… a glorious sight for Saskia and the rest of the female population, but a grim one for me.

Poltergeist side effects may cause intense paranoia. Not exactly conducive to the sane conversation I needed to have with Ryann.

Then again, around her I was never really sane. More like a babbling moron.

I jittered the whole way to the Smiths', riding shotgun in Daisy while Harley drove. This car had seen some things. Our road trip to San Francisco, for one. Ah, the fragrant scent of stale fast food and sweaty bodies, a ripe odor not easily forgotten.

Still, it was nice to ride in her again. Harley had asked Remington to deliver her car back from San Francisco, where she'd left it after we'd snuck through to the San Francisco Coven, and he'd been only too happy to scoot this vintage beauty to San Diego the old-fashioned way.

"You okay there?" Harley cast me some serious side-eye.

I nodded. "Yep, fine. Just reminiscing."

"You were?"

"About our trip to San Fran. Good times." I was struggling to string a whole sentence together.

"You still haven't told me where those secret tunnels are." She smiled.

My knowledge of old passageways was formidable. I hadn't wasted my cult time, no sir. That tunnel leading into San Francisco had probably crumbled by now, though. They'd been around for so long, and had been forgotten by so many people, that there was no upkeep. Like any interdimensional space, they were disintegrating, slowly but surely.

"Hey, you tell me when you need one, and I'll try and find one that's still usable. Wouldn't want you getting squished by a collapsing passage." I snorted, my anxiety dissipating for a minute.

Harley rolled her eyes. "Finch."

"What?"

"Do you ever take anything seriously?"

I grinned at her. "When it matters, yes. But 'collapsing passage' is never not funny."

"I'll be the judge of that."

Harley turned onto the Smiths' street, and my nerves shot through the roof. *Keep it cool, Finch.* I'd spoken with Ryann a thousand times. All I had to do was take her to one side, keep it casual, and get those invitations. Without explaining why, or who was involved, or that I was beholden to Erebus in a life-or-death contract that might see all my friends and my sister dead if I didn't manage it. No pressure, right?

Seconds after Harley rang the doorbell, the door opened to reveal the glory of Mrs. Smith, all aproned up and ready for Sunday dinner. The sight of her instantly made me calmer. She had that energy about her, an easy domesticity that made her home feel like your own home. I'd spent enough time here to be able to call it something close to that. Plus, they knew about the magical world, so there was no tiptoeing around.

When I'd first discovered my Elemental abilities, there'd been a few accidents, and some had bled out into the Smiths' ordinary world. Namely, I'd made the barbecue flames rise to about twelve feet one afternoon. There'd also been an incident where I'd almost caused a hurricane at their Christmas party, because Ryann had whipped out some mistletoe, and my heart—and powers—had gone into overdrive. But Mrs. Smith had quickly assured the rest of her guests that it must have been a freak snowstorm. Without the snow. Or the weather reports to back it up.

Humans liked to believe what they could understand, so they'd bought it, and the Smiths hadn't held any grudges. That was the beauty of them—they never did. They were some of the most loving and forgiving people I'd ever met. I only realized how much I'd missed them when I was swept into Mrs. Smith's loving arms and given a hero's welcome.

"You made it!" Mrs. Smith cried. "Ryann told me you might not be able to, because you weren't feeling well. I almost made you soup, but she said you wouldn't want to be fussed over."

I smiled and kissed her cheek. "I like a bit of fussing if it's coming from you, Angela."

"You see!" she shouted back to Ryann, who'd yet to make an appearance. "I told you he wouldn't mind me making him some soup!" I waited for Ryann's reply, but it didn't come. "She must be out back with Adam. He can't stay, but he dropped in. Such a sweet boy."

"I suppose kids keep dying, even on Sunday." I hid my delight. This would be way easier without Jeffrey Dahmer prowling around all afternoon.

"Finch!" Mrs. Smith gave a horrified gasp.

"Sorry about that. I might be feeling better, but I've got an eternal case of no-filter between here and here." I tapped my head and then pointed a finger at my mouth. She laughed, letting me off the hook.

"It's been so long since I've seen you, I forgot how dark your sense of humor can be." She gave me a playful nudge in the shoulder.

"Pitch black at times." Harley flashed me a knowing wink as she went in for her own hug, mouthing *be nice* over Mrs. Smith's shoulder.

I'm always nice, I mouthed back, getting a customary roll of Harley's eyes.

"Is that the Merlins I hear?" Mr. Smith appeared from the garden wielding a grilling tray. He'd learned to cook before I arrived, to prevent more mishaps with the barbecue.

"It certainly is, George, my main man!" I walked over to him and found myself pulled into a big, beefy bear hug.

"What did we say about not being a stranger?" He grinned as he released me. "I'd forgotten what you looked like."

"It hasn't been *that* long." Warm and fuzzy feelings swelled, like hot fudge on a sundae. My cheeks were practically glowing with happy embarrassment. I'd meant what I said—I liked being fussed over, by the right people.

"My darling wife was going to send a whole care package when she found out you were sick. Are you feeling better now? I see you've got a couple of scrapes and bruises—nothing too serious, I hope?" Since their capture by Davin the Ass-Wipe, they immediately jumped to the worst-case scenario when something came up with Harley or me.

I shook my head. "I got in a fight, but don't tell Angela."

He put his fingers to his lips. "Your secret is safe with me. Nothing... magical, though, right?"

"Just your ordinary, run-of-the-mill fisticuffs." I flashed him what I hoped was a genuine smile, and he seemed to buy it.

"Well, I hope the other guy looks worse than you."

"Oh, he does." *Being dead for a couple hundred years will do that to you.*

"Ryann, come in and say hi to Harley and Finch!" Mrs. Smith called out.

My whole body clenched. It was like this every time I saw her.

A moment later, Ryann appeared through the back door with her six-foot Canadian. They were holding hands and smiling in that secretive way that lovers do. I forced myself to keep smiling as Adam made a beeline for me, sticking out his enormous hand. I didn't make the obvious joke. It would only have given me another complex.

"Hey, man, why so Sirieux?" I joked. A little wordplay on his French surname. The room fell silent. Oh, the shame.

Adam chuckled. "The older kids love telling me that one. I laugh every time."

The tension broke and everyone joined in, giving their pity

laughs at my expense. Ryann, on the other hand, just folded her arms across her chest and shook her head. But in a funny way, like she was sort of amused by me. *I'll take it.*

"Good to see you two, anyway. It's been way too long." Adam shook my hand, his palms hockey-player rough. After almost disjointing my wrist from its socket, he went straight over to Harley and bundled her into a hug before doing the rounds with Mr. and Mrs. Smith. "Sorry I can't stay, Mrs. Smith. I wish I could, but duty calls."

That's right, get outta here.

"I hope you have a good shift." Mrs. Smith took a brown paper bag off the kitchen workbench and pushed it into his hands.

He beamed from ear to handsome ear. "You shouldn't have!"

"I couldn't let you go off to work on an empty stomach. It's nothing, really, just some sandwiches and a slice of my apple pie to keep you going." Mrs. Smith blushed.

Apparently, every single member of this family was in love with Mr. Perfect. Even Harley was staring. *I'll tell Wade about that...*

"You're too kind, Mrs. Smith." Adam leaned down and kissed her cheek, and I swear I heard her squeal. "Thank you for this, and sorry again about not being able to stay. I'll see you all on Wednesday though, right?"

"You certainly will," Mr. Smith replied, equally enamored.

"Enjoy your dinner." He glanced at Ryann in a way that made me squirm. "I'll see you later. I love you."

"I love you, too." Ryann smiled back.

No embarrassment, no hesitation, just a gut-wrenching "I love you" that hurtled across the room, piercing my heart along the way. I guessed they'd already said their farewells in the garden, since she hadn't answered when her mom called. *Ugh.*

He barely fit through the door with his giant body. As soon as he was gone, I felt as if I could breathe properly again. Well, more or less. I still had some trouble around Ryann, but I could keep it together as long as I didn't have the boyfriend to deal with. Besides, this wasn't an ordinary Sunday dinner at the Smiths' house. I had a reason for being here, and I had to make this work.

"Let's eat before all of this gets cold." Mr. Smith led the way to the already-set table. Harley and I took our seats without being told, the two of us always together on the far side of the table. We actually had regular seats here, which was always a novelty for me. I'd never had a seat anywhere before.

"Angela, you'd put Martha Stewart to shame." I looked across the almighty spread on the table. The barbecued food took center stage, with a cast of creamy mashed potatoes, sautéed green beans, honeyed carrots, buttery corn, and a fresh green salad in supporting roles alongside.

My mouth was already watering, and I hadn't even tasted anything yet. I was already looking forward to dessert. If there was apple pie in John Wayne Gacy's lunch sack, then the rest of it had to be around here somewhere.

"I have to spoil you when I get the chance," Mrs. Smith replied, clearly pleased. "Go on, help yourselves!"

As I loaded my plate, the conversation started to flow. That was another awesome thing about the Smith family—there were never arguments across the dinner table. There were jokes, laughter, and intelligent discussion, but no insult-hurling or harsh words. The first time I'd come here, it had been a revelation. After all, the only family dinners I'd known involved cult talk, the persistent crushing of my self-worth, and a few extra digs just so my mother could really bring home how pathetic she thought I was.

I breathed a sigh of relief and settled more comfortably into my seat. The evening was starting perfectly. Plus, without Adam here, we could speak more freely about magical society, and the Smiths seemed just as interested to know what Ryann had been up to as I was.

"Is everything going all right at the SDC, Ryann?" Mrs. Smith asked through forkfuls of mashed potato.

Ryann nodded. "I love it, I really do. Some of my work is mind-blowing. At the moment, Miranda has put me in charge of a few of her charities, so I'm actually getting to make a difference. I wish I could tell Adam, but having to stay quiet is worth it as long as I'm doing something I love, right?"

"Absolutely, sweetheart," Mr. Smith replied. "Do you think you'll ever be able to tell him?"

"The coven has some pretty strict rules on that," Harley interjected. "There are all these forms and hearings you have to go through if you want to tell an unauthorized human about the magical world. But, if everything's going well, I don't see why it wouldn't be possible one day."

Traitor. I shot my sister a look, but she just shrugged.

"Does that mean we're authorized?" Mrs. Smith chuckled to herself.

"You had to be, after the Davin incident," I replied.

Ryann nodded. "They could have wiped all of our memories, but the legislature around that changed after Katherine died. It's no longer legal to just wipe a human's mind without their consent, which is why we were all allowed to keep our memories."

"It was always a bit of a moral gray area," Harley agreed. "I'm just glad things are progressing. I still don't think humans are ready to learn about the presence of magicals, but not wiping everyone's memory after they encounter one is a good place to start."

"I just think it's all so fascinating," Mrs. Smith said. "I understand why people would be scared or worried, but I happen to think you magical folks are all exceptional."

"You may be a little biased, my love." Mr. Smith chuckled as he tucked into his potatoes. Finishing his mouthful, he turned to Harley. "And how are things with you and Wade? Are your projects going well?"

"They're keeping us both busy, which has been a good thing. It's nice to have a purpose. And it's obviously great to have Ryann around."

"Isn't it, Finch?" Ryann added.

I almost choked on a carrot. "Uh... yeah, it's... interesting to have a few more humans around."

"Is that all we are to you? Humans?" Ryann arched a savage eyebrow at me.

"Well, it's not like I can call you magical. Can you waft your fingers and make things fly across the room?" I retorted.

"If you could try not to do that, I'd be grateful," Mr. Smith teased. "Remember what happened the last time?"

I sighed. "That was almost a year ago."

"And I haven't forgotten the state you left my grill in," he replied, laughing heartily.

"It really is a shame that you can't tell Adam, though," Mrs. Smith lamented. "I'm sure he would take it well. He's such an open-minded, sweet-natured guy. I'm sure he'd have no problem with it... but I suppose rules are rules."

"Yeah, I mean, our director hasn't even told his wife, so not sure how easy it would be to swing a boyfriend being in the know," I said, getting a curious stare from Ryann. "Not that I don't think it's a good idea. I just mean it'll be a lot of hoops to jump through, and if there's no ring, then they might not go for it." *Smooth, Finch... very smooth.*

Ryann smiled. "Speaking of my boyfriend, you were actually reasonably nice to him today. You sure you're feeling better?"

"Ryann!" Mrs. Smith chided.

"What? He's never nice to Adam!" she protested. "I'm wondering if he hit his head or something."

I shrugged. "Nope, head's fine. I just decided to be respectful, like you asked." Plus, this was the closest I'd ever get to a real family, and I'd never do anything to jeopardize that. If I had to play nice with the Zodiac Killer, so be it. But I wasn't going to say that out loud.

Harley nudged me in the ribs and whispered to me. "She's got a point. You didn't call him a serial killer once. What are you up to?"

I grinned. "Up to? I'm not up to anything. I just felt like being more civil tonight, after what you said. Might as well be nice, if I can't do anything else." I cleared my throat. "Now, Ryann, why don't you tell us more about your humanitarian work? I know you humanitarians *love* to go on about it. The floor is yours." I was genuinely curious, and it would get Harley off my case.

"Okay, now I know you hit your head." Ryann laughed.

"I'm not saying I won't start snoring halfway through," I replied.

"That's more like it." She smirked. "You had me worried for a minute."

"I'm touched."

"What are you two even doing?" Mr. Smith shook his head in playful despair. "I can never tell if you care about each other, or if you can't stand one another."

I smiled at Ryann. "I think it's a bit of both."

"I was just about to say the same," she said, her eyes twinkling.

A couple hours and a stuffed belly later, I saw my opportunity to speak with Ryann alone. Harley was busy laughing with Mr. and Mrs. Smith in the kitchen, all three of them singing Springsteen like strangled cats and dancing as they did the dishes. I was fairly sure they were trying to emulate "Dancing in the Dark," but it was anyone's guess.

Ryann sat on the porch swing, cradling a mug of coffee and staring up at the clear, dazzling sky. Somehow, we'd both been let off cleanup duty. I knew I'd been let off because of the swollen size of my stomach and my constant groans every time I moved, but I wasn't sure about her.

"Hiding out, are we?" I leaned against the porch post and followed her gaze up to the sky. It was a beautiful night. The sky looked as if someone had dropped a bag of diamonds onto a stretch of black velvet. The moon peeked out of the darkness in a thin crescent.

"Says you." She chuckled, making room for me on the swing.

"I can barely move, let alone wash dishes."

"Then you shouldn't have eaten three slices of apple pie."

"You were counting?"

She grinned. "It was like an episode of *Man v. Food*. How could I not?"

"Well, I think food won this one." I sank down onto the swing and let out an unholy groan.

"When's it due?" She prodded my distended belly.

"I wouldn't do that if I were you. You might not like what comes out," I warned.

She crumbled into laughter. "Maybe it's a good thing you never come to Sunday dinner. You'd be the size of a house."

"It's going to take days to get back to my normal size. Harley's probably going to have to roll me into the car."

I shifted to make myself more comfortable, and froze as my leg brushed hers. She didn't seem to notice, but then, she didn't see me that way. No matter what Saskia said, there's no way she could. I mean, what did a sixteen-year-old girl know about these things?

A lot more than you. Shut up, brain!

"Moby Dick, off the port bow!" Ryann said.

"Hey!" I smiled. "Don't tease the wounded. My stomach really hurts. I might die."

"You won't die—you're just full of pie."

"Poetic. I've heard people can explode from eating too much, so you never know." I started to move my legs, swinging us gently. "So… are you really enjoying your time at the SDC?" It wasn't the smoothest of segues, but it was all I could come up with, considering my blood was half sugar right about now.

She nodded. "I love it."

"What's Miranda like? I don't know much about her."

"That's because you're hardly ever there," she replied.

"Touché."

"She's cool, though, once you get to know her. Intimidating, and way smarter than I'll ever be, but she's inspiring."

"She's got some weird interests though, right?" Another shaky segue.

Ryann glanced at me quizzically. "What do you mean?"

"Well, I heard through the grapevine that she's into Dark Tourism stuff."

She shrugged. "She is, but it serves a purpose. That's one of the other awesome things about her—she never does anything without a reason. Everything is planned out to the smallest detail."

"Oh?" *Yeah, I knew someone like that… didn't turn out too well.* "So, why does she do the Dark Tourism stuff? Is it for the auctions?"

"Yeah. I'm not the biggest fan of it, to be honest, but Miranda donates all the money she earns from the events to charities that support human rights in the magical world. Plus, she always vets potential buyers, and she uses the events as a chance to mingle with influential people. Like I said, her actions always have a purpose."

I frowned. "But they sell creepy things at those auctions, don't they?"

"Sometimes." She took a sip of her coffee. "But it's out of her control. All she can do is make sure dangerous items get struck off the auction list. It's just a way of making money to give to charity, in the end, and it's not causing anyone harm, so I don't have a massive issue with it."

"Won't she get into trouble, going to these things?"

"No, they're not illegal. And she's more of a mediator, to make sure it stays that way." Ryann paused. "Although, I wouldn't tell anyone about that side of her charitable endeavors."

"You just told me."

She laughed. "I mean, I wouldn't tell anyone I didn't trust."

"You trust me?" That threw me for a loop. Earning someone's trust was as valuable to me, these days, as breathing.

"Of course I do. You're family." She nudged me in the ribs.

"Ow. Injured, remember?"

"Surely you can find someone at the SDC who can kiss it better?"

If only. "I prefer more sanitary methods of healing. You know, *actual* medicine."

"Fair enough." She stared back up at the sky. "Why are you so interested in this Dark Tourism, anyway? That doesn't really seem like your thing."

"I'm looking to get an artifact for some work I'm doing, and I heard they might have one at an auction. An Ivan Trap, specifically."

Her expression shifted into one of disappointment. "So, what, you're using me for intel?"

Dammit! Stop being so perceptive! "I just thought you might know more about it than I do, and it's always better to ask for the right help instead of scrambling in the dark, right?"

She paused for a moment before finally relaxing. "Why do you want one of those trap thingies?"

"Just some work I have to do, but I wouldn't be asking you about it if it wasn't serious." I was trying to be as honest as the limitations allowed.

"Does this have something to do with those injuries from the poltergeist?" She turned and stared me dead in the eyes.

I gave a low whistle. "News really does travel fast, huh? Who told you that?"

"Harley. After I saw you all bandaged up, I asked what was wrong with you, and she told me you'd been in a fight with a poltergeist." She gave a small smile. "My life really has changed. Before I knew about magicals, I'd have thought it was a horrible prank, being told something like that. Now, I don't even bat an eyelid when I hear that kind of thing."

"Even though I was the one on the receiving end?" I couldn't help myself. I wanted to know if she worried about me.

"No, that freaked me out. As soon as I saw you, I had to know what was up. Ever since Davin, the moment I hear something happened to you or Harley, I think it's Katherine part two, or worse." She lowered her gaze. "But that's not so far from the truth for you, is it?"

My eyes widened. "What?"

"Harley told me about your deal with Erebus, and she told me why you made it. Honestly... I'm really worried about you, Finch. You looked all right at breakfast that morning, but then Harley explained about the dead-men's poison, and that you'd almost died, and that this wasn't the first time you'd come back to the SDC in a bad state."

Ryann exhaled deeply before continuing. "That's when she told me about the deal. I wanted to find you and tell you off for not saying something to me, but after I thought about it, I understood why. You want to protect everyone on your own. I can admire that... but I can also admire that you've finally reached out for help."

My jaw was on the floor. Harley could've at least given me a heads-up about Ryann knowing. I mean, she seemed to know *everything*. I felt silly for thinking it, but this deal was mine to handle, and I didn't like that someone else had told Ryann. And after Harley laid into me about not dragging Ryann into anything Erebus-related!

I shook my head, not knowing what to think. I could've kept it vague if Harley had stayed quiet about it, and Ryann and I could have gotten through this without the Prince of Darkness ever coming up. My sister had thrown a wrench in the works, that's for sure.

"I don't want you knowing any more than you already do," I said firmly. "You shouldn't even know about Erebus in the first place. If you learn any more, you'll be at risk."

"Does that mean you *are* doing something dangerous?"

"No, it's just a matter of principle," I replied. "I don't want you getting too close. I promise you that what I'm doing won't get me killed, and that everything I'm working on is necessary and fully legal. Would I be speaking to a woman in pre-law if it wasn't?"

I was lying through my teeth, and I hated the sick feeling it gave me. Further proof that I was as far as possible from being Mr. Perfect.

Ryann stared at me while I sat there feeling awful. "Do you swear it's not going to end up with you back in the infirmary?"

"I swear."

"Then I'll look into the Ivan Trap for you." Her brow furrowed, as if she couldn't believe what she was about to say. "I'll check

Miranda's documents and emails and let you know if there's an Ivan Trap being auctioned anywhere."

I wanted to hug her. "Thank you, Ryann. Thank you so much. You're a lifesaver."

"I hope I am," she murmured. "I don't want to see you in bandages again, okay?"

"Why, because you'll have to cart me off to your boyfriend?" I smirked. "How is Jeffrey Dahmer, anyway? Have you found the bodies yet? Any weird smells you can't quite get rid of? Lampshades made of strange material? Did you check the basement of his house? The freezer in his garage? Does he have a freezer in his garage? If he does, then he's for sure a serial killer."

My defense mechanism had kicked in, regular as clockwork. I meant what I'd said about her not getting close, just not in the way it sounded. I didn't want her getting too close to me, not with Erebus hanging over my head. I didn't want him adding another name to his list of possible victims if I couldn't get this job done.

Ryann gave an exasperated sigh. "On that note, I'm going back inside." She tossed the rest of her coffee into the grass and got up. She walked to the door, then paused on the threshold. "Oh, and Mom has a freezer in the garage, so maybe you want to accuse her of being a serial killer?"

I grinned. "No, I know that's where she puts all the pies. The only person she's at risk of killing is me, with obesity and cholesterol. Maybe that's where your boyfriend keeps *his* special pies! Sweeney Todd, anyone?"

"Sometimes I don't know whether to laugh or cry with you, Finch." Her voice sounded strangely sad, without the usual bite she had when I spoke about Mr. Perfect. Her shoulders sagged as she turned on her heel and disappeared inside the house.

Neither do I... I sat on the swing, pushing it gently to and fro while staring up at the night sky. I felt alone again, a single figure on a swing built for two. At least by chasing her away, I didn't have to be with her. The longer she was around, the greater the risk I'd say something I'd really regret. Don't get me wrong, I wanted to be near her all the time, but she was with someone else. I had to accept that.

Yeah… it was better this way.

FOURTEEN

Finch

S till contending with my colossal food baby, I leaned out of
Daisy's window and let the breeze soothe my forehead. It was
one of those perfect nights—not too cold, not too warm, with the
stars putting on their finest display. I should've been anxious about
what Ryann knew, but I wasn't. If anything, it had taken a weight
off my shoulders.

She cares... That was my takeaway from our conversation, now
that I'd had a chance to think about it. And it had literally been all I
could think about since she'd gone inside. I'd already accepted
there was nothing I could do about the Boston Strangler, but that
didn't mean I had to put Ryann out of my thoughts altogether. I
wouldn't dare to hope—I'd just let myself be happy she gave a crap.

"How are you doing over there?" Harley smiled, but she focused
on the road.

"I'm in pain," I murmured.

"At least I know you're not going to go hungry." She nodded to
the Tupperware container loaded up on my lap. A parting gift from
Mrs. Smith, filled to the brim with a week's worth of leftovers.

I grimaced. "I can't even look at it right now."

"How's the rest of you?"

"Not too shabby. A few aches and pains, but pretty much back to normal."

"We've seen some things, haven't we?" She chuckled, leaning her head on her hand, her elbow propped on the open window. One hand on the wheel, like a proper Bonnie, though Clyde was thankfully absent, having stayed at the SDC to deal with paperwork.

I nodded. "We sure have."

"What you said before, when we were driving to the Smiths'—it got me thinking about everything we've been through. You and me." She kept her eyes forward. "It's weird to think that we probably wouldn't be here if it wasn't for you. If I'd never gone back for you, and broken you out of Purgatory, and given you a chance... do you ever wonder what might've happened?"

"I'd either be dead or Katherine's slave," I replied. "Like everyone else."

"I'm so glad you joined our side, Finch."

I smiled. "That I came over to the Dark Side, you mean?"

"I'm serious. I think back on all the times we spent together, trying to stop Katherine. None of it could've happened without you."

"Don't sell yourself short. You helped a bit." I flashed her a wink.

She laughed, but I could hear a hint of sadness in it. "Was there ever a time when you doubted me? When you wondered if you'd made the wrong choice?"

"Never." I didn't miss a beat. "When you agreed to infiltrate the Cult of Eris to find your mom's spirit, I realized I'd found someone just as nuts as me. A kindred spirit—more than just siblings. I mean, we weren't really siblings back then. We didn't know each other. You had no reason to take that risk, but you did. Nobody ever trusted me the way you did that day, and I know how much you must have fought to make the others agree. I'll never forget it."

"You made it worth the risk," Harley replied, her expression soft. "When I found out Katherine had offered to bring Adley back and you'd told her where to stuff it, I knew you were with us for good. I'm still sorry for what she did to Adley. And I'm sorry if Wade and I are too sappy around you. It can't be easy, seeing couples and knowing what you've lost."

I closed my eyes to stop the tears coming. "Don't ever censor yourselves for my sake. I can cope with seeing other people in love, even if it's hard sometimes. Contrary to popular belief, I actually don't mind seeing everyone else happy."

"I love you, Finch."

"Right back at you, Sis." The wind whipped away the moisture from my eyes.

"Do you remember our chats in the bathroom in that hut on Eris Island?"

I smiled. "I still can't walk into a bathroom without expecting the Spanish Inquisition."

"Ah, well, that's because nobody expects the Spanish Inquisition."

I cackled. "Looks like I've rubbed off on you after all."

"More than you know."

"Where's all this coming from?" I turned to her. "I'm not complaining, but this feels like one of those conversations we've had, when we thought we might never see each other again."

"Maybe that's because I feel that way," she replied quietly. "We've done so many crazy things to protect each other— answering the Chains of Truth, fighting and running away from our enemies, facing the Committee about keeping you out of Purgatory for good. And I feel like I can't protect you this time."

She sighed. "It hurts, because I *should* be able to protect you, no matter what. You protected all of us when you dove in and read the spell that killed Katherine. I want to return the favor, but you're keeping me at arm's length."

"You don't need to return any favor. You've done more for me than I can ever pay back." Just saying she loved me, without hesitating for a moment, was proof enough of that. I had a life, and a home, and friends, and family because Harley had taken that chance on me, a chance that could've gone horribly wrong.

"Still, humor me. What are you doing for Erebus? A problem shared is a problem halved, right?"

I shook my head. "It's easier if you don't know more than you do already. For your own safety. Erebus is a Child of Chaos, and those kids aren't worth messing with. He's insanely powerful, and he has a thing for us Merlins. I don't want to give him an opportunity to make it a two-for-one." I paused. "But... I will tell you everything when the time is right. When it's all over."

"What if that takes years?" She clearly didn't like my answer.

"I'm hoping it won't."

She sighed. "Can you at least tell me what you were talking to Ryann about while you were outside?"

"You mean, while you were wrecking my eardrums with your rendition of 'Dancing in the Dark'?" I chuckled.

"It wasn't that bad!"

"The ringing in my ears said otherwise."

"Ryann isn't in any danger, is she?" Harley flipped the conversation back, suddenly dead serious.

I shook my head. "I already told you I'd never put her at risk. Although, I'd have appreciated a heads-up that you'd told her everything about my deal with Erebus. That gave me a shock."

"Sorry." She looked sheepish. "She was freaking out about you, and it came out before I could stop myself. I didn't give her any details. I just explained what happened in Elysium and told her you were still dealing with it."

"I guess she'd have found out sooner or later. I've learned lately that the SDC *loves* to gossip." I offered a forgiving smile. "But I'm not involving her in anything. I just asked her if she could help me locate an Ivan Trap—they're used to capture poltergeists. She won't be doing any of the heavy lifting. She's just getting me some information so I can get my hands on one. Hopefully. You know I'd have asked Kenzie, but... well, she's got enough on her plate. I mean, I did ask her, but she'd never heard of the thing, so it didn't make sense to try to send her after it."

I figured it would be easier to appease Harley with a sliver of the facts. She didn't have to know the minutiae; a bit of honesty would be enough. At least I hoped it would be, because I didn't feel like lying to my sister tonight, as well as Ryann.

Harley furrowed her brow. The pieces were visibly coming together. "So that's why you ran after Kenzie?"

"Yeah, but I didn't want to say at the time."

Her frown deepened. "And it's just about information, with Ryann?"

"Just information. No danger necessary."

"And for you?"

I shrugged. "I've got it all covered. Nothing I can't handle." *I said I didn't want to lie!* Oh well, it was better than her losing sleep over me trying to hunt down the Fountain of Youth. And flooring an uber-powerful poltergeist while I was at it.

"You'd ask me for help if you needed it, wouldn't you?" She glanced at me.

"Eyes on the road." I forced my voice to sound chipper. "You know I would. We've been through enough together. If I was struggling, I'd call you."

"You mean it?"

No... "Of course."

Harley had done enough for me. I didn't want her to risk her neck for me again. Plus, if Erebus got wind of Harley being involved, he'd have a field day. If I had asked for her help, I wouldn't need to do this cloak-and-dagger stuff with Garrett and Saskia, but this was the way it had to be. Saskia wouldn't even be coming along for the ride if she hadn't shanghaied us into agreeing. *Sly weasel.*

"You've changed." Harley snapped me out of my internal babbling.

"Is that a good thing?"

She laughed. "A very good thing. You've gotten... softer around the edges. Not as spiky as you used to be."

"That's because you've all been putting mushy marshmallows on my spikes."

"I don't even know what that's supposed to mean." She grinned as she turned down the street leading up to the Fleet Science Center. "But it's a nice change. It suits you. I don't think you were ever supposed to be hardened by life. You just got dealt crappy cards."

"So did you," I reminded her.

"I guess I've softened up, too." She turned to me for a split second. "Maybe you and I are getting more and more alike each day."

I snorted. "Do you want me to heave apple pie all over your dashboard? Because you're headed in that direction."

She snickered. "You do that, and *my* spikes might come out again."

"Love you, Sis." I stuck my head back out of the window to enjoy the last wafts of fresh air.

"Love you, too."

After parting ways in the living quarters, I headed back to my room. The moment the door was shut, I flopped down onto the bed and groaned. I grabbed my pillow and held it against my swollen tummy, willing the indigestion away. As I lay there, my eyes squeezed shut, I went over the events of the past week.

My talk with Ryann had reminded me to make a mental list of everything I'd checked off, and everything I still had to get done. Unfortunately, the latter was longer than the former.

I had Garrett on my side, and Saskia too, whether I liked it or not. She definitely had the ruthless drive we would need. And spirit skills to boot, which we *definitely* needed. Ryann was going to search through Miranda's documents and emails for any sign of an Ivan Trap. And, if I managed to get this done, I'd have my freedom at last.

On the other hand, there was Erebus's threat if I failed this mission, and Ponce de León had almost beaten Erebus to that particular punch. My wounds were healing, but they were a reminder of what I was up against, and they were going to scar. The one across my chest had turned a weird purple color, with little black veins creeping away through my skin. I told myself it was just part of the healing process, but I worried it was going to stay like that.

On top of that, I was basically conning Ryann into getting me access to a Dark Tourist auction so I could steal an Ivan Trap. From what I'd been told about these gatherings, rare artifacts didn't come cheap, and I didn't have that sort of money lying around. Turns out, there's no compensation for ridding the world of the greatest evil known to mankind. Not even a bonus or a golden handshake.

Maybe you deserve this. My brain kicked in, just to have a dig while I was down. *Maybe this is your punishment for your past crimes.*

My alternative Purgatory? I thought of the girl in the Crypt who'd died because of my actions with the gargoyles. I couldn't fix that, or a lot of other things. Katherine would never have reached near-goddess status if I hadn't helped her. I helped create her. People were dead or maimed because I'd been at my mother's side, executing her missions. Tess Crux, for one, Nomura for another— and so many more whose names I couldn't even remember. That only made it worse.

As I was about to sink into the depths of a long-overdue wallow, a crackling sound splintered from the bathroom, making me sit bolt upright.

What is it with bathrooms?!

My heart lurched as I edged toward the bathroom door. I pushed it aside, right in the middle of my very own horror movie, and stared at the mirror. It was covered in frost, the ice thickening slowly. Another sign from the Lord of Darkness. That psychopath just loved mirrors.

Calming my nerves, I approached and lifted my finger to the icy surface. Like a delinquent in winter faced with the blank canvas of car windows, I carved in two words: *Making progress.* I wanted to write a different two words.

The mirror broke, the shards exploding outward. I ducked and covered my head as the fragments rained down. A few bit into me, to add injury to insult. Once they'd stopped falling, I raised my head, half expecting to see a floaty shadow of wispy black bobbing around the room. Instead, there was nothing but the aftermath of Erebus's warning.

I understood loud and clear. If I failed, it wouldn't be fragments of mirror surrounding me. It would be the remains of everyone I'd ever cared about, and I would be forced to stand alone to face the blow that would destroy me, too.

FIFTEEN

Finch

_____

Waiting on Ryann to bring me news about these Dark Tourist auctions, I rendezvoused with Garrett in his office. He was housed in Wade's tiny old shoebox, as Wade had received a fancy upgrade coinciding with his new SDC status. Garrett didn't have any particular status to go along with the office, but it'd been given to him as a base of operations for his day-to-day business at the coven, which included helping Harley and Wade hunt down cultists, whenever they needed advice from his LA days.

Garrett had done his best with the décor, but interior design wasn't his strong suit. It still looked like he was unpacking. There were random bits of furniture scattered around and cardboard boxes piled up against the walls. But he had chairs, at least. I took a seat on one of the wheelie office chairs and tried hard not to Telekinesis Saskia right out of there.

We need her... we need her... we need her. I rinsed and repeated.

"Did you draw the short straw with Diarmuid or something?" Saskia asked.

I'd started to notice that she used a lot of idioms when she spoke. Apparently, she'd learned English by watching TV shows, so I put it down to that. She had barely a hint of an accent, unlike Tatyana, whose accent was considerably stronger. Not that Saskia could ever have passed for American-born. She had a Russian flair in the way she acted. Cold, bold, and decisive. No room for niceties. I wasn't tarring every Russian with the same brush—*she's got me doing it now!*—but she lived up to certain stereotypes.

"It's small, but it's fine for what I need," Garrett replied.

She snorted. "I've heard that before."

"Where's your office?" I chimed in.

"I don't have one," she said.

I smirked. "Exactly, so don't go picking on other people's. When you've taken over O'Halloran's office, then you can comment."

"Why so testy?" She eyed me.

"Who's testy?" I smiled sweetly. "Anyway, what were you saying about poltergeists? That's why you're here, isn't it?"

"Garrett yawned when I was trying to explain before. I figured I was boring you." A flicker of defensiveness peeked through her polished exterior.

"I'm just tired," Garrett replied. "It wasn't you."

"You were telling us how they come into existence," I prompted.

She skidded along the floor in her office chair, coming to a halt by the narrow desk. "Poltergeists aren't ordinary spirits. They manifest from traumatic events or unfinished business. Most spirits eventually move on from those, but poltergeists don't. They're almost always magicals who died tragically or had more they wanted to do, which makes it impossible for them to move on. Over centuries, their souls fester, and their spiritual forms contract and implode into full-blown poltergeists."

"Like a supernova?" I replied.

"In a way, yeah. A ghostly supernova, and just as deadly if they want to be." Saskia swung her legs like a kid. "They don't really abide by the same rules as ordinary spirits. They're in between— that's the best way I can describe it. Not alive, not a spirit, and not a creature of Chaos. That's why controlling them or trying to exorcise them is super difficult."

"I have trouble with exercise, too." I grinned.

Garrett stifled a laugh. "Good one."

"Thanks," I replied, pleased with myself.

Saskia sighed. "You're like children, the pair of you. I probably have more maturity in my little finger than you have in your entire bodies."

"I'm not disagreeing with you." I chuckled.

"Anyway, I'll have to tread carefully with Ponce," Saskia continued in a disapproving tone. "A poltergeist can still possess a Kolduny by force. I'm not as inviting as my sister, but that might not stop him. He doesn't even need permission; he can just sweep in without buying me dinner first."

"Can you stop that from happening?" Garrett asked. We'd learned to ignore her more inappropriate comments. It was easier for everyone.

Saskia delved into the neckline of her T-shirt.

"Whoa! What are you doing?" Garrett ducked down behind the desk and shielded his eyes. I had an urge to do the same.

She snickered. "Relax, I'm just showing you this. Honestly, who'd have thought the two of you would be so scared of a woman?"

I glanced at the small silver locket she'd displayed over her shirt. It was shaped like a Celtic knot, with tiny inscriptions all over it.

"What is it?" I asked.

"It's a Celtic Shield Knot," she replied. "Designed to ward off evil spirits. In the old days, warriors used to paint this or carve it onto their shields for protection before they went into battle. Maybe you remember it?"

I snorted. "Very funny."

"It'll keep the poltergeist away, at any rate, according to some of the Kolduny elders I grew up with. They gifted it to me so it would keep me safe." Saskia toyed with the locket, flipping it over to show more inscriptions. "They didn't give Taty one, though. They knew she was a lost cause, even then."

"What's their beef with Tatyana?" Garrett stood up again, brushing himself down as if that would rid him of his embarrassment.

"People don't just leave the Kolduny. If they do, there's always hell to pay. Sure, they may go away to learn more and experience the world, but they always go back."

She put the locket back under her T-shirt. "Tatyana was supposed to spend six months here, then go back to Moscow with everything she'd learned. But the deadline passed, and she refused to go back. I think it's why they let me come here on the exchange program—so I could persuade her to come back home. I doubt she will, though. She's too Americanized now. Our parents don't mind so much. Mom wants her home, for sure, but she's okay with Taty staying here as long as she keeps learning. It's our grandparents who are laying the guilt on thick. They're old school; they don't like it when the youth disobey. And they're putting the pressure on Taty and our parents to keep tradition."

"What happens if she doesn't go back?" I wondered aloud.

Saskia looked suddenly sad—just a glimpse. "Nobody speaks her name again."

"What, like she's dead?" Garrett gasped.

"Pretty much." Saskia nodded, before visibly pulling herself together. "How are things with that human minx of yours, Finch? Any news about the Dark Tourist auctions?"

I had more questions, but I knew when someone didn't want to talk. Saskia evidently had a soft spot for her big sis, no matter how hard she tried to pretend she didn't. If Saskia went back to the Kolduny without Tatyana, she might never see her sister again. That knowledge must have been pretty rough for both of them.

I shook my head. "I'm still waiting for Ryann to come back with useful intel. That's her name, by the way. You seem to have forgotten." I shot her a smile. "I told her what to look for, though. She knows we need an Ivan Trap."

"What do you see in her, anyway, that has you so head over heels?" A glint of mischief darted across Saskia's eyes.

I stiffened, going into Ryann-panic mode. "I'm not head over heels! You need to stop saying things like that!"

"Your cheeks say you are," she retorted. "Beet red, if I'm not mistaken. I'd have thought someone like you would've gone for a powerful magical. Someone a bit more fitting."

My hands balled into fists, my cheeks on fire. "Does everybody know I like her?! Seriously? Am I that transparent?" The words exploded out of my mouth in a blurted barrage.

"Not as smooth as you thought you were, huh?" Saskia howled with laughter, which did nothing for my searing cheeks. "Plus, the spirits like to have a little gossip with anyone willing to listen. A.k.a., me. They know a lot, and they see a lot. I listen to them almost all the time, even when they think I'm not. *Especially* when they think I'm not."

She wheeled her chair forward, almost crashing into me. "In fact, one of the spirits said they saw you checking me out. I had that red Bardot dress on, if I remember correctly. How could you not take a peek?"

Sweat started to pour down my face. "I didn't peek at anything!"

"I don't mind," she purred. "What would you say to going out for drinks sometime? You'll find me a lot more willing than Ryann will ever be. More fun, too. I'm the sort of powerful magical you should be head over heels for, not her."

She leaned in, dangerously close now. I was seconds away from bolting across the room when the door burst open and Ryann strolled in.

Oh, COME ON!

"Harley said I might find…" She trailed off, staring at me like I'd just grown tentacles.

I froze. Saskia grinned at me like the devil she was, and Garrett wasn't helping, cackling away in the background. The universe really had it in for me today. First, getting hit on by an underage pest, and then the woman I was interested in wandering in to watch. Man, she was going to get all the wrong impressions from this.

"Saskia was just messing with me," I sputtered. "I would *never* flirt with her. Categorically, never! She likes to freak me out. I don't know why. Maybe she needs her head checked or something. Maybe her dad didn't love her. Maybe she's lacking a decent role model. I don't know. But this isn't what it looks like!"

Ryann said nothing, aging me about fifty years in the process.

"Seriously, she was just messing around."

I sounded pathetic, I knew I did, but I needed her to believe me. Otherwise, I looked like a sick old dog who entertained underage weirdos. And I wasn't. I hadn't so much as glanced at Saskia that way. Ryann, on the other hand… she could walk up in an ancient band T-shirt and baggy, ripped jeans after suffering a week of gastroenteritis, and I'd still think she looked like a friggin' angel.

Ryann smiled at last. "It's cool, Finch, you don't have to pop a vein trying to explain. I know all about Saskia. Tatyana has already warned every male in the coven over the age of eighteen." She cast a cold look at Saskia. "I've heard she likes to toy with guys, but she's all talk and no action. Which is probably a good thing, considering the legality issue."

Saskia pouted. "A few more minutes and Finch would've been on his knees."

"On his knees laughing, for sure." Garrett stepped in, finally. "Do you have some news for us, Ryann?"

I could have kissed him for saving my ass, even if he'd taken his sweet time.

Ryann nodded. "I do, indeed. There's an Ivan Trap being auctioned two nights from now, at one of Gerard Daggerston's parties."

"Gerard Daggerston? Bit much, don't you think? Does he have a cloak to go with that name?" Saskia snorted, recovering quickly from Ryann's comment.

"Who is he?" Garrett translated from teen-speak.

"He's Miranda's... uh... beau," she replied awkwardly. "Fortunately for you, he always sends Miranda twenty or thirty invitations to pass around to her trusted friends. And I got my hands on a few for *my* trusted friends." She whipped out a handful of invites, brandishing them with a triumphant grin.

"Ooh, burn." Saskia cast me a smug glance. "Did you hear that, Finch? Trusted *friend*."

I tried not to show anything on my face. I wasn't going to give her the satisfaction of riling me up. But it did sting. A lot.

Ryann looked puzzled for a moment before continuing. "These were on Miranda's desk. She won't miss them—she loses count. So, how many do you need?"

"Three." I took the first one while Garrett took the second. Saskia then scooted forward on her chair to swipe the third right out of Ryann's hand, prompting Ryann to frown.

"What? I'm part of the crew," Saskia said defiantly.

"And underage," Ryann shot back.

"Age doesn't matter when you're rich and popular." Saskia beamed. "People know me. I'll be welcomed at the party and the waiters will just pass me some fizzy, fruity stuff instead of champagne. I know how it works. This isn't my first rodeo. And besides, I'll have two sexy chaperones, so I'll be perfectly safe."

Ryann groaned. "You wouldn't know sexy if it hit you in the face."

"Neither would you, apparently." Saskia grinned.

Ryann frowned again, looking as if she was missing something. Shrugging it off, she turned to me. "Just be careful, Finch, okay? If you're going to this thing, you should use disguises and fake IDs. The invites are blank, but people have to sign in before entering the party so they can bid on the auction. I'm guessing you're trying to stay off the radar with this, so you and Garrett should use your Shapeshifting skills. As for you, Saskia, you might have to get creative."

I smiled in surprise, though I shouldn't have been thrown by her wit and quick reactions. She was one of the smartest people I knew. "Oh no, don't worry about her. I've got her covered."

"What do you mean?" Ryann replied.

"Looks like some secrets haven't wound up in the gossip mill." I was about to flex, and I had no shame about it whatsoever. *Take this, Mr. Perfect!*

"I got another level to my Shifting, after my Suppressor broke. It's part of the Mimicry skill I can use. It allows me to spread the Shifting net a little wider, putting a glamor on people whose appearance I want to change. Folks will be able to get right up close to Saskia, and they won't recognize her. It takes a lot of effort, but it'll be worth it."

"I bet you've used that for personal reasons," Saskia taunted. "You can spend time with a supermodel just by changing someone's face. Pretty neat trick. I wouldn't mind a bit of that. I could look at a Hemsworth whenever I wanted."

So much for my flex. "I only use it for professional reasons."

"Sure you do." Saskia spun around in her chair, clearly delighted.

Ryann, to my relief, ignored her. "If you've got the disguises covered, the only thing you've got left to worry about is money. You'll need at least fifty-thousand dollars handy for the auction. That's what an Ivan Trap usually goes for, from the research I've done."

I was at least two zeros short. *Yeah, in my dreams.*

Garrett chuckled. "We're not buy—"

I cut him off quickly. "Sure, we'll scrape the money together and have it ready to go. No problem."

I gave Garrett a warning look. I wasn't about to tell Ryann that we were planning to steal the Ivan Trap. She might've been cool with the under-the-radar aspect, but she definitely wouldn't have been cool with outright theft. That wasn't her nature, and I didn't want her flipping out on me. Or thinking badly of me.

"If you've got everything in order, I should head off. You wouldn't believe the mountain of work I have to get through before I can clock out." Ryann gave me one last nod before she exited. As soon as she was gone, I turned to Saskia. She might've been the devil, but she could well be our saving grace.

"I don't suppose you've got some secret millions, do you, so we can buy this Trap? You can obviously keep it once we're done."

Garrett laughed. "Seriously, we're not even stealing rare artifacts these days? I don't even know who you are anymore, Finch. You sure that poison didn't rot your brain?"

No, actually, I'm not sure it didn't. I held my tongue. I was still seeing shadows where there weren't any, but telling my colleagues that my mind gremlins were on the wild side at the moment wasn't an option. They needed to believe I was in the best health I could be, or at least *compos mentis*.

Saskia flicked her wrist. "I'll check my accounts and see what's left of my monthly allowance. My parents keep me on a fairly tight leash, and they don't send me more money unless it's some kind of emergency. Naturally, this wouldn't qualify, since I'd have to tell them everything."

She paused. "But I do get a hefty annual sum from my uncle which I've barely touched. What can I say? He's fond of me. Sees a lot of potential in me and knows I need money to spread my social wings, so he caters to those eventualities. My parents don't know about that, but it's there so I can make a name for myself. I suppose this *does* qualify for that."

"Who the heck is your uncle?" Garrett gaped.

"Anatoly Rasputin," she replied, not missing a beat.

"Shut up! You're pulling our legs!" Garrett's eyes widened.

"Oh, you know the name?" she said. "He takes care of me, since I've always been his favorite. A generous Christmas present, every year without fail. It goes without saying, but don't say a word about it to Taty. She doesn't know about his financing either, and she doesn't get the same generosity. I wouldn't want her getting jealous."

"Or telling your mom and dad." Garrett scoffed.

She sneered. "You'll need to dress the part. I don't want you embarrassing me at an event like this. I don't mind being a rose between two thorns, but the two of you are a little too thorny right now. Prep-school dropout and biker wannabe won't fly." She raised her hand. "Oh, and fake identities. You two will definitely need those."

"So will you," I reminded her. "If you don't want Tatyana finding out you've been at a Dark Tourist party, it wouldn't be too smart to have your name right there on the list."

Saskia chuckled. "Don't worry about my ID. I've got my methods. And you're not putting your glamor on me, or whatever it is. I don't trust you, Finch. You'll probably saddle me with some ugly face just to piss me off. So, you two deal with yourselves, and I'll figure out my own solution. Besides, I like myself too much to pretend I'm someone else."

I'd give you a face that matches your swollen ego. I was almost disappointed that I wouldn't get the chance to land her with some ugly mug so I could get a laugh out of this. I didn't like her being in control.

"And you're going to need some etiquette lessons. Like I said, there's no way you're embarrassing me in public," she said firmly.

Garrett and I exchanged a glance.

"Some what now?" I asked her.

"You'll find out." She grinned.

My to-do list was getting longer by the day.

SIXTEEN

Garrett

"Remind me what we're doing here again?" I whispered to Finch as we stood in a dingy waste unit in the darkest depths of Waterfront Park. Dumpsters lined the back wall, and sewer grates were embedded in the ground. The whole place stank, and creatures scuttled through the shadows.

"Getting ourselves dolled up, my friend." He nudged me in the arm.

"Can't we just Shift some suits onto ourselves?"

He shook his head. "It'll be easier if we just have to deal with our faces. You know what Shifting is like, and we don't know how long we'll have to keep it up for."

"Yeah, but there are stores *inside* Waterfront Park. Why don't we just buy a suit from there, or borrow a couple of Wade's designer outfits?"

"Apparently, there's a very specific dress code. Neither Wade nor those stores have what we need." Finch lifted his palms in mock surrender. "Don't shoot the messenger. Saskia just told us to meet her here."

I snorted. "You trust her?"

"We have to. She wants to help, and we need her." He shrugged. "She's harmless enough, as long as we ignore all the flirty stuff."

"There's nothing harmless about Saskia," I murmured.

He smiled. "It's an act."

"What?"

"It's all an act. I know one when I see one. She's probably lived in Tatyana's shadow most of her life, and this is her way of rebelling—making herself stand out by being the opposite of her sister. I'm pretty sure she's an innocent soul, deep down."

"It's your funeral if she's not." I gave a nervous laugh. To me, Saskia was an enigma. An alarming one. But then, I didn't have much experience with her vein of the female species—the teenage, temperamental kind. So, maybe Finch had a better sense of her than I did.

At least being here meant we could delay the next step in our mission. To get into the Dark Tourist party, we would need fake IDs, and there was only one person at the SDC with the skillset to make good ones. Astrid. Just thinking about speaking to her made me nervous. *But I have to keep trying.* I'd promised myself that.

The door to the waste storage room opened and Saskia came in, with a familiar figure in tow. Finch's face instantly fell. He clearly hadn't anticipated Ryann joining the fashion show. I shared his dismay. Finch had wanted this to be a close unit of need-to-know associates, and for good reason, but he seemed to be losing control over who was involved.

"Well, someone's got some explaining to do," Finch said.

Saskia smiled sweetly. "I called Ryann because she knows the etiquette for the party we're going to. Plus, I thought it'd be good to have feminine backup, to make sure you look good enough to eat."

And you couldn't resist making Finch squirm? I gave her a disapproving look, which only made her smile wider. I wasn't buying

Finch's assertion that this was all just an act. Saskia definitely liked messing with people and had no qualms about twisting the knife when it suited her.

"Does Harley know she's here?" Finch narrowed his eyes at Saskia.

"No, and Ryann isn't going to tell. She understands why you're keeping your sister out of this, so you can stop harping on about it. It's getting old, just like you."

"I wanted to keep Ryann out of it, too," Finch replied under his breath.

"I'm just here to make sure you guys look your best." Ryann looked nervous, like she was worried a fight would break out. "I get why you want to protect Harley, and it's up to you what you tell her. That's not my business, and I'm not in the habit of breaking confidences. I'm just going to tell you how to behave and what to wear so you don't get in trouble. That's all."

I stepped in to ease the tension. "Then we should get these suits and go. Where are we getting them from, by the way? I don't see any high-end stores around here."

"That's because you don't know where to look," Saskia replied haughtily. She headed for one of the sewer grates and lifted it. I was surprised to see a staircase that led underground. "Welcome to Xander Bandersnatch Couture."

"Didn't he play Doctor Strange?" Finch smirked.

"You know, if you spent less time being a secret nerd and more time focusing on the fairer sex, you might have a girlfriend by now," Saskia shot back.

"Ouch." I grinned at Finch, but he just looked sad, like she'd hit him right where it hurt.

"There's nothing wrong with nerds," Ryann interjected. "It's good to have a passion. Maybe if you had a hobby, Saskia, you wouldn't be running around terrorizing the SDC's male population."

Finch's eyes instantly brightened. *She's got your back, buddy. We both do.*

Finch and I had clashed over the years, but I didn't like to see him in a bad state. Saskia was new to the group, so she didn't know Finch's history. In fact, even now, very few people knew about the pills he took every day just to keep himself even-keeled. I'd never mentioned them, because it wasn't my business, but I'd seen him take them when he thought no one was looking.

With Saskia silenced for the moment, we descended into Xander Bandersnatch's hidden store. A spiral staircase led to a sparse shop floor, the kind where one would expect sales assistants to sneer at anyone who didn't look rich enough. Instead of racks, there were elegant mannequins spread out and displayed in a weird gallery arrangement. And all the way down the spiral staircase, glass windows revealed embedded cases, like sartorial fish tanks, containing suits and clothes of all kinds: casual wear, elegant three-piece suits, tailcoats, top hats, flowing cloaks, shining watches, and suspended pocket squares that looked like kites in midflight. Everything about this place was like an art installation.

"Xander?" Saskia called to the empty room.

A door opened and a suave gentleman entered the store. He wore a dark purple suit with a lavender shirt, an emerald green pocket square, and a tie of the same shade. His bright white hair fell past his shoulders. His intense black eyes, smoked out with purple-and-green shadow, scrutinized us, and I immediately felt *very* underdressed.

"He's like fashion's answer to the Joker, or maybe Willy Wonka," Finch whispered to me. I clamped my hand over my mouth to stop a laugh from exploding out.

"Saskia, darling!" Xander cried, smothering her in air kisses. "I thought you'd forgotten our little rendezvous."

"Never," she replied. "I'm sorry we're late. These pesky boys delayed me."

"Ah, I see." He waggled a finger at Finch and me. "You must never keep a lady waiting. Didn't your mothers teach you anything?"

Finch snorted. "She taught me a lot of things, but she definitely didn't teach me that."

"At least they have divine faces. They could use an intensive skincare routine, but the raw materials are pleasant to look at." Xander approached, lifting my chin up and turning my head from side to side. He moved on to Finch and did the same, making both of us deeply uncomfortable.

"And such excellent figures. Broad shoulders are a must to pull off one of my suits. Why the young men these days wear such atrocious clothing is beyond me. They waste their exceptional figures in T-shirts and jeans and, heaven forbid, *polo* shirts. I suppose they don't realize that one day, they will have exchanged defined abs and taut muscles for flab and paunch."

"Perhaps they will be as lucky as you," Saskia cooed. "You always look beautiful."

Xander clapped his hands together. "You flatter me, Miss Vasilis. I love it! Please, flatter me more! And who is this rare bird?" He swept toward Ryann, rearranging the strands of hair around her face.

"Ryann Smith," she replied, holding out her hand to shake his. Instead, he caressed it and lifted it to his lips, planting a dramatic kiss.

"Am I to be adorning you today?" Xander looked at her hopefully, but Saskia interjected.

"Just the boys."

"Very well." Xander returned to scrutinizing Finch and me. "I'm rather disappointed not to be dressing you today, Saskia, you luscious creature."

"I've got a very specific idea in mind. I'll give you the details once we've sorted these two out, and I'm happy to pay for a quick turnaround, as always. As you can probably tell, they're in greater need of a fashion upgrade than I am." She shot us an amused look.

"I quite agree." Xander smoothed his hands across Finch's shoulders, mentally sizing him up. "If you will give me a moment, I will make choice selections that will suit them perfectly. Pardon the pun." He cackled so loudly I almost jumped out of my skin. "I will call you to the dressing arena when I have made my selections."

As he strode away, muttering to himself about jackets and pants, Finch cast me a side glance. "A dressing *arena*? Are we supposed to fight to the death for a suit?"

I chuckled. "He's... interesting."

"He's a genius," Saskia snarked. "So show him some respect. He's going to turn you two sow's ears into silk purses."

"I like him." Ryann grinned.

"You can't afford him," Saskia retorted. I noticed her aggression amped up when Ryann was around, like a cat marking her territory.

"So, Xander is sorting out our clothes," Finch cut in. "To be honest, when Saskia said we needed to dress up, I was thinking more Halloween. You know, SFX makeup, scary masks, that sort of thing, what with this being 'Dark Tourism.' Although, I've got to ask, what's the point of us trying on suits with our own faces, when we're going to be other people on the night?"

Saskia grinned. "I have an idea of what you're going to look like, so you leave it up to me to pick the right one. I just want to see how you move in nice clothes, since your bodies are going to be more or less the same. Wearing an elegant suit is as much about how you carry yourself as it is about the overall look."

"Are you sure you're not just doing this to amuse yourself?" I replied.

Her grin widened. "Call it an added perk."

"Right, so speaking of 'carrying ourselves,' what else do we need to know about this kind of party?" Finch asked.

"Is this going to be a pinkies-up affair?" I added. I'd gone to a good school, the same one as Wade, and had an expensive education under my belt, but the social occasions had never been my forte. I used to stick to the sidelines and try my best to avoid dancing. I was already getting traumatizing flashbacks thinking about those days. My teenage years hadn't been my finest.

Hmm... maybe Finch has a point about Saskia. Being a teenager was tough, and being so far from home couldn't have been easy for her. It was all about trying new things and figuring out where you fit in. If you suddenly found you didn't fit in anywhere, it could be even harder. Maybe the way she acted was Saskia's way of figuring things out.

"For starters, it's rare you'll call anyone by name," Ryann said, diving into education mode. "They like to take on the titles of ancient heroes, heroines, villains, or criminals who came to a nasty demise. It depends on their taste. You'll find Joan of Arc and Vlad the Impaler arguing over who had the worst ending. You should probably come up with historical names too. They get testy if you pick the same as them, so go obscure if you can—they love an obscure reference."

She tapped her chin as she looked at us. "You also need to know backstory about your name, or they'll figure you out instantly. These people study hard. There's not a lot they don't know about historical figures who've met grisly ends."

"*Two* fake identities?" I groaned. One was bad enough.

Ryann smiled. "That depends on how much talking you intend to do. You can always avoid it altogether, but they might single you out if you seem evasive. They don't like wallflowers. These gatherings are all about showing off—your wealth, your intellect, and your knowledge of dark history. It's funny you mentioned Halloween, because there are some who go all out in period dress."

"Of course they do," Finch muttered.

Ryann laughed. "We're talking Georgian ballgowns with sky-high wigs and beauty spots, or perfectly replicated suits of armor from the Crusades. The ones wearing that kind of attire are usually the richest."

"What else?" Finch prompted, hanging on every word.

Bless him. I knew, firsthand, nothing was worse than impossible love. He had Ryann. I had Astrid. And we were both paddling hopelessly in the same boat.

"There'll be tricksters who try to make deals, so just make your excuses and stay away from them, because you might not know what you're getting into. Sometimes, they'll try to make exchanges or expand their 'collection.'"

"Collection?" Finch frowned.

"A collection of Ephemeras, each containing a sliver of a powerful magical from history. If they get a whiff that you're powerful, they might try to buy a sliver of your abilities from you. That's why it's so important you use fake identities. If anyone found out that you were Finch Merlin, they'd swarm you like flies. Garrett, you might be safe, since you don't have rare blood, but you can never tell with these people."

I shuddered. "So, this is more of a freakshow we're attending?"

"Just because people have unusual tastes doesn't make them freaks," Saskia retorted.

"I thought it did," Finch shot back.

Saskia gave him a withering glance. "These are classy pursuits, not pieces of plastic in pristine condition and comic books."

"How do you know about those?" Finch stared at her.

She tapped the side of her nose. "That's for me to know."

"Have you been in my room?!" He looked like he was about to burst a blood vessel, and I didn't blame him. Trailing Finch around and harassing him was one thing. Breaking into his private space was another.

Wait... has she been in my room, too? I was about to ask when Xander came striding back with a fancy flourish.

"Your path to sartorial excellence awaits!" He grinned, his teeth so bright they almost blinded me.

Saskia flashed me and Finch a mischievous look as Xander grabbed our wrists and dragged us to the back room. He was surprisingly strong.

Before we even had time to protest, Xander yanked us into another expansive space. In the center was a large, circular pouffe in gunmetal velvet. Tucked into all four corners were chrome cubicles with heavy metal doors. Two of the doors were open, and an array of suits had been hung up for us to try on.

"These are for you to select from." Xander ushered me toward the right-hand cubicle before shoving Finch into the one opposite. "And these are for you."

Ryann and Saskia headed straight for the central pouffe and sat down. Xander buzzed around them, bringing over some drinks for Ryann and Saskia. As they sipped happily, Finch and I exchanged a glance.

"Is it too late to make a run for it?" he whispered.

"Yes, it is!" Xander cried, hurrying back. "Come now, get inside, or I'll be forced to come in with you to make sure you try on these beautiful creations."

Finch jolted as if he'd been stung. "That won't be necessary."

"Excellent news." Xander smiled. "I think you'll look divine in the emerald green—your complexion is so very suited to green."

"No green," Finch replied sharply.

"You don't care for the color?" Xander sounded disappointed.

Finch shook his head. "It brings back a lot of bad memories."

I got what he meant. Even with his changed hair color, if he put on a green suit, he'd look too much like the son of Katherine Shipton.

"That's a shame," Xander lamented. "But there are plenty to choose from. And you, Mr. Kyteler, I think you would look charming in the slate gray."

Wait, how do you know my name? I supposed it was on the reservation that Saskia made, though it still took me by surprise.

"Noted." I stepped into the cubicle before he could offer help. With the door closed, I took a deep breath and glanced at the array of clothes. I had no idea where to begin. And I didn't know what he'd meant by "slate gray." There were at least four gray suits lined up.

I selected a dark gray one with a matching waistcoat and a white shirt. I stripped down and put it on, choosing a black tie to pair with it. As I looked at my reflection in the mirror, I wasn't sure what to make of it. The suit felt restrictive and uncomfortable, and it didn't look much better.

"Show us!" Saskia's voice called from outside. "Don't be shy!"

Wishing the ground would swallow me up, I opened the door and stepped out. Finch did so at the same time, wearing a weird, dark red number with enormous lapels and glitzy buttons. The shirt was orange, and it was paired with a tie the same color as the suit. Finch's cheeks matched his suit, too.

"Elton John is in the building!" Ryann howled, clutching her stomach as tears rolled down her cheeks. "And what are you, Garrett, his butler?"

"When I said you were on fire, Finch, I didn't mean literally."
Saskia giggled, throwing her head back.

Xander folded his arms across his chest, assessing us. "I agree,
you look ridiculous. There aren't many who can wear orange,
although I admire you for taking such a bold fashion risk. And that
gray is much too drab on you, Mr. Kyteler. And it certainly
shouldn't be paired with a black tie. And for that matter I said slate
gray, not hematite gray."

"How am I supposed to know the difference?" My shoulders
sagged. I hated this. Clearly, Finch did, too.

"I would've thought it was obvious." Xander tutted. "Go on,
back inside with you. And please stick to the pairings I've set out;
otherwise, you'll never look the way you ought to."

The next two hours passed in a carousel of "Not that jacket, try
another one" and "What the hell is that tie?" and "No way! Get back
in the cubicle before you burn out my retinas." It was doing
nothing for my self-confidence, and I was running out of options.
I'd even tried on the slate gray suit only to be told I looked like I
was going to a funeral. Still, I was grateful that my selection was
more muted than Finch's. Xander had really gone to town on him,
giving him a full rainbow of suits to try.

I reached wearily for a dark, sapphire-blue suit and put it on
with what little energy I had left. The jacket was double-breasted
with dark silver buttons, and a dark gray military stripe ran up the
pant legs. The accompanying shirt matched the gunmetal of the
buttons and the stripe, and it had a dark blue tie to finish it off.

I stared at my reflection, hardly able to believe what I was
seeing. I looked… wealthy. Even Wade would've lost his mind over
this suit.

"Anytime today!" Saskia yelled impatiently.

With a bit more energy than before, I opened the door and stepped
out. Opposite me, Finch did the same, dressed in a sleek suit of

maroon red with a collarless black shirt underneath and a matching waistcoat. An unusual, short, black-and-gold-patterned scarf-type thing was draped around his neck. The ends lay flat against his lapels, and a gold chain came out of his pocket, connected to his buttonhole.

Silence echoed from Ryann, Saskia, and Xander.

"That bad, huh?" Finch sighed.

"You look... beauteous!" Xander practically screamed, dabbing at his eyes with the corner of his pocket square. "I knew I could make you both into handsome young devils, but this... this is exquisite!"

Saskia's jaw was on the floor, her glass of fizzy juice tilting at a precarious angle as she stared. Even Ryann looked speechless.

"You... look... I mean... WOW!" Ryann finally managed to produce words, though not quite a sentence.

Finch shot me a pleased look. "You do scrub up pretty good."

"So do you," I replied. "I wouldn't have thought maroon was your color."

"Listen to you." Xander applauded wildly. "I've made fashionistas out of you."

"I wouldn't go that far." I chuckled, smoothing down the front of my jacket. Now I was starting to understand why Wade loved these things so much. If you found the right one, it made you feel... powerful. And this one definitely made me feel cooler.

"You look all right." Saskia snapped out of her daze. "Considering what we had to start with, anyway."

"High praise, coming from you," I replied.

"You might even get the girl you want in that suit, Finch." Saskia flashed him a sly smile, one that made his evaporate. "Who could resist you, looking like that? Any girl in her right mind would come running. But I guess not all girls can see what's right in front of them, can they?"

Finch paled, while Ryann frowned.

"Who's the lucky girl?" she asked, eyes darting between the floor and Finch.

Interesting...

"Saskia's just bored," I answered on Finch's behalf. "She's trying to wind him up. You think he's got time for a love interest?" I laughed.

"I wasn't just talking to him, Garrett," Saskia purred. "What about the girl *you* want? She'd fall at your feet if she saw you right now. You can keep the suit on, if you like, when we go see your little broken bird to get those fake IDs."

My heart sank. "I almost forgot about that." After this, our next stop was getting Astrid's help with our fake identities.

"Good thing I'm here then, isn't it?" She smirked, loving this.

"*Is* there someone you like, Finch?" Ryann surprised us. Finch, most of all.

He shrugged, recovering quickly. "It's no one you'd know. And Garrett's right—I don't have time for that right now. Even if I did, I don't know if I'd bother."

"Why not?" Ryann scrunched her eyebrows, seeming genuinely curious about his answer.

He sighed. "The people I love always end up in danger. I'm not trying for a sympathy vote. I just mean… it's easier for everyone if I don't bother. I lost someone once, someone I loved. I won't go through that again."

Even Saskia didn't say anything, the mood had turned so sad. Xander openly sobbed into his pocket square.

"That's so heartbreaking!" he wailed.

I wanted to comfort Finch, but I didn't know how. So we all stayed silent and let the weird atmosphere stretch between us. I knew exactly how he felt. What if I couldn't protect Astrid? What if all I did was hurt her, simply by existing in her father's place? There was so much I wanted to say to her that I couldn't.

"Before we all end up in therapy, why don't we buy these suits and get on with those fake IDs?" Saskia said. "I could do with a laugh, and watching Garrett try and fumble his way through a conversation with Astrid should do it."

The change in mood was so welcome I couldn't even get annoyed with her.

"Agreed." Ryann nodded. "The Dark Tourist parties thoroughly vet their attendees, so they'll have to be good."

"I'm sure if Garrett asks nicely, she'll make the very best ones she can." Saskia grinned, but I could see a hint of sadness in her eyes. As if she'd actually been affected by what Finch had said. A slight chink in her armor showed for a fleeting moment.

Maybe Finch was on to something with her. Regardless, this meeting with Astrid was going to be a nightmare, and I could almost guarantee that Saskia was going to twist the knife for her own amusement.

Yeah, I'm screwed. And no fancy suit was going to save me.

SEVENTEEN

Garrett

B ack in normal clothes, we made our way to the SDC. Saskia had taken Xander aside for a quiet word before we left, probably to make arrangements for her own outfit. Now, all we had to do was get fake IDs, and then we'd have nothing to do but wait for the auction.

I was dreading talking to Astrid. It wasn't as if we could tell her everything, and I knew she'd be suspicious. But I hoped she'd help us without asking too many questions.

With that in mind, we made our way to Astrid's computer lab— an upgrade, courtesy of O'Halloran, which had been gifted to her after Alton's death. I knocked while Saskia grinned, evidently looking forward to the imminent exchange. Fortunately, Ryann had left us to return to her work with Miranda Bontemps, so at least Finch was in a less nervous state.

"It's open!" Astrid's voice echoed.

Taking a breath, I pushed the door open and entered the lab. Finch and Saskia followed. Astrid sat in her usual leather chair, staring at a myriad of computer screens. Smartie kept her company on the desk. It sounded stupid, but sometimes I got jealous of that thing. I wished she'd show me the same attention.

Her eyes widened. "Oh… hi. I wasn't expecting to see you guys today. Is everything okay?"

I nodded. "Yeah, everything's fine. We just… uh… well, the thing is…"

"We need your help with something," Finch interjected, saving my ass.

"Oh?" She cocked her head to the side. A cute trait of hers.

"We were wondering if you could fix us up with some awesome fake IDs—cards and everything, the whole shebang?" Finch took a seat in one of the other chairs and leaned on the armrest.

She frowned. "Why?"

"We've got some business to deal with. Nothing major, but we need to do a bit of sneaking," he replied.

"What sort of business?" she pressed.

"None of yours," Saskia whispered under her breath, but Astrid didn't seem to notice. Or, if she did, she didn't show it.

I cleared my throat. "You know I've never asked you for anything in my life, right?"

Her frown deepened. "Right."

"I know you'll have a lot of questions, but this business we're dealing with has to be discreet. The fewer people who know about it, the better. And I really need you to come through for me now, if you can. I know it's a big thing to ask, but it's important."

"I'm not sure I like the sound of that," she said.

"I'll tell you everything when it's over and done with," I promised. "We just need to keep it quiet for now. And we can't do it without your help on these IDs."

She didn't say anything for a while. She just sat and stared at me. Finally, she sighed. "You promise it's nothing illegal?"

"I promise." I could say that honestly. We weren't stealing the Ivan Trap anymore, since Saskia had confirmed she'd be the one footing the bill, and the Dark Tourist parties weren't illegal—just frowned upon. Aside from the occasional appearance of black-market goods.

"I won't get in trouble for this?" She turned around and picked up Smartie.

"Not if you make them *really* good," Saskia chimed in. For all her huffing and puffing about making me uncomfortable, she seemed to be behaving herself. Perhaps Finch's words made more of an impact than I'd thought.

Astrid smiled. "I always do. I just want to make sure I'm not going to get you in any trouble, either, if I do this for you."

"No." That was stretching the truth, but I hoped things would go smoothly.

"I can come up with something," she replied. "What do you need, exactly?"

"Make us filthy rich!" Saskia chirped.

"You already are," Finch muttered.

"Can I get a bit more detail?" Astrid looked nervous.

Saskia hurried forward and crouched down by the desk. "I'll help with the creative side. I know rich people, and I've got a few perfect candidates."

Half an hour later, Saskia and Astrid had produced decent profiles for us to use. Saskia perched on the edge of Astrid's desk, and the two of them worked while Finch and I twiddled our thumbs. It was interesting to see Saskia invested in something besides herself, and she really did seem to enjoy the creative side of this.

Astrid even laughed at some of Saskia's suggestions, and the two women seemed to really be getting along. I'd never witnessed a stranger pairing, but as long as Saskia didn't start making comments about me and Astrid, I could deal with it.

"Garrett, how's this for you?" Saskia glanced over her shoulder. "Mr. Ernest Pompadour—a magical with a mountain of money who's been living in St. Tropez for the past forty years. Same height and same build as you, so you only have to worry about the face and stuff. See if you can Shift into this guy."

She pointed to the computer screen, which showed a middle-aged guy with a perma-tan and sweeping blond hair that couldn't have been natural. At least he was good-looking in a rich, well-groomed way, with a subtle air of ruggedness, as if he'd been an explorer, or at least gone on safaris. If he'd been an ugly, fat, old guy, there'd have been no point in me wearing that sharp-looking suit.

"I need some hair or an item of clothing from the guy," I replied. "Something with his DNA on it."

Finch looked surprised. "You do?"

"You don't?"

He shook his head. "No, I've never needed it."

"Then how do you make it work?" I was puzzled.

"I just look at the person and Shift," he said. "I've always been that way."

"Maybe that was your Mimicry poking through," Astrid suggested. "Traditionally, Shapeshifters need DNA in order to Shift. Unfortunately, I don't have anything from Ernest Pompadour, and it would be a while before I could get my hands on some sort of DNA fragment. I'm guessing you don't have time to wait for that?"

"Not really," I murmured.

"Here, let me try something." Finch stepped closer and put his hand on my shoulder. Immediately, I felt a rush of Chaos twist through my veins, my cells jangling as they altered to fit the image. He was manipulating my Shifting ability to bend to his will. I felt the familiar ripple across my skin as the Shapeshifting took hold. After a moment or two, I opened my eyes. My hands weren't mine—they were larger and speckled with freckles and blond hairs.

"How's my face?" I asked.

"Perfect!" Saskia replied.

"Glad I could help, though you'll have to stay close to me so I can top you up with Mimicry here and there." Finch grinned. "Now, what about me?" He anxiously edged closer to the computers.

Saskia grinned. "You're going to be Mr. Martin Maddelson, of the Australian Maddelsons. Again, same height and build as you. Officially, he went missing on a Caribbean cruise, but rich people are always faking their deaths for insurance purposes. Believe me, it happens way more often than you'd think. So it shouldn't be too much of an issue."

Astrid nodded. "I've altered the profile so that if you get checked, it'll seem like Maddelson faked his disappearance so he could become a full-time Dark Tourist. Saskia suggested it. People don't take kindly to that kind of hobby, which makes it a perfect cover."

"His parents and sisters would be furious if they learned he was into that." Saskia gave Finch and me a knowing look. Astrid didn't need to know that it was related to what we were up to.

"Give me a sec." Finch pressed his palms to his chest. In literally a second, his face changed to match the picture on the screen—a suave-looking guy with a silver fox vibe, a hint of designer stubble running across his jaw, and piercing blue eyes, a different shade from his usual blue. I envied how quickly Finch could Shift.

"Looks good to me," Saskia said.

"You think any man with a pulse looks good." Finch grinned back with his new mouth and teeth.

"What about you?" I turned my attention to Saskia.

She stretched like a cat. "I told you, I've got everything covered."

"Why does that worry me?" I shook my head.

"It shouldn't. I may be young, but I know what I'm doing." She flashed a wink that made me want to rip out my eyeballs. Astrid laughed, somehow charmed.

"When will the IDs be ready?" Finch asked.

Astrid thought about it. "I can have them done by tomorrow. Did you need anything else?" She blinked up at me, making me feel all kinds of awkward.

I balled my hands into fists and braced myself. "Actually, yeah, there was one other thing."

Finch and Saskia looked at me oddly.

"I was wondering if you'd like to go out for brunch sometime. It seems we've got a lot of catching up to do." I Shifted back to my regular face and gestured around the computer room. This was my first time in her new domain, and I was interested in what she was doing here. Plus, if I didn't ask her now, I probably never would. Sure, I'd rather have done it without a gaping audience, but at least it'd shut Saskia up.

But, seriously... brunch? My mind started to whirr. I could've gone with dinner, or a movie, or a walk. Why did it have to be brunch? It had been the first thing to jump into my head, since Astrid loved brunch.

Astrid fidgeted with Smartie. "Uh... sure. If you make it out of wherever you're going alive."

"Really?" Finch, Saskia, and I chorused. I definitely should have asked without an audience.

Astrid chuckled quietly. "Why not? We're friends. We should see each other more often."

That hit me right in the solar plexus. I'd been thinking of a more date-like scenario, not buddies hanging out. If I'd wanted that, I'd have asked Finch out for brunch. *Dammit.* Even when I was trying to be straightforward with my feelings, it didn't pan out. Unless she just didn't want to date me, and this was her way of letting me down gently?

"He wasn't asking you as a friend!" Saskia blurted out, to my horror. "Am I the only person around here who understands guys? He wants you to go on a date with him. Why else would he have asked you to *brunch*? Guys don't do brunch unless they're trying to impress a girl. Everyone knows that!"

"That's not true. I love brunch. Who doesn't love iced tea and some quiche?" Finch smiled. "But she's right. I don't think he was asking as a friend."

Way to throw me under the bus! I glared at them, but they just shrugged.

Astrid blushed furiously, fumbling with Smartie's screen.

"You won't find the answer on that thing," Saskia chided. "Just say yes and put us all out of our misery. You're both getting on my nerves!"

"I... I guess," Astrid stammered. "I guess that could be nice. I'll have to... check my schedule and stuff, but... uh... I'll text you or something?"

I gave her a strained smile. I hadn't meant to pressure her into it. "Yeah, that sounds good."

"That's more like it!" Saskia punched the air and leapt off the edge of the desk. "Now, let's get out of here before she changes her mind and I have to smash your heads together."

"See you later," I said, rubbing the back of my neck.

Astrid smiled at me, and I nearly melted. "Yeah... see you later."

It wasn't a definite yes, but it wasn't a no, either. At least now, Astrid had a better idea of how I felt. I hated to admit it, but I was grateful to Saskia for putting it out there. Maybe the little brat wasn't completely terrible after all.

I breathed a sigh of relief. The ice was beginning to thaw, and maybe we'd finally get the fresh start I'd been hoping for. The ghost of Alton would never entirely fade, but perhaps we could find happiness in the midst of loss.

EIGHTEEN

Finch

"There's a TV in the armrest!"

I'd never been in a limo before, and it showed. These things were the stuff of celebrities and overzealous teens on prom night, and since I wasn't a celebrity and I'd never had a prom night, the novelty was fresh. I was like a kid in a candy store, fiddling with every button.

"Can you not?" Saskia cast me a withering glance. She had those down to perfection. I imagined she practiced in front of the mirror to keep from getting rusty.

I found another secret compartment and opened it to reveal a compact refrigerator filled with drinks. "There's a fridge!"

Garrett laughed. "Your first time, huh?"

"Limos weren't exactly on my mother's agenda, back in the day." I clinked the bottles together as I rummaged through the selection. I thought about pulling something out but worried it might get added to the tab, so I left them where they were. "Does everyone have their tragic characters on lockdown?"

Saskia stroked the white faux fur she was wearing. "I'm Hypatia of Alexandria, a famed and respected academic who was the world's leading mathematician and astronomer back in her day. Naturally, this caused her a lot of trouble, being a woman in a man's world."

"What happened to her?" Garrett asked.

"One day, five hundred monks—or so the story goes—descended on her and dragged her from her chariot by her hair. They hauled her into a church and told her to kiss the cross and join the nunnery if she wanted to live. She refused, so they stripped her naked, scraped her flesh from her bones with oyster shells, tore her limbs from her body, and then burned the evidence of what they'd done."

I shuddered. "That's dark."

"She was the first feminist icon. A martyr for the right to female education." Saskia smoothed down the front of her shimmering black dress and glanced out of the window. Even though she wasn't disguised, she didn't look like the Saskia we knew and tolerated. She was completely made up, her features defined with products I wasn't even going to try to list. Foundation and stuff. It made her look like she'd just waltzed off the cover of *Vogue*. Her blonde hair looked almost silver, flowing past her shoulders in kinked waves.

"Now mine seems stupid." I sighed.

"Who did you go with?" Garrett asked.

"Sigurd the Mighty," I replied.

Saskia gave a derisive snort.

Garrett frowned. "What did he do?"

"He was the second Earl of Orkney—a Scottish Viking. He got into a battle with another local leader called Mael Brigte, for Viking reasons. Territory and so on. It was meant to be forty men against forty, but Sigurd brought eighty. He put two on each horse, sly devil that he was. So, he obviously won. They beheaded the enemy, and Sigurd took Mael's head as a trophy, tying it to his saddlebag so everyone could see what he'd done. Only, as he was riding, Mael's teeth rubbed on an open wound on Sigurd's leg. That pesky zombie bite infected Sigurd's leg, and he died from it."

"Ah." Garrett chuckled.

"Not quite a feminist icon." I chuckled back, a little dejected. "Just a stupid Viking with no disinfectant handy. What about you, G?"

"Mine's somewhere in between cool and stupid," he replied. "I went with Eleazar Avaran."

I smirked. "Sounds like you're about to pull a rabbit from a hat."

"No rabbit, but there is an elephant involved." Garrett smiled.

"Color me intrigued." I propped my arm against the window and listened intently, though I realized his story probably wouldn't beat mine for silliness.

"During the Battle of Beit Zechariah, Eleazar was fighting, and he spotted a war elephant, which he thought was carrying the Seleucid king, Antiochus V. The elephant was wearing fancy armor, which made it stand out. Anyway, it would have ended the battle if he killed the king, so he charged the elephant and thrust a spear into its belly. The dead elephant collapsed and crushed Eleazar." Garrett laughed to himself grimly. "Some people say his body was discovered crushed in the elephant's... uh... poo, but that might just be the storytellers trying to paint him in an even worse light."

"Why am I not surprised?" Saskia sighed. "Of course the two of you would go for dumb deaths. At least they're obscure, so you each get a point for that."

We arrived at an enormous mansion. It had towering gates with two bronze gargoyles, one perched on each post. Not the Bestiary kind, but just as intimidating. Rubies flashed in their eyes as the car drove past and we headed up an obnoxiously long driveway. I had a feeling those rubies were entirely real and probably cost more than I'd make in my lifetime.

After a few minutes, the limo reached the end of the drive, where the road looped and curved back the other way. An elegant stone fountain stood in the center of that circle, decorated with devils and angels in perpetual battle.

For a moment, I thought we'd gotten the wrong address and stopped by a hotel. I'd never had any reason to visit Beverly Hills, and seeing such opulence left me in a silent stupor. Nobody needed a house this size! Others might have been jealous of a house like this, but it just turned my stomach. Rich folks weren't my favorite, and that was putting it lightly. There were exceptions, of course, but this place just screamed "asshole."

Around us, other cars dropped off guests in a conveyor belt of wealthy elite. The darlings of this world, clad in pricey suits and dresses that glittered like the sky overhead. Some were in costume, as Ryann said, but these were no dime-store, off-the-rack outfits. One woman wore a wig so large she couldn't fit through the front door and had to be maneuvered by four other people. Another woman wore a dress with a skirt so huge and bulky she could have hidden a fifty-inch flat screen under it.

There were a couple of guys in armor, and another in a mass of silken robes that pooled down the front steps. Naturally, he tripped, and had to be caught by one of the underlings manning the door. Not a very cool entry, but he didn't seem bothered. I was sure his wealth provided a decent cushion for any and all embarrassments.

"Showtime." Saskia grinned as the valet opened the car door. She exited first, and Garrett and I clambered out behind her. We had our new faces on—Mr. Ernest Pompadour and Mr. Martin Maddelson, respectively—with our fake identities safely stowed away in our expensive suits.

I had to hand it to Saskia. She'd gone all out for this party. As she sashayed up the stairs, she looked like she belonged here. The sparkling black of her dress moved like it was part of her, the train swishing and drawing attention from most of the male population. Diamonds dripped from her throat and wrists. Real ones. They flashed no matter which way she turned, drawing in the wealthy magpies around her.

But it was as much about her attitude as her clothes and jewelry. Garrett and I might've looked the part, but we didn't have the natural sense of privilege to go along with it. Garrett was closer to it, but I had never wandered in the upper echelons before. Not even in the cult. Katherine hadn't let me talk with the bigwigs, preferring to be the one to put on a show for them. And they lapped it up. Just like they were lapping up Saskia's presence right now.

She's one of your own... Even the magical guards at the top of the stairs needed to winch their jaws up from the floor as she approached. At least she provided a good distraction from Garrett and me. If they focused on her, they might pay less attention to us, her "chaperones" for the night.

"Good evening, miss," the first security guard said, staring like he wanted to eat her.

She's underage, you perv! I wanted to yell at him, but I didn't want to ruin the effect of Saskia's hard work. Or draw unwanted attention. So far, this was the good kind. The useful kind.

"Good evening," Saskia purred in reply.

"Might I have your invitations?" The guard's eyes shone, as if he were under some kind of spell.

"Of course." Saskia pulled the invitations from her diamond-encrusted bag. A "clutch," as I'd been informed by the mistress of fashion. She handed them to the guard, who added our names to a hefty registry that sat on a lectern beside him. He was about a third of the way through the massive book, making me wonder just how many of these parties there'd been over the centuries.

"Do you have identification?" The guard smiled. "It's just a formality."

"Certainly." Saskia gave a coy giggle and handed her card to him. She gestured for Garrett and me to do the same, which we did without hesitation. The guy was barely paying us any attention, but that didn't mean we'd get through the door. I trusted Astrid and her technological wizardry, but my cheeks still clenched a little as he waved the IDs under a scanner. He seemed to frown at mine and Garrett's for a moment, which made me sweat.

This suit is silk! Xander had warned us that the fabric would be ruined if we dared to perspire, but I couldn't help the beads forming.

"Crikey, it's bloody hot, isn't it? Feel like I've just wandered into the outback." I took out my pocket square and dabbed my forehead. That was the beauty of Mimicry—I took on the nuances of the person I was playing, down to the pitch of their voice and their littlest quirks. I'd never have said the word "crikey" in my life, but apparently Martin Maddelson enjoyed a bit of "crikey" and stereotyping to go along with it.

"I'd have thought you'd be used to hot weather." The security guard smirked, checking the ID. "Being Australian and all."

"It's the suit. Personally, if I'm going to be roasting my proverbial beef, I prefer to be on a beach in nothing but my finest pair of budgie-smugglers, so I can cool off when the mood strikes. None of this suited and booted lark," I replied, in a voice that didn't belong to me. Deep and inviting, with a confused flavor of Australia, America, and Britain. A Trans-Oceanic accent.

"Well, Mr. Maddelson, I hope you find something to your taste here in LA," the guard said. "With company like this, how could you not?"

"Not sure you should be looking at the merchandise, mate." I flashed him a warning smile. "But what do I know? I'm just a guest."

The guard paled. "Of course, Mr. Maddelson. Please, go on in. And here are your cards back." He fumbled with the IDs, shoving them back into our hands. I'd put the fear of God in him. No, worse... I'd put the fear of his employers in him. I doubted Mr. Daggerston would be too happy to discover that a lowly guard had been hitting on someone like Saskia Vasilis.

Smiling, I strode past the guard with Saskia and Garrett in tow. I'd barely walked a few steps when it was my jaw's turn to drop. *Well, well, well, what do we have here, old sport?* I felt like I'd stepped into *The Great Gatsby*. The mansion had a modern exterior, but inside, it contained sparkling diamonds, gaudy chandeliers, brushed gold fixtures, lustrous velvet chaises draped with tipsy revelers, and endless plates of hors d'oeuvres. Or horse's doovers, as I'd always called them.

The display looked like we'd stepped back in time to the roaring twenties. There was even an actual goose, sitting on a table right in the middle of the entrance hall.

"Risky move, Mr. Maddelson," Saskia muttered.

"Huh?" I pulled my gaze from the goose, but it snagged on an aerial artist performing a daring somersault between chandeliers. Everywhere I turned, I found a feast for the eyes.

"Talking to the guard," she hissed. "You could've gotten us all in trouble."

"But I didn't." I grinned at her. "Everyone likes an Australian."

"We should explore," Garrett said, his eyes like saucers.

"It's called 'mingling.' Use the right words unless you want to stand out like a sore thumb," Saskia chided. She headed down the hallway to the right, and we followed.

"I think all those sparkles have gone to her head," Garrett whispered as we walked.

I smiled. "I think it's the bank account. I thought you were used to this kind of shindig."

"Me?" Garrett gaped at me. "No way. I used to avoid them like the plague, and they were *never* this fancy."

"Looks like we're both on a learning curve tonight, then."

He nodded. "At least you don't have to worry about getting the voice right."

"You sound fine."

"Do I?"

"Yeah, Astrid did a great job on the voice-box distorter. Don't worry about it."

"I don't sound like I'm autotuned?" He smiled back nervously.

"It's fine, honestly."

We continued through the long hallway and emerged into another room. This one was themed as a Regency ballroom, with a small orchestra in one corner playing an old-timey tune on violins and flutes. Meanwhile, dancers flew about the room in a dance that definitely wasn't Regency. Far too much physical contact. And too much kissing in the shadows on the sidelines. I guessed not everything had to be era-appropriate.

Through French doors that lined one side of the room, I could see into the enormous gardens. A pool took up the immediate outdoor space and had been decorated to emulate ancient Arabia. Candles floated on the water in bronze dishes alongside clusters of red-and-orange flowers, and wooden bridges crisscrossed the surface. Tents and yurts had been set up on the poolside, and haunting music floated through the French doors.

The curtains of two of the tents were tied back, revealing a hookah bar and a regular bar, although there wasn't much of a line for the latter. There were enough servers in this mansion, running around with fresh trays of booze and food, to make up a small army.

I kept looking around, in a daze from the visual feast, trying to figure out where the auction was going to take place. There was an open terrace that didn't seem to have anything on it, aside from a covered plinth. *Maybe that's it.* But it could have taken place anywhere—the choices were endless. Another room resembled Versailles, while another had Japanese geishas performing a traditional dance, and yet another looked like an Ancient Greek or Roman forum. It seemed like there was a setting perfect for everyone's historical fetish, and the space to accommodate all.

Beyond the pool, an open lawn had been converted into a medieval jousting ground. Huge warhorses charged up and down, various colors flying from their riders' lances, representing the women whose honor these knights were fighting for. Although, it wasn't just men getting involved. As one of the riders pulled off a jet-black helmet, long blonde hair tumbled down and one of the most beautiful women I'd ever seen raised her lance in victory. The crowd sitting in the raked chairs roared in applause.

"Erin St. Cloud, in case you were wondering." Saskia nudged me in the arm.

"What?" I sputtered.

She chuckled. "You were staring."

"I've never seen a joust before!" I protested, but she kept laughing.

"She's one of the most famed magicals in the world. They think she might be the next director of the Edinburgh Coven, and who would stop her? Look at her; she's got everyone eating out of her palm." Saskia looked as transfixed as I was. A bit of heroine worship.

"They have dragons!" Garrett hissed, practically twisting my head off to get me to look. It seemed I wasn't the only one distracted from the Ivan Trap by the visual display.

"Where?" I peered across the lawn, but I couldn't see any dragons.

"There!" Garrett jabbed his finger at the more distant gardens.

Sure enough, two hulking dragons sat amidst quaint rosebushes and manicured hedges, smoke billowing from their nostrils. One was red, the other white, and neither seemed impressed to be there, which likely had something to do with the fact that they were chained up. It was like looking at sad circus animals who'd been forced to perform.

I was about to come back with a scathing comment about the state of them when a vision in orange distracted me. Ryann walked along the far side of the pool, dressed in a glittering cocktail dress with a sweeping silk train attached at the waist. It trailed behind her, making her look like a friggin' princess. The bronze circlet on her head completed the image.

What is she doing here? I was happy to see her, but she wasn't meant to attend. Had she come to keep an eye on things, or had Miranda demanded her presence?

Speaking of which, Miranda Bontemps walked beside her, decked out in a vivid gown of reddish purple that wouldn't have looked out of place on a red carpet. Her black hair had been arranged in an updo that glittered with amethysts. I didn't know much about her, but she made quite an impact.

"Keep it together, Mr. Maddelson," Saskia warned. "Your Finch is starting to peek through."

"Huh?" I glanced at my hands. They'd smoothed out, de-aging in front of my eyes.

I focused Chaos back through my veins and allowed it to re-cement the portrayal of Mr. Maddelson. I didn't want to mess up just because Ryann looked smoking hot. I hadn't even realized I was doing it.

I looked down and breathed a sigh of relief. My hands had aged back. And not a moment too soon—Miranda and Ryann were heading straight for us.

"Good evening to you all," Miranda said, pausing in front of us. "It's always a pleasure to see new faces at these little soirees."

"Thank you for welcoming us," Garrett replied in the creamy voice of the wealthy elite—thick and rich. Astrid really had done a killer job with his voice box distorter.

"I'm terrible with names," Miranda prompted.

"My real one or my character?" Garrett replied.

She chuckled. "Your real name."

"Ah, then I'm Ernest Pompadour." Garrett bowed. "And I know old Daggerston has his name on this party, but I imagine *you* are the creative genius."

Miranda flushed with pleasure. "I'm glad you like it. It was nothing, really, and it's all for such a good cause. Which is always the main thing."

I barely restrained myself from rolling my eyes. I knew her type. The kind who threw fundraisers in the Hamptons and expected a Nobel Peace Prize for rustling up a few deviled eggs and draining plump bank accounts from the same vein of elitists. But, in this case, she was useful. A little flattery definitely wouldn't hurt.

"Martin Maddelson." I took her hand and kissed it lightly. "It's a good thing you're not part of this auction. If you were, Miss Bontemps, I don't imagine any man would leave this house with a single penny to his name."

She giggled. "You rogue!"

"What's a fella to do, in the face of such beauty?" I winked at her.

"Are you *that* Martin Maddelson?" Miranda eyed me curiously.

"As far as I know, there's only one of me." I gave a deep belly laugh. "If you're talking about the faked death, then I'm your man. Had to find a way to indulge my hobbies without having the family on my back. It's a bloody shame more people don't understand these things. A bloody shame. But at least now I get to roam around Dark Tourist spots without hassle, so it's not all bad."

Miranda nodded sympathetically. "It's a very real shame. It's my hope that, one day, Dark Tourism will reach the mainstream."

"Well, until that day comes, it's their loss and our gain." I planted another kiss on her hand, though I kept Ryann in my peripheral vision. "Who'd be boring enough to miss out on something like this?"

"Precisely." Miranda smiled.

"And who's this?" I glanced at Ryann, allowing myself a proper appraisal. She looked breathtaking.

"This is Ryann Smith, my assistant. She's very good. Very discreet," Miranda replied, casting me a conspiratorial glance.

"As any good assistant should be, especially where our mutual interests are concerned," I agreed.

Miranda's gaze moved to Saskia and lingered for a moment. Her brow furrowed. "I've seen you before. Yes... you're Saskia Vasilis, if I'm not mistaken. I know your family. But what are you doing here? You're underage, aren't you? Oh, I hope this won't cause a stir." A note of concern edged into her eloquent voice.

Saskia stroked her faux-dead-cat scarf. "I'm an aspiring Dark Tourist, and it's my firm belief that we should start as young as we can. I didn't think it would be too much of a problem as long as I had chaperones. And I swear I haven't touched a drop of alcohol." She chuckled. "Just don't tell my family. They'd disown me, and I wouldn't be able to buy any of the wonderful things I've heard will be auctioned tonight! My uncle, Anatoly Rasputin, is the only one who encourages this kind of thing, but he's always had the most discerning taste."

Oh, you're good. She had Miranda—hook, line, and sinker. Dropping the Rasputin bomb in company like this was like dropping a fresh chunk of meat in a den of lions. That name was power, wealth, and influence personified.

"Anatoly Rasputin encourages you in this pursuit?" Miranda's eyes glinted with dollar signs.

Saskia nodded. "Although, it'd be best if you didn't tell him I was here. I was hoping to snag a gift for him, and I wouldn't want to ruin the surprise."

"No, of course not! What a charming, thoughtful girl," Miranda cooed. "It's always good to have new members, and I'd be only too happy to see you at more events. Perhaps you might bring your uncle one day?"

"I'm sure he'd love to come." Saskia was pulling Miranda further in with every word. "He's always spoken so highly of them, which is why I really wanted to come to this one. There aren't as many in Russia, so I thought I should take advantage while I'm in America."

"Then I'm very glad you're here!" Miranda cried, her nerves apparently forgotten. There was power and money in a name, and Saskia had just proven that. It no longer mattered that she was underage, as long as she planned to buy, and buy big.

"If I had my way, there'd be one of these parties in every city in the world on a monthly basis," I said. "People are so narrow-minded, aren't they?"

Saskia flashed a winning smile. "They're scared of what they don't understand, while we embrace it. It's what sets us apart. It makes us truly elite."

"I should put that on the invitations." Miranda grinned. "It has been an absolute pleasure to meet you all, it really has. And I hope to see you again at my little parties."

Little parties?! I'd have hated to see what her big parties looked like.

Ryann hadn't said anything throughout this entire encounter. She just kept staring at Garrett and me. Shapeshifting could be a little difficult to wrap your head around when seen in action for the first time. Plus, I guessed Miranda preferred her to be a seen-and-not-heard assistant. That's what these rich folks liked best.

"If you're not otherwise engaged, you *have* to come and meet Gerard. He'll be thrilled to meet you!" Miranda exclaimed. She started dragging Saskia away, which gave us no choice but to follow. As her chaperones, where she went, we went.

I took a deep breath and put on a huge fake smile. I hoped we weren't getting too close to the fire. This wasn't the time, or the occasion, to get burned. We had an Ivan Trap to buy, and we needed to get out of here in one piece.

NINETEEN

Finch

D aggerston was as sleazy as I'd imagined. Slicked dark hair and beetle-black eyes, with a laugh that swallowed up every noise around him. And man, did he like to talk. He was babbling away, downing drinks like there was no tomorrow and snapping his fingers for another glass whenever his got empty. I hated people who snapped at servers. *Hated* them. But I had to play nice.

On the plus side, it meant I always knew when the servers were coming, so I could shoot a warning glance at Saskia. She'd been trying to swipe flutes for herself all evening, and I had to keep taking them away from her.

Meanwhile, Garrett was digging into the canapés as if he hadn't eaten in weeks. With Daggerston doing all the talking, there wasn't much else to do but eat. Still, he was getting a few choice looks from the other rich folks at our table.

"Take it easy there, pal. You can't just pop open a button in company like this." I nudged Garrett in the arm.

He looked up at me, his cheeks bulging.

"Sorry, it's just so good." He swallowed his mouthful but didn't reach for more.

"A man should have an appetite in all things," Daggerston protested in his booming voice. It sent a shudder up my spine. "Although, perhaps it's best you listen to your friend, Pompadour. You used to be huge, back in the day! And you look so good now. I have to get the name of your PT."

Garrett stiffened in his chair. "I like to train alone. Keeps me motivated."

"If only I had that kind of motivation." Daggerston sighed.

I glanced at Ryann, who was sitting beside Miranda, opposite me. I wanted to speak to her in private. I supposed I should've realized she'd be here tonight, being Miranda's assistant and all, but it'd still been a surprise. She'd hardly batted an eyelid at Garrett and me, with our new faces on. She would have recognized our clothing.

"So, which character did you pick?" Daggerston bellowed at Garrett.

I turned to look at my friend, eager to hear him ramble on about elephants. My heart stopped. Over his shoulder, I saw a face I *really* didn't want to see. Mingling in the gardens was Davin Doncaster.

I squinted, in case it was the party atmosphere playing tricks on my head. But, nope, it was definitely him. I'd have known that smug grin from a mile off. He looked like he was in his element. Smiling, laughing, having a blast.

With a puzzled look, Garrett turned and followed my gaze. As soon as he caught sight of Doncaster, the Shapeshifting mask over his face phased out for a split second, prompting me to surge some more of my Mimicry into him before anyone noticed. His eyes went wide. I knew he was feeling the same emotions—anger, hatred, disgust, and a sudden urge to start flipping tables.

Saskia leaned into me. "What are you both gaping at?"

I nodded discreetly toward Davin.

"Who's he?" she asked.

"Davin Doncaster," I hissed back.

Saskia frowned. "Ah, so that's the immortal douchebag?"

"Not immortal, just extremely hard to keep dead," I told her under my breath. "Although, with my mother gone, keeping him dead might be a little easier. How about we test the theory?" I was certain Katherine had been the one resurrecting him, before her demise. Who else would've gone to that kind of effort to keep Davin alive?

I stood sharply, and Garrett rose with me. There were no words necessary. Davin was here, and we were going to knock the living daylights out of him. Finding this serpent and getting him thrown into Purgatory had been Harley and Wade's mission for the last year—the least we could do was help them cross it off their list.

Daggerston coughed, distracting us from our path of destruction, and he didn't look too pleased. "Is this conversation boring you?"

"Not at all, Daggerston," I replied, trying to keep up the pretense of nonchalant Aussie. "I've just seen an old pal I wouldn't mind catching up with."

Daggerston peered over my shoulder. "You and Doncaster are friends? I had no idea! It's nice to have him back. He's been away for so long, and I'm obviously not the only one who's missed him."

Nice to have him back? Why wasn't I surprised that Daggerston and Doncaster were friends? They sounded like the co-owners of some overpriced store, selling watches or something else that hardly anyone could afford. Although, this raised some pretty worrying questions about Miranda, if she was in on this, too. Letting a known enemy of the magical world, not to mention the

SDC, saunter about didn't really coincide with the morals of someone working *at* the SDC.

"Not friends, exactly," I replied. "We have a vested interest in some of his past behavior."

"Do you always invite criminals on the magical most-wanted list to these parties?" Garrett cut in. "You know he should be in Purgatory. He was Katherine Shipton's right-hand man."

Easy, G. I nudged his arm lightly, a gentle reminder that we were playing characters. But he looked ready to burst a blood vessel.

Daggerston laughed. "I hope you're not thinking of doing something foolish."

"Foolish?" Garrett parroted.

"It wouldn't do to have the authorities swarming the place, now, would it, given the nature of the evening?" The threat was thinly veiled at best. "I understand your concern, as you've likely been misinformed. You should know not to believe everything you read. The magicals in politics needed a scapegoat, and poor Davin had the axe fall on his head."

I wish a real axe would fall on his head.

"The allegations that Davin was Katherine's subordinate are massively fabricated. Davin is, and has always been, a good man. We go way back, he and I, long before the Katherine situation." Daggerston paused. "I'd hate for there to be any unpleasantness."

I bet you'd have been at Katherine's side, too, given half a chance. This was why I despised rich folks like Davin. If you had friends in high places, you could get away with just about anything. Being the stooge of a psychotic killer, for one.

I wondered if Miranda had been brainwashed by her boyfriend's diatribe and his assurances that the sun shone out of Davin's behind. Or maybe she was just afraid of disagreeing with him, since Daggerston paid for all this. She hadn't been a part of the coven when all the Katherine business went down, but she'd definitely heard about it afterwards. Maybe Daggerston had done some convincing, to make her believe the lies. People did a lot of stupid things when they were in love. Glancing at her, I noticed she looked uncomfortable, as if she didn't like the line of conversation. That gave me some hope that she wasn't rotten to the core.

"Perhaps I should call Davin over, so we can put any worries to rest?" Daggerston said. "Truly, I think you'd find him very worthwhile company, if you just spoke to him yourselves instead of listening to vapid rumors."

Well, that was the worst idea possible. I didn't want Davin getting anywhere near Ryann or Saskia. The latter he might not recognize, but he would definitely remember Ryann. He'd trussed her up like a Christmas ham, for Pete's sake. Plus, even though Garrett and I were in our disguises, he might get suspicious if he saw us hanging around with known members of the SDC, especially a Vasilis.

"Actually, I was enjoying hearing about your character. Was it Mad King George?" I knew Daggerston wouldn't be able to resist having the spotlight on him again.

Daggerston tutted. "I take it you don't know your kings and queens. It was George Plantagenet, the Duke of Clarence, not Mad King George. Apparently, he drowned in a barrel of wine after choosing that as his means of execution. What a way to go!"

It did the trick. Daggerston started crowing about himself again, defusing the situation before Davin could be called over to blow our cover wide open. Or, at the very least, to bring him closer to Ryann, which would only end badly. Even if Davin was on his best behavior, that wouldn't change the suffering that Ryann had endured at his hand. I didn't want her to have to remember all of that.

Garrett pretended he was picking something up off the floor.

"Tell me we're still dealing with Davin? There's no way he's leaving this party a free man."

I sat back down and twisted my napkin in knots. "We can't do anything about it right this second. Not while we've got his best pal sitting at our table. You can bet your ass the Duke of Clarence over there would make sure neither of us saw the light of day again, if he caught us murdering his bestie or trying to shuffle him off to Purgatory on the sly." I didn't need Daggerston *and* Erebus on my plate. It was already overstuffed as it was. "But he's not getting away with it. By the time this party is over, he *will* be dead or on his way to Purgatory."

"What are you thinking?" Garrett sat back up and leaned over as though he were selecting another morsel, a move which brought him close to my ear. "We go for him once we have the Ivan Trap?"

I nodded. "After the auction, we deal with him in private. We lure him out and get him alone. We can say we've got a deal for him, or we want to find out if any of the cult is still standing."

"I want to rip his stupid face off," Garrett muttered.

"So do I, but we have to wait," I replied, though I hated saying it. He was right here, wandering around like he owned the place! And worse, people were lapping it up. I guessed he was the living, breathing, impossible-to-kill epitome of Dark Tourism. He'd been at Katherine's side for so much of her destructive sweep, and I would've bet my entire figurine collection that he was indulging everyone in his awful tales. The guests considered Katherine a point of fascination, just like people who were obsessed with serial killers or unsolved murders. They'd immortalized her, all for the sake of a dumb rich-person hobby.

"That doesn't mean we can't keep an eye on him, though," Saskia whispered. I hadn't realized she'd been eavesdropping. "You wouldn't want him running off before you get to him. But, damn, why does he have to be so freaking cute?"

"Don't make me march you out of here," I warned. "He's a toad in a nice suit, believe me."

Garrett lifted another canapé to his lips and used it to hide his mouth. "Saskia's got a point. We should take advantage of our... characters and watch him. Like you said, he won't recognize us like this."

"I agree. I'll be watching that bastard like a hawk." I twisted my napkin some more. It took every ounce of self-control not to cross the gardens and take him on. After everything he'd done to us, I was surprised I was still sitting. *Patience... patience is key.* Making Davin pay was important, but so was the Ivan Trap. We needed both. And rushing in would only see us behind bars.

All I could think about were the million ways I wanted to kill that sucker. He hadn't paid for his crimes. He'd just crept away without a trace and hidden under a rock for the past year, while Harley and Wade had tried to track him down. *And I bet you've been laughing at us all, huh?*

"What did that napkin ever do to you?" Saskia gestured down at the shreds in my lap.

"You'd understand if you knew him," I replied. "This napkin is stopping me from doing something very stupid, now that we've decided to be careful."

I felt a hand on my shoulder. I jumped, half expecting to turn around and see Davin staring down at me. Instead, Ryann was the one doing the staring. I hadn't even noticed she'd gotten up. She crouched down like she was about to tell me something private, placing her other hand on my leg. That certainly distracted me from Davin for a moment.

"Is everything okay?" she asked, looking up at me.

I gave a small shake of my head. "Davin is here."

Her face paled. "What?"

"He's over there."

She turned to look for herself, but I reached for her face to keep her looking at me. It wasn't quite as romantic as it sounded. "Don't look! He could recognize you. Stay as far away from him as possible."

"He's really here?!" Her voice rose in panic.

"You should go home. Make an excuse. Women's troubles, or whatever, and get the hell out of here before he sees you. Although, next time you're in work, you might want to have a word with Miranda about him—see if she's bought into this tripe that he's a 'good man.'"

I didn't think Davin was stupid enough to repeat his past horrors, especially not in full view of a party, but I wasn't going to let him get within a mile of Ryann. Not after what he'd done to her and the Smiths. He wouldn't be able to resist taunting her over their last encounter, especially if he somehow caught her alone. Something else I wasn't going to allow.

Ryann's gaze hardened. "I *will* be having words with Miranda, but I'm not going to let him scare me. Not today, not any day. Let's not forget the most important factor here: he lost. He chose the wrong side. He knows that. If he tries anything, he'll get a second taste of what it's like to lose, and he'll find out what Smith payback feels like."

Saskia stared at her with shining cartoon eyes. "Did you just come up with that?"

"With what?" Ryann tilted her head at Saskia.

"Awesome," Saskia breathed.

Nobody was more surprised than me. These two women had been unimpressed with each other since they met, and now Saskia gazed at Ryann like she was her favorite person on Earth.

"Sorry to interrupt." Miranda's silky voice cut through. "The auction is about to begin, if you'd like to take your places on the terrace. Make sure you pick a good spot—we wouldn't want you missing out, Miss Vasilis."

Saskia smiled. "No, we wouldn't."

"After this, we get him," I whispered to Garrett.

He nodded, his mouth set in a grim line. "Then let's get this done quickly."

We got up from the garden table and headed for a marbled expanse nearby. It was the only place that didn't have a theme. Chairs had been set up in neat rows, and guests seated themselves, vying for the spots near the front. The seats faced a solitary podium at the far end of the expanse, complete with display tables, cases, and a microphone for the auctioneer.

Hold on to your Stetsons, fellas—it's about to get crazy in here.

TWENTY

Finch

I'd never seen a weirder collection of objects in all my life. I didn't even know what half of them were. An older dude in a white tuxedo and top hat brought each item to display on the velvet-covered table. Other objects were shown in display cases, each odder than the last.

Some of the choice prizes: a haunted pendant belonging to Mary, Queen of Scots, and a cuckoo clock that held the spirit of a famed Dutch clockmaker. He'd been executed after experimenting with clockwork mechanisms on human victims. It was possible he'd been trying to find a way to save his sick son, who'd had a heart defect, but the clockmaker hadn't come out of it looking good.

There was also a signet ring that gave the power of poetic verse, exhumed from Oscar Wilde's grave in Paris. A tube of lipstick belonging to Coco Chanel, which made the wearer irresistible. A dusty old lamp with a tamed djinn, a.k.a. a genie, inside. But there was nothing deadly on display, per se. These weren't things you'd hand over to your kids to play with, but they weren't going to make anyone explode, either.

I scoured the congregation for Davin, spotting him close to the front. I meant what I'd said about keeping an eye on him. If we lost him, even for a moment, he'd have a chance to skip away into the sunset, and that wasn't going to happen this time. Tonight, Davin would pay for his crimes, one way or another. His bigwig pals wouldn't be able to save him. Purgatory or death, I didn't mind. The outcome would depend on how slippery he tried to be. But, until this auction was over, all I could do was watch and wait, and let my anger build, so it could feed my Chaos when we faced him.

"How do they have all this stuff?" I whispered to Ryann, who sat beside me. I was having to concentrate twice as hard due to that fact alone.

"Miranda is a collector," she whispered back. "Well, she's more of an acquirer, since she hardly ever keeps the objects that come to her. She has people working for her all over the globe, finding these rare artifacts—items that have been lost in the human world."

I looked up as the assistant placed a golden longbow on display. "Why not give them to museums? That'd be better for her reputation."

"She wants magical items to be put back into magical hands, where they can actually be of some use, instead of being stared at by tourists. Human or magical," Ryann explained.

"Yeah, but there are some risky items here, and some actual weapons." I nodded to the longbow that people were now vying for.

"It's more for status, and it brings in the money that Miranda needs to fund her charities," Ryann replied. "With museums, there's a lot of red tape that would stop her from being able to do that. You go to all the effort of finding something like that longbow, and the museums can turn around and say, 'It's a heritage piece—it belongs to the state,' which means you don't get a dime."

I examined everything on display. Every item we'd seen so far was ridiculously rare and jaw-droppingly expensive. The guests were practically *throwing* their money at the auctioneer. A fight broke out close to the front as two bidders battled it out over the golden longbow. It had already gone north of 250k, and the price just kept rising, the bidding paddles flapping wildly.

"Doesn't it all seem a bit... sick to you?" I whispered to Ryann as I looked around. "Squabbling over some dead person's belongings?"

Ryann shrugged. "I might not entirely agree with everything Miranda does, but I understand why she does it."

"I didn't take you for a 'the end justifies the means' kind of woman."

"I'm not, but I've seen the good these auctions do. There's not much of a difference between the state getting their hands on these things and letting them go dusty in glass cabinets, and private bidders adding them to their collections. Although, I guess the items see a little more daylight with the latter."

I wasn't convinced. This whole thing left a bitter taste in my mouth, especially the squabbling. The initial sourness definitely came from Daggerston's denial of Davin's history, as if rich people could just pay their way out of heinous crimes like talking their way out of a parking ticket. As if they could just buy up dead people's things because they felt like it. As if they could just do whatever they damn well pleased, because it was their birthright. And, like Ryann had said, this was just a show of status—a way of peacocking and displaying how much money you had. It didn't serve a cultural purpose. People couldn't just waltz into the buyers' houses and view the collections and gain education from viewing them. It was just rich people showing off.

I looked back at the miserable dragons in their chains. They were victims of the same thing, no more than an amusement in the lives of the wealthy.

"Darling, when are you going to get something more current?" I overheard Daggerston saying to Miranda. The two of them were seated a few rows ahead. It was hard not to eavesdrop on him, since he didn't seem to have a whisper setting. Just that same, booming baritone.

"What do you mean, Gerald?" Miranda replied, her eyes shining as the price of the longbow continued to skyrocket.

We were almost at half a million. That got me worried. We had fifty thousand at our disposal, and it was starting to seem unlikely that it would be enough.

"There's just nothing here to tempt me," he said. "Now, if you could get ahold of Katherine Shipton's Grimoire—I'd pay everything I had to add that to my collection."

"Perhaps that's why I haven't." Miranda chuckled.

My stomach turned. How could they be so damn casual about the woman who'd almost destroyed the world? I wasn't exactly surprised; it just made me feel like throwing up the canapés I'd forced down or flipping these chairs and calling them out for being stuck-up, self-obsessed, disgusting sycophants. Or maybe "psychophant" would've been a better term. I supposed they thought they wouldn't have suffered under Katherine's rule, as they were so powerful and influential.

"Can you imagine what such an item would go for?" Daggerston sighed, as if he were picturing having the evil thing in his hands at that very moment.

Part of me hoped, if the book ever fell into these peoples' hands, that it'd melt their flesh the moment they turned the first page. *That'd teach you a lesson you'd never forget.* For my part, I had no idea where the book was. Maybe the UCA had it, after their raid on Eris

Island. Or maybe nobody did. Maybe it was hidden away, somewhere no one would ever find.

"It would be priceless, my love," Miranda replied. "Completely priceless, to have the Grimoire of Eris."

"Everything has a price." Gerald erupted with laughter, startling the people to his left.

You make me sick. I had to hold on to my Mimicry to stop my face from phasing out. Once again, I had no doubt Daggerston would've joined my mother's cause, had she become what she'd wanted to be. He was probably jealous that Davin had been getting all the idolatry from their peers, for knowing Eris herself, in the flesh. It was taking everything I had not to go and cave in the back of Daggerston's head, to take him and his pal down together. Speaking of Davin, he just seemed to be sitting passively at the front, watching everyone fight it out for the longbow.

I jumped as I felt Ryann's fingertips on my neck, rapidly bringing me out of my bitter reverie. "What the—!"

She had a napkin in her hand and was drawing it gently across my skin. My throat constricted, and I almost lost control of my Mimicry.

"You're bleeding," she whispered, her face close to mine. I could've kissed her if I'd just leaned an inch.

Sweeney Todd! My brain screamed at me, serving a blunt reminder of Mr. Perfect. The invisible force between us.

"I am?" I stared down at the napkin as she drew it away. A streak of red spread across the white fabric.

"The collar must've caught on one of your cuts."

"Oh... yeah, of course. One of them keeps opening. It's in a funny place, so it's taking ages to heal," I rambled, trying to calm my rapid breaths. I pressed my hand to the spot where she'd wiped away the blood and transformed the skin farther down my neck than I had before, right to my chest.

She didn't sit back, as I expected her to. Instead, she kept her arm across the back of my chair, her body turned toward me, her thigh against mine. I could smell her perfume—sweet and dark, like burnt sugar or vanilla. *Man, is it getting hard to breathe in here, or is it just me?* She was too close. I didn't know what to do with myself.

"So which poltergeist are you going after?" Ryann held my gaze until I thought my lungs might burst. I didn't want to take a breath if it meant getting a nose-full of that heady scent. It was too much.

I stared into my lap. "I can't tell you any more than you already know, Ryann. I won't put you at risk, so please don't ask me to."

Ryann looked unsatisfied. But a few moments passed, and she didn't say anything. Instead, she finally sighed. "I understand."

"You do?"

She nodded. "You want to do the right thing. I can admire that, even if it's mega frustrating."

"Thank you." I thought about putting my hand on hers, but I resisted.

"Although, it's nice to know you care about me." She flashed a mischievous grin, the tension breaking.

"Don't feel special. It's more of an umbrella of care. There are a *lot* of people under it." I grinned back, wishing I could just forget about Ted Bundy and pull her in. *You* are *that special.* In my head, she had an umbrella all of her own. One nobody had stood under since Adley.

She laughed. "Noted."

"Lot twenty-six, the Ivan the Terrible Trap!" the auctioneer called.

I hadn't even noticed the golden longbow being purchased, with Ryann distracting me. It had probably gone for a stupid amount of money. My head whipped around as the guy in the white tux brought up a charmed glass box, similar to those used in the Bestiary. This one was frosted, which made it hard to see what was inside. I could see the vague outline of a smaller box, with four spikes sticking up from the top, but that was about it.

"Belonging to Tsar Ivan IV Vasilyevich, more commonly known as Ivan the Terrible, this trap was created for use in the Massacre of Novgorod to frighten and incapacitate his enemies through the entrapment and manipulation of poltergeists," the auctioneer went on. I noticed Davin sit up in his seat, a smirk on his face. That was nothing new, but it was enough to make me sit up a little straighter, too.

I turned to stare at Saskia, who sat on the other side of Garrett. "Any relation? Vasilis, Vasilyevich?"

She shrugged. "A distant relative."

"Well, start thinking and make it less distant. We might need that if it comes down to the wire," I whispered.

The auctioneer carried on. "This item's creator was one of the most prominent Russian magical inventors in the sixteenth century. It was used in several campaigns until Ivan the Terrible's death, which occurred while he was playing chess in 1584."

A roar of applause rippled through the crowd. *Sick leeches.* Davin clapped like a seal, the arrogance flowing off him like oil.

"This object subdues violent spirits and forces them to obey their captor for a brief time." The auctioneer smiled, playing up to his audience.

"We can't see it!" a voice shouted.

"There is good reason for that, sir," the auctioneer replied. "As you can see, the Trap is enclosed in a charmed box. The safety mechanisms will be removed when it's given to its new owner, but, for all your sakes, they must remain on for now. One can never tell if there is already a poltergeist lurking within."

A theatrical "ooh" drifted across the gathering.

"Now, I'll begin the bidding low, at five thousand dollars. Do I hear five thousand dollars?" The auction began without warning.

"Six thousand!" Saskia yelled, drawing gasps from all of us.

"Go easy. We don't want to look desperate," I hissed at her, but she was fully in the moment now. A hungry glint shone in her eye. I looked to Davin, but he was sitting quietly, taking it all in.

"Seven!" A guy so large he took up two seats shouted.

"I hear seven—can I get a half?" the auctioneer rattled back at lightning speed.

A wiry woman who resembled an ostrich lifted her paddle. "I have the half."

"Do I see eight? Anyone for eight?" the auctioneer asked.

"Eight thousand!" Saskia waggled her paddle in the air. At least someone was enjoying themselves.

"Eight and a half!" Chubster retorted.

"Nine!" another bidder—a dwarf in a top hat—bellowed suddenly, startling me.

"Nine and a half!" Chubster fired back.

"Ten!" Ostrich said, lifting her paddle.

The bidding went up and up, Saskia on the edge of her seat as she kept up the pace. Before I knew it, we'd hit twenty-five thousand, with no sign of stopping. I was starting to feel jittery, and Garrett was gnawing his fingernails down to the skin, his eyes fixed on the flashing paddles as they went up and down like a wave. It continued at breakneck speed, and soon we were crossing right over the thirty-thousand threshold as if it were loose change.

"Thirty-five thousand!" A new bidder had entered the battle. I knew that voice. *You've got to be kidding me.*

Peering over the crowd, I found him again. He perched right at the edge of his seat, an even smugger smirk on his stupid face. Davin, that son of a bitch.

"Lord Black, a pleasure!" The auctioneer gave a small bow. "We have thirty-five from His Lordship in the front. Do I hear thirty-six? Anyone for thirty-six?"

Lord Black? My eyes bulged with rage. If I'd felt sick during the conversation with Daggerston, I was ready to hurl now. The crowd clearly felt the same way about him as Daggerston, staring at him with adoring gazes. He was as much a hero to them as Katherine was a goddess in their eyes.

Adore him all you want. We're going to take him down. Once this auction was over, we'd make sure he got what he'd earned. It was a torment to sit through this.

Straining for control, I forced myself to pay attention to the bidding. It had gone up again, with Davin and Saskia now the only horses in the race. *What the hell does he want with an Ivan Trap?* I'd have said he was just doing this to piss us off, but he didn't know who we were.

"Forty thousand!" Saskia shouted, shooting a glare at Davin.

"Forty-one," he replied.

"Forty-two!" Saskia countered. We were getting close to our limit, and everyone was perched on the edge of their seats.

"Forty-three." Davin turned and glowered at Saskia, showing signs of his own frustration.

"Forty-four!" She met his gaze defiantly.

"Forty-five," he growled.

Saskia smirked. "Forty-six."

"Forty-seven."

"Forty-eight." Saskia cast a quick look at Garrett on her right and whispered, "I can't go much higher. Fifty is my monthly allowance. I've got more in savings, but I don't want to drain my bank account in one go."

"*That's* your monthly allowance?" Garrett gaped at her. "I thought that was your *yearly* allowance."

Saskia snorted. "And I thought *you* came from money."

"Not that kind of money!" he squeaked.

Daggerston raised an eyebrow, catching the end of our conversation. "What's so shocking about that? My daughters have similar allowances. They may not spend it all, but I always ensure there's at least forty thousand in their accounts on the first of the month."

"It's another world, pal," I whispered to Garrett.

"Yeah, you're telling me."

"Fifty thousand!" Saskia yelled, silencing us. "This is a family heirloom of mine, and I'd like to see it returned to its rightful place."

Ooh, nice move. A ripple of intrigue passed through the crowd.

Davin's brow furrowed, clearly unbothered. "Fifty-one."

"Fifty-two." I heard the reluctance in Saskia's voice and hoped Davin hadn't.

"Fifty-two and a half," he replied, keeping his eyes on her. The entire audience held their breaths. This might not have been the highest price that night, but it was the tensest bidding war. And we were running out of funds fast.

Saskia clenched her jaw. "Fifty-three!"

"We've got some money. Well, I've got *some* savings," Garrett said. "You can go up to fifty-five."

She nodded, as Davin called out: "Fifty-four."

"Fifty-five!" *Well, that buffer lasted all of two seconds.*

"Fifty-six!" He was shouting now.

"Fifty-seven!" Saskia snapped back.

"You've got to stop," I hissed. "We don't have enough. Quit now, or we'll be in trouble."

"Fifty-eight!" Davin boomed.

She shook her head. "We can't let him get it."

"There are other ways we can get our hands on it," I replied. "Let him win. I hate saying that, but we have to. We can't have you getting on his radar, and if you keep going, he's going to want to have words. Stop. You've got to stop."

"Fifty-nine!" she shouted regardless.

"No more, seriously!" I reached out and grabbed her arm. "He clearly wants it for something. If you win, he'll come after you."

She looked back at me in panic.

"Sixty!" Davin declared.

"What do I do?" All of her grown-up façade fell away, leaving a frightened girl who was in over her head. I softened my grip on her arm.

"Let him have it. We'll take it another way," I said. We already planned to take him down, so why not get the Ivan Trap at the same time? It made more sense than offering a bid we couldn't afford.

"Do I hear any more than sixty?" The auctioneer asked. Saskia dipped her chin to her chest, her knuckles white as she held on to the paddle. "We have sixty. Do I hear any more?"

Saskia said nothing.

"Sixty—going once. Going twice." The auctioneer looked at Saskia one last time. "And... SOLD, to Lord Black, for sixty thousand dollars."

Davin smirked and turned back around. It pissed me off that he'd managed to win this auction, but the game wasn't over yet. He might've known who Saskia was, given her family name, but he'd have no idea that she was with me and Garrett. Ryann had ducked behind the person in front so he wouldn't see her sitting near us. As far as he knew, we were Ernest Pompadour and Martin Maddelson. And that would work in our favor when we moved to end him. Hopefully, he wouldn't see it coming.

"Lord Black, you can collect your purchase at the end of the evening," the auctioneer said. A moment later, Davin nodded and stood up, then headed back into the house.

You won't be the only one coming to collect. I watched him go, an idea coming into my head. In an hour or two, he was going to have to go and fetch his purchase from wherever the items were stored. Ryann would know about that... at least, I hoped she would. If we were already there, waiting for him, then it could be the opportunity we needed—the Ivan Trap and Davin, both in the palm of our hand. My nerves were teetering on a knife's edge. He'd escaped us one too many times before. This time, if I could help it, he wouldn't get the chance.

TWENTY-ONE

Garrett

Pretending we were peeved about losing the auction to Davin, which wasn't actually untrue, Saskia, Finch, Ryann, and I moved to a more secluded part of the garden while the auction carried on.

"I've got an idea." Finch looked at us, vibrating with nervous excitement.

"Hiding in the pick-up room until he comes to collect?" It'd come to me the moment the auctioneer had mentioned the goods needed to be collected.

Finch smiled. "Great minds, my man. Great minds."

The last time I'd seen Davin Doncaster, he'd put a Necromancy-laced blade in my back... and I'd died. That wasn't something I could forgive, considering the ripple effects. If Davin hadn't killed me, Alton wouldn't have sacrificed himself to bring me back. And tonight, I was going to get some of that long-awaited revenge. Not just for me, but for everyone he'd hurt along the way.

Saskia tapped her foot impatiently. "The question is, where do we go and how do we get you both in there without being seen? If Davin senses something is wrong, he'll run a mile."

"It's weird seeing him here, acting like everything is fine," Ryann said quietly, like she wasn't quite with us. "I kept thinking someone would do something, or someone would call the security magicals, but they seem glad that he's here. I don't get it. They have to know who he is, right?"

"Oh, they know," Finch grumbled.

I nodded. "Yeah, they know, all right. He's their sort of person. Of course they won't turn him in to the authorities. That's why we're doing it for them—bringing some morality to the party."

"They look after their own." Saskia looked confused. Perhaps this party and these people had lost some of their shine for her, too. She'd seen a glimpse behind the pretty front, and I got the feeling she didn't quite like what she'd seen.

Finch turned to Ryann. "We need your help if we're going to get that Trap."

"My help?" She raised a surprised eyebrow.

He moved closer to her. For a second, I thought he was going to hold her hand, but he didn't. "I'll tell you more when I can, but for now you have to trust us. This is serious. If we don't leave here with the Ivan Trap, then I'm in trouble. You remember what I said to you before?"

She nodded slowly. *What did he say to you before?*

"Everyone under that umbrella might be in trouble, too." He held her gaze, and she seemed to understand, even if I didn't. "I need you to tell me where the Trap is being kept. That's where we'll hide and wait for Davin. Where do they put the auction items after they've been sold?"

She frowned. "Is anyone going to be hurt if I tell you?"

"No," he replied. "The only person you'll be harming is Davin, and he deserves it. You know that better than anyone. Think about what he did to your family. Think about what he did to you. You've got every right to help us take what he bought, after all of that, and you've got every right to have some payback of your own."

A steeliness came into Ryann's eyes. "It's in the study room on the first floor, at the farthest end of the hallway. Last door on the right. Miranda and Daggerston like to keep the auction items close and secured until they're handed over to the bidders."

"Will Davin have paid by now?" Finch pressed.

Ryann paused. "I imagine that's why he walked off. All transactions have to be made with Daggerston's private accountant. He's in one of the back rooms, but there'll be too much security for you to try and nab him there."

"Then we stick with the pick-up room," I said.

"That's probably your best bet." Ryann nodded, though she looked nervous. "And you should take this, or you won't be able to get in. Just try to give it back to me before you go, okay? Miranda will probably expect it back." She dug into a small pouch that hung from the waistband of her dress and took out a keycard. She handed it to Finch, who brushed his fingertips against Ryann's as he took it.

"Thank you." Finch quickly kissed her on the cheek. She blinked in surprise, and he looked away as if it were nothing at all. He didn't see the small smile that turned up the corners of her lips, but I did.

Ah, Finch... why did it have to be her? He knew it couldn't go anywhere, but he couldn't help himself. The poor guy was smitten, and her smile made it all the more confusing. I was glad he hadn't seen it; otherwise, this mission to snatch the Ivan Trap and get Davin might not be the only thing that ended badly tonight. Assuming that Ryann was as happy with her boyfriend as she seemed to be, Finch would only be rejected and heartbroken if he had a hint of encouragement. Not that I was worried about stealing the Trap—after swiping the Merlin Grimoire from the New York Coven, security protocols didn't concern me much these days. Confidence was key.

"Here, take these, too." I delved into my pocket and took out three earpieces. I handed one to Ryann and one to Saskia and put the last in my ear.

"Why don't I get one?" Finch asked.

"You and I have to stick together, remember? You're running this show." I gestured to my Pompadour masquerade. "It makes more sense to give the other two to Saskia and Ryann."

"This is all very cloak and dagger." Saskia smiled. "I like it. But what's the actual plan?"

Finch paused for a moment before answering. "You'll go up the stairs first. Do something teenage—pretend to take selfies or Snap-speak, or whatever it is you kids do."

Saskia rolled her eyes.

"Whatever it is, make a good show of doing it. Once you see the coast is clear, let Garrett know it's safe to move," Finch continued. "Ryann, you stay close to Miranda and Daggerston for the rest of the night. Let us know if they act strangely, and keep them away from the pick-up room until we've dealt with Davin."

Ryann gave him a hard look. "That sounds an awful lot like you're trying to keep me out of the way."

"It'll just be… safer. Okay?" He lowered his gaze.

Fortunately, she didn't make a fuss. "Okay. I'll keep an eye on them and run interference. It'll also give me a chance to speak to Miranda, to find out what she really thinks of Davin. It has to be Daggerston's influence. It has to be."

"Thank you." Finch looked back up, and Ryann blinked as if she thought he might try to kiss her cheek again. I saw the realization hit him. A millisecond of embarrassment in his eyes, and then it was gone.

"Do you want me to go now?" Saskia interjected. It served as a distraction for any awkwardness between Finch and Ryann.

"Yeah, go now," Finch urged.

Swiping a glass of fizzy peach juice from a passing tray, she sauntered up to the house with Ryann. Finch and I turned to each other as if we were deep in conversation. Us watching the two women would've drawn too much attention. Instead, I just listened to Saskia chattering away through the earpiece and relayed information to Finch to make it look like we were talking.

"She's in the entrance hall," I told him. "Moving toward the stairs. Yep, she's going up the stairs now… okay, she's at the top of the stairs, and she's talking about summer vacation. No idea what that's supposed to mean. Still talking about vacation. Okay, now she's talking about a guy called Fred who's in love with a girl named Sally, but Sally has a boyfriend and he doesn't know how to tell her how he feels."

Finch stared at me. "She's not."

I grimaced. "She is."

"I swear, if she—"

"She says the coast is clear." I cut him off before he could get worked up. He needed a clear head, and Saskia was just messing with him. Besides, if Ryann *hadn't* picked up on all the signs up to now, she wasn't going to think anything of this. At least, I hoped not.

"You've got this." Saskia's voice came through again. "Ryann's heading off to rejoin Miranda and Daggerston, but I'll make sure no one comes up here."

"How will you do that?" I asked.

"There are bathrooms on the ground floor for guests to use. I'll just say one of you clogged the one up here, so it's better if they just keep their distance until the stench goes away." She gave a smug chuckle while I relayed the info to Finch.

He grimaced. "And she wonders why people don't like her?"

"Come on, we should get going. That imaginary stench is only going to last for so long." I started to walk toward the house, with Finch in tow. Making our way back through the themed rooms and hallways, we reached the grand foyer. It was nearly empty now, with most people outside still invested in the auction. But there were enough stragglers to make me cautious.

"Act drunk," I whispered to Finch.

"Huh?"

"Act like you're drunk." I dragged his arm over my shoulder, and he got the picture.

Jumping into character, he lolled against me, covering his mouth with his hand as if he might be sick. I didn't know if this was just his acting skill or part of his Mimicry, but it was insanely believable. I had to remind myself not to worry about him vomiting on me as I dragged him up the stairs, his feet snagging on every step. He weighed a ton.

At the top of the stairs, we passed Saskia, who was chatting loudly into her phone about how cool the party was and how dreamy some of the guys were. She was the epitome of an obnoxious teen, no acting skills required. She didn't even look at us as we staggered by, even though Finch was behaving like he'd downed a bottle of tequila by himself.

"I need the bathroom," Finch groaned. "I'm going... to be... sick." He gave a realistic retch as I propped him up, readjusting my grip.

"Just hang on." I peered down the hallway Ryann told us about, before I hauled Finch toward the last door on the right. Coming to a halt in front of it, Finch swiped the keycard in front of the lock. The entry panel beeped and flashed green, and I pushed the door open before it could lock again. We stepped into the room, where we were surrounded by items from the auction. The frosted glass box with the Ivan Trap sat on the desk. If it wasn't for Davin, we could've taken it and run. But we'd made our choice.

"Where do we hide?" Finch asked, shaking off the drunk act.

"Wherever we can." I looked around and spotted a hefty vault. There was a small gap between it and the wall, and it would give us cover from anyone coming through the door. I made my way over and crouched behind it, testing how much room I'd have. It was a perfect fit. But not for two. I liked Finch, but that might've been asking too much of our friendship.

"I'll go over here, then." Finch strode toward a coat closet behind the study door. He opened it and disappeared inside.

"Should we keep our disguises on?" I hissed.

"What?" Finch's muffled voice replied, as he peered out of the closet.

"For facing Davin, should we keep our disguises on, or let him know it's us?"

He paused. "Keep them on. That way, if anyone suspects us in the aftermath, they'll think it was Pompadour and Maddelson, not Merlin and Kyteler."

"Good thinking." I ducked back behind the vault while Finch hid himself in the closet again.

"Garrett?" Finch reappeared.

"Yes?"

"I've been wondering about Davin and his resurrections. I know we think it was Katherine doing the trick, but what if she already gave him, like, nine lives and he's only on his eighth?"

"What are you suggesting?"

He pulled a face. "I'm guessing he'll make it too difficult for us to escort him to Purgatory, so we should probably just go straight for his head—while we have the chance. If we mess around trying to play gentle and contain him, it'll give him the opportunity to hurt one of us, or escape. It's grim, but cutting his head off might be the only way to avoid him bobbing back up again, if she did grant him a full deck of lives in one go."

"Behead him?" I wanted Davin dead, possibly more than anyone, but cutting someone's head off wasn't exactly a walk in the park.

He nodded. "Zombie style."

I sighed. "Okay then, we behead him. Do you think Telekinesis will do it?"

"If I pull hard enough."

Ugh. "If not, there'll be something around here we can use." I crept out from behind my vault and took another look around. It didn't take long until I found what I was after. A long, shining dagger hung on one of the walls, with a twisting golden handle—not an auction item, but part of Daggerston's personal collection.

"What is it?" Finch leaned out of the closet.

"A dagger," I replied.

Finch shook his head. "Of course Daggerston would have a dagger. Be rude not to, with a name like that."

"Do you think it'll do the job?" I swiped it through the air, trying not to imagine it slicing through flesh and bone and sinew. The blade looked dangerously sharp, glinting in the low light of the study.

"I think we're going to find out. I mean, even if you have to stab him first, you can always saw through his neck afterward."

"When did this go from *us* beheading Davin, to *me* sawing through Davin's neck?" I had to remind myself of all the terrible things he'd done, to steel my resolve. Stabbing seemed easy in comparison, though I imagined both would haunt me. He was an awful human being, sure, but killing was killing.

"I'll be there to help. This is just in case popping his head off like a daisy doesn't work," Finch assured me. "Now, take that dagger and get back into your hiding spot. We don't want to lose the element of surprise."

"Let's just hope a cramp doesn't get me first," I muttered. Holding the dagger, I returned to my position. A clock ticked loudly, sounding out the trawling seconds until Davin appeared.

This was going to be a long night.

TWENTY-TWO

Finch

Time became an abstract concept, cooped up in the coat closet. Every sound made my nerves jolt. But it was never Davin. Nobody had come in since we'd left the garden, but Ryann and Saskia kept us informed about the doings of the outside world. No sign of Davin, and no sign of Daggerston coming to check on things. The party was in full swing, and we were like the cloakroom attendants, just waiting for the revelers to collect their designer gear. Well, one reveler. The rest needed to stay the hell away, for the time being.

"He's coming!" Garrett whispered. "Just had news from Saskia."

I took a breath and listened. A moment later, the door opened. Peeking through the slight gap in the closet doors, I saw Davin come in and make a beeline for the Ivan Trap. He stood there, smoothing his hands over the glass box, caressing it like an old lover. I still didn't know why he wanted it, but he wasn't getting his prize. Instead, he was going to get more than he bargained for.

Before I could move, Garrett exploded from behind the vault and unleashed a quiet hell, evidently aware that too much noise would bring unwanted attention. Air tore out of his hands and hit Davin square in the chest. The British ass-wipe went flying, arching over the desk and smacking into the back wall. He even managed to do that elegantly, leaping right back up like a prima ballerina.

"What the—what is the meaning of this?" he spluttered, raising his hands to retaliate. He'd focused in on Garrett, gussied up as Pompadour, giving me my moment to strike.

I darted in and took Davin by surprise, using everything in my arsenal that wouldn't cause a ruckus. Drawing Water from a nearby potted plant, I sprayed it into his eyes to blind him. As he swiped at his face, I launched a lasso of Telekinesis at his legs and yanked it. He went down again and hit the ground with a thud. I thought about adding Fire, but there were too many rare artifacts in the room, and I didn't want to toast them. I had respect for these objects, just not for the people buying them.

Purple light swept over Davin's body, evaporating the lasso. I felt the tug as it was severed. He was up again in no time, like a really irritating Weeble that just wouldn't stay down. I hurled a second lasso at his waist, but his hands shot out. Somehow, he managed to catch the shimmering tendrils with wisps of his violet energy. Before I knew what was happening, he'd pulled hard on the strands of Telekinesis and sent me sprawling forward.

I was shocked. He'd used my magic against me, and I had no idea how. All I knew was I had a mouthful of carpet.

"Who are you?" Davin spat. "You'd best start talking."

"Call us a concerned third party." Maddelson's voice came out of my mouth, reminding me to keep Finch pushed down, out of sight. One whiff of who I really was and Davin would try and finish the job that Mother Dearest couldn't. One last homage.

I lashed out with another lasso of Telekinesis, managing to wrap it around his waist so I could pull him toward Garrett.

Understanding what I was doing, Garrett took out the blade he'd borrowed and swiped it at Davin. The Necromancer craned away, the dagger just missing anything vital, as a thin stream of blood trickled down his throat.

More purple sparks shot down the length of my Telekinesis. I snapped my hands away from the violet energy hurtling right at me, my fingertips stinging as a sudden heat scorched them. I had no idea what the purple magic would've done if it managed to reach me, and I didn't want to know. There was no time for that. Garrett hurled a blast of Air at Davin, but he raised a shining force-field, and the Air bounced right off. *Man, he's quick.* I'd forgotten how skilled he was, what with all the hatred and loathing.

"Who are you, and what are you doing here?" Davin glowered at us from behind his forcefield.

"Maddelson and Pompadour, at your service." I slammed a barrage of Air into him, but it did nothing. He was all snug behind his shield of power.

"That's just not true, though, is it?" Davin smirked.

Garrett leapt at the forcefield with his dagger raised, the edge of the blade poking through the sparking fabric of his magic. A white light shimmered across the edge of the dagger. *So, not just an ordinary knife, then?* Davin stared at the blade in horror as it cut right through the shield, leaving him exposed.

"I don't know what you mean." I lunged back in with a lasso, grabbing him around the knees and yanking him down. This time, he was slower on the bounce-back, giving Garrett a moment to slam a blast of Air right into his face. He groaned loudly. As Garrett stood over him, Davin clasped his hands together, forming a purple dagger between his palms. Garrett's eyes widened as Davin threw the knife at him. I hurled my Telekinesis at it, grabbing the handle when it was about a split second from plunging into Garrett's face. I flung it outward, where it hit the far wall and disappeared in a burst of purple sparks.

The distraction gave Davin an opportunity to crawl, like a nasty little spider, under the desk and out the other side. It wasn't much, but it gave him cover. And he seemed to guess we wouldn't risk hitting the Ivan Trap. Anger pulsed through me, riding a wave of adrenaline.

"I don't know about you, Mr. Pompadour, but I know that you, Mr. Maddelson, are dead. Utterly dead," Davin said.

"I don't feel very dead." I hit him with a round of Water, dragging it out of every available plant pot and spraying it in his eyes.

He ducked, firing two more purple daggers. They skimmed past my shoulders as I twisted out of their way.

"I spoke to Maddelson's ghost some years back, through a Kolduny. He is naught but bones at the bottom of the ocean." He sent out two more daggers—one at me, one at Garrett. Neither hit their mark, but they kept us on our toes. "Now, I know my way around a Necromancy trick or two, and it is impossible to piece raw bones back together in so seamless a fashion. Which begs the question, who *are* you?"

I'd forgotten how much you love the sound of your own voice. Another thing he and my mother had shared. I bet they'd had soliloquizing competitions, just to get them in the mood. *Ugh.*

"Maybe you got the wrong guy." Garrett picked up the golden longbow that'd been on auction before the Ivan Trap. It came with a quiver of golden arrows. Lodging one into the string, he pulled it back and fired at Davin's head. The arrow moved like a homing missile, twisting right at him. Realizing he was in trouble, Davin started to run. With him distracted, I tried to hit him with my Elementals, but he was too quick.

He reached the closet and dove into it, slamming the door behind him. The arrow thwacked into the wood, its target escaped.

Garrett and I sprinted for the closet as the doors flew open and Davin came back out, guns blazing. He had more daggers ready, and he flung them this way and that, making Garrett and me feint and crouch and wrench our bodies away.

"What are you doing here?" I demanded. No more Mr. Nice Finch. "Why aren't you under a rock, where you ought to be?" He could ask questions, but so could I. Though, it was hard when there were magic knives coming for your face.

He smiled as he dodged our joint Air efforts. "As you've probably guessed, I have been keeping something of a low profile since the Katherine debacle."

"Yeah, tell us something we don't know!" Garrett barked, as he tried to tackle Davin. But Davin was ready for him, using his Telekinesis to send Garrett flying. Garrett bounded up in seconds, but it took me a moment to re-energize his disguise. A few flecks of his real face were showing through, but not enough to give the game away.

"It still breaks my heart, how such majesty was crushed so cruelly. Nevertheless, I still had a few friends and called in favors," Davin replied. "Most of them were secret admirers of my beloved who moved through these Dark Tourist circles—for obvious reasons. Katherine was the living embodiment of Dark History."

"And that'd make you the dumb sidekick?" I glowered at him, as I returned to the action. His Telekinesis and mine met in the center of the room, sending a shower of sparks downward, singeing the carpet. I pushed harder, and so did he. Our Telekinesis suggested we were evenly matched, but he wasn't even breaking a sweat and I was panting hard.

"Far from it. They revere me as much as they revered her," he replied. "Only those with true power get to write the history books."

"You know, I'm stunned no one's managed to find you, in all

this time, when all you do is talk on and on and on." I delved deeper into my well of Chaos, still holding off his attack. Time to stretch these newfound abilities further.

"What can I say, I enjoy a captive audience." He snickered to himself.

"Presumptuous to believe we're the captives," I shot back. "What do you want the Ivan Trap for? Give us a good answer and I might not snap your head off and bury it where you and your sneaky Necromantics won't ever find it."

He frowned. "So, the Vasilis girl was bidding on your behalf, was she? I'm not sure that makes sense to me, considering your supposed wealth. But then, I don't believe you are who you say you are. I will figure it out, though. Mark my words."

"That's also none of your beeswax." I let more Chaos bristle into my palms. This sucker wasn't going to take me by surprise. Beside me, Garrett had the same idea and charged his Chaos as well. "What do you want with it?"

"Now, that is none of *your* beeswax. I'm certainly not going to let you have it, if that's what you think." He smirked and pulled away his Telekinesis. I sprawled backward from the shock of the release, but Garrett dragged me back up a moment later.

"Funny, we had the same thought." Garrett lashed out with more Air, knocking Davin back into the desk.

His head snapped up, clearly infuriated. "Do you have any idea how difficult these things are to come by? And so inordinately expensive. I bid far more than I wanted to, and that's all your doing."

"You're going to lose more than money by the time we're done with you." I hit him with a supercharged round of Fire, focusing intently on the flames so they wouldn't touch anything other than Davin. Mental gymnastics at its finest. I coaxed the Fire into a ring and had it surround Davin, but he just laughed.

"Did you think it would be easy? A few paltry displays of power and I'd just give in?"

"It's not over yet." Garrett leapt past me, firing off a barricade of Air. Once again, Davin had already pre-empted it, somehow. I watched as he sent up a blockade of his own, and the Air bounced harmlessly off his forcefield. A moment later, the forcefield disappeared, and I managed to jump to my feet.

Going into desperation mode, Garrett dropped the Chaos altogether and hurtled across the room. He lunged at Davin with old-school brute force, the dagger in his hand. The Necromancer lifted his hands sharply and gripped Garrett in a blinding vise of purple light. The next thing I knew, Garrett was sailing right over me. I heard him hit the floor.

"Tut, tut. I thought you might listen to my word of warning." Davin glared at me. "You're not going to beat me, so why don't we sit down and talk like gentlemen? If there is something you want, perhaps we can come to an arrangement. I am a reasonable man. But you should know the Ivan Trap isn't for sale."

Garrett groaned as he got back up. "Is this you trying to buy time, Davin?"

Davin grinned. "You look like the ones who need a pause."

A cool draft touched the back of my neck. I whipped around to see Ryann sprint through the slightly open door. I froze, unable to move or think. But she seemed to have a plan of action. Delving into the waistband that attached her train to the rest of her outfit, she pulled out a small pistol-looking weapon and raised it. She fired, giving a startled Davin zero time to react.

A dart shot out the end and hit him in the throat. He gasped, scrabbling at his neck, trying to get the foreign object out of him. But whatever that dart had on it, or in it, it worked fast. Davin stopped struggling, and his eyes rolled back into his head. He collapsed in a satisfying heap on the floor.

Not that I could feel much satisfaction. Every part of me was shaking.

"Are you insane?" I stared at Ryann.

She smiled. "Earpieces, remember? I heard everything, and I wanted to make sure you didn't get hurt. I know what kind of guy Davin is. I wasn't going to let him take the Ivan Trap and kill the pair of you while he was at it." She looked over Garrett and me. We were both panting hard. "Clearly, I have good timing."

"You mind telling us what that is?" Garrett nodded to the gun in her hand.

"Nifty little peashooter," I muttered, still baffled and a little miffed that she'd had to save our asses.

Ryann put the dart gun back in her waistband. "It was a gift from Harley. She had Krieger make it for me after finding a blueprint for it on one of her cultist hunting missions. I carry it with me most of the time. The poison doesn't kill, but it knocks out any kind of magical. Even Purge beasts, though they don't stay down for very long—that's more of a stun thing."

"How long will he stay down?" I glanced at Davin.

"Long enough," she replied.

"Think again." Davin jumped up and hammered us all with a violent blast of Telekinesis. Garrett and Ryann went flying into the walls, while I hit the desk with a thud. I put my arms around the Ivan Trap and gripped it for dear life, in case he tried to come and wrestle it from me. But he seemed to have escape on his mind, realizing this was more hassle than it was worth. Before any of us could do anything, he sprinted for the window and cleared it in one leap.

"We need to get after him!" I yelled, as Garrett and Ryann dragged themselves to their feet. I grabbed the box and tucked it under my arm, transforming it into part of my disguise. Immediately, sirens blared all around us, some kind of alarm triggering.

Ah... CRAP! This wasn't good. But if we let Davin get away, then we'd never have a shot like this again. And one thing was certain now: we definitely couldn't let him live. Purgatory had been tossed about as an idea, but that had swiftly been kicked off the table. Davin had to die. Now.

I tore toward the window and leapt through, cushioning my fall with a pillow of Air. *You might have a head start, but it won't help you now.* We had the Ivan Trap, and now it was time to tie off those pesky loose ends. And rid this world of Davin Doncaster, once and for all.

TWENTY-THREE

Finch

Garrett leapt from the window behind me, following me down to the ground floor and cushioning his fall with another pillow of Air. I had Davin in my sights, but that didn't mean I was forgetting about my team.

I glanced at Garrett. "Tell Saskia to get Ryann out of there. Put on another show—drunk teenager, maybe. Daggerston's goons are going to be on those sirens in about ten seconds flat." I tore the keycard out of my pocket and dumped it in a nearby window box, outside the room that had been decorated French-Revolution style. Guillotine and all. "And tell Ryann I'm leaving the keycard in the flowerbox outside Versailles!"

He relayed the information to Saskia and Ryann as we darted into the extensive gardens, following Davin's trajectory. Rose gardens, winter gardens, Japanese-style water gardens—we raced through them all, gravel crunching underfoot. I tried to leap across a pool to gain some ground but misjudged the distance. I plunged into the water and gasped at the sudden cold. Immediately, I was up and out, gripping the Ivan Trap tighter under my arm as I flipped algae and lotus petals off myself. I had to soldier on, no matter what.

Garrett didn't even pause, and for good reason. Behind us, Daggerston's private security guards were surrounding the house in response to the blaring sirens. They would be coming into the gardens, too, once they realized something had gone awry in Daggerston's study. A pretty big something. Presumably, one of Daggerston's folks was supposed to take the charms off the Ivan Trap's box before it got taken away, and since those alarms weren't shutting up, they'd know something was going on.

That massively narrowed our chances of getting out unscathed. But we had to get Davin before they found us, or we'd lose our opportunity.

His shadow darted ahead of us. It felt way better to be doing the chasing, instead of being chased. Poltergeist flashbacks bombarded me as I ran through the gloom. Davin had taken to extinguishing the torches as he escaped.

Everywhere I turned, a tree branch or a statue made me jump into a defensive stance, expecting a surprise attack from Davin— only for me to break back into a sprint when I realized it wasn't him. He was going to run out of garden soon, which meant we just had to keep running until then. We seemed to be closing in, as the sounds of his footfalls were getting louder. Seemed to be, that is, until we came to the towering heights of a hedge maze.

Of course they have a hedge maze. Ahead of us, Davin sprinted inside. We barreled in after him.

I kept catching sight of his heels as he rounded corner after corner, apparently knowing where he was going. My lungs were on fire and my thighs were burning. It wasn't easy, doing all this *and* keeping up my disguise and Garrett's.

My eyes struggled to focus on the twisting path ahead. I almost careened right into a hedge or two, with Davin turning at the last second. Pretty quickly, I realized I'd been wrong about the running thing. It was useless to keep chasing him like this. He was faster than us, and my stamina was waning.

I lifted my palms and sent out a wave of Earth. It exploded into the hedge, and the intertwining branches shrank into saplings. I jumped through the shortcut and saw Davin up ahead. He turned again, and I opened up another gap in the hedge. I was putting landscapers out of business with all this last-minute topiary manipulation.

Garrett was close behind me, running at full pelt. With every pathway I opened, we got closer to Davin. He was struggling to stay ahead of my Earth game.

Gathering a cushion of Air beneath me, I used it to spring unnaturally high. It gave me a glimpse of the whole maze. Davin had just entered one long line of path, which led to the farthest hedge wall. When I swiped the Air cushion away, I landed awkwardly. I ignored the throb in my ankle and sprinted for a line of hedgerow to my right.

"This way!" I called to Garrett, realizing I could circle back on Davin.

I cut through the hedges until I reached the outside world, only to realize we were right back where we'd started, at the sprawling lawn, where the party had come to a screeching halt. *Eh?* Still, the private security guards were busy at the house, and the ones who weren't there were probably running loops through the garden, trying to find us. Which meant we still had a shot.

Listening for footsteps, I seized my moment. I bombarded the hedge with Earth, tearing open a gap and leaping through it. Davin was running too fast in my direction to stop. To my surprise, he didn't even try. Instead, he brought up his palms and hit us with a blast of Telekinesis that sent us stumbling backward. He raced past us, heading for the house.

"Time for a quick change," I gasped. Touching my palm to my chest and my other palm to Garrett's shoulder, I surged a fresh bout of Mimicry into the two of us. Miranda's face stared back at me a second later, and her shocked expression told me all I needed to know about mine. For the next however many minutes, I would be Gerald Daggerston.

"He's getting away!" Garrett hissed in Miranda's guise.

"Then grab your stilettos and get running, G!" I put my money where my mouth was and hurtled after Davin, with Garrett in hot pursuit. Our target had slowed slightly, clearly thinking he was safe now that he was among a crowd. *Wrong move, dingus.* He paused on the lawn and scoured the doors that led into the house, choosing Versailles.

As we burst through the French doors, which had gotten even Frencher, considering our surroundings, Davin was making his way up onto the guillotine platform. A crowd gathered around him, obviously thinking this was part of a performance or something. But we knew better. He wanted to call us out. *Well, that's not going to happen.* Davin had barely opened his mouth to speak, when Garrett raced past me and lunged at him, knocking him to the ground. Through some divine twist of fate, his head and neck hit the lower half of the stocks. I leapt to my friend's aid and slammed the top half down, locking Davin in place.

"Is this thing real?" Garrett whispered. Davin groaned, disoriented by the blow.

"It looked pretty real with the watermelons," I hissed back.

"Here goes nothing." Garrett yanked on the string that held the huge, glinting blade in place. It plummeted down in front of the crowd's eager eyes, slicing straight through Davin's neck.

For a moment, his head stayed exactly where it was supposed to be. And then… it toppled into the basket just in front.

Screams and applause mingled in the air as blood began to

spurt. A few people in the crowd looked confused, as if they weren't quite sure what they were seeing. I had to admit, it wasn't easy to look at. But we'd certainly gone zombie-style on his ass. There was no way Davin could claw himself back into the land of the living after this. His brain wasn't attached to anything anymore, so it wasn't as though he could get his hands to just stick his head back on.

I cleared my throat. "This is just one of the spectacles we have arranged for you this evening!" Daggerston's voice came out, crystal clear. That hideous, booming baritone. "Please, don't be alarmed. It's all part of the show. We have to go and prepare the next, so do look out for it."

Garrett looked at me. "Are we getting out of here?"

"Yep, and now, before they realize that blood is the real deal." I gave a bow as more applause reverberated around the room.

With it echoing in my head, I took Garrett's hand in a show of sweet, sweet love and dragged him out of Versailles and back into the gardens. Our timing couldn't have been more perfect. The real Daggerston and Miranda were just passing through the main entrance, no doubt heading toward the sound of sirens. By the time they realized what we'd done, we'd be long gone, and they'd have no idea who'd done it. At least, that was the hope I was pinning everything on.

"Tell Saskia and Ryann to meet us in the maze, through the big gaping hole," I said, as we kept moving toward the hedge maze.

Garrett did as I'd asked. His brow furrowed. "Ryann is staying, but Saskia's on her way."

"What? Why is Ryann staying?" Now wasn't the time for heroics.

"She says it'll look too suspicious if she vanishes, and she needs to make sure we've got rock-solid alibis. She's sorting it out for us," he replied.

"What does that mean?!" I snapped.

He shrugged. "I guess it means she's sorting it out for us."

"This is ridiculous! She's going to put herself in danger."

Garrett smirked.

"What's so funny?"

"She says you should remember she was pre-law. She's used to talking her way out of tricky situations."

"Yeah, but not ones that involve someone being decapitated!"

"Put it this way—we need to make sure we don't take the rap for this, and Ryann is Miranda's assistant. She's smarter than most people I know. If she thinks she can handle it, then I trust her."

I grimaced. "Fine, but if anything happens to her, I'm blaming you."

"Do you want to let go of my hand now?"

"No. I need it to stop me from running back to the house and getting Ryann out." I hated leaving her behind, to face whatever music we'd created. There was one comforting point, though. Ryann was a human. And people like this looked down on humans. Hopefully, they wouldn't think her capable of being part of this.

He shrugged. "Do what you have to do."

Garrett and I slipped through the gap that I'd made and found the nearest shadowy spot to wait for Saskia. Everyone had gathered by the house, meaning we were entirely on our own.

Saskia came around the corner a few minutes later, scaring us out of our skins. She had some stealth to her, that was for sure.

"What happened?" She jumped right in. "I heard screams, then applause, then more applause. Weren't you running off to kill that guy?"

I nodded. "We did. We guillotined him."

"You *what?*" Saskia's eyes bulged.

"We can explain later. Right now, we need to vamoose," I urged.

"Wait." Garrett held up his hands. "Saskia, how far does your Kolduny power reach?"

She frowned. "Pretty far. Why?"

"Can you check and see if Davin's spirit is around?" Garrett asked. "See if he's floating somewhere."

She sighed and lifted her hands. Her eyes turned bright white, and her whole body glowed as she put out her spiritual feelers. Less than a second later, she snapped out of it, heaving in breaths like she'd just seen a ghost. Which, I guessed, she had.

"Well?" Garrett urged.

"He's near the house. He's pissed." She shuddered visibly.

"If we cut his head off, can he still come back?" I figured it was best to ask the expert.

"Near impossible, from what I know. He'd need very powerful resurrection magic, which he wouldn't be able to perform on himself—so, his Necromancy wouldn't work," she replied.

I smiled. "Then it looks like there's no more Davin Doncaster. Man, does that feel good to say." If his spirit had loosened itself from his body, it stood to reason that he wasn't coming back. "Not so easy to come crawling back when you don't have your head and body attached, huh? Or Mama Dearest to put you back together again, Humpty Dumpty. I hope she's saved you a toasty spot in Hell."

It'd been a pretty safe assumption that Madre had been the one doing the resurrecting—or at least giving him the juice he needed to do it. Sweet, really, in a sick, twisted way. My mother's signature style.

Garrett jumped to his feet. "We'd better get out of here." He glanced at me. "You've still got the Ivan Trap?"

I brandished it. "Safe and sound."

"Then let's move." He drew a chalk door on the ground and whispered the *Aperi Si Ostium* spell. We'd leave Daggerston and his

security to try and figure out what had happened here. It'd definitely leave them scratching their heads. The Ivan Trap was gone,
and the buyer had his head in a basket.

Sorry, Daggers. Claim it on your hefty insurance policy.

We fell through the air and landed with a thump on the floor of
Garrett's shoebox office, with no time for me to fashion an Air
cushion. One of the perils of opening chalk doors on the ground.

I lay there for a minute, staring up at the ceiling. The door had
closed by itself, thanks to the forces of gravity. Now that adrenaline had left the proverbial building, I felt every ache and sting
from our encounter with Davin. I finally let our disguises fall.

"Ow," I wheezed.

"Seconded," Garrett replied.

"Honestly, look at the state of you both." Saskia sat up. "You'd
think you'd just gone into battle. You had a little scrap and a bit of a
sprint, that's all. Stop complaining."

"Hey, you don't know what Davin can do—he's a tough, snaky
toadstool. Well, he *was*." I grinned. "You'd be whining if you'd been
there. You just need a cough drop for all the chatting you were
pretending to do."

"I was pretty convincing, wasn't I?" Saskia got up and opened
her clutch. She took out a small first-aid kit, producing a little
brown glass pot. Kneeling beside Garrett first, she scooped out
some milky gel and smeared it on his visible cuts and bruises.

"This stuff smells great. What is it?" Garrett murmured. He
stayed flat on the floor, his eyes closed, breathing deeply.

"You don't want to know." She chuckled. "If you did, you might
change your mind about the smell."

He opened one eye. "Now I have to know."

"It comes from the mucus membrane of the *Magicis cochlea*." She scooped out some more gel and started smearing it across my injuries before I could reel back.

"The who-said-what-now?" I grimaced as the cold substance touched my skin. Garrett was right—it did smell good, but I wanted to know what was going on my face. That was a rule I liked to live by.

"Magical snail. Stop squirming." She held my head as she dabbed the gel on my last few bruises.

"Snail snot?" Garrett scrunched his nose.

"It'll help you heal quicker," she replied. "People will ask fewer questions if you're not covered in scrapes. Tatyana and Harley-type people."

"Good thinking." I finally sat up, relieved to be home.

"How did you end up guillotining Davin, of all things?" Saskia sat back.

Garrett shrugged. "He ended up with his neck in the right place, at the right time."

"You could say we got him in the neck of time." I grinned back at my pal.

"Hello?" Saskia interjected. "You *guillotined* a guy, and the two of you are cracking jokes. What's wrong with you?"

"You get a macabre sense of humor when you've been through the things we've been through. And don't go getting all soft—Davin doesn't deserve your sympathy. You can trust us on that. He got what was coming to him." I set the Ivan Trap on the ground between my bent legs. I put my palms flat on the box's cold surface and started unlocking the charms engraved across it. Unlocking charms and hexes had been a specialty of mine ever since my cult days. And these were surprisingly simple, for something so rare and potentially dangerous. Focusing hard, I continued unraveling the charms so we could remove the Ivan Trap. As the last one unfurled, I opened the glass lid and took out the trap, putting it on the floor in case it tried to attack me.

I turned to Saskia. "What do we do with this thing, maestro?"

Saskia shrugged. "That depends on where we're headed next."

"Morro Castle, so we can confront Ponce de León's poltergeist," I replied.

"Doesn't 'ponce' mean something rude?" She cocked her head at me. "I know English isn't my first language, but I'm sure I've heard that somewhere."

"If you were sauntering around the British Isles, then yeah. But in this case, no—it means something dangerous. Very dangerous." I tapped my chest, where the scar was still healing. "Like, ripped apart by shadow claws dangerous."

"Don't worry, I won't let him hurt you." Saskia winked. "Although, I wouldn't mind nursing you back to health."

"Head in the game, Vasilis," Garrett muttered.

"I'm guessing you know how to get the poltergeist into this thing?" I smoothed my fingertip across the bronzed box and felt energy thrum back.

She nodded. "In theory, yes."

"What happens once he's inside?" Garrett peered at the spiked contraption. It was a perfect bronze cube, about the size of a jack-in-the-box. I hoped there wouldn't be any ghosties jumping out to the tune of "Pop Goes the Weasel."

I looked closely at the box. Sigils were etched into the metal sides, while cogs covered the top panel. I guessed that was the mechanism that opened it. The four spikes at the corners were each topped with a ruby, and they looked like four miniature Eyes of Sauron.

The Trap felt powerful. Really powerful. Just putting my hand on it gave me a headache, but I didn't know if that had something to do with Ponce de León's attack on me. Perhaps that made me susceptible to this thing's energy.

"He'll have to obey," Saskia said. "Usually, these Traps are only used to get a poltergeist to perform some action—terrifying villagers and that sort of thing. But if I use my abilities on him, once he's in the box, I should be able to compel him to speak and give any answers you want."

"You make it sound so easy," I said dryly. This was going to be anything but. Still, I was confident we could pull it off with a Kolduny's help. It was definitely better than going in unprepared and clueless, like I'd done the last time. *Cheers for that, Erebus.*

As I stared at the Ivan Trap and thought over our next move, my gremlins started pelting my brain with thoughts of Ryann. She was still at the Dark Tourist party, dealing with the fallout of our bloody little performance. As we'd given the guests no indication that she actually knew us, I hoped that would be enough to get her out of any suspicion that might come her way. Miranda would hopefully keep her assistant out of the line of fire. But I had to be sure.

Taking out my phone, I sent her a quick text: *All good?*

A few moments later, my phone pinged with a reply: *Yep, all good. A lot going on. They figured out which keycard was used to get into the room, but I told them I no longer have it and someone must have pick-pocketed it from me. They don't seem to suspect me. Just helping D and M deal with the mess then I'll head back. Might be a while. Did you get out? I can't find you, so I'm guessing yes.*

I smiled and typed back: *Escape successful. Hope they don't keep you there too long.*

Now that I knew she was okay, a different kind of thought infiltrated my head. I kept thinking about Ryann's fingertips on my neck, wiping away the stray blood. And how close her face had been to mine. I could still smell her perfume and remember the smoothness of her cheek as I'd kissed it. The way she'd looked at me and half-smiled. Was I just imagining that I'd seen something else in her eyes—something more than caring for a friend?

Please stop... please, just be quiet, I begged my brain. I couldn't deal with this now. The Fountain of Youth was waiting for us, and there was no point getting all worked up about Ryann if I wasn't sure I was going to survive what came next.

"Can you believe he's dead?" Garrett broke me out of my head.

I chuckled. "Can you believe we guillotined him?"

"I just hope he's really gone this time."

"Saskia said it's near impossible for anyone to come back from that," I replied.

Garrett grimaced. "I just don't like that 'near' part."

"Then we have to focus on the impossible part. This has been a long time coming. Killing him means we finally get to properly close that chapter of our lives," I said, waxing lyrical. "But I get what you mean. It's hard to imagine he's actually gone. It's like a phantom limb, a really irritating one. We need to believe he's really dead this time, or he's just going to keep haunting us."

Garrett nodded. "So we focus on the impossible part."

"That shouldn't be too difficult for us. Isn't that what we always do?"

"You've got me there." Garrett laughed, and it really did feel like that chapter had closed for good. No more Katherine. No more Davin. No more cult. And I would believe it with all my heart, because I was done being haunted by the past.

TWENTY-FOUR

Garrett

Succeeding in any task required the appropriate tools, and facing Ponce de León was no exception. Even though we now had the Ivan Trap in our possession, there was no telling how our encounter would go, and Finch definitely didn't want to go in underprepared this time.

Luckily, the Armory would give us what we needed, which meant that was our final stop before heading to Cuba and making our way to the lighthouse at Morro Castle. We made a quick detour to the living quarters to change into something less flashy.

Dressed more casually in dark jeans and dark T-shirts—a uniform of sorts, ideal for those who didn't want to draw attention —Finch, Saskia, and I gathered on the ground floor of the living quarters. I had the Avenging Angel slung over my shoulder, nestled in the strapped sheath Astrid had made for me.

"Compensating for something?" Saskia smirked, eyeing the weapon.

"We're going to the Armory to get magical weapons. I figured this one would work just as well." I ignored her comment. "It's designed to work against all of Chaos's creations."

She shrugged. "I didn't know you were packing heat, that's all."

"I got to keep it after the Battle of Elysium." I shouldered the strap to make it more comfortable.

"A gift for dying in the line of duty?"

"Something like that," I replied.

"You should see him use it." Finch waggled his eyebrows. "If you think he's sexy now, just wait until he starts swinging that magnificent thing. Hotflush inducing."

"Thanks... I think." I laughed. Finch had a way of breaking the tension in any situation, and I was often grateful for it. Even Saskia chuckled, her gaze lingering a minute too long on Finch. If she were a couple years older, I wondered if she might've turned his head. Then again, I was pretty sure Finch was a lost cause as long as Ryann was around.

We made our way through the SDC to the Armory. It was at the far end of the grounds, close to the infirmary, but it was already way past midnight and there was no one around to ask any questions about what we were up to. I envied the sleeping souls, who didn't have to worry about what else the night might hold. But I'd promised to help Finch, and I wasn't backing out now.

As for what my night had held so far, dark twinges of disgust and sickening realization kept creeping into my mind. It was lucky I had something else to focus on, or I might have sunk too deep into my thoughts.

I killed someone tonight.

I wasn't usually the "eye for an eye" sort of guy. It didn't matter how evil my enemy was—killing was killing. It wasn't easy. The only comfort I could take from it was knowing that Davin wouldn't bother us again. That counted for something, regardless of how it twisted me up inside.

I didn't like that I'd had to pull the string that had sliced Davin's head right off his shoulders; I could still hear the organic thud, separating flesh and bone. It made me shudder just thinking about it.

It hadn't just been vengeance for me. Astrid, Alton, and so many others had suffered because of him. It would've been stupid for me to have a crisis of morality over ending someone like that. Harley and Wade had been trying to find him for the better part of the year. We'd have to let them know what happened. But that could wait until after we'd dealt with the pesky spirit.

"What are we looking for?" I whispered as we approached the Armory door. It was a big, metal blast door designed to keep people out.

"Magical weaponry. You said so yourself," Saskia replied.

I cast her a stern look. "I mean, is there anything specific we're after?"

"Anything that can hold back a rampant poltergeist. Plain old Chaos doesn't work. I tried." Finch got to work on the lock, feeding his magic into the mechanism. "Saskia, any thoughts? You're the spiritual guru here."

"I'll know them when I see them," she said.

Helpful.

The door clicked, and Finch pulled it open. "Open sesame!"

"Do you ever take anything seriously?" Saskia muttered.

"Everything except myself," he replied, with a grin. She looked like she was about to cast him a withering look, but instead a reluctant grin tugged at her lips.

The Armory looked more like a museum than a place to pick up weapons. Guns, blades, scythes, bows, arrows—everything a warrior could need all neatly organized into sections. Swords hung from the walls with square cards underneath describing what the weapons were and where they had come from. Guns were mounted in the same fashion, while glass boxes held some of the rarer objects—the Indonesian keris that O'Halloran had used in the Battle of Elysium, a twin set of Okinawan sai, a cluster of poison-barbed shuriken, a display of silver bullets, and a white-hilted dagger, among others.

Finch seemed drawn to the dagger, while Saskia went straight for an elegant sword that hung on the wall, mounted on a wooden shield. It was curved, like a saber. She took it down without hesitation and started spinning it skillfully, as if it were a baton or something, her body twisting as she ducked underneath the twirling blade. It looked like she'd spent years training with the thing.

"Something you want to tell us?" I asked, a bit awestruck.

She smiled. "Kolduny training isn't just about the spiritual. It's about the practical side, too. And this is one of Russia's finest exports—aside from me, of course. I've been training with one of these since I was old enough to grip the handle."

"What is it?" I replied.

"This is a *shashka*." She tutted loudly. "Looks like the SDC has been borrowing things that don't belong to it."

I frowned. "What do you mean?"

"This is a Kolduny weapon." She slashed the air, the blade shimmering with a white glow. "See that? That's Kolduny magic embedded in the metalwork. I guess that's why there's no card to go with this—wouldn't want anyone finding out they'd been stealing. Especially not my family."

"You can take that up with O'Halloran later. Just leave your arguing for after we've faced Ponce, okay?" I glanced at Finch for backup, but he was staring at the white-hilted dagger. He looked hypnotized.

"Fine by me." She cast me a sly grin. "Anything grab your attention?"

I glanced around, but nothing caught my eye. "No, I'm okay with the weapon I've got."

"I bet you are." She chuckled before turning to Finch. "How about you? What are you gawping at?"

"Carnwennan," he replied, in a weird, faraway voice.

"Huh?" Saskia edged closer to the box. The dagger inside didn't look like much, just a simple blade with a handle of smoothed white bone. But Finch gaped as if it were made of diamond.

"It's called Carnwennan." Finch lifted the lid and took out the dagger. "It belonged to King Arthur. Apparently, he used it to slice some dark witch in two."

"Sounds like the kind of weapon we need," Saskia said. "Funny that it's here, though, what with you Merlins running around. Looks like it found its way home."

Finch smiled as he turned the dagger over in his hand, a glint of purple shining off the blade's edge. "Come to Papa."

"Is that what you're settling on?" I was antsy for us to get out of here before anyone showed up. It might have been late, but O'Halloran ran a tight ship, with night guards who patrolled the entire coven at regular intervals.

He nodded. "Oh, yes."

"Then let's get out of here," I urged.

Saskia darted forward, took down the scabbard and strap that went with the shashka, and slid the saber inside. She slung it over her shoulder, mirroring me, while Finch slipped his dagger into its sheath and attached it to the belt loop of his jeans.

A moment later, we were back in the hallway with the Armory door locked tight. We'd be back before anyone noticed the weapons missing... if everything went according to plan. Armed and ready, we crossed the hall to a narrow side corridor. I'd just taken out the charmed chalk and lifted it to draw our gateway to Cuba when a voice called out. All three of us froze.

"Would you mind telling me where you're going at one in the morning?" Astrid stood at the entrance to the corridor. She looked tired, like she'd been waiting up. For us, probably.

"Would you believe us if we said 'nowhere'?" Finch smiled sweetly. Meanwhile, I felt like a little schoolboy who'd just been caught playing hooky.

She shook her head. "You know I've got cameras everywhere, right?"

"Friggin' Smartie. What is this, *1984*?" Finch muttered under his breath.

"Can I have a word, Garrett?" Astrid ignored him and fixed her eyes on me.

I forced a smile. "Sure."

"Anything you want to say to him, you can say to us," Saskia protested.

"You don't want to get caught in this crossfire, kid," Finch whispered. He took her by the arm and led her down the hall, giving me and Astrid a chance to speak in private.

"I'm not a kid!" I heard Saskia complain. She clearly wanted to help, which was sweet, but not the best idea. I needed to hear Astrid out if we wanted to make sure she didn't say anything to Harley or the others. She'd already helped us without asking too many questions. The least I owed her was an explanation.

"She's got a crush on you," Astrid said, with a sad half-smile.

I gave a strangled laugh. "She's got a crush on any male that moves and has most of his teeth. But that's not why you came to talk to me, is it?"

"No." She paused. "What were you doing in the Armory? Don't lie to me... please. I know when you're lying. And I'd really like for you to tell me the truth. The whole truth. Not just bits and pieces."

I sighed. "It's not that simple. It's not my secret to tell."

"Then tell me what you can," she replied. For once, her eyes stayed focused on me. "You can't expect me to sit by while you go sneaking around, stealing things and acting suspiciously. I'm not saying I think you're up to no good, but you're up to something. And it worries me. If you're striding into danger, I can't pretend I'm not watching. If anything were to happen to you, and I realized, after the fact, that I could've stopped you or helped you, that would... it would break me, Garrett." Tears glittered in her eyes, threatening to fall.

"If you've been watching the cameras, then you know we went somewhere tonight," I said, deciding to be honest.

She nodded. "The Dark Tourist party."

"What gave us away?" I smiled nervously.

"Saskia's dress, and your suits. Plus, it was pretty easy to piece together from the fake IDs and Ryann carrying invitations. What happened there?"

"Well, at the party, we ran into Davin. He caused trouble for us, as he always does, so we decided to put an end to him while we had the chance." I kept it as vague as I could. "We chased him. We ended up in a room themed around the French Revolution. There was a guillotine, we took him by surprise, and I... I killed him."

Astrid gasped. "You killed him?"

"It was sort of a joint effort, but I dealt the last blow. We had to stop him, or he would've caused more problems for us, and others. But that wasn't the only reason I did it." I took a breath before I went on. "I killed him because he killed me. And because he killed Alton."

"You... killed him for Alton?" Her voice shook and her eyes widened.

I nodded. "He won't be bothering us anymore."

"That's a... relief. At least, I think it is," she murmured, clearly trying to decide whether she was pleased or not. "Are you all right? That can't have been easy."

"It was the right thing to do."

"But that doesn't mean you have to feel okay." She looked concerned, her eyebrows knitted together above the bridge of her glasses.

I smiled. "I'll be okay."

"But won't you get into trouble?" Her voice shook with anxiety. I smiled, showing more confidence than I felt. "No, I'm not worried. Nobody saw us, and nobody knows it was us. We kept our disguises on." I took a small step closer to her. "And, at least, this means it's over now."

"Are you sure about that?" Astrid frowned. "He didn't seem to be capable of dying the last few times. After Marie Laveau's church, you thought he was dead. After the fight at the inn, you thought he was dead. But he kept coming back."

"Saskia sensed his spirit afterward, and it wasn't attached to him anymore," I replied. "You've theorized about it enough, and you agreed with the rest of us—it had to be Katherine who was providing his immortal lifeline."

Astrid fidgeted. "And if we were wrong?"

"If Davin does somehow find a way to come back, then our visit to the Armory is even more warranted. Saskia sensed his spirit was pissed, so if he does resurrect himself, which I highly doubt, he'll be out for blood."

Astrid's expression softened. "You understand why I'm here, asking you this, don't you?"

My heart lurched. "I... uh... sort of?"

She paused, biting her lower lip. "The truth is, I can't bear the thought of you dying again," she said after a moment. "It really would break me beyond repair. If I see you acting weirdly, doing strange things, I get worried. I get worried that you're going to disappear through a chalk door and never come back." She hung her head, no longer looking at me.

"You've never said that before." I didn't quite know how to feel. "I just want you to know that I'm not being ungrateful for Alton's gift. I'm not deliberately risking myself. I feel terrible about what happened, and—"

She stopped me abruptly. "My father made his decision. It's taken me a long time to come to terms with it, and it hurt me deeply, but... at least you got out of it alive."

A tear slipped down her cheek, and I wanted to brush it away. Instead, I let her go on.

"It doesn't matter how strained things are between us right now," she said softly. "The grief will become manageable, eventually. Until then, I need you to stay alive. Not because you owe it to anyone, but because you deserve to live. Because I want you to live."

My throat tightened. I'd never expected to hear that kind of hopeful talk from her—talk that wasn't riddled with the memories of what she'd lost. A thread of possibility lingered in her words. And I was eager to seize it with both hands and hold on.

I lifted my hand to her face and let myself brush away the tear. "I promise you, I'll be careful."

I meant it. Even if she said I didn't owe my life to anyone, that wasn't true. I owed it to her to take care of myself. I owed it to her to survive so we could keep building this bridge between us. And maybe, one day soon, we'd finally meet in the middle.

TWENTY-FIVE

Finch

"Everything peachy?" I asked as Garrett walked toward us.
Astrid had just parted ways with him, which I guessed
meant she wasn't going to stand in our way like a bespectacled
terrier. Unless, of course, this was him headed our way with his tail
between his legs, coming to tell us we weren't allowed to continue
—Astrid's orders.

He was giving off slightly jittery vibes, but that could've been
from just about anything. She might have smiled at him funny and
turned his brain into a mass of seething nonsense. I knew that
feeling all too well.

I hope you're really okay, Ryann.

Garrett nodded. "She's not going to say anything."

"Yes, Hepler-Waterhouse! I knew we could rely on her." I gave
the air a quick one-two.

Astrid had changed her name after Alton's passing; a fitting
homage from a girl who wanted her dad back. Her mom had
encouraged it, likely hoping it would make Astrid feel closer to her
father. I understood that, too. I'd changed my name to get away

from the Shipton smear, preferring to associate with the less psycho side of my family, but people were finding it hard to think of me as Finch Merlin. My former moniker had a nasty way of sticking.

Garrett smiled weirdly. A secret smile. "She says we have to replace whatever weapons we took, though."

"Spoilsport." Saskia pouted.

"But we're good to go?" I pressed. That was the important part. Astrid could monitor us all she liked as long as she didn't tell anyone what we were up to.

"Yeah, we're good to go." Garrett took out a stick of charmed chalk and drew a shaky rectangle onto the nearest wall. He glanced at me. "You're the one who knows where we're going."

I stepped forward and whispered the *Aperi Si Ostium* spell. The lines crackled, sinking into the solid wall and opening up the doorway with a hiss that reminded me of a cartoon fuse rushing toward a massive pile of TNT. Heading into Morro Castle gave me a similar feeling. I just hoped I'd be more successful this time.

"Three express tickets to Cuba, coming up." I reached for the handle and wrenched the door open, my stomach experiencing a little churn as I looked out upon the familiar terrain of the castle. A flicker of déjà vu joined the anxiety party as I realized I'd pretty much opened the door exactly where I'd closed the last one—the one where I'd narrowly escaped being slashed to ribbons by Mr. Ponce.

Taking a deep breath, I focused on the mission at hand. The lighthouse sat ahead, all flashy and protruding. *The bulb still works, after Ponce trashed the place?* Apparently, it did—it cast its glow onto the distant ocean, like a super-slow strobe, warning away any stray ships that ventured too close.

I liked this place even less in the dark. A bright moon bathed the old fortress in a stark, silvery glow, fading then shining brighter as clouds passed across it, almost like another beacon. The scene was beautiful, but I knew what lurked at the top of that lighthouse.

"Do you guys feel that?" I whispered. The air felt thick, like someone had turned it to syrup. It hadn't felt this way the first time I came here, but I figured I must have pushed some poltergeist buttons, and this was the aftermath. A warning not to disturb him.

Saskia nodded. "It's the spirit."

"Well, I didn't think it was Santa Claus." My gaze flitted up to the lamp room. This felt... off. Entering that lighthouse and facing the poltergeist again was the last thing I wanted to do.

"I don't see any guards. Do you?" Garrett peered across the open expanse.

"No, but that doesn't mean they're gone. We need to get inside." I led the way across the sandy ground before ducking beside the lighthouse door. I peered around the edge of the building, making doubly sure no guards were going to jump out at us. Satisfied, I reached for the door handle and pulled hard.

The door rattled but stayed exactly where it was, locked in place with a shiny new padlock.

"Was it locked the last time you came?" Saskia whispered.

I shook my head. "Not that I remember, but my head's been a little foggy lately."

"Try a chalk door," Garrett suggested.

I took out my trusty stick of charmed chalk and drew the usual lines. But, as the *Aperi Si Ostium* spell came out of my mouth, nothing happened. I tried it again. Still nothing.

"Well, that's never happened to me before." I frowned at the door, trying to figure out what was going on. "And don't even think about cracking a joke. We have exactly zero time for that, not unless our poltergeist pal is a secret fan of bad comedy."

Saskia snorted. "Actually, I was going to say that this place must have been warded against magical interference."

"The guards might've seen the mess in the lamp room and realized there'd been a trespasser," I mused. "Only problem with that theory is human guards can't ward a place against magical interference."

This was a magical's work.

But who? A two-bit exorcist who'd strung up some charms to help out the humans? A magical who just happened to be on the security team, maybe placed there by Havana's coven? Or someone else, maybe? Someone who knew what they were doing.

"Is the poltergeist still inside?" I whispered, sliding my Chaos into the lock to see if I could unpick it with my Telekinesis. The tendrils came up against the equivalent of a two-foot-thick steel wall. And this wall had some extra touches to really make its point that we were *not* welcome. A spark shivered down through the strands, giving me a nasty jolt. I snapped my hand back from the lock.

"Ah, son of a—it bit me!"

"It didn't bite you, it shocked you. Another security measure to stop folks from picking the locks." Saskia's eyes turned white for a moment. "I can feel the poltergeist. It's still up there."

Garrett glanced sharply over his shoulder, which kind of freaked me out. He seemed to be scanning the area, as if he'd heard something.

"What is it?" I hissed.

"Do you... feel like we're being watched?" His eyes darted along the darkened fortress walls. It was almost four in the morning here.

As terrifying as that was given our vulnerable state, there wasn't actually anyone in sight. It was just us, scaring each other stupid. And yet, Garrett wasn't the type to let his irrational fears get the better of him. If he thought someone was watching us, they probably were.

"Forget about what's going on out here. We need to get in there." I nodded at the door and reached for Garrett's bag. He had it slung over his shoulder, beside his great big sword. Unzipping it, I pulled out the item I was looking for. "Nothing like a pair of good, old-fashioned bolt-cutters."

Saskia frowned. "What are you doing with bolt-cutters? Do you moonlight as a thief when you're not helping Finch?"

Garrett shrugged. "I never actually thought I'd have to use them, but I keep them in my toolkit in case magic isn't available." He paused. "After the whole Katherine debacle, I figured it was a good idea to think about all potential scenarios, not just magical ones. Looks like bolt-cutters come in pretty handy."

"Always, my good man—always!" I put the scissor-like head of the cutters against the arc of the padlock and clamped it shut. The sharp edges chowed through the metal until it collapsed.

I pocketed the padlock—not that it'd be much use after this. Human tools had their uses, but magic was a lot easier to cover up than a great big slice through solid metal.

With the door open, we quietly headed inside. I ushered the other two ahead and was about to close the door behind us when I heard footsteps outside. My head whipped around, my hands up and ready for a fight. Nobody was there.

My hands itched to get a ball of Fire ready, just so I could be sure. But we couldn't use Fire or flashlights, not unless we wanted to bring a bunch of panicked guards down on us. I doubted they'd be in an "ask questions first, shoot later" kind of mood after what had happened to the lamp room last time.

"Everything okay?" Garrett whispered.

I forced myself to nod. "Just thought I heard something."

Swallowing my nerves, I closed the door and kept an eye on it for a second, half expecting it to swing open and scare the bejeezus out of me. When it didn't, I took in a deep breath. *Mind gremlins, you need to pack it in.*

"Are you two coming up or what?" Saskia was already up the first twist of the staircase. It was too dark to make out her face, but she sounded impatient.

"On our way," I whispered back.

We climbed the spiral steps up to the very top. The entire way, the winds howled outside, screeching past the shuttered windows like banshees.

At least we have the Ivan Trap this time. Hell, at least we were a "we" this time. I felt a fuzzy warmth at not having to do this alone, somewhere underneath the bubbling sense of dread that Ponce was going to shred us all.

Saskia waited for us on the platform with the ladder, which led to the lamp room. The trapdoor was shut. I tried to remember whether it had been closed the last time I'd been here, but my mind had filled with nightmarish memories of a gaping mouth and a hooded, screaming figure. I literally couldn't think of anything else.

"You'll be needing this." I delved into Garrett's bag, using him as my personal packhorse. Carefully, I took out the Ivan Trap and handed it to Saskia.

She smiled at it in admiration, like it was one of those fancy dresses of hers. "It's a beauty."

"You've still got your Celtic Shield Knot, right?" I eyed her.

She showed me the chain with her free hand. "Let's get this poltergeist to obey us before it senses what we're up to and decides to make the first move."

She clambered up the ladder. I was already braced for the trapdoor to be locked—another hoop to jump through in my endless obstacle course—but Saskia pushed it open without any trouble at all. *Weirder and weirder...*

Why go to the trouble of magically reinforcing the entrance if this door was just going to be left unlocked for anyone to climb through? I supposed whoever had made the initial barriers had hoped it'd be enough to deter people from going farther, so they didn't bother locking the trapdoor.

Ignoring the nagging doubt in the back of my head, I hauled myself up through the trapdoor and into the oh-so-familiar dome of the lamp room. Someone had cleaned up. The table and chairs, and every object that had been launched at my head, were back in their places, aside from the ones that had shattered or torn or plummeted to their demise.

At first glance, it looked as if my last encounter had never happened. Had it not been for a few cracks in the dome and the wall, and a few fairly fresh scuffs on the floorboards, I might've believed I'd been a bit dramatic about recounting the damage Ponce had caused.

Speak of the devil. As the lantern shone onto the ocean, sending a powerful beam out again and again, a shadow stretched across the floor of the room. Without the lamp, it would've been nearly impossible to see Ponce de León standing by the central bulb. Hooded and ominous, he was once again staring out to sea.

I fixed my eyes on Skullface, my chest tightening with fear as I remembered those cloaked arms getting longer.

Saskia edged forward and placed the Ivan Trap on the floor. She touched the sides and whispered something in Russian, a spell I didn't understand. My grasp of Russian had never been great. I was more about the Romance languages.

Nevertheless, the spell made the hairs on the back of my neck spike up. The Trap whirred quietly, and the top panel unfurled like an ugly metal flower.

"Hey! Ponce de León, right?" Saskia called. My heart lurched.

What are you doing? I would've said it out loud if I could've gotten my words to tiptoe past the enormous lump of terror in my throat. Why was she yelling at it? That was only going to make it angry. I started to wish I'd put Krieger on call, so he'd be ready if we had to come tumbling into the infirmary like last time.

"Hey! Ponce!" Saskia shouted. "Here I am, trespassing on your sacred ground. What are you going to do about it? I'll tell you what you're going to do about it—nothing! I'm here, and I'm walking around, and you can't stop me."

She made a show of hopping backward and forward, though she never got too far from the Ivan Trap.

Ponce de León turned to face his tormentor. His gray, ghoulish face stretched out in a silent, hollow scream.

Crap...

Around the dome, the wind howled louder than ever, reaching a fever pitch. A gust tore through the room, Ponce de León's cloak billowing as his shadowed limbs expanded. The same glinting black claws that had slashed my chest extended from hands that no longer held a proper shape.

He turned to wisps and sharp edges. Danger and death. Doom and gloom. And I couldn't help but worry about how the hell this was going to turn out.

TWENTY-SIX

Finch

"**G**ET OUT!" Ponce de León roared, as the first bits of furniture went flying.

Saskia ducked behind a chair that had been duct-taped back together while Garrett and I skidded to our knees to avoid getting whacked by a table. With every object he flung, the poltergeist edged closer to Saskia.

"GET OUT!" he boomed again. My eyes flitted to the box on the floor. The edge of Ponce's shadowy figure had just reached the trap.

Come on, you beautiful box! Show us you were worth the hassle!

The rubies that topped the Trap's four spikes glowed red. A second later, crackling beams shot across in two diagonals, making a red "X" between the gemstones. Where the lines met, a vortex formed. It spiraled downward into the darkness of the box and dragged in the tail of Ponce's shadow.

The moment the vortex grasped him, it sucked him inside until there wasn't a speck of him left in the room. Not even a thread of cloak. As soon as the last of the poltergeist vanished into the Trap, the top panel sprang shut, sealing him in.

"Release me!" he howled. "Release me! Please, release me!"

In the space of one spiritual vacuuming, Ponce de León had gone from insanely terrifying to pitiful. His voice no longer packed an echoey punch. It just wailed from the box in a thin, weak waver.

"Please, release me. I will do as you ask as long as you free me from these confines."

Saskia rolled her eyes. "Oh really? Are you going to grant me three wishes and do my laundry, too? I've heard it all before, Ponce. You should've thought about behaving *before* you sliced my friend's chest and tried to poison him. Just because you're a poltergeist doesn't mean you can't be reasonable, but you lashed out. And now you need to learn a lesson or two on how to obey before I even think about letting you out of this box."

She picked up the Trap and whispered a brief Russian spell to each of the four rubies. As she reached the very last one, the gemstones glowed blue. And so did her eyes. No more red; the rubies now looked more like sapphires.

"Whoa," I said.

Garrett nodded in appreciation.

"He's ready to talk now. I have compelled him to obey."

Saskia's voice came out all kinds of wrong. It sounded warped and distorted, as if it were being played through ancient-ass speakers. I wasn't an aficionado in the world of the Kolduny, but I could put the pieces together. The only way to get the poltergeist to speak truthfully was to inject the Trap with some Kolduny juju. And Saskia had done just that.

I stepped up to bat. "Mr. Ponce—first, let me tell you what a pleasure it is to finally speak with you. I know we didn't get off on the right foot last time, but I meant what I said about you being awesome. You are Ponce de León, the famed explorer, right? I suppose that's the best place to start, so nobody's wasting anyone's time."

"*You* are wasting my time," Ponce shot back. "And yes, I am Ponce de León."

Grump de León might've been a better name for him. Then again, decades and decades of unfinished business festering like a big, nasty boil weren't exactly conducive to a sunny disposition.

"Okay, next question. Let's take this honesty policy for a test spin or two before we get into the juicy stuff." I tapped my chin in thought. "Where were you born?"

A low growl erupted from the box. "Santervás de Campos, Valladolid, Spain."

"What year?"

"1474," Ponce replied.

"Were you the governor of Puerto Rico?" Garrett chimed in.

A deep sigh thrummed from the Trap. "I was the governor of Puerto Rico thrice. I was the first, the third, and the seventh."

"Were you pals with Christopher Columbus?" I added.

"We were friends and colleagues. Like-minded gentlemen. It was his son, Diego, I could not abide. Because of him, I first lost the governance of Puerto Rico."

I cast a tense glance at Garrett. "And you explored the Caribbean?"

"Every corner of it," Ponce replied.

"And did you find the Fountain of Youth there?" I waited, my heart in my mouth.

The now-blue gems pulsated for a second. "No."

"But... you *did* find the Fountain of Youth?" If he said no again, I may as well have kissed my butt goodbye.

The gems glowed brighter. "Yes, I found it."

"Why didn't you drink from it? Couldn't you have spared your-self all this poltergeisting?" I couldn't help asking. My curiosity was nagging at me.

The glow faded slightly. "I did not dare."

"I'm going to need more details, Mr. Ponce," I pressed.

"I thought about it for a long while. Courage failed me. I worried about the cost of such a gift. But, in time, my mind changed. I decided that I would drink from it, after all, and attain immortality. But before I could... I died. A poisoned arrow to the thigh."

The gems throbbed angrily. "I died as the only person on Earth who knew where it was. It was that thought that transformed my tortured spirit into a poltergeist. To have almost reached for some-thing wondrous, only to have it slip away through hesitancy... There is nothing more painful than that. A chance that might have been mine, and mine alone, all because I was afraid—afraid of all that immortality entailed. Fate decided for me, and I shall never forgive it for doing so."

"So, where is it?" Garrett interjected.

The gemstones crackled, and I could sense Ponce's resistance bristling through the Ivan Trap. But Saskia had him by the atoms, and she wasn't about to let go until we had everything we needed.

As if hearing my thoughts, her eyes burned a brighter shade of blue, and the gemstones began pulsing more evenly.

"The Fountain of Youth is deep beneath a diamond mine called Jubilee, in the region of Yakutia in Russia," he replied, his voice straining. "You must go beyond the very bottom of the mine. Dig holes, as deep as possible, until you reach the true bottom—as I call it. There is a chamber beneath. The Fountain Chamber."

"Wait... what? It's in Russia?" I frowned. "How did you find it there? My history isn't great, but I don't remember you ever being in Russia."

"I had avenues open in many countries, even those I rarely visited myself. However, I did visit Russia during my extended European excursions. Do not believe everything you read," Ponce answered curtly. "I employed scouts to investigate and uncover sites of curiosity and unusual interest—places of myth and legend and local stories that happened to come my way. After all, even fairytales are based in some truth."

Garrett folded his arms across his chest. "And this was one of those sites?"

"Before the Fountain was discovered, the Jubilee pit was simply a strange area that drew some people to it and scared others away. It had a magical, mythical quality that could not be denied by any who walked into its domain."

The gems glowed brighter. "It took countless paid scouts and many, many years to locate this strange place. Once I settled upon the spot, I began to dig and dig, and dig some more, until I found the Fountain located beneath the layers of the diamonds."

"How come you're the only one who's ever reached it?" Another question I couldn't resist.

The gemstones dulled slightly, as though Ponce didn't want to talk about it. Then he continued.

"Others made their attempts, but all died in the endeavor or gave up. In the winters, it grew too cold to dig through the frozen earth. In the summer, the ice thawed and the ground turned to slush, causing landslides that collapsed the tunnels. People were injured, and many were swallowed whole by the earth, vanishing into obsoletion—a cautionary tale, nothing more."

Saskia's eyes shone vividly. "I believe the Jubilee mine was opened in the 1980s, which means the current depth that's been reached must be deeper than ever before. What's stopping the diamond miners from digging through?"

I was glad she was back with us. Her blue-eyed hypnotic staring had me worried for a minute.

"The dangerous terrain upon reaching deeper levels deters most, as the soil simply caves in at the slightest vibration. I also put my own measures in place when I finally discovered the Fountain —though that was long before the diamond mine opened. I covered the Fountain Chamber with a protective layer, then added another solid layer many feet above. I called it the 'white floor.'"

"So, if we find the white floor, that means we're on the right path?" I asked.

The gemstones fizzed. "Yes, it does."

"What about the other layer?" That part I was finding hard to visualize. I didn't know if the Fountain was going to be massive, tiny, or somewhere in the middle.

"That will become clear upon seeing it," Ponce replied.

"Who created the Fountain of Youth?" Saskia chimed in. Her voice still sounded like it was coming through a tinny, used car lot boombox, but she was asking some decent questions.

Ponce and his box gave a little light display, flashing wildly. "It is thought that Gaia is the creator, though no one is certain."

"So, if it's in Russia, how come everyone thinks it's in Bimini or some mangroves in the Caribbean?" *Myself included.*

"I spread a multitude of stories and rumors to make sure no one else ever uncovered it. I was not only an explorer and conquistador, but a skilled magical, too. Planting false leads was not so difficult. People enjoy a treasure hunt, even if it has no ending."

The box thrummed quietly, the clockwork whirring slightly as though in laughter.

"I went to a great deal of trouble hiding the Fountain after I finally found it. Immortality should not be easy to attain. In fact, in my time here, I have come to the conclusion that it should not be attained, under any circumstances."

"Yet here you are, giving it the full poltergeist pizzazz because you regret not having attained it yourself. Did I miss something?" I arched an eyebrow. "Why not cut yourself some slack and cross over, safe in the knowledge that you did everything you could to stop folks from getting their hands on it?"

"My mind can never be at peace while the Fountain exists, thus making it impossible for me to cross over," he replied. "I would destroy it if I could, but I am bound to this lighthouse."

"*Has* anyone ever attained immortality?" Saskia asked, her eyes still glowing.

The box thrummed a little louder. "Not that I am aware of. I took the secret to my grave. I would know if someone had broken through the white floor, but I have not felt the threshold break."

A thought stabbed the back of my mind. "What about Davin Doncaster? Have you ever heard of him?"

I mean, what were the odds that Davin wanted an Ivan Trap for a different poltergeist? How many of these gangly, slashy creeps could there be?

"I have seen this Davin Doncaster," Ponce replied. "He also wanted to know the Fountain's whereabouts and received a similar response to the one you first received. Yet he did not manage to evade me, as you did. I killed him, but he came back again, as if it had never occurred. It is not true immortality—it cannot be—but it is the closest I have ever witnessed."

The gems glowed sporadically. "I have killed Davin three times in as many months, but the fiend simply will not die."

Garrett and I looked at each other in horror, while Saskia's eerie blue eyes seemed to burst with light. Garrett broke the silence first.

"That's got to be why Davin wanted the Ivan Trap. He was looking for the same thing as us—the Fountain."

I nodded, feeling sick. "He must have been the one to put the new charms on the entrance." Another thought struck me. "Also, if he's been coming back like the rancid waste of space that he is, then it clearly wasn't Katherine who was doing the resurrecting."

"Do you think that means we didn't kill him at Daggerston's?" Garrett looked like he might punch something.

"I think we have to keep the faith. I'm sure that a decapitation did what nothing else could." I wasn't going to sink into despair. "In all the other instances, his body was still intact. We took his head off, which means there's a good chance it worked."

"And if it didn't?" Saskia chimed in.

"We need to find out how he's been resurrecting himself up until now and how to kill him, permanently, if he comes crawling back," Garrett said. "Do you know, Ponce de León?"

"I do not," he replied. "It has continued to baffle me. Although, I always suspected other magicals would come looking for me one day. That is why I was so diligent in planting all those false paths and extensive rumors."

The lights paused for a moment before starting back up. "You have come here twice, despite the dangers. Tell me, do you really desire immortality so badly?"

Do I? It hadn't crossed my mind a whole lot. To me, this was just another task for Erebus. I had no personal stake in the actual content whatsoever. I only cared about giving him the goods and getting my sweet, sweet reward of freedom.

Garrett chuckled. "I wouldn't mind it, personally. Who wouldn't want to be immortal?"

"But that's not why we're after it," I added quickly, in case that was some kind of deal-breaker. I'd come to learn that spirits and deities could be testy little pains in my butt when they wanted to be. Sneeze in a way they didn't like, and there was no telling what they'd do. Then again, this ghostly pest was being compelled to obey, so I was probably okay for once.

Ponce hissed, a weird concept considering he was still inside the box. It was more like the box did the hissing. "Erebus... I will never get used to that sensation. I can feel him all over you, Finch Merlin. It sickens me still."

"Really? I thought I'd washed the last of his stink off with that bathtub of bleach." I forced a laugh, but Ponce's reaction made me nervous.

"Stay away from Erebus, Finch. He is naught but bad news," Ponce warned, sounding stern even through the Ivan Trap.

This time my laugh was real. In a sort of "if I don't laugh, I'll cry" kind of way. "It's a little too late for that, Mr. Ponce. Erebus has me dancing on the end of his hook, and all I can do is shimmy away like a good little worm and hope I don't die doing it." I paused. "Hey, I don't suppose *you* know what Erebus wants with the Fountain, do you?"

"I do not, but I have crossed paths with that Child of Chaos before." Ponce wheezed inside his box. "You must be careful. I urge you to extricate yourself from this mess before it is too late. Erebus is not to be trusted. *None* of the Children should be trusted."

"Gaia has been nothing but good to us," Garrett interjected. "We owe her a—"

"Gaia is a decent exception, at best, but she can also turn against you if she deems it necessary. Her loyalty lies with the higher order of things—with creation and destruction. Do not be misled into thinking she has a soft spot for humanity," Ponce urged.

"What about Lux?" I'd been hoping I might get Lux to help me in the whole bid for freedom thing.

The box thrummed, rocking violently. "Avoid any and all Children, without exception. They each have their own agenda, and they do not always coincide with those of the living or the magical. As I said, they serve a higher order. And, above all, they serve themselves."

Well then, it looked like gaining some cosmic help was out of the question. After all, they'd probably want to strike another deal, and I'd learned my lesson on that one. If I wanted my freedom, I was going to have to get it with my own two hands.

TWENTY-SEVEN

Finch

With nothing left to ask our ghoulish friend, Saskia let him go, whispering more Russian that went right over my head.

Ponce floated across the lamp room and took up his usual spot by the central bulb. He didn't move, and he didn't try to retaliate. No huffing and puffing or blowing our houses down. I guessed he was feeling a little sensitive after getting sucked into the Ivan Trap and now preferred to pout instead of tearing us all into shreds.

Leaving him to his brooding, we clambered down the trapdoor and headed all the way back down the lighthouse spiral.

Fresh air beckoned. Being stuck in a room with a trapped poltergeist had left a weird, metallic smell deep in the crevices of my nostrils, and I needed to clear that out before it was all I could smell for the rest of my life. My hair was standing on end, too, in a tufty mess that no comb would fix.

"Why'd you let him loose? Isn't that just asking for trouble?" Garrett turned to Saskia as we made our way through the lighthouse door. A wind whipped up across the fortress. I braced, ready to unsheathe my dagger and use it on Slashy-Hands McGee if he decided he wanted a slice of revenge after all. But it was just the wind and the lap of the ocean waves beyond the wall.

Saskia shrugged, clutching the now-empty Ivan Trap. "He's more or less harmless, and I think he was secretly relieved to get that off his chest after so long. I could feel his sadness... all the conflict and torment that's been festering inside him for centuries."

"Does that mean he might be able to cross over?" Garrett replied.

"No, I doubt he'll ever be able to do that. Poltergeists fall into two categories: A, they don't want to cross over, ever. Or B, they need a helping hand to do it, which ends up being pretty impossible when they lose their temper every time someone comes near. Ponce is a mix of both, from what I could sense." Saskia smiled. "Plus, I don't want to affect the local economy."

"Eh?" I cast her a confused look.

She gestured up at the lighthouse. "Chances are, he's part of the reason so many tourists visit this place. Everyone loves a ghost story, right?"

I chuckled. "Ponce gets his poltergeist on, spooks the tourists, gives everyone a heart-stopping anecdote to take home to the fam. The stories spread, curiosity nips a few heels, and they can sell T-shirts and fridge magnets with ghosties painted on the front for ten times what they're worth."

"Precisely. It's part of the local charm." Saskia smirked.

"Although, you're forgetting one pretty key thing."

She frowned. "I am?"

"The part where he tried to kill me." I pointed to my chest. "These puppies are still healing, by the way, and believe me when I tell you it was a close shave to get to the infirmary before his dead-men's whatever turned *me* into a dead man. We're talking cutthroat close."

Saskia just chuckled. "If he wanted to kill you, he'd have killed you. Sounds to me like he was just sending you a warning, for poking your nose where it wasn't wanted."

"Says you. If I'd had a magic box, I wouldn't have gotten slashed either," I shot back.

"You sure about that?" She flashed me a grin as we reached the wall that looked out onto the ocean.

As Garrett and Saskia caught their breath, gazing at the churning water and the flash of the lighthouse's glow on the waves down below, I glanced back at the dark fortress. I still couldn't shake the feeling that we weren't alone. And I didn't mean Ponce. He was accounted for. This was a different kind of shadow. One I couldn't see.

Whatever it was, it was seriously disturbing. I could feel its presence in my brain like a childhood trauma. I'd taken my pills to keep my usual list of issues at bay, but that hadn't done anything to quiet down the gremlins this time. Something had them on edge. Or rather, someone.

Who's out there?

I tried to peer into the gloom, but there was nothing but walls and turrets and cannons. No darting figures or stalking enemies, not even any guards to worry about. Clearly, the security guards here weren't taking their jobs very seriously, which suited me just fine. Trying to forget about it, I turned back to face the ocean... and what was coming next.

"Saskia, you've been a literal lifesaver," I started. "But this is where our collaboration has to end. You helped, you got a freebie Ivan Trap out of it, and now you can get back to the coven and resume your pestering."

"Yeah, the eligible bachelors are probably wondering where you disappeared to," Garrett added.

"I know you're trying to be funny, but I'm not laughing," Saskia countered. "You couldn't have done this without me, so what makes you think you can do the rest of it without me?"

I folded my arms across my chest, trying to look like a worried big brother. "It's too dangerous. Facing Ponce was one thing, but trekking into Russian territory and trying to dig our way to the bottom of a friggin' diamond mine, where everyone else who's tried it has died or gone MIA, is a situation I'm not going to put you in."

"Plus, Tatyana would use our guts as a hair tie," Garrett muttered.

Saskia snorted. "As the only actual Russian in this little party of three, if anyone can get us safely across Russian magical territory without getting caught, it's me. And you're not putting me in this situation—I'm putting myself in it so you two idiots don't get yourselves buried under a hundred feet of rock and diamond."

"No, Saskia. Being Russian doesn't mean you've got some immediate advantage. It's not going to happen." It wasn't just getting to the Fountain that had me worried—I was worried about what we might find when we got there.

What if it was cursed? What if it was hexed? What if there were great, hulking beasts guarding it? Ponce had alluded to some safety measures. Saskia may have had her devil-may-care hat on, but this devil did care, and I wasn't letting her put herself in any more danger.

"Well then, I think you're *really* going to like this part." She held my gaze with a determined smirk. "The Jubilee mine belongs to the Rasputins—my uncle's family. I can get us inside without a hitch. How's that for an advantage?"

Garrett cast me a nervous look. "That *would* give us an easier way in."

I stared back at him. "Just because it's easier doesn't mean it's the right thing to do. My fortune cookie told me so."

I didn't want to give in. I didn't want to put Saskia through what was coming. But she'd played a trump card with the Rasputin business. If she had a direct line into that mine, then that changed things, especially as Erebus wasn't going to sit around twiddling his thumbs, waiting forever for me to get myself together. He wanted me to find that damn Fountain for him, and he wanted me to find it now, like the spoiled Child that he was.

A piercing squawk made my head snap up. A flock of seagulls had appeared out of nowhere, their eyes flashing red in the darkness. They circled overhead before diving like arrows, their pointy beaks ready to strike.

Ah, there you are—couldn't resist checking in, huh? I guessed this was his way of pushing me to move on to stage two. Finding the Fountain and making sure it was where Ponce said it was.

The hairs on the back of my neck raised as a creeping cold edged through my veins—my body's allergic reaction to Erebus popping up unannounced. At least he hadn't frozen the ocean to get his point across, or exploded any mirrors.

More seagulls joined the swarm in a full-on ornithological barrage.

"Get to the wall!" I yelled. "We need to chalk-door out of here before Erebus Hitchcock decides to go in for the grand finale!"

We raced for the castle walls. The flap of a thousand wings thrummed behind us as the world turned dark. The moon's silvery glow vanished, replaced with pitch blackness. From inside the gloom, the din of the screeching gulls grew louder and louder.

My eardrums nearly reached their breaking point as I looked over my shoulder, unable to see anything through the horde of potentially deadly birds. I mean, I'd seen one of these suckers nearly tear a child's hand off to get at his fries, and another one force a burly dude to relinquish his baguette. Hundreds of these diseased scavengers could peck us to pieces in less time than it would take to say, *Erebus, you asshat!*

We skidded to a halt in front of the wall, and Garrett whipped out his chalk. As he drew, I kept my eye on the descending horde. They were almost on us—then they stopped suddenly. Silence echoed across the grounds of Morro Castle. No squawking, no fluttering, no screeching. The birds were, literally, frozen in the air.

My heart pounded as I waited for them to start up again, knowing this was just Erebus's way of freaking me out even more. But instead of flying toward us, they stayed suspended, and their bodies twisted through the air. They clearly had zero control over themselves as Erebus pulled them around in a feathery kaleido-scope, bending them to his vision.

As we watched, a curious pattern of bird bodies formed in the sky, illuminated by the silvery glow. The shadow that spread on the ground underneath felt like a warning: a giant eye, the birds creating its seamless lines and curves.

"The Eye of Erebus," Saskia whispered. "I've seen it before, in textbooks."

"This is textbook Erebus, all right." I sighed. "He sees us. He wants us to move on with the task."

Saskia shuddered. "I've never seen a Child of Chaos in action. I thought they couldn't cross over to this world by themselves."

"Does that scare you?" I replied. *It should.*

Her expression hardened. "No, it doesn't scare me. When you've seen screaming ghosts and crypt ghouls since you were four years old, it takes a lot more than a flock of frozen birds to get creeped out."

"He has people working for him—magicals—all over the world. One of them is probably doing this for him."

I wondered if it was the same person who seemed to be

following us. If that was the case, then perhaps they'd buzz off once they'd finished the bird origami.

"If he knows you're involved, you're putting yourself in his line of fire. I'm trying to keep you out of that," I warned Saskia.

"Still not scared, and still not backing down. Erebus conjuring a party trick isn't going to make me go running," she replied. "You need me. I'm the one who can get you a way in, no muss, no fuss. Speaking of which—"

She turned around and put her hand against the chalk lines that Garrett had drawn. Before he could say a word, *she* whispered the *Aperi Si Ostium* spell in his place. The edges sparked, cutting into the solid stone and creating a door.

Where's she taking us?

Saskia seized the door's handle and yanked it open. Stepping through first, she turned back to look at Garrett and me. His shocked face was comedy gold, and I doubted mine looked much better.

"Come on, before these birds start flapping again," she urged.

Garrett and I exchanged a dubious look. "I don't really feel like getting pecked to death," he said after a moment.

"Me neither. Dying as a seagull's pincushion—no, thanks." I walked through the chalk door before I could change my mind. Garrett followed, and the door closed behind him.

Erebus had sent his message, loud and clear. Get on with it. Stop messing around. Take the easier route if it comes along. And that meant giving in to Saskia.

Without the murderous birds to worry about, I glanced at Saskia's chosen destination. My jaw damn near hit the intricately patterned floor, which had been polished to such a shine that I could see my shocked expression when I looked down. Aside from the floor, everything was covered in gold wherever possible. Elegant engravings, hand-cut patterns of gold leaf, and golden sconces adorned the expanse. Gold-and-white domed archways curved overhead, with golden chandeliers dangling from every apex.

Elegant candles flickered from the chandeliers. There were no bulbs—that would've been tacky. Actual candles, rows upon rows upon rows of them, cast their glow on the stunning room. The light intensified as the reflections bounced back, making the place seem like it belonged to another world entirely. A fairytale world of castles and damsels.

With so much gold and white, the black birds carved into the archways stood out. I wasn't quite sure what species they were, but I was sick of anything winged after the seagull incident. The depicted bird looked like a cross between an owl and an eagle. One clutched some kind of shield to its chest.

An owgle? An owlea? An eawl?

French window-doors opened into an equally grand and mesmerizing room. And through the windows, I could see more of the same beauty and obnoxious wealth, splattered throughout like someone had just vomited the contents of Versailles. It was stunning, sure, but this much gold had to have come at a pretty price. And it was *everywhere*. Even the grouting between the tiles was gold.

"Where are we?" Garrett gasped.

"Welcome to the Grand Kremlin Palace," Saskia replied. "Otherwise known as the Moscow Coven."

I'd never felt more intimidated and awestruck at the same time. I didn't even want to take a step, in case my boots smudged the floor and scuffed the sheen.

"Did you mean to bring us here, or did you panic?" I asked. "I've done that a couple times. It's nothing to be ashamed of."

She shot me a withering look. "No, I didn't panic. This is where we're going to start our journey toward the Fountain. You need my help and you need my contacts, and this is where we begin."

"We still hadn't agreed on that." I sighed.

"While you were having your heroic little crisis, I made the decision for you." She glanced at Garrett. "Besides, someone needs to keep this one alive. If I don't, Astrid will hack into every social media account I own and ruin my life. So I'm doing this as much for myself as for the two of you. Astrid told me you have a habit of throwing yourself into dangerous situations."

"You and she have talked about me?" Garrett looked dismayed.

"It's woman code. When you see a girl crying, you eavesdrop in case you need to step in. Astrid was crying, and I was just following female protocol. I thought it was about her dad, and then... it wasn't. Not totally, anyway. So I'm protecting you. She's been through enough without her lover boy winding up dead, too." Saskia paused, and her lips widened in a mischievous smile. "Again."

I stared at Garrett, ready to leap into action if he snapped. Astrid and Alton were touchy subjects for my old buddy. Sometimes I got the feeling he wanted to talk more about his resurrection but he didn't feel like he could. Like the topic was somehow forbidden, because he had gained something from Alton's death.

To my surprise, Garrett's mouth turned up in a grin. A chuckle escaped his throat, deep and genuine and startling.

"Then I pity anyone who gets in your way."

TWENTY-EIGHT

Finch

E very room was more elaborate than the last. The Kremlin had incredible works of art on display, seemingly just for the hell of it. As if, instead of putting up a five-dollar IKEA special, they'd roped in the finest artists just to paint some masterpieces on the walls. No biggie.

All the murals depicted scenes of heroism and war and ancient magic. I didn't know the stories behind those scenes, but viewing them was like walking through a gallery. I had to stand in front of the artwork and pretend I knew what I was doing.

Incredible use of color. And those brushstrokes—sublime. I think the artist must have been feeling... some stuff when they painted this. Somebody needed to pass me a beret so I could complete my bohemian vibe.

"This coven is epic," I whispered in awe.

Saskia chuckled. "Why are you whispering?"

"I feel like the custodian might jump out and shout at me if I don't," I replied, shaking my head.

"Relax. This is home sweet home." She flashed us a smile, one that oozed confidence. This was her territory, and being a Vasilis, she was probably the equivalent of the Homecoming Queen.

"And here I was, thinking you'd grown a soft spot for the SDC." Garrett smiled at Saskia.

She shrugged. "I like it a lot, don't get me wrong, but there's no place like home."

"All right, Dorothy, let's get this show on the road," I said. "Otherwise, I'm going to wind up with an art history degree and a serious headache from staring at all this gold. Do your people not realize there's such a thing as 'too much'?"

Between the filigree and the dancing candlelight, the environment was starting to get a little trippy. Almost like the gold was starting to melt off the walls. But that might have just been my brain, buckling under the pressure of a million thoughts and worries. Erebus's warning had hit home, big time.

"They're not ashamed of their wealth," she replied curtly. "If you've got it, flaunt it. Right?"

"Ah, so this is the root of all your problems?" I chuckled.

Saskia rolled her eyes and led the way to the next room, where the first signs of life emerged. Elegantly dressed people sauntered around us, no one giving us more than a passing glance. They certainly weren't afraid of flaunting their designer gear. The whole place looked like a runway.

One woman was even decked out in a ballgown. You know, just keeping it casual on a Saturday morning. I preferred track pants and a T-shirt; this woman preferred Yves Saint Laurent, or whoever the super-fancy designer was. I only knew about Yves Saint Laurent because Adley used to have a ticket to one of his Paris shows pinned to her wall.

It suddenly occurred to me that I'd never found out where Adley's belongings had gone. I hadn't been around when she'd died, what with Purgatory and everything. I sighed, shaking off a deep pang of sadness. It didn't matter. Presumably everything had gone to LA, with her.

"Saskia?" a voice called out from across the palatial room. It came from a looming, silver-haired guy in a three-piece suit that matched his hair. It wasn't silver in an old person way, not unless he'd been sipping from the Fountain of Youth on the sly. He couldn't have been older than thirty, and his bright blue eyes reminded me of a wolf.

"Dmitri!" Saskia beamed, shifting into flirtation mode.

"Who's that?" I whispered.

"Dmitri Peskov—Physical Magic preceptor," she replied quickly. He stopped in front of us. "Long time, no see. You're looking good! New workout regime?" she gushed. He replied in Russian. Garrett and I stared at him like clueless idiots. There was something about the Russian language that always sounded angry. I didn't know if he was telling her he'd bench-pressed two hundred pounds, or if he was yelling at her for suggesting he wasn't always at the peak of his physical prowess.

"I hate to ask, Dmitri, but could you speak English? My friends here don't understand Russian, and I'd hate for them to think we were sharing secrets." She cast him a wink, and he burst into laughter.

"Of course, though I do loathe speaking it. I have such trouble with the English tongue, and I always feel as though I am making an utter fool of myself." Dmitri gave Garrett and me a quick bow.

"Are you serious?" Garrett gaped. "You speak English better than I do!"

"That's because you're American," Saskia shot back.

"If I make any mistakes, please correct me. It's the only way I'll learn," Dmitri replied. His voice revealed a faint accent, but it was hardly noticeable. To be honest, I didn't know if this dude was pulling our legs or if he really thought he sucked at English.

"And who are your friends?" He looked from Garrett to me inquisitively.

"Finch Merlin." I stuck my hand out. His grip almost tore my fingers off as he jolted my hand up and down.

"And Garrett Kyteler." Garrett avoided the handshake, giving a polite nod instead.

Good choice. Krieger would have to give my digits physiotherapy after this.

"Sorry we don't speak Russian," I blurted out.

Dmitri smiled. "It is a difficult language to learn. Don't worry. I'm sure we can all manage well enough with English." He turned back to Saskia. "What brings you back here? I thought you were on an exchange program in San Diego. Is this a reverse cultural switch —you show your friends your home, after they have shown you theirs?"

Saskia nodded. "Sort of, yeah. Think of it as a field trip."

"Excellent. We see so few Americans here in Moscow. It's almost as if they do not trust us." He grinned at Garrett and me. "You should not always listen to propaganda. Moscow, and Russia, have a great deal to offer."

Like the Fountain of Youth, for one. Russia's best-kept secret. So secret that apparently no Russians knew of it.

"I've always wanted to visit," Garrett said. "When I was younger, I wanted to spend a summer traveling around Europe and work my way east, but it never happened."

"Oh? Why not?" Dmitri seemed genuinely interested. I was, too. I'd never known that about Garrett. This whole mission was turning out to be a learning experience.

Garrett shrugged. "Life got in the way. You know, you finish school, you get pressure from your parents to start college or get a job. Then, summer passes and you end up doing something else, like an internship in Los Angeles."

I noted the hint of regret in his voice when he touched on his parents. His mom ran the San Francisco Coven, his dad was on the Texas Mage Council, and they'd each spoiled him in their bid to be the better parent. He'd gotten away with a lot because of his parents' divorce. But their high positions put pressure on their son. They'd always expected him to do well, which was probably why he'd rebelled in the first place. Some of us hadn't forgotten why he'd come to the SDC. He'd caused problems in San Fran and been shipped to San Diego until the dust settled. Although, that had clearly become permanent. It made me realize that, although we were friends, there was a lot I didn't know about Garrett. He'd had a wealthy, high-class upbringing: good schools, good grades, sports trophies, magical achievements, the works. And then it had all been torn away, because of a prank gone wrong in San Francisco. I knew when someone was lashing out, and I would've bet my life that was why Garrett had done it. I'd teased him about it often enough. San Francisco was pretty laid back, so he had to have done something pretty damning to get kicked out. But I didn't know what made him tick now, or even when we'd first met. Our conversations had never gotten that deep.

What were his passions? What had he wanted to be? It wasn't stuff guys tended to ask, and I felt bad about that. I wasn't saying his parents were on Katherine Shipton's level, but maybe he'd bowed to their parental pressure all the same, trying to be a good son. And failed miserably when it became too much. Weren't we all just trying to make our parents proud, one way or another?

"That is a very real shame," Dmitri said, regarding Garrett warmly. "I hope that spending a short time here may make up for some of those missed opportunities. And there are always open internships here, if you ever felt like making a lengthier stay."

"That's good to know." Garrett smiled.

"Where were you off to?" Dmitri turned toward Saskia. "It's

strange seeing you in such ordinary clothes. I hope your time in America hasn't dulled your divine sense of style."

Saskia laughed. "It's laundry day."

"Ah, that makes sense. Though you are all dressed *very* alike. Is it laundry day for all of you?" He eyed us curiously.

"This is how we dress at the SDC," I replied, trying to cover our asses. We did look like we were wearing some kind of undercover uniform, with all of us in black. "Saskia usually stands out, but we're becoming a bad influence."

Dmitri frowned. "I do hope not. It would be like clipping the wings of a bird of paradise."

"Don't worry. Next time you see me, I'll be back to my usual self," Saskia assured him. "We were just on our way to visit Maksim."

"He'll be pleased to see you," Dmitri replied, nodding. "I won't distract you any longer, as I'm sure you have a lot to do and not a lot of time in which to do it. It was a pleasure seeing you back here. Don't be gone too long, will you? There is already uproar about your sister—I should hate to see you dragged through the same mud."

Saskia smiled sadly, no doubt thinking about her sister's issues. "I'll be back soon enough."

"Send my love to Tatyana when you see her, won't you? I know the old folks are angry, but the rest of us miss her."

"I will." A hint of bitterness lingered in Saskia's words. I guessed she had probably lived in Tatyana's shadow for most of her life. Being an only child for most of *my* life, I'd missed most of the competitive sibling rivalry stuff. But I'd been compared to Harley enough to know that it had to sting Saskia, having her spotlight taken away by her sister's legacy.

After a quick farewell, we followed Saskia through the Moscow Coven, moving from golden room to golden room. As we headed farther back into the headquarters, the grandeur ebbed. Not much, but things started to look more normal.

"Who's Maksim?" I asked, breaking the silence.

Saskia glanced back at me. "Think of him as a male, magical version of Astrid."

Garrett stiffened. "Good with computers?"

"*Very* good."

Saskia didn't say anything else as she led us through the labyrinth. She was clearly stewing, but I figured the walk would clear her head. Plus, it gave me a chance to stare at all the pretty sights. This coven was quickly becoming one of my favorites, aesthetics-wise. Although, I pitied the person who had to light all the candles every day.

We reached a wide, arched corridor about ten minutes later. A frieze of magicals in mid-battle had been painted across the ceiling. Saskia stopped in front of a mahogany door with a brass knocker in the shape of a bird's head. She rapped on it once and waited.

"*Voyti*," a voice replied. I guessed that meant "come in," since that's exactly what Saskia did.

Stepping into the room was like entering a CIA hub. All around us, monitors blinked and videos streamed, while numbers tumbled down computer screens. A lone techie sat in a plush office chair. He was younger than I'd expected, with a long mane of dark hair and a set of strange amber eyes that reminded me of Tobe's.

He wore thick specs pushed to the bridge of a pointy nose and had dark circles under his eyes that suggested he was a night owl. The usual requirements for a technological genius. The black turtleneck and high-waisted jeans completed the look.

"*Saskia, kakoye udoyol'stvye videt' tebya snova!*" His face lit up, an effect which changed his features completely.

"*Maksim, prostite za vopros. Ty budesh' govorit' po angliyski? Moi druz'ya amerikantsy,*" Saskia replied, with a cursory look at Garrett and me. I understood the word "American," which was pretty much all I needed to know.

Maksim looked at us disapprovingly. *"Razve ty ne uchil ikh russkomu yazyku?"*

Saskia chuckled. *"Tam ne khvatayet vremeni v den'. Dazhe yesli by u menya byla tselaya zhizn', eto ne pomoglo by."*

"You want to translate for us?" I whispered. I had a feeling they were having some fun at our expense.

"He asked if I'd taught you Russian. I said there's not enough time in the day—even if I had a lifetime, it wouldn't help." She grinned, amused with herself.

"She has a point." Garrett smirked.

"My English is not so good. Forgive. Is what you get, if asks to speak in a language I don't know well." Maksim shrugged. "At least I know some. Is more than can say for you."

Easy, tiger. "Sorry about that." I forced a smile. This guy wasn't nearly as welcoming as Dmitri.

"What you want?" Maksim looked at Saskia.

"Can you open up a line to Astrid Hepler-Waterhouse at the SDC?" she replied.

He nodded. "You think I am child? Is easy."

He tapped a few buttons on his ergonomic keyboard. A moment later, a window opened, and a camera emblem appeared. It rang for a couple of seconds before the stream connected and Astrid's face peered at us. To my surprise, she wasn't alone. Ryann sat beside her.

Relief overwhelmed me. Man, was it good to see her in the flesh, unharmed.

"Ryann? You're okay!?" I darted forward and leaned over Maksim's shoulder to get a better look. I had so much I wanted to ask, but I was very aware of the nerdy Russian in front of me. "Hey, would you mind giving us a moment, Maksim?"

He snorted. "No. Is my office. I don't leave."

"We could really do with some privacy," I urged.

"Is not my problem. Is my office. I stay, you stay. I go, you go." Stubbornness must be in the water here.

Saskia put her hand on my shoulder. "It's fine if Maksim stays. He's trustworthy."

"You hear that, American? I am trustworthy." Maksim beamed.

Ryann looked nervous. "It's okay to speak?"

Saskia nodded. "Knock yourself out."

Ryann focused on me. "Okay," I grumbled.

"I'm fine," she said, after a pause. "But you left a pretty huge mess back there."

"Did you get interviewed?" I pressed.

"They talked to me when they realized my keycard was used to get into the artifact room, but they bought my explanation that someone must have pick-pocketed me. I made sure I was nowhere near the study, and I told them I didn't see anything. I was too busy getting a drunken teenager into a cab with her chaperones." She flashed a wink at Saskia. "I also took out my earpiece in case they checked me over. So I'm sort of in the dark about what happened after Saskia went to you."

"Do they think we're involved?" Garrett appeared at the other side of Maksim's chair.

"In the Ivan Trap going missing?" Ryann asked.

Garrett shook his head. "No, in Davin's death. And, yeah, I suppose the Ivan Trap business, too."

"Davin's death?" She sounded puzzled.

Astrid nodded. "The guys told me they'd killed him. I thought you knew."

"Davin isn't dead," Ryann insisted. "He was part of some performance, apparently, though there was a lot of confusion about that. Security tried to speak to him, but he took off before they could do a proper interview. I only caught a glimpse, but he seemed spooked. Davin *didn't* get away with the Trap, right?"

"No, he didn't," Garrett said.

My gremlins started to clamor again. That weird feeling I'd had back in Havana, of being followed. The shadows in the corner of my eye. The footsteps without a figure attached. If Davin wasn't dead and had gotten out of LA not long after we did, that meant he was on the prowl.

What did I need to do to bury that smarmy git and keep him there? The fact that he was alive burned in my chest like a white-hot knife, but getting angry wasn't going to make him any deader.

"Are you okay?" Astrid was staring at Garrett. "When you didn't check in, we started to worry. We haven't gone to bed yet."

"What time is it there?" I asked.

"Nearly three in the morning," Ryann replied. "Where are you?"

"Yeah, why is the call coming from Moscow?" Astrid added.

"Moscow?" Ryann turned to Astrid in shock.

"Yes, Moscow." Saskia popped up and gestured to Maksim. "And this is my good friend, Maksim Volanski."

"Nice to meet you," Ryann replied.

Astrid nodded. "Likewise."

"Is pleasure to meet you." Maksim smiled. "Is beautiful girls. Very nice. Very beautiful. I think American women not lovely. I am wrong. America is keeping secrets of lovely girls."

Ryann chuckled. "Thank you."

Eh, less of that. "Don't you want to know what happened?" I reeked of desperation, but I didn't care.

"Obviously," Ryann replied with a smirk. "We've been going out of our minds. I only heard snippets, but it was mostly running and applause, which was odd."

"Well, we had a fight with Davin that ended with us guillotining him. We thought he was dead, but apparently he's up to his old tricks." Venom dripped from my mouth. "He just won't stay dead. It's infuriating!" It was a lot more than that, but I didn't want to swear, even though those words were teetering on the edge of my tongue. "Anyway, we took the Trap and went to face our spooky friend."

"How did it go?" Astrid asked.

I kept it vague, with Maksim listening. "Everything went smoothly. We got what we needed, and now we're here. I'm not quite sure why, but Saskia seems to have a plan."

"If you could cover for us while we're gone, that'd be swell," Saskia chimed in.

Ryann's expression changed. No more giggly Miss Nice. "This wasn't part of the plan, Finch."

In all fairness, you didn't know the whole plan...

I couldn't say that. "No, but plans change. And this is where we have to be. I know it's not ideal, and we wouldn't ask you to cover if it wasn't important, but trust us—we're getting there."

Ryann shook her head. "You can't keep hopping around like this, just the three of you. Come on, this has to be enough now. Bring Harley and the Rag Team in, before you get into trouble. They can help you."

I was about to answer diplomatically when Saskia cut in. And she definitely wasn't feeling diplomatic.

"Or, you know, you could just trust that the three of us know what we're doing. Have a little faith in Finch and Garrett, maybe? This isn't their first rodeo. Everyone seems to forget that Finch was the one who killed *Katherine Shipton*. It's not like he needs his hand held, so how about *you* help him, and cover for us, and let us get on with it."

Ryann looked startled. "What about your sister? She's not stupid. Do you think you can just disappear, and she won't notice?

The same goes for Garrett and Finch. People notice when they're not around."

People? I couldn't take my eyes off her. She was trying not to look at me.

"Don't bring my sister into this," Saskia snapped. "I can make something up if she calls. I'm home, after all. She's got nothing to worry about. Besides, none of that matters right now. I'm actually doing what I can to help Finch, which is what you should be doing instead of getting in his way and making things more difficult."

Maksim gazed at Saskia adoringly. He was clearly head over heels for her. That was useful for us, as it meant he wouldn't go yapping about what he'd heard today. And, to be fair, this bold display made me look at Saskia in a slightly different light. Not a romantic one—*geez, no*—but I hadn't expected her to stand up for us this way.

She was like a protective little sister, or a feisty chihuahua who'd nip at the heels of anyone who tried to stop us. Somehow, she'd become one of us, and she definitely wasn't mincing her words.

"I just don't want to see anyone get hurt," Ryann said after a brief, shocked pause.

"Then keep quiet," Saskia retorted. "If you know even a shred of why Finch is doing this, which I'm guessing you do, then you know why it has to stay secret. More people will be in danger if they know. So, do them, and us, a favor, and hide where we are and what we're doing."

"Are you sure that's a good idea?" Astrid peered through the camera at Garrett.

He smiled reassuringly. "We've got everything in order, and we're armed. I promised you I'd come back, and I meant it. I know you're both worried, but this is something we need to do—alone."

Astrid frowned. "I don't like it... but I suppose we don't have much choice. Promise me you'll get in touch as soon as you finish? Neither of us will be getting much sleep until it's over, so keep us in the loop as much as you can."

"And you'll keep your mouths shut if we do?" Saskia interjected.

Astrid's frown deepened. "Yes, we will."

"Then we'll drop you a line when it's done," Saskia replied. Apparently she was our new, savage mouthpiece.

"Be careful." Ryann looked at me.

"We will." I looked back, trying not to show how much I adored her. "But we should be going now, if we want to get this task completed sometime in the next millennium."

She nodded slowly. "Okay."

"Hope to see you all soon—"

I was about to say more when Saskia leaned forward and pressed the button to end the call. The screen blinked off, leaving a black mirror reflecting our faces back.

"I didn't get to say goodbye," Garrett protested.

Saskia shrugged. "You can say hello instead when we're finished." She turned to us. "I hope you both packed your big-boy boots, because we've got places to go, and it's going to be rough."

"Sorry, I must've forgotten my pick-axe." I kept staring at the screen. "I guess this means we're hi-ho-ing our way out of here?"

Saskia arched an eyebrow. "No idea what that's supposed to mean, but yeah, we should move ASAP."

"You're starting to sound like O'Halloran," Garrett said.

Saskia chuckled. "Good. Every group should have a leader."

"You think that's you?" She had gumption, this one. *Great word.* I thanked my brain for bringing it back into my vocabulary.

"You think it isn't?" she shot back, grinning.

"Are you going somewhere dangerous?" Maksim looked up at her.

She shrugged. "No more dangerous than usual."

"Be safe, *malen'kiy solovey.*" He stared down into his lap, like he'd just said something cringey. Saskia didn't seem to mind. She basked in it.

"You know me, Maksim. I'm always safe."

"You call me if needs help. If is problem, I fix it," he replied, looking up at her earnestly.

"I will, Maksim. Thank you." She leaned over and kissed his cheek. He turned bright red. I had to hand it to her—her flirtations might not have gotten her too far at the SDC, but they worked like a charm here. Maksim was putty in her hands.

Now that we'd checked in with Ryann and Astrid, there was only one thing left to do: head to the Jubilee mine and find this friggin' Fountain before Erebus's patience wore too thin.

We were getting closer. I could almost taste it. Not that I planned on sipping from the fount. Everything supernatural and powerful in this world came with a hefty price tag, and I could only imagine what the cost of immortality would be. Likely more than I was willing to pay.

I didn't even want immortality. I just wanted freedom. And if I could pull through this intact, freedom would be mine. After this, Erebus would give me what I desired most. He'd sworn it.

Once this was done, I could actually start thinking about building a life for myself. A real one, with no deal hanging over me and nobody threatening the people I cared about. I would finally find some peace in this messed-up, chaotic world.

I'd been merely existing for far too long. Soon, it would be time to start living. And I couldn't wait.

TWENTY-NINE

Garrett

We had decided to travel the human way, since our destination was close. Sitting in the back of a cab, I watched the city of Moscow flash past in a blur. Beautiful red-and-white architecture stood beside towering glass skyscrapers, the ugly grays of the blocky Soviet buildings blended in between. The mix of styles gave a fairly clear picture of the strata of the city's history—the modern, the old, and the important moments in time that had built this city.

I'd assumed we were going straight to the Jubilee mine. Instead, we were heading to the outskirts of Moscow to make a last-minute stop at the Vasilis house.

"Tell me again, why are we going to see your parents?" I gazed out of the window.

Saskia seemed anxious. "If they find out I was here and didn't go to see them, there'll be trouble. You can bet someone in the Moscow Coven will say something to them. Plus, we need access to the mine, and my parents are the ones who can get in."

"You don't think they'll find it suspicious when you turn up with two handsome devils on your arm?" Finch leveled his gaze at her. "Last I heard, they weren't particularly fond of us SDC types. Aren't we keeping your sister hostage?"

"They like you," Saskia replied. "You saved the magical world. Even if they didn't, they'd still welcome you into their house with open arms. You get a free pass, after killing Katherine."

"Ah, the perks," he said sarcastically.

I knew he was still having trouble with the fact that he'd killed his mother. He didn't regret it, no way, but matricide was a big thing to deal with. And those issues in his head could get overwhelming sometimes, even if he tried to hide them.

I could see the cogs in his mind whirring—it was written all over his face. It had to be loud in there. I didn't envy him that.

Half an hour later, after traveling most of the way in a semi-comfortable silence, the cab pulled up outside two enormous black gates. Black birds perched on the stone pillars at either side—the same black birds from the Moscow Coven, part of the Russian coat of arms. The black, double-headed eagle was, if my memory of Russian history served, a lingering relic from the empire.

The cab driver rolled down his window and spoke into the intercom by the gates. "Miss Vasilis *zdes'*."

A moment later, the gates opened, and my jaw hit the floor. A long driveway cut through an entire estate of manicured grounds and distant greenery, bordered by a dense forest. Uniform trees lined the drive, standing like dutiful guards all the way up to an enormous mansion. It had been built in the same white stone as the main body of the Grand Kremlin Palace, with similar architecture —very grand, very old, and very impressive.

I was in awe. The place looked like something out of a period piece, with the windows shining in the bright afternoon light. My body clock was in a state of confusion, since Moscow was ten hours ahead of San Diego. It should've been the middle of the night, but the sun was shining. And I had no idea when we'd actually get to sleep.

"*This* is your house?" Finch gaped.

"What were you expecting?" Saskia replied casually.

"I knew you guys were rich, but damn... you must be loaded!" I exclaimed. I'd thought the mansions in Beverly Hills were incredible, but they had nothing on this. This estate oozed old money. No nouveau-riche bourgeoisie here. This was the type of property that was inherited, not purchased.

The cab came to a stop in front of the house's grand entrance. A set of marble steps led to a sheltered archway where more birds perched, forever set in stone. Saskia paid the driver and got out first. Finch and I followed her onto the gravel. I felt very underdressed.

As she headed up the steps, she stopped and turned back after us. Finch and I hadn't moved, staring up at the house in disbelief.

"Are you coming or are you going to keep standing there, catching flies?"

"We're coming," I replied, heading after her. She didn't even bother to knock—she just turned the handle and stepped inside. For people so filthy rich, it surprised me that they wouldn't bother to lock their doors. They must have had more security than Fort Knox.

"Mama, Papa?" Saskia called.

We stepped into a cavernous entrance hall, where a winding staircase led to the upper floors. Following the pattern of the Moscow Coven, there was a lot of white and gold to take in. Oil portraits of the Vasilis clan adorned the walls. Statues and vases dotted the hall, all of which probably cost more than I'd ever make in my life. Velvet chaises sprawled along the borders, and the floor was polished white marble with veins of gold.

"Saskia?" Mrs. Vasilis appeared on the balcony. Her eyes

widened as she saw Finch and me. "What an unexpected surprise!" Seeing us, she evidently figured it would be easier if she spoke English. Something I appreciated.

"*Kto tam?*" Mr. Vasilis emerged from a corridor upstairs.

"It's Saskia, and she's brought two friends with her." Mrs. Vasilis nodded to us.

Mr. Vasilis peered down. "Finch, is that you?"

"Hello, Mr. Vasilis," he replied awkwardly. "It's been a while, huh?"

"Much too long!" he cried. "And Garrett, too."

It had been a year, in fact. Neither I nor Finch had seen the pair since the final showdown with Katherine and the subsequent testimonies the couple had given in Finch's favor. They'd returned to Moscow, and we hadn't heard anything from them. I realized now that it probably had something to do with Tatyana's grandparents being so adamant about her returning to Russia. She was likely doing her best to avoid the entire situation.

"What brings you here?" Mrs. Vasilis looked to her daughter inquisitively.

"A cultural exchange," Saskia replied without missing a beat. "We're on an exploratory field trip to see the Jubilee mine, but we can talk about that later. What's for lunch? Do you have enough for a few extra mouths?"

Mr. Vasilis smiled. "There's always too much, and we'd be happy to have you all dine with us. I hope you're hungry. Cook has been working away all morning, and I've heard whisperings that it's going to be a huge roast."

On cue, my stomach growled. "Roast sounds great."

An hour and three courses later, with no sign of the food stopping, we were seated around the table in the Vasilises' ornate dining room. It felt weird to see Saskia and her parents acting so casual in a room that had gold cherubs playing harps in every corner and four chandeliers dangling down, illuminating a tapestry of more gold and a whole wall of mirrors. But this was their home, and they were comfortable here, amongst their insane wealth.

"And how is everything going at the SDC?" Mr. Vasilis dabbed the corner of his mouth with a napkin. "I imagine it's more peaceful, with Katherine gone?"

Finch snorted into his glass. "I wouldn't say that, exactly."

"Oh?" Mr. Vasilis frowned.

"Things always crop up, don't they?" Finch recovered quickly. "We're pretty busy."

"I was surprised you weren't promoted, Finch," Mrs. Vasilis interjected. "If you were part of a Russian coven, you would be a director by now, after everything you did. I suppose things are different in America."

Finch shook his head. "I wouldn't want to be a director. Too much work."

"I like your honesty!" Mr. Vasilis grinned. "That's why I have my lovely wife. She's the brains, and I just do what I'm told."

Mrs. Vasilis gave him a gentle shove in the arm. "That is not true!"

"Ah, you know it is, you just won't admit it." He chuckled as he set down his napkin and patted his stomach.

"Have you been working in LA much, Garrett?" Mrs. Vasilis asked.

I shook my head. "Not really. I get called there occasionally, but not as much as before."

"And has Saskia been behaving herself?" Mr. Vasilis cut in.

"She's doing well," I replied. "She's fitting right in."

Mr. and Mrs. Vasilis exchanged a worried look. "But you still intend to come home after six months, don't you?" the latter asked quickly.

I could only imagine her concern. Having one AWOL daughter was one thing, but two? It seemed parental influence didn't just affect the young. I didn't know which side of the family was piling on the pressure to bring Tatyana back, but there was a definite air of worry, more from Mrs. Vasilis than her husband.

Saskia nodded. "Yes. Don't freak out."

"What about Taty?" Mr. Vasilis chuckled. "Is she still dragging her heels?"

"She's about as American as these guys now," Saskia replied, with a hint of sass. I couldn't tell if she was just winding up her parents.

"Don't let your grandparents hear you say that. They'll vow vengeance on all of America." He grinned, but Mrs. Vasilis looked less than amused.

"Don't say that!" she scolded. "It's very serious."

"No, it's not. It's your mother and father throwing their weight around. The minute they see Taty again, they'll forget every nasty thing they've said. They aren't really going to renounce her." Mr. Vasilis put his hand on his wife's, a small gesture that made me smile.

"That's because you don't know them like I do." Mrs. Vasilis sighed. "They think I've lost my mind, sending Saskia too."

"Our two little escapees," Mr. Vasilis teased.

It was becoming obvious to me that Saskia took after her dad—mischievous and sometimes blunt. Meanwhile, Tatyana was definitely more like her mother—aloof, but quite nice once you got to know her. Mr. and Mrs. Vasilis clearly cared very much about their daughters. I imagined they'd have been happy to let their girls do whatever they pleased if they weren't being hassled by external influences.

"Perhaps I should let you answer one of my mother's calls, and then you won't be laughing so much." Mrs. Vasilis gave her husband a stern look.

"Anything but that!" he replied, laughing more.

"It's a good thing I love you." Mrs. Vasilis sighed again.

"Oh yes, it is a very good thing you love me; otherwise, I'd be a very sad and lonely man," he said, lifting her hand and kissing it.

"Can you not?" Saskia rolled her eyes, but she fought a smile.

"Well then, if I can't even kiss my own wife, perhaps we should discuss why you're here." Mr. Vasilis smiled. "What's this cultural exchange you were talking about?"

Saskia glanced at Finch and me. "We're doing an exploratory investigation into the Jubilee mine. Garrett has an interest in geology, and he wants to see the purity of the diamonds there. So I was hoping you could speak to my uncle, Mama, and see if he can get us access to the mine tomorrow?"

Saskia really knew how to exploit her relatives. I wasn't complaining. So far, it had gotten us everything we needed. I didn't know if I could convincingly feign interest in geology, though.

Mrs. Vasilis paused for a moment. "I suppose I could. I don't see why he'd object—you've always been his favorite, able to twist him around your little finger." She clamped her hand over her mouth. "Don't tell Taty I said that. It's not right to have favorites."

"She won't care. She doesn't like Uncle Anatoly, anyway. She thinks he's corrupt."

Mr. Vasilis snorted. "Well, she's not wrong."

"That's my brother you are talking about!" Mrs. Vasilis nudged him again.

"Am I wrong?" he replied.

"No, but he is family. And we speak kindly of family." She flashed him a smile. "Even if they are a little crooked."

"So, you'll ask him?" Saskia pressed, without seeming desperate.

Mrs. Vasilis nodded. "I will, once we've worked our way through dessert."

"Out of curiosity, how many courses do we have left to go?" Finch looked a little green.

"Four," Mr. Vasilis replied. "Welcome to Russian hospitality. Your metabolism will never be the same."

"That's what I was worried about." Finch sighed. I saw him discreetly undo the top button of his jeans.

Stifling a laugh, I focused on the task at hand. If everything went smoothly and Mrs. Vasilis got her brother's permission, we'd be on our way to the Jubilee mine tomorrow. We were all set for the last part of our mission, and, frankly, it couldn't come quickly enough.

THIRTY

Finch

After enduring a second six-course smorgasbord for dinner, courtesy of the Vasilis family, I stepped outside to try and walk some of my arteries back into fully functioning blood pipes. All I really wanted to do was curl up on a plush chaise and stay there until my tummy deflated. But I was terrified there might be another secret course. I wouldn't survive it.

I pulled the collar of Mr. Vasilis's coat closer to my chin. It might've been summertime, but there was a definite nip in the air, and it was having a good old nibble on my cheeks as I stood on the back terrace, gazing at the vast gardens.

"Gardens" was a bit of an understatement. This was like a national park masquerading as an estate. In the distance, I saw deer grazing in the clear moonlight. Ordinary, run-of-the-mill deer—none of those brightly colored, glowing creatures that Gaia had created in Mexico. I often wondered how those animals were doing. If any scientists happened upon one, they'd wet their pants with excitement.

Despite the chill, it was stunning outside. Moscow had a cool, ancient vibe that I was really starting to like. It brimmed with history. Not all of it good, of course, but what country had a perfect track record?

I shoved my hands into the pockets of the woolen trench coat and took off across the lawn, headed for the walled garden nearby. I'd heard the telltale trickle of water and wanted to investigate. As I entered the garden, I saw a massive stone bird in the center, spewing crystalline water from its mouth. It arched down into a pool below, where strange charms had been embedded into the marble mosaic beneath. Gold... of course.

The charms were sigils associated with the Kolduny—symbols of life and death, resurrection and protection. Not my forte, but they were familiar enough.

I ambled to the edge of the walled garden, where a wooden bench looked out toward the forest. Groaning from the heft of the food in my stomach, I sank down and tried to relax. I didn't relax easily, I never had, but the atmosphere was so peaceful and beautiful that I hoped my mind might cut me some slack, just this once.

I was settling into it, drawing the cool, crisp air into my lungs, when something darted across my peripheral vision. My head whipped around, but nothing was there. Just fluttering roses and the rustle of leaves. Out of the corner of my eye, I saw another shadow shoot across the lawn. My head snapped toward the distant forest like an anxious guard dog. In the gloom between the trees, something moved. My heart stopped, and it wasn't because of the huge quantities of ice cream and cake I'd eaten at dinner.

Davin wasn't dead. And he'd gotten away before security could catch him. How he'd resurrected himself without my mother's help, I had no idea. But the facts spoke for themselves. It made me want to scream at the top of my lungs. Still, I'd keep killing him until that colossal waste of skin stayed the hell down. There had to be a way.

I reached beneath my borrowed trench coat and closed my fingers around the handle of Carnwennan. I had tucked it into my belt.

Dread coursed through me as I waited for the shadow to move again. But it seemed to have vanished, which was infinitely worse.

I tightened my grip on Carnwennan. I didn't know if a magical weapon would have more effect on Davin than a guillotine. Maybe it would be enough to keep him dead next time. If it could slash a dark witch in two, it could certainly make a mess of him.

A deafening crack sliced through the air behind me. I ducked on instinct, thinking it was a gunshot. Staying low, I turned around and peered through the slats of the bench. But there was no shooter, and no smoking gun. Instead, one of the mansion's windows had splintered. The silvery lines shone like a spiderweb as they caught the moon's glow.

Shaking violently, I dragged myself to my feet and walked over to investigate. There, in the center of the splinters, a bloody hand-print dripped. I reached out and found that the blood was on the inside.

I shuddered. *I hope you're going to pay for that window, Erebus.* I guessed those darting shadows had been nothing more than one of my evil overlord's minions and my overactive gremlins, conspiring together to freak me out... and leave another grim message, summoning me to him.

Heaving a nervous sigh, I placed my hand over Erebus's ruby signet ring and whispered the spell that would take me to Tartarus. I understood what the bloody handprint meant. I was being summoned. Why? I had no clue. Clearly, I was working on his task, and him interrupting me wasn't doing either of us any good. But my master had called, and I had to go running or risk his wrath.

I shouldn't have eaten so much. Trying to sprint through a horde of Purge beasts with my stomach swollen and a ton of dairy in my veins wouldn't be easy. I was already bracing for the stitch.

Damn your delicious pirozhki, Mrs. Vasilis.

My body twisted through the modified portal, and I landed in the hissing, snapping, slavering darkness of Erebus's otherworld. I gave in to second nature and lit up a ball of Fire, using it to guide me through the pitch black as I took off, racing for my life. Glinting eyes and razor-sharp jaws flashed in the gloom as I ran, following the faint path to the Sisyphean mountain where I'd find my boss.

The beasts were getting bolder—several tried to block my route. With one hand holding the flaming ball, I shot out barrages of Telekinesis to keep the creatures at bay, flinging them back into the shadows when they lunged for me.

My lungs were ready to burst as I neared the base of the mountain, my ribs trying to accommodate both oxygen and indigestion. But I didn't stop. I couldn't, with these savage beasts closing in with every step I took.

This might be one of the last times I have to do this.

I focused on that as I sprinted the last few yards to the mountain. Once I found the Fountain, I wouldn't be Erebus's whipping boy anymore. He'd have to get his kicks elsewhere instead of watching me run this gauntlet.

As soon as I crossed the invisible threshold between the flat terrain and the mountain, the Purge beasts backed off. I could still see their eyes flashing and hear their grumpy snarls and growls, irritated that their prey had managed to get away. Again. With the risk of getting chomped minimized, I skidded to a halt and stooped to catch my breath.

After a few moments, I sighed and looked up toward the summit. Gripping my ribs and mopping my brow with the back of my arm, I continued up the incline at a slower pace. Erebus might've summoned me, but that didn't mean I had to run the whole way. He could wait.

A short while later, I reached the spotlighted ruins. Erebus was lounging about in his usual state, draping his wispy self against the pillars. This time, I had no patience for niceties. Him splintering a window and smearing a bloody handprint on the glass hadn't put me in a friendly mood.

"What's with the creepy message, Erebus?" I launched right in. "Can't you see that I'm a little busy right now, running around like a headless chicken for *you*, in case you'd forgotten? I know the Fountain shebang is urgent. I'm on it, for Pete's sake! I couldn't be more on it unless I was drenched in the water itself! I got the location; we just have to check it out, so you really need to chill your beans."

Erebus swept forward. All his wisps were churning violently, with little threads spiking into the air. I didn't know if I was reading too much into it, but he seemed... nervous. Even his movements were jerky, instead of the usual smooth flow he prided himself on.

"Seriously, what the hell's got you so impatient?" I tried a calmer angle, as his nerves were ramping up mine.

"You're being followed, Finch," Erebus replied in a serious tone. "This shouldn't be happening. Who have you told about what you're doing?"

"Like, two people, and they don't even know the full story. Plus, they're working *with* me, so they're not following me."

Erebus drifted back to the pillars, clearly agitated. "There is a fierce energy pursuing you. I don't know if it's Lux, or someone else, and it has me gravely concerned."

"Look, I *know* I'm being followed. I noticed something wasn't quite right after we got the Ivan Trap," I told him. "I'm keeping an eye on it, and we're armed, so we can defend ourselves. But can you see who's doing the following?" I had my suspicions, obviously, but I hoped Erebus might be able to clarify.

"No, I can't pinpoint them. I have tried, but they keep evading my gaze. It is almost as if they are cloaking themselves. That is what has me so concerned—it is not often I happen upon someone who can avoid my ever-watchful eyes."

"I think it might be Davin Doncaster. He was at this party that we were at, the one where we got the Ivan Trap. I'm guessing you know all this, with your ever-watchful eyes?" I paused, and he nodded. "We thought we'd killed Davin, but he's got this sneaky way of not staying dead. He managed to get away, and nobody knows where he is, so it's likely he's the one on our tail. Are you sure you can't see him?"

Erebus grumbled. "As I have said, they are cloaked from my gaze."

I frowned. "Say it is Davin—that means he's looking for the Fountain of Youth, too."

"If the Necromancer is the one following you, then you must dispense with him," Erebus said, after a pause. "It can be done, I assure you."

"How? We've tried everything, including chopping his head off."

Erebus gave a hollow chuckle. "You must destroy the object to which Davin has bound his life. If it is powerful enough to continue resurrecting him, then it must have taken a vast amount of Dark magic to create."

"An object? What kind of object?"

"I do not know. But, if he is this malevolent presence, you must find it and destroy it. He can't be allowed to follow you to the Fountain."

"You think I don't know that?" I shot back.

Erebus's wisps spiked outward before settling back down. "Davin isn't your only problem."

I dug my fingernails into my palms. "Why, what else do we have to worry about? Is the sky falling? Is the Fountain really a massive monster we're going to have to pound into the ground? Am I going to self-destruct in ten minutes?"

"No, it is far worse than that." Erebus hovered anxiously. "Lux might suspect something."

"Well, she didn't hear it from me!"

"I know," he replied quietly. "I can't be sure what she knows, but I have known her long enough to tell when something is amiss. She is acting strangely, and that leads me to believe she is suspicious of what I'm doing."

What you're doing? Pfft, don't make me laugh. Erebus hadn't lifted a wispy finger.

"Why is that my problem?" I eyed him coldly. "Why are you so worried about your wife finding out? Aren't married people supposed to share everything?"

"Spoken like a single man." He chuckled stiffly.

"I'm serious, why is that a problem?" I pressed. I wanted answers.

Erebus flicked his smoky wrist. "Just know that it *is* a problem and behave accordingly if she confronts you. Be wary. Get this job done as quickly as possible, or I can't promise something awful won't happen to Ryann Smith."

A shiver of dread shot up my spine. "What did you just say?"

"I might not be able to see who's pursuing you, but I see everything else. I've noticed your feelings for that human girl. Silly of you, to flaunt it so obviously." Erebus edged closer. "You'll get to see just how vulnerable these humans are if you don't complete this job within the next few days—*before* anyone catches up to you."

I knew this would happen. I'd tried so hard to keep Ryann out of it, and for what? Erebus had seen it anyway and backed me into a corner, using her as his cattle-prod. I'd tried to protect her, and I'd failed.

It twisted me up inside and reminded me of all my former failings, all the people I hadn't been able to save. This wasn't a savior complex; it was a failure complex.

Katherine had always told me I was useless, that all I'd do was disappoint, no matter what I did. I couldn't have cared less about disappointing her, but it hit me deep to think that I was letting down the people I loved. Ryann shouldn't have been on Erebus's radar, but my embarrassing fumbling in her presence had put a target on her back.

I stared at him in horror, my heart hammering. "I... I'll get it done."

"See that you do. Human bones snap like twigs, and I'll make you listen to each one break if you disappoint me."

I'm sorry I couldn't keep you out of this, Ryann. I'd be damned if I was going to let him hurt her. I wouldn't fail again. Even if I had to dig through the diamond mine with a teaspoon, I'd do it to make sure no harm came to Ryann. She had my heart.

THIRTY-ONE

Finch

I took a portal back to the Vasilis estate. By some stroke of luck, I appeared where I'd left instead of in the forest miles away from the house.

As I made my way through the darkness, I paused to collect my thoughts. I couldn't face going back into the house yet, in case my face gave me away. "Terrified" didn't even begin to cover how I felt. Erebus probably thought he was Billy Big-Balls, swinging his weight around to try and get me to work faster. And yeah, I was going to get it done, but that didn't mean I wasn't going to stew about it.

So what if his wife was curious about what he was up to? If he wasn't telling her the truth, that was his problem. Why did he have to bring Ryann into it? Shaking off my distress and rage, I turned and prepared to go back inside. Just as I did, a shadow moved against the windowpane and I damn near rocketed out of my skin. *Not now, Davin. Please, not now!*

Then I realized the furtive figure was too small to be Davin. And too feminine.

"You almost gave me a heart attack!" I exhaled as Saskia emerged from the French door beside the splintered window and strolled out onto the terrace.

"Garrett sent me to find you. He thought you might've gotten lost. Bless him, he worries about you." She nodded to the bloody handprint. "Let me guess. Erebus's handiwork?"

I nodded. "A gentle message of hope and fuzzy feelings."

"Where did you go?"

"Huh?"

"You just appeared a minute ago, so you must've been somewhere. Did Erebus summon you or something?" She chuckled. Her expression changed the minute she saw my face. "Oh... he *did* summon you."

"He has a nasty habit of doing that, usually after leaving something as comforting as that handprint." I gestured to the window. "Sorry about the breakage. I'd ask Erebus to cough up, but he doesn't have any pockets. Even if he did, I'm sure they'd be shallow."

"Don't worry about it. There are so many windows in this place, it'll be weeks before anyone notices. When they do, they'll probably assume a big bird flew into it." She cast me a reassuring smile. "We might want to wipe the blood away, though. That might raise a few eyebrows."

"You should see what he's done to my room back at the SDC." I gave a bitter laugh. Suddenly weary, I walked over to the garden bench and sat. Saskia followed and perched next to me. The two of us stared out at the nighttime forest.

She broke the silence. "I didn't realize it was so bad. I knew you were working for him, obviously, but I didn't know he had so much control over you. I suppose I should've guessed, him being a Child of Chaos and all."

I shrugged. "It is what it is. It's the price I paid for killing Katherine and saving the world."

"That doesn't mean you can't hate it," she replied.

"No… but it's hard to admit that, knowing what it bought." I dipped my chin to my chest. "I just wish it didn't have to be him. I know Ponce said they're all as bad as each other, but Erebus… he's a nasty piece of work. Particularly nasty."

Saskia side-eyed me. "What's he done this time?"

"Who says he's done anything?"

"Your face." She chuckled, but it was a sympathetic sort of laugh.

"I suppose it doesn't matter what I say anymore." I sighed. Keeping secrets hadn't helped me protect anyone. "He's been threatening people I care about, more so than usual, and using them against me. He doesn't seem to get that we're working as hard as we can, as fast as we can. He wants his cake and he wants to stuff it in his wispy, stupid mouth."

"He threatens you a lot?"

"When he wants something, yeah."

She frowned. "But why's he adding all this extra pressure now? What's different? I don't get it."

"I guess he wants this more than he's wanted the other things," I replied. "Plus, this might be my last act as his cosmic slave, so he's getting all his jabs in while he can."

I didn't know why this was pouring out of me. I supposed I needed to share the load before it snapped me in two. *Like Erebus might do to Ryann, if I'm not careful.*

Saskia shuffled closer. "This is your last task for him?"

"If I survive, he's promised to reward me with what I desire most— my freedom." I glanced at her and noticed she was shivering. "I thought you Russians had skin of steel. Isn't this tropical weather to you?"

She laughed. "America must have made me soft."

"Take this." I took off Mr. Vasilis's coat and put it around her shoulders. "I doubt anything could make you soft, Saskia. You're the toughest cookie I've ever met, and I've met some bruisers in my time."

"Thanks... I think?" She pulled the edges of the coat around herself.

"I mean it as a compliment. Just because you're tough doesn't mean you're not a warm person," I said. "It's the best of both worlds, as long as you don't let life harden you. I've seen where that leads, and I wouldn't want you headed down the same path."

"Do you mean your mother?"

I smiled sadly. "Among others."

"I'd never be like her. There's a difference between strength and insanity, and she was way over the crazy line." Saskia looked back out at the forest. "What else has Erebus had you doing? I've heard the others talking, though they stopped when they realized I was eavesdropping."

"He's had me collecting a never-ending list of artifacts, spells, objects, that sort of thing. I've been all over the world: India, South Africa, China, Bali, Tunisia, Jordan, Azerbaijan, Ireland, Portugal... You name it, I've probably been there on some errand for Erebus."

"Has it all been like this? Danger, threats, risk of death, constant harassment?"

I laughed. "And more."

"How are you not in a straitjacket?"

"You know what, I ask myself that every day." My words came out sadder than I'd intended. I didn't want this to be a pity party, but it was hard not to wallow when I remembered the year I'd had.

"I've seen you taking pills," she said hesitantly. "Are you sick?"

I tapped the side of my skull. "Since birth. I've got a severe case of the brain gremlins."

"I didn't know." She peered at me. "Do you mind me asking about it?"

"Not really. It's sort of an open secret."

"Is it... natural? Or something Katherine did to you?"

Ouch... That stung. It was a question I'd asked myself repeatedly since my issues had first made themselves known. My mother had told me it was the result of a hex, always saying she'd find a cure for it, but that had been a lie. Another means of controlling me. In a way, it was worse knowing these gremlins had come into my head the old-fashioned way. No magic, no hexes, no curses.

More recently, I'd been wondering if my mind gremlins were an aftereffect of having the adapted Dempsey Suppressor put in me, but I'd never know. And it didn't matter. The gremlins were here to stay, and having the Suppressor broken hadn't made them go away.

"Sorry, I'm asking too many questions, aren't I?" Saskia asked quietly.

"No, it's okay. I think they're from natural causes, but that's more difficult to deal with. Part of me wishes it *was* something my mother did, because then I'd have an explanation for them. But I don't. It's just me—I was just born wrong."

Saskia's eyes glittered with tears. "Hey, you weren't born wrong. Don't say that! I hear what everyone says about you when you're not there, and they're not gossiping behind your back or saying mean things. Sometimes I want to roll my eyes so hard my eyeballs will fall out, because they're always singing your praises and saying how much they miss you when you're not there. Harley's the worst. Wade's a pretty close second. Even Santana mopes, and that snaky thing of hers mewls when she mentions you."

I frowned. "Really?"

"Would I lie about something like that? I'd be more likely to tell you that they bitch about you, just to amuse myself," she replied, the corners of her mouth turning up just a little. "Honestly, I didn't get what all the fuss was about until I started spending time with you and Garrett. I thought you were hot, for sure, but I also thought you were a bit grumpy, and sometimes you tried too hard, but that was usually when Ryann was around. And your jokes... I never know whether to laugh or cry at how bad they are."

I snorted.

Saskia's voice softened. "But you're actually pretty cool, now that I've gotten to know you a little better. I'm not sure what this boyfriend of Ryann's is like, but I can't imagine he's any match for you."

"Believe me, if you met him, you'd have cartoon hearts floating over your head." I tried to laugh, but I couldn't manage a full one.

She shrugged. "Maybe I've got more refined tastes than Ryann."

"Or maybe she just knows me too well," I replied. "Or she's heard too many of my exemplary jokes."

"You do that a lot, you know."

"Do what?"

"Get all self-deprecating. You shouldn't."

I paused. *When did she get so mature?* "Anyway, I'm tired of talking about me. My brain hurts. So, how about you? How are you holding up on your first SDC mission? I'd say it was official, but it's clearly not."

She drew the coat closer around herself. "It's nice to feel useful for once, instead of being a nuisance or an afterthought."

"You feel like an afterthought?" That surprised me. She never gave off that vibe, but I guessed we'd entered the confessional stage of our blossoming friendship.

She nodded uncertainly. "I do there. At least, I did for a while."

"What do you mean?" I pressed.

"Taty was always the golden child. She's got more raw energy in her little finger than I'll ever have. That's why she's always getting possessed. She's a magnet for spirits. A Kolduny superstar. It's why our grandparents are so eager to have her home—they don't want to lose one of their finest to America."

I smiled. "Now who's the self-deprecating one?"

"You didn't know you had a sister until just over a year ago, so you never had to deal with living in her shadow. If you had, you'd know what I'm talking about. Imagine how cast aside you'd have felt if you'd had to compete with Harley. Taty never made me feel like I was living in her shadow, but she didn't have to. Everyone else loved to remind me. Especially our grandparents."

"That must've been hard." It was odd seeing this side of Saskia. I'd guessed there was more to her, lurking beneath the surface—a vulnerable teenager trying to find her place in this world. I had been right.

She nodded again. "It sounds awful, but I was glad when Taty left. Without her, I had my parents' undivided attention, and more of the Kolduny started to focus on me. I guess they hoped I'd be their next protégé, and I like to think I haven't disappointed. I might not be as powerful as Taty, but I work damn hard, and it has paid off."

Saskia paused. "But then I started to miss Taty, and all the perks and all the attention couldn't fix that. So, when the exchange program came up, I jumped at the chance. I just wanted to be with Taty again, but it wasn't quite what I expected. I didn't think she would've built a life without me... but she has, and that's where the nuisance part comes in. Sometimes I think she's ready to ship me back so she can get on with her life."

It was my turn to offer a supportive shoulder. "That's not true. Your sister cares about you. People can act really weird when they're worried about someone, and I know she worries about you pretty much all the time."

She glanced at me, puzzled. "You think so?"

"I'd bet my life on it. I've seen what it looks like when someone pretends to care, and that's not the case with Tatyana. My guess is she's concerned about what your grandparents are going to say if you decide to stay at the SDC. She probably doesn't want you to suffer the way she is. Plus, they'll definitely blame her for it, and all hell will break loose if two Vasilis sisters refuse to go home."

"I hadn't thought of it like that," she murmured.

"I'd also bet that if she had to choose between all of us and you, she'd pick you in a heartbeat. She'd probably come back home to spare you a barrage from the elderlies. Maybe that's why she's been a bit off? Maybe she's trying to decide what to do under all that pressure."

Saskia dipped half her face into the collar of her dad's coat. "I guess it hasn't been easy for her."

I was about to make a stinging remark about family being a gigantic pain in the ass when Garrett came around the corner of the house and spotted us. He made a beeline for the bench and skidded to a halt, out of breath.

"Everything okay?" I asked. *Of course it's not.*

He shook his head, as I'd known he would. "I was out looking for the two of you when I saw something moving in the rear courtyard. It didn't see me, and it didn't look like it wanted to be seen. It was moving weirdly, darting behind walls and pillars and things. I came to warn you that we're being followed again."

A very familiar voice cut through the tense atmosphere. "Does someone want to explain to me what on earth you're all doing here?"

It wasn't Davin's British brogue. Nope, this was more local. And way more frightening at that moment.

All three of us turned in shock to find Tatyana striding toward us.

THIRTY-TWO

Finch

"Taty?" Saskia shrieked as she shot up from the bench.

My thoughts exactly. Erebus might as well have slapped another bloody handprint on the window, because this was about as convenient as his badly timed summoning. If it wasn't one thing, it was another. A few more days and we could've finished our job without anyone figuring out what we were up to. That simple hope was whizzing right by my head and out the proverbial window.

I mean, come on... Was the universe conspiring to screw me over?

"Someone had better start explaining." Tatyana stopped at the bench, giving us all the stern-eyed treatment.

"There's nothing to explain," I said quickly.

Tatyana scowled at me. "Don't you dare lie to me, Finch. This is my sister we're talking about. Did you think I wouldn't find out? I should've known the minute you mentioned a poltergeist that you'd go running to her instead of me. Why is it that wherever you go, trouble follows?"

Wow... That one hurt. I could forgive her, since she was clearly pissed and worried. Even if I wasn't convinced she hadn't meant it.

"Who says he was the one who came running to me?" Saskia leapt to my defense.

"I overheard that conversation you had with Astrid and Ryann. I heard Finch talking about your 'spooky friend,' which I know means the poltergeist. I'm not an idiot." Tatyana shot a warning look at her little sister. "Finch didn't come to me because he thought I'd tell Harley. Again, not an idiot. Why else would you be with him, Saskia? It's not like you'd have known what he was up to, so he must have roped you in."

"Do Ryann and Astrid know you're here?" Garrett asked, clearly trying to defuse the ticking timebomb of Vasilis sister nuclear warfare.

"No, they don't. They've got no idea I overheard, but I'm glad I did." She was getting madder by the second. "I noticed them sneaking around, whispering, making sure nobody saw them. Their version of stealth is suspicious beyond belief. Plus, I'd already heard about Saskia being at Mr. Daggerston's party. It wasn't hard to put two and two together, Saskia, once I found out you'd been spending an awful lot of time with Garrett and Finch. Poltergeists equal Ivan Traps, and the only place to get one of those is from weird, dark, corrupt people like Mr. Daggerston."

I held my ground. "Don't you know it's rude to listen to people's conversations?"

"Don't you know it's wrong to manipulate people's little sisters into doing your dirty work for you?" she shot back.

Touché.

"He didn't manipulate me. I manipulated him—both of them." Saskia took a step closer to Tatyana. "They just wanted information, but I was the one who insisted on coming along for the ride."

"Then you're even more foolish than I've given you credit for," Tatyana raged. "What do you think you're playing at, Finch? No matter what she said, you should've kept her out of this."

"I'm standing right here, and I can answer for myself." Saskia lifted her chin. "You know, it's kind of sad that you decided to follow us. You should've known Garrett and Finch wouldn't let anything happen to me."

"I didn't follow you, Saskia. I knew where you'd be, and I used a chalk door to come here when I figured you'd be done playing house with our parents. They'd go out of their minds if they knew what you were really doing here, and I didn't want to bring them into it."

Saskia crossed her arms but said nothing.

"I heard Maksim's voice during the video call you had with Astrid and Ryann and knew you were at the Moscow Coven. There's no way you would've gone on with whatever you're doing without coming home first, or you'd have been dealing with a million calls from Mom and Dad." Tatyana nodded toward the house.

"You didn't follow us to the lighthouse, did you?" I interjected.

Tatyana looked confused. "Lighthouse? No, I didn't follow you to any lighthouse. I came straight from the SDC."

So, you're definitely not our pesky shadow, then? That meant it had to be Davin. Another flaming hoop for me to leap through. I wasn't even surprised. This was an Erebus mission we were talking about. When had they ever been simple?

I'd been chased by native tribes through the Amazon and narrowly missed getting skewered by poison spears. I'd faced monsters that would've boggled Tobe's mind. I'd worked my way through security systems more complex than the FBI's and sprinted from countless booby traps. I couldn't even laugh at "booby traps." None of this was funny.

And worst of all, I knew Tatyana was right. I should've kept Saskia out of it. I'd wanted to, but had I tried hard enough? Garrett and I had buckled at the first sign of pressure without thinking through the validity of her threats. Would she really have gone yapping to Tatyana? Maybe not, and it was too late to find out.

I tried to imagine how I'd feel if someone had roped Harley into doing something dangerous and then kept it secret from me. Tatyana had every right to be furious.

"You shouldn't have come." Saskia glared at her sister. "I'm sixteen, not five. I can handle myself better than you think. I'm fine —you can see I'm fine. So open up another chalk door and go right back to the SDC. I've started this, and I'm finishing it, whether you like it or not."

"If I'm going back to the SDC, you're coming with me," Tatyana replied, mirroring her sister by crossing her arms.

"Oh yeah? Are you going to make me?" Saskia's cheeks went beet red. "Maybe you're more like Grandpa and Grandma than you think."

Oh boy. Garrett and I exchanged a look. We would've done just about anything to slink off and leave the sisters to battle this out. But that wasn't going to happen. We were the guilty parties here, and we needed to see it through.

Tatyana's mouth straightened into a grim line. "*Some* of us are trying to protect you. I don't know what Finch and Garrett are up to. That's their business. I'm just here to keep you safe." She shot Garrett and me a look. "I still can't understand why you two didn't just ask for my help and let the Rag Team in on this. Clearly, things have gotten more complicated than you expected. It's stupid to try and do it all alone."

"See, this is exactly why Finch didn't go to you!" Saskia cried. "You'd have just blabbed everything to Harley, when all Finch is trying to do is protect the people he cares about. You'd know that if you bothered to take a step back and think about it. Why else would he be so adamant about doing it alone? Or just with Garrett, anyway?"

Tatyana frowned. "What?"

"Any normal person would be able to see there was a reason for that, but not you," Saskia pressed. "All you're worried about is protecting me, even if it means stunting my progress as a magical. Funny, really, since that's all Finch is worried about—protecting the people closest to him."

I stepped in before things turned really ugly. "Tatyana, I'm sorry. You're right to be mad. I know Saskia is trying to defend me, but bringing her into this isn't defendable. I shouldn't have done it, but... I was desperate. That's not an excuse. I just want you to know that I didn't intend for this to happen. I didn't want to put your sister in danger any more than I wanted to put you, or Harley, or anyone else in danger."

Saskia whipped around to face me. "Are you serious right now?"

"Very serious." I nodded. "That's why you have to stay here, Saskia. Garrett and I will handle the rest. I know you're disappointed, but it has to be like this. I've put you through enough— through things I shouldn't have. Your sister is right. Your part in this has to end tonight."

I looked at Tatyana, who still looked miffed. "As for the rest of the Rag Team, just... just don't tell them anything, okay? No one else needs to get involved. Please. I know I have no right to ask you for a favor, but if you could keep it quiet until our mission is over, it'd mean a lot. Saskia's right, too. I'm just trying to keep the people I love safe. And I can't do that if they know I'm up to something risky. You know Harley. You know she'll try to help, and I don't want that."

Tatyana's expression softened slightly. "I suppose I could—"

"Forget it!" Saskia interrupted, her tone razor sharp. "You're not casting me off like yesterday's trash now, Finch. No way! How far do you think you'd get without me, hmm? You couldn't have tied your own shoelaces without me. You'd still be moping around the

SDC, wondering what the hell to do or getting another dose of dead-men's poison from a poltergeist. So don't you dare try and shove me off now. You *need* me, unless you want to get your asses whipped!"

"We're not—"

Saskia snorted. "Yeah, right! What, are you going to downplay my part now that my big, bad sister is here to yell at you?"

Tatyana observed her sister, listening silently to the tirade. *You don't want to jump in here?*

"You need to calm down," Garrett chimed in.

"When has anyone, in the history of calming down, ever calmed down after being told to calm down?" she fired back.

The whole scene would've been hilarious if I hadn't been so pissed. A few minutes ago, we'd been having a mature conversation and I'd been marveling at how grown-up Saskia was. Now she was kicking her rattle out of her stroller because she didn't like the way things were going. The endless roundabout of the teenage psyche. Not quite a kid, not quite an adult, flitting between both at the drop of a hat.

"Then at least think about what we're saying," Garrett said in an even tone. "You've been helpful, but it's time for you to go home now, before things get dangerous. Nobody is downplaying your part."

Tatyana said nothing, her expression unreadable.

Saskia laughed coldly. "Then they'll be bringing your bodies back in bags, if they can even find them. What would you have done without my money? I know we didn't use it, but you thought you were going to need it. Where would you have been if we had? Or was that why you brought me on this trip, so I could be your cash cow?"

"Enough, Saskia." Garrett had his dad voice on.

"No, it's not enough. I'm just getting started. You two idiots probably wouldn't have made it back to Cuba without me. I'm the reason you know where you're going. I'm the reason you didn't both die in that lighthouse. I'm the reason we got into the Dark Tourist party. You couldn't have done any of it without me."

I almost felt a vein pop in my head. "I don't remember you dying in the Battle of Elysium. I don't remember you giving up your freedom to kill the greatest evil this world has ever known. I don't remember you taking on monsters, and cultists, and tasks more dangerous than this one. Don't forget who you're talking to. We've seen things you wouldn't believe. We've done things that would make you cower under your bedsheets and sing friggin' lullabies to yourself."

Saskia nearly growled. "I—"

"We're not idiots and we're far from useless, so stop being such a spoiled, immature brat because you're not getting your own way." My vision turned red. "If you continue the way you're going, you'll negate every good thing you've done for us. So I suggest you pull it back and listen for once in your damn life! Not everything is about you! And, frankly, I can't be bothered to babysit your attention-seeking ass anymore."

Silence echoed across the Vasilis estate.

Too much? Sure, I regretted everything the moment it came spewing out of my mouth, but I couldn't shovel it back in. Instead, it lingered in the air like a rancid smell, getting fouler by the second. Even Garrett looked shell-shocked.

Tatyana turned to me slowly, her voice low. "Just because my sister didn't fight against Katherine doesn't mean she's some inept kid. She may be young, but she's remarkably capable for her age, and I wouldn't be surprised if there's a whole lot of truth in what she's said. And if I hear you speak to her like that again, I might be the one taking you back to the SDC in a body bag."

Huh? What just happened? Here I was, trying to give Tatyana the opening she needed to get Saskia away from this mission, and now she was lecturing me? Sisters… I'd never understand them. I didn't even understand my own half the time.

"Did I miss something?" Garrett gave me a sympathetic glance.

"A few of your brain cells, maybe." Saskia scoffed, sidling up to her sister.

"You wouldn't have known where to find the Ivan Trap without her," Tatyana said. "And I know they don't come cheap, so she's likely telling the truth about the money. If I find out you were just using her, there's going to be trouble—you can count on that. Plus, we all saw the state that poltergeist left you in the last time, Finch, so how about showing some respect where respect is due? Do you think you could've faced the poltergeist without her help?"

"Maybe? I mean, no?" I fumbled the words, not sure of the right answer to a rhetorical question. My head was about ready to blow. "Hang on, I thought you wanted her out of this mission. Isn't that why you're here?"

"No, that's not why I'm here, but I didn't get to explain with all the mud-slinging going on," she replied. "I'm not here to take Saskia away. I just wanted to know what she'd gotten into so that I could help. And, yes, before you ask, without telling Harley or anyone else. I still don't understand why you don't want her to know, but if you have your reasons, then you have your reasons. I, unlike you, have some respect for other people's feelings."

"That's not fair," Garrett interjected. "You might be upset, but there's no need to get personal. How about we all take a breather before something gets said that you're all going to regret in the morning?"

Haven't we crossed that line already? I knew it was a bad idea to add fuel to the fire, so I held my tongue.

Having reached a stalemate, the four of us stared at each other, no doubt wondering who was going to break the tense peace first. To my surprise, it was Saskia.

She took a deep breath, though some irritation lingered in the curl of her lip. "Taty, I appreciate you wanting to help me out, but you don't need to do that. If they don't want me around anymore, that's fine, but I'm not going to let them put themselves at risk just because I'm annoyed." Her shoulders relaxed. "How about this—I'll guide them to the mine, but after that, they're on their own?"

"Mine?" Tatyana frowned.

"Ah… right. We'll need to fill you in a bit."

Saskia gave Tatyana a quick rundown of the plan, and how our poltergeist pal had given us the location of an "artifact" I was looking for. I was grateful she didn't mention Ponce de León specifically, or the Fountain of Youth. That was a can of worms I didn't want opened. I might've spoken too soon about Saskia being immature. I mean, she could've spilled everything to Tatyana, but she hadn't. That showed class—more than I'd shown her in return.

"So that's what you're after? Some artifact?" Tatyana glanced at me. "Is this part of the Erebus deal?"

I smiled. "No, I just felt like coming all the way out here to pick up some random object for fun."

"Sorry, that was silly of me." She gave a quiet laugh.

Am I off the hook?

"Anyway, that's why Finch has been trying to keep you and the Rag Team out of it—because Erebus doesn't want a lot of people to know about his requests," Saskia continued. "I don't want to end up his target, either. So, I'll just take them to the mine, and then… I'll come back." She sounded bitter about it, but it was nice to see some of that maturity floating back to the surface.

"Just promise me one thing, Finch," Saskia went on.

I frowned. "What?"

"Don't try to minimize what I've done for you. I've loved coming along on this trip with the two of you, and I don't want us falling out over it. I don't want to look back on it with bad memories, either." She lowered her gaze.

I put my hand on her shoulder. "We wouldn't be here without you. I mean that. I'm sorry for what I said."

Way to go, being the bigger person! I half expected her to grin at me and say, "Ha! I knew it!" Instead, she just smiled back.

"Thank you. That's all I wanted to hear." Her attention flitted toward Tatyana. "So, how does the new plan sound to you?"

Tatyana paused for a moment. "I guess that works for me."

"Glad to hear it, but we do have one other problem," Saskia said.

"Oh?" Tatyana switched back into panicked sister mode. I knew it well.

"You need to get the whole Vasilis estate on high alert. We were followed here by Davin Doncaster. He needs to be caught, or he might ruin everything."

"Davin is here?" Tatyana gasped.

I nodded. "Unfortunately, that's looking more and more likely. He gave us the slip at the Dark Tourist party. And he's got a bone to pick with us that's brought him all the way to your motherland. We need to catch him and find an object on him—apparently that's what's allowing him to cheat death."

"An object?" Tatyana looked puzzled.

"Yeah, I don't have anything more to go on. I just know he has something that he's bound his life to. And it's resurrecting him like nobody's business. We break it, we kill him. Job done."

Saskia and Garrett frowned at me. "What? I didn't have time to tell you before the Ice Queen rolled in," I said.

"Nobody's called me that in a long time." Tatyana chuckled. "But I'll see to it that the whole estate knows we have an intruder, and I'll get the security protocols heightened so we can find that devil and end him, once and for all."

I sighed with something like relief. "Thank you."

"As for this mine, when are you going? Not before we've found Davin, I hope." Tatyana glanced at us.

Saskia shook her head. "I'll take them in the morning, to make sure they can get past the guards. Mom said she'd clear it with Uncle Anatoly, but security won't buy it if I'm not there to make it official."

"Ugh, it's Anatoly's mine?" Tatyana grimaced.

Saskia grinned. "Your favorite."

"After you've seen them through security, you'll come back?" Tatyana ignored the sass.

"I'll leave them to it, yes. It's their funeral." She gave a sharp laugh, but it didn't reach her eyes. There was sadness there instead, like this wasn't the outcome she had wanted.

"But, Tatyana, you have to remember that no one can know what we're doing," I urged.

Harley and the others deserved as much peace and quiet as they could get, after facing Katherine. I didn't want to offload my problems onto them. I mean, Garrett deserved some peace too, but I'd roped him in for his lack of savior complex, so he was sort of stuck with me now.

Tatyana sighed. "Fine. But when it's done, you *have* to tell Harley and the others. They're worried about you."

"I will," I promised.

At the end of the day, Tatyana and Saskia were doing the same thing I was: trying to be a good sibling. It wasn't always easy, and there would always be missteps, but it was the thought that counted.

Now, Saskia was more or less out of trouble. And, soon, I'd be able to take the targets off the backs of everyone else. Harley, the Rag Team... and Ryann.

Tomorrow, you son of a bitch, you'll get what you want. I glanced at the splintered window and saw more cracks appear.

THIRTY-THREE

Finch

The next morning, we gathered on the terrace again. Apparently, this was the perfect place to solve all of our problems. We'd be getting out peace pipes and guitars next.

Garrett and I were wrapped up in blankets like pre-butterfly pupae, with coats underneath, trying to keep out the dawn chill. Saskia and Tatyana were faring better in light sweaters, already having acclimated to the temperature. Just looking at them made me feel cold. It seemed a short stay at home had reacquainted them with their Russian roots.

As promised, Tatyana had instructed her parents and the staff to boost the security at the estate, but slimy Davin hadn't shown his face or his shadow. Alarms and charms had been set around every possible perimeter, but the snake hadn't bitten. This put us in a bit of a sticky situation.

"So they still haven't found him," I grumbled into the collar of my trench coat, borrowed from Mr. Vasilis's endless supply. This was proper undercover wear, secret-agent style, though it was slightly concerning that Mr. Vasilis owned so many. Who needed twenty trench coats?

Tatyana shook her head. "I'll stay here and keep an eye on things, in case you're right about Davin, but that doesn't mean I can't help from afar. I'll put some charms on you all. That way, I'll know if you're in trouble and I can bring backup."

Saskia rolled her eyes. "Sounds like an excuse to put charms on us."

She smiled. "Maybe it is. But it's either this or I call Harley in right now."

"Why am *I* being punished?" I exclaimed.

"Do you really want me to answer that?" Tatyana replied.

I buried my mouth deeper in the coat collar. "Get on with it, then, so we can leave."

Tatyana stepped forward and took three necklaces out of her pocket. She'd come prepared. *Very sly, Miss Vasilis.* She placed one over each of our heads and covered the plain silver pendants with her hand, one by one.

"*Zashchiti eti dushi. Pozvoni mne, yesli oni v bede. Otpravit' slovo cherez prostranstvo I vremya. Dukhi, sledi za nimi.*"

She whispered the spell until her eyes glowed, and each silver pendant followed suit. I didn't know what it was supposed to do, but I guessed it had created a link between us and her. She was already wearing a pendant of her own, which glowed each time the spell was whispered. She finished the last pendant.

"Okay, let's go," I said.

Tatyana reached for her sister's hand and held it. "Be careful."

Saskia sighed. "It'll be a piece of cake. Uncle Anatoly has already given his permission, so we'll be expected."

"Go on, then." Tatyana let go of her sister.

Saskia walked to the garden wall and drew a doorway with a

stick of charmed chalk. Puzzled, I patted my pockets only to find my own chalk missing.

"Hey! Did you steal that from me?"

Saskia flashed a grin back. "Like taking candy from a baby."

"I want that back," I protested.

"Duh. How will you get back without it? Think of it more as borrowing."

Smiling to herself, Saskia whispered the *Aperi Si Ostium* spell. The lines ignited, cutting a door into the stone. Once it had fully appeared, she tugged on the handle and opened it wide. Garrett and I followed her through to the Sakha Republic of Russia.

Tatyana lingered on the threshold, watching us leave. She stayed there until Saskia closed the door, and then the three of us were alone in the wilderness. I stared at the landscape in awe, mesmerized by the stark beauty. A flat, green expanse stretched as far as the eye could see, with rugged mountains and a glint of water in the distance. A town of some kind lay to our right, the houses squat and square, as if they were only supposed to be temporary. I guessed they belonged to the mine employees, since we were in the middle of nowhere.

Beside the town, I found one of the most striking sights I had ever seen. A huge crater disappeared into the earth like a gaping mouth. Ridges had been cut into the sides, giving the impression of an enormous stone tornado working its way deeper and deeper into the ground.

"Is that…" I trailed off, gobsmacked.

Saskia nodded. "The Jubilee mine, boys."

She led the way across the flat terrain toward a metal fence that surrounded the gaping crater. Two guard towers rose up on either side of a chained gate. Gruff faces peered out as we approached, followed by the business end of some pretty nasty guns. I supposed not everyone here could be a magical, considering the purpose of this place was to dig up shiny diamonds. It was a money-spinner, not a center of magical excellence.

"*Chto ty zdes' delayesh'*?" one of the guards demanded. From his tone, it was clear he wasn't asking us our favorite colors.

"*Ya Saskia Vasilis. Moy dyadya, Anatoly Rasputin, dolzhen byl pogovorit' s vami?*" Saskia replied. I heard her uncle's name and knew she was dropping it to get us in.

The guard's expression changed. "*Konechno, Miss Vasilis. Vy mozhete voyti.*" He gestured for his colleague to go down and open the gates. The other guard practically stumbled over himself in his rush to obey. The Vasilis name had power here, too.

Once the gates were open, Saskia strode toward the perilous edge of the mine. Swallowing my nerves, I went after her, with Garrett in tow.

We walked for a long time, until we came to a small hut perched near the lip of the crater. The corrugated iron doors stood wide open, revealing a metal platform with two crosshatched shutters tucked into the sides. My stomach plummeted when I realized what it was. This was an elevator that would carry us deep below the ground, into the mine.

"When did they last check this thing?" I kicked the metal shutters and the whole thing groaned. *Comforting.*

Saskia shrugged. "The eighties? I don't know."

"And we have to go down in it?" Garrett gulped.

She chuckled. "How else did you think we were getting into the mine?"

"Magic?" he said hopefully.

"Nope, we have to do this the traditional way," she replied. "The bottom of the mine is unchartered territory. I can't visualize it, so we'd probably end up stuck in the rock if we tried a chalk door."

I grasped Saskia's arm. "Hang on, what do you mean 'we'? This is where you go home, like you promised."

She grinned. "I must be a very good liar if you bought that. I thought my sister was the gullible one—apparently not. I only said that to stop her from freaking out."

"Saskia!" Garrett gasped.

"I told you, I'm finishing this. Now, since I'm the only one who knows the code to get us down there, I suggest you put up or shut up. Without me, you don't get into the mine. It's as simple as that." She leaned against the hut, giving us devil-may-care attitude.

I shook my head. "You're unbelievable."

"I like to think of it as tenacious," she replied.

Garrett and I looked at each other with mutual despair. But what could we do? She had us against the ropes again. I had to hand it to her, her manipulation skills were second to none. What was worse was that reality echoed the comments her swollen ego had made the previous night. We genuinely couldn't get down there without her, and she was loving every minute of it.

"And they say working with babies and animals is bad. Try teenagers," I said, defeated.

"Does that mean you're letting me come with you?" She fluttered her eyelashes at me.

Garrett sighed. "You haven't given us much choice."

"You're right. I haven't." Grinning, she stepped into the elevator and tapped numbers into a pad. "You'd better move quickly if you're getting on."

As if to bolster her point, the mechanisms started to creak and whirr, prompting Garrett and me to jump onto the metal platform before it descended without us.

"We'll be having words if we make it out of this, Saskia," I said, leaning back against the railings as she hurried to close the shutters.

"Whatever you say. You'll be jumping for joy if we make it out of this, so I might catch you in a generous mood." She locked the shutters and stepped back as the elevator began to descend beneath the earth.

Being trapped inside a tiny metal box within four walls of solid rock wasn't exactly my idea of a good time. If it caved in, we'd be crushed, and I didn't have much faith in the rickety machinery pulling us down. I gripped the rail and closed my eyes as we descended deeper and deeper, the air getting stale. It was surprisingly hot, too, the atmosphere stifling and oppressive. It wasn't long before my clothes stuck to me uncomfortably.

Gasping the stale air, I untied my trench coat and threw it over my shoulder, trying to shove down the panic that threatened. I'd always been borderline claustrophobic, but this was a brand-new level of hell. Fitting, since we were sinking deep into Earth's underworld.

"Are you okay?" Garrett's hand gripped my shoulder.

I nodded. "Yep… peachy with a side of keen. Just trying not to let the existential dread sink in. The usual stuff."

"Take deep breaths," he urged.

"Of what? This isn't air, this is vaguely oxygenated lung syrup." I gripped the rail tighter.

Saskia chuckled, a sound that made me want to draw a chalk door back to Moscow and shove her through it. "We're almost there. Stop being a drama queen."

Ten minutes of panic later, a loud clank rang in my ears as the elevator jerked to an abrupt halt. Shaking violently, I managed to open my eyes, and the sight was worth the struggle it took to get down here.

The cathedral-esque dome of the cavern's ceiling had been chipped away by years and years of digging. Wooden walkways lined the walls, and an array of machines and tools were scattered around. Apparently, the miners weren't scheduled to work here today. After a moment or two, I could breathe easier. It probably had something to do with the huge air conditioning units pumping fresh air into the cavern.

"This way," Saskia said. She headed away from the elevator and made for a narrow corridor hewn into the rock.

The corridor led to a smaller cavern. There were no workers here, either, and the wooden walkways were falling apart, as if they'd been abandoned. The lack of air conditioning units in this section was doing a number on my lungs. But at least we weren't trapped in that stupid box anymore.

"What are we doing here?" I asked.

"Going deeper." She pointed to a small hole in the ground nearby. The ends of a ladder stuck out of the top, a sight that filled me with dread.

"You're joking, right?" Garrett hissed.

She shook her head. "Nope. If we want to go deeper, we need to climb. Nobody goes down this shaft at this time of year, because of the soil softening."

"You're not making me feel better." Garrett looked green.

"Ponce said the Fountain was at the very bottom of the mine, and we're nowhere near it. If we want to reach it, this is the only way. It's been colder this year, so we might get lucky," Saskia replied nonchalantly.

"What, and *not* have the whole thing crash down around us?" I gaped at her.

"Exactly." She walked toward the open shaft and started to climb down.

That got our asses in gear. If we didn't follow her, we'd be leaving her to who-knew-what, and I wasn't about to get torn to pieces by Tatyana if anything happened to her. We were bound to her now, whether we liked it or not.

Saskia, I'm going to spread some juicy rumors about you having webbed feet and a stamp collection when we get back to the SDC.

I took a deep breath and started to climb, conscious of Saskia beneath me. Electric lamps hung at regular intervals across the rock, casting an anemic glow on our descent. It wasn't much, but at least we weren't in pitch darkness. I didn't fancy climbing down this ropey-ass ladder with one hand while wielding a fireball in the other to light our way.

What felt like a lifetime later, we reached the end of the ladder and found ourselves in yet another cavern. This one was even smaller than the last, only a few feet taller than me, with a couple halogen bulbs hanging overhead. There were no walkways here, just wooden posts to support the rock.

I'd done dangerous things in my time, but this had to make the top three. I was painfully aware of the fact that the soil could collapse at any moment.

"Is this as far as the mine goes?" I asked.

Saskia nodded. "This is where we start digging. I'm going to go ahead and say that's your job, Finch, since you're the one with the Earth abilities."

"Oh… yeah." I knelt and placed my palms against the rock floor. I gathered a measured quantity of Chaos into my palms, not eager to blast a hole in the unstable earth, and fed it gently into the ground. Threads of it sank into the soil and stone, cutting it away little by little and sending the remnants spiraling up in a vortex of dirt.

When the vortex got too dense, I dropped the contents nearby until there was a hefty pile. I kept digging and dropping, digging and dropping, digging and dropping. Soon enough, I'd created a crater almost as deep as I was tall.

"Any sign of that white floor yet?" Garrett peered over my shoulder.

"Not yet," I replied. Saskia had taken to pacing, which was doing nothing for my nerves.

I dug until sweat poured off me. I could taste the salt on my tongue as it dripped into my mouth, and my forearm was slicked with it every time I tried to mop it off my brow. But I couldn't stop now. Feeling Chaos jangling through my veins and knowing I was pushing myself hard, I kept at it. I'd keep going until I dropped dead of exhaustion or this cavern crumbled—whichever came first.

I was close to losing hope when I noticed a faint glimmer under the dirt. Adrenaline thundered through me as I pushed a little more Chaos into my palms and removed another chunk of the earth. My heart sprang into my throat.

"It's white!" I yelped. Garrett and Saskia hurried to the lip of the small crater and craned to look for themselves.

"You're right! It's white!" A wave of relief washed over Garrett's face.

Saskia gaped at it. "You did it, Finch."

"Well, not quite. We've still got to dig through *that*." I eyed the mysterious white glint and channeled my Chaos toward it.

At first, there was resistance, a magical pushback that wafted my Chaos away. *Not today, thanks.* Gritting my teeth in determination, I felt across the white stone with my powers until I found a crack in the surface. I poked a strand of Chaos into the minuscule gap. It filtered downward, evading the resistance. Like water frozen in a pipe, I expanded my magic inside the crack and let it spread outward, cutting a hole in the solid white rock.

I paused as the earth trembled, panicked that I'd pushed too hard. But the vibrations faded as quickly as they'd come, so I kept cutting away at the stone.

Black spots danced in my vision as I worked. I was close to my limit. Suddenly, the resistance that kept fighting me disappeared. I toppled forward, the gaping hole rushing up to meet me. Fortunately, a sharp yank tugged me back. Garrett gripped my T-shirt and hauled me away from the edge.

"Easy there," he said. I sank back, panting hard.

"What happened?" I couldn't catch my breath, and I definitely didn't have the energy to lean forward to look.

Saskia glanced over the edge. "I think you broke through."

"I did?"

She nodded. "There's something dark down there. It's not white anymore."

"Thank God for that." I tipped all the way back and lay flat on the floor, staring up at the ceiling. All the tension left my body as I drew in deep breaths, trying to return to normal. *I'm definitely speaking to Dylan after this is over.* Although, I doubted he'd have a training regime for digging through piles and piles of solid rock.

"How do you feel?" Garrett loomed into my line of sight.

"Like I've just shifted fifty tons of rock," I replied.

He laughed. "Aside from that?"

"Achy. Sore. Like my arms are about to fall out of their sockets. Like I've got a thousand ants with boxing gloves going ten rounds with my cells. Like my blood froze, then thawed, then froze, then thawed again. How many more would you like? I can keep going." I managed a thin smile.

"Can you stand?" Saskia appeared beside me. "We can wait a while, if you're not feeling too hot."

I shook my head and forced myself to sit up. "We've come this far. I'm not napping now."

"I have a question." Saskia raised her hand.

"What is it?" Garrett replied.

"How are we supposed to get down there?"

I groaned. "I guess that'll be me again."

"Can you manage?" Garrett looked at me, worried. "I've got Air. I can do it."

"Mine is stronger, not to brag or anything, and we don't know how far down that hole goes. It's going to take a powerful cushion of Air to stop us from getting smooshed. I've got some fumes left in the tank."

I shuffled to the edge of the crater and dangled my legs over the edge. Before the others could stop me, I dropped off the end and pushed a cushion of Air out ahead of me. I slipped right through the hole like I was riding some sort of terrifying waterslide and disappeared into the darkness beyond.

Fortunately, the Air cushion broke my fall a few seconds later, caressing me in its pillowy embrace. Once I let go, my feet hit solid ground. I stared at the light shining above.

"I'll catch you!" I shouted.

"Are you crazy?" Saskia yelled back.

"How else are you getting down here?" I smiled. The shoe was on the other foot. With my last burst of energy, I created another cushion of Air and held it beneath the hole, ready for the next rider. "Come on! I can only hold this for so long!"

I heard rude muttering, followed by a figure slipping through the hole and hitting the cushion. Saskia had jumped first, though she rapidly clambered out of the way as a second shape came hurtling down. The cushion caught Garrett, too. As soon as it had them, I released the pocket of Air and lowered them gently to the ground, taking more care than I'd done with myself despite Saskia's rude mutterings.

"All good?" I asked.

"All good. How about you?" Garrett replied.

I shrugged. "I'll be fine."

"Wow..." Saskia gasped.

No longer focused on keeping the other two from breaking their necks, I took in our surroundings. "Wow" was an understatement.

We were standing in a strange, wide tunnel with a carved set of steps just ahead, spiraling down toward the center of the Earth. At least, that was what it looked like. There were no manmade lights, but that didn't matter. The tunnel itself glowed, which resulted in a beautiful display. The walls were covered in clusters of raw diamonds and gemstones of all colors, but they were somehow luminescent. The soft, steady light pulsated as if the gemstones were alive, a collective beating heart.

"Does anyone else think this place is a bit... creepy?" Garrett asked, looking around.

Saskia shook her head. "I think it's beautiful."

"Personal taste, I guess," I added. "I think the tunnel is beautiful, but that staircase is giving me major eerie vibes."

"I didn't realize I was coming down here with two scaredy-cats." Saskia shot us both a withering look.

"And we didn't realize you were coming at all," I fired back. "So I guess it's surprises all around."

I edged toward the top of the spiral steps and looked down. If there was a bottom down there, I couldn't see it. More clusters of gemstones pulsated in the rockface, shedding gentle light on the stairs.

I had no idea what we were going to find down there in the darkest depths of the Earth, but there was only one way to find out. Drawing from my reserves, I took the first step into the unknown.

THIRTY-FOUR

Garrett

The steps carved into the rock were slippery and uneven. And the farther we descended, the less light emanated from the glowing clusters of gemstones.

Finch led us with a ball of Fire in his hands, trying to pick his way carefully from step to step. I'd have given anything for a guide rope or a bannister—something to stop us from slipping to our deaths. In the center of the staircase's spiral, there was nothing but a steep drop into pitch-black oblivion.

"Careful on this one! It's a slimy mess," Finch announced.

My heart thudded in my chest and the blood rushed in my ears as I stepped onto the narrow plinth. My boot had just settled on it when my foot slid out from under me. I grasped wildly for support as I hit the ground with a thump.

Fortunately, I landed on my ass. I put my heels down and dug them into a ridge in the stone to stop myself from skidding all the way down the staircase.

"You okay?" Saskia's voice came from above.

I nodded and picked myself up. "All good, but Finch was right—

be careful on this one." A thick slime covered the back of my jeans, but at least I was alive.

"I hate to be the bearer of bad news, but they're all as slippery as—"

Finch suddenly yelped mid-sentence. Silhouetted against the ball of Fire, I watched him lurch forward and flail as he struggled to keep his balance. He was too close to the edge, too close to toppling right into the darkness.

Blind instinct kicked in, and I leapt and tackled him around the waist, slamming the two of us into the curved wall of this never-ending pit. I braced my feet against another ridge in the rock floor and held him there until I was sure he wasn't going to slide away. He breathed hard, the whites of his eyes showing.

"I've got you." Gingerly, I released him.

"That's the most action I've had in years." He gave a nervous chuckle, trying to cover the fact that he could've been seconds from plummeting to his death. Humor was Finch's panacea, but I could see he was rattled.

"Are you okay? What happened?" Saskia peered down from above. She sounded as panicked as I felt.

"It's these steps." Finch exhaled. "They just get worse. It's like the aftermath of an explosion in a French cheese factory."

I frowned. "Huh?"

"De-brie everywhere." He forced a smile, and Saskia gave a quiet snort. "We really need to watch our step. There's fallen rock, some mystery mulch, and a slick of water that must be dripping down from somewhere."

"Can't we just jump and make a cushion of Air?" This was getting ridiculous, and I had the horrible feeling that one of us was going to wind up breaking their neck.

Finch shook his head. "I don't know how far down that thing goes, and I can't see jack. If I just freefell down that hole, I'd have no idea when to open the chute, so to speak. Cue a splattered Finch, with his insides as outsides."

"I've got an idea." I reached back and pulled the Avenging Angel out of its sheath. It seemed a waste to use it as a walking stick, but the situation called for it. Jabbing the blade into the ground, a flame licked up the edge, casting more light on our descent.

"Good thinking." Finch took out his dagger and stabbed it into the wall like a crampon, before taking out his Esprit and transforming the lighter into a second dagger. He used both to brace himself. Behind us, Saskia took out her shashka and did the same as me, using it like a cane. She looked nervous, and I had to wonder if she was regretting her decision to disobey Tatyana.

"You sure you want to come with us?" I asked.

Her nervous expression turned into a scowl. "Of course."

"Won't your sister be getting suspicious about where you are?" I pressed.

She hesitated. "I sent her a text to buy some more time."

"Must've been a doozy of a text," I said, dubiously.

"I said we'd been held up by the guards. They wanted to interview us first, that type of thing." She dug her blade into the stone as she kept moving.

A bit more stable now, we continued down the precarious steps. Even with the blades digging into the stone, it didn't feel remotely safe. One false move and we'd be goners.

We'd been taking our time, slowly moving down, when a tremor thrummed through the pit. It started small, barely a vibration. My head whipped around as I heard rocks falling behind me. It was hard to see anything beyond the light given off by my sword.

Is the pit caving in?

Adrenaline pounded through my veins. I fought with the gloom to try and see what was going on. I'd just fixed on the faint shape of Saskia when a bloodcurdling scream pierced the air. Before I could react, Saskia tumbled backward into the central hole, and the ground disappeared beneath her.

"Saskia!" I yelled.

"What?" Finch shouted above the din.

"Saskia fell!"

He darted to the edge and dropped to his knees. Tendrils of Telekinesis shot from his hands, snaking into the gloom. I moved to his side as quickly as I could, to shine the sword's glow over the gaping void.

My heart stopped as Saskia's scream echoed, bouncing off every wall until it started to play tricks with my head. It sounded as though she was all around us.

"I can't reach her!" Finch panted. His brow furrowed as he forced more and more Telekinesis down the hole. It was a risk, as his magic could cause the whole place to collapse, but those risks seemed tiny in comparison to losing Saskia.

"Keep trying!" I urged.

A bombardment of emotions crossed his face as he stared into the abyss: frustration, terror, grief, panic... I experienced them with him. Weirdly, there was a vague comfort in Saskia's screams. As long as she was screaming, she was alive. And as long as she was alive, we had a faint hope of catching her.

"I... I think I've got her!" Finch knuckled down and pulled his hands into fists. Yanking back, he recoiled the Telekinesis tendrils to where we stood. It was like a twisted fishing trip, and we just had to hope we had the prize fish on the end of the line.

Sweat dripped down his face as he drew the coils in, his shirt stuck to his back. I wanted to help, but I didn't know what I could do. I just had to stand there and pray.

Minutes later, Saskia's body rose from the pit, limp and lifeless, with the sword miraculously gripped in her floppy hand. The sight made my throat close in fear. *Was he too late?* What if she'd already hit bottom before the tendrils reached her? She wasn't moving. And the screams had stopped, the last of them merely echoes from her terrified throat.

With a gentle motion that showed his insane control over these powers, Finch lowered Saskia onto the steps. I hurried to her while Finch got his breath back.

"Saskia? Saskia, can you hear me?"

She didn't look broken. I smoothed the damp strands of hair away from her face and laid my fingers on her cheek. Her face was warm and pink under the firelight of my sword, but that didn't mean anything. Taking Finch's knife from him, I put the blunted side under her nose and waited. A second later, it fogged up.

She's alive... thank God.

"How is she?" Finch asked.

"Alive. I think she fainted," I replied, overcome with relief as I handed Finch's knife back.

"Yeah, thinking you're about to die will do that." He sank onto the step beside her and pulled her into his lap. I tried my best to play doctor.

"Saskia?" I shook her shoulders gently. "Saskia?"

Her eyelids fluttered. "Hmm?"

"Saskia, you're okay. I need you to open your eyes for me," I urged.

"Am I... dead?" Her voice was so small and childlike, it broke my heart.

"No, you're not dead. Finch got you in time." I gave her hand a squeeze, to let her know we were here. That she was still in the land of the living. "Come on, open your eyes for me."

Eventually, she did. They shone with tears. "I... I thought I was going to die."

"I know, but you're safe now." I held on to her hand, and she gripped mine in response.

"At least I know this isn't heaven," she said faintly. "They'd never let the two of you be angels." She managed a quiet laugh, but it didn't reach her face. Everything about her demeanor screamed panic and fear. That had been a very near miss, and we were all feeling it.

"I'm sorry I wasn't quicker," Finch said. "It was all the rocks and stone. I didn't know if I was grabbing them or you, and I didn't want to get it wrong."

She stared up at him. "Thank you."

"You're welcome," he replied.

I waited for the punchline, but it didn't come. He meant it. And the moment had been too serious to start wisecracking.

Once Saskia was steady enough to get back on her feet, we started our descent again. This time, Finch and I kept her between us. But the atmosphere had changed. Finch had gone quiet, like he was deep in thought, and Saskia wasn't saying anything, either, no doubt dealing with the fact that she'd almost died.

The silence was interrupted only by our boots scraping against stone and the chink of our blades as we used them for purchase. We were taking it painfully slow, but there was no use in rushing.

After another half-hour of endless, hesitant creeping, the terrain changed. It was like heading downstairs and expecting there to be one more step, only to find that there wasn't. I edged my foot out in the gloom and shone my sword on the ground, just to be sure. But no, there were no more steps. Just solid, wonderful, incredible flat stone.

"Is this the bottom?" Saskia didn't seem convinced either.

"Looks like it," Finch replied as he felt his way around the walls.

"I swear, if there's another secret staircase, I'll have to cover your ears."

"Is it just me or is it shiny?" I crouched low to the ground and swept my hand across the smooth surface. A fine blanket of dust from all the years of crumbling rock had settled across it. But, underneath, the floor gleamed.

It looked like glass. No, not glass—diamond. If I turned my head, it sparkled from the glow of my sword.

"It's made of diamond!" Saskia's eyes flew wide.

"Not naturally, though, right? I mean, what kind of diamond grows A, this big, and B, this uniform?" Finch shone his fireball over the incredible floor, kicking the dust away. "Man, I could live the rest of my life on my own private island if I took a chunk of this."

"Don't you dare," Saskia warned. "I'm not having this place collapse because you got greedy."

He chuckled. "I wasn't going to; I was just saying. Easy there."

"Wait a sec…" As I leaned closer to the diamond, I saw something move beneath. A subtle glimmer, like reflections of water shining on a ceiling.

Finch peered over my shoulder, breathing loudly in my ear. "That's water. Is that water? I don't know what anything is anymore."

"I think it is." I sat back on my haunches and watched the water swirl beneath the diamond. The only clue that it was special was the way it shone with a strange blue light. "This must be the second covering that Ponce talked about. We broke through the white floor, but he mentioned he also built a second layer."

I couldn't believe Ponce had done this. He must have been an intense magical back in his day. His geological manipulation abilities were stronger than ordinary Earth, for sure.

Finch suddenly erupted in hysterics, scaring the life out of me.

"What's funny?" Saskia stared at him.

"This whole thing," he replied, weeping with laughter.

"I don't see how," I interjected.

Finch just lay flat on the floor and continued laughing, tears streaming down his cheeks.

"Is there some airborne disease down here that's gotten into his lungs?" Saskia looked to me. "Should we be worried? Like, should we cover our mouths or something?"

Finch shook his head. "You don't get it, do you?"

"Get what?" I pressed.

"There was one thing Ponce neglected to mention. A pretty massive thing."

Finch sat back up and wiped the tears from his eyes. "He built this second layer, right? But what did he build it out of? It should only take a second for the irritating friggin' penny to drop."

I sucked air through my teeth. "He's right."

"Can someone tell me what's going on? I feel like I've come down here with two lunatics," Saskia snapped. "What am I missing?"

"The floor is made of diamond," I said flatly, understanding sinking in.

She frowned. "And?"

"We can't cut through a diamond floor, Saskia. Hardest natural thing on Earth." Like Finch, I didn't know whether to laugh or cry.

"But… the Fountain of Youth. It's right there!" She jabbed a finger at the swirling water beneath the diamond layer. I could feel its power even through the covering. It vibrated through the chamber around us, rippling with raw magic. The hairs stood on the back of my neck, and a sensation of relaxing calm drifted through my body, even though nothing was soothing about our current problem. That had to be the Fountain, spreading its energy.

"Yep, and we can't get to it," Finch replied.

"Use your Earth ability or something. It cut through the white layer—why not this one, too?" Saskia gestured to the diamond.

Finch sighed. "I can cut through rock and stone, but diamond is a different ballgame. The white layer must've been made of something softer. I could pummel Earth into this thing for hours and not even make a dent."

"I thought you had mad powerful skills, after your Suppressor broke?" Saskia waited, as if she expected him to demonstrate.

"It won't work." Finch flexed his palms and forged a ball of swirling bronze. Brow furrowing, he fed the energy downward, sliver by sliver, the way he'd done with the white marble. As if repelled, the strands slithered across the diamond, having no effect whatsoever.

"See what I mean?" He slammed his fist into the hard surface and immediately winced. "How did he make this thing, anyway?"

"He must've been a Geode, when he was alive." That was my guess, anyway.

"Why are you talking about Pokémon?" Saskia folded her arms across her chest.

Finch snorted. "A Geode, not a Geodude, though it's nice to see you had some semblance of a childhood."

"A Geode is a magical who can manipulate minerals. Ponce must have been a very skilled one if he could create something like this," I explained. "The question is, *why* didn't he tell us that we'd have trouble when we reached this? Shouldn't the Ivan Trap have forced him to tell us everything?"

Saskia shrugged. "It's more of an 'ask a direct question, get a direct answer' kind of deal."

"So he just decided to keep this to himself," Finch muttered. "He doesn't want Erebus to get to the Fountain. He doesn't want *anyone* getting to the Fountain, period."

"Ah." I stared at the water. So near and yet so far.

Just then, rocks peppered the diamond floor. My attention snapped to the staircase, where a shadowy figure hurried down the stairs toward us. Right now, I'd have given everything for it to be Tatyana coming to her sister's aid. But it wasn't.

It didn't shock me that Davin had gotten past the security guards. The slippery weasel had a way around everything, including death, which was supposed to be one of the only certainties in this world.

"Why am I not surprised?" Finch hissed. "Here he comes to wreck the day."

Rage exploded through me in a wave I couldn't control, coursing through my veins like wildfire. The intensity of it startled me.

He'd escaped us for much too long, but this time, we knew the secret that brought him back to life. If we found his object, we could kill him. And man, was I ready to kill that son of a bitch for good.

THIRTY-FIVE

Finch

Davin staggered down to the true bottom of this pain-in-the-ass Cave of Wonders.

Him against us. Us against him. Hopefully, for the last friggin' time. The man might as well have been made of grease. He certainly had enough of it slicked through his hair. The moment we'd gunned for the Ivan Trap, he'd clearly started tracking us. So here we were, about to fight it out once again.

But why?

What was drawing Davin to this place? A personal quest? Was he doing this for Erebus, like me—was he a backup?

Or was he working *against* Erebus? Maybe he was working for someone else. None of the ideas ricocheting through my skull sat well with me.

"I was wondering when you'd drop by." I stared at him as he skidded to a stop on the smooth diamond floor. "Don't you know it's polite to bring a gift? I thought you British folks were the height of propriety."

The three of us rallied, weapons in hand. I had to say, I'd never fought anyone on top of a priceless quantity of diamond before.

"You're like your sister, always talking when you should be acting," Davin shot back. To my amusement, the guy was breathless. It seemed the Jubilee mine was a match worthy of even the great, wormy Doncaster.

"Don't you see the blades in our hands? Did you not manage to piece your optical nerves back together?" I retorted.

"It is not my intention to enter fisticuffs with you, not after that foul stunt you pulled at Daggerston's. Do you know how painful it is to reattach your head to your body?" Davin scoffed. "Not everything has to result in violence, though that has always been your first and last resort, has it not, Finch?"

I flipped the dagger in my hand. "I'm clearly missing something. If you're not down here to fight us, then why've you been following us?"

"Why are we talking?" Garrett hissed. He took a step forward, the Avenging Angel raised and ready.

"I wouldn't do that if I were you," Davin warned him. "I have information that you'll want to hear. It is of particular interest to your friend, Finch. Perhaps you ought to give him the deciding vote before you attempt to lop off my head again?"

Garrett might as well have had skulls in his eyes. Anger had taken over. His knuckles whitened on the handle of his sword. I could tell it was taking every ounce of his willpower not to stab the guy before he could breathe another word. He shot me a dark look, as if waiting for me to wave the flag to let him go ape on Davin.

"We can hear him out," I finally said. "If we don't like it, you can do it your way."

I wanted to see Davin dead as much as Garrett did, but that smarmy jackass had a way of manipulating people. Now I *really* wanted to hear what he had to say, as much as I hated to admit it.

Garrett's face twisted up in fury. "You've got five seconds before I burn that mouth of yours shut."

"A wise choice." Davin smirked. *Not doing yourself any favors there, pal.* "I know that you are here on an errand for Erebus, Finch. What he might want with the Fountain of Youth has given me pause for thought, and I believe I have come to a solid conclusion, through my own intimate knowledge of our mutual acquaintance."

"What intimate knowledge?" I asked. Creeping thoughts tugged at the back of my mind, trying to pull all these threads into one logical line. Did Erebus and Davin have some kind of history? It sounded like it, but this could've been another of Davin's weaselly get-out-of-jail-free clauses.

"Let's address that later," Davin said. "I will explain what Erebus is truly after... *if* you stand down and let me have this victory."

"What victory?" Garrett growled. "We haven't even fought yet."

"The victory of sipping these immortal waters, and ruining Erebus's plans whilst I'm at it," he replied smoothly.

"You want to drink from the Fountain?" I cocked my head.

He chuckled. "Why else would anyone come here?"

Gotcha!

Davin didn't realize that he'd just given away a very important fact. If he needed to sip from the Fountain of Youth, then that meant whatever object he'd bound his life to was definitely a temporary solution for avoiding death. If he drank from the Fountain, that would make his immortality permanent.

"Your five seconds are up." Garrett took a step closer, and I had to get in his way.

I'd never loathed Davin more than in this moment, forcing me to step between him and my friend. By rights, I should've let Garrett loose, but Davin had dropped enough breadcrumbs to make me think twice. Sneaky of him, to know that this Hansel was starving for a way to get back at Erebus.

Even so, the heat of the Avenging Angel brought beads of sweat to my forehead.

"Get out of the way, Finch." Garrett meant business.

"Not yet. I'm sorry." I brought my dagger up and heard the grate as my blade met his.

His glare sparked. "We're not accepting any offer this bastard gives us. He dies, and he dies now!"

"Take it easy, Garrett." Saskia stepped in beside me, her shashka drawn.

"Both of you get out of my way. I don't want to hurt you, but I will if you stop me from skewering this weasel!" Garrett was losing it, big time. And who could blame him? This creep was the root of his problems.

Davin snickered in the gloom. "Then how about this, to whet your whistle? This floor is made of diamond, something I am sure you have already discerned. The Fountain is also warded against chalk doors and the like, so it will do you no good to take that path. You will wear yourselves out before you have even managed to chip the surface, unless one of you has suddenly become a Geode overnight?"

Even Garrett seemed to freeze for a moment.

"You can get through?" I asked, controlling my tone of voice.

"Unlike you, I did my homework regarding the protections Ponce de León put in place. There is truth in legend, if you ask the right people—spirits of Ponce's comrades, who heard his whisperings. They are still around, if you know where to look. A Necromancer's sensibilities," he replied, smug as ever. "One of his former men said he'd witnessed Ponce trying to manipulate diamond, so I prepared for such an eventuality. The only thing I didn't know was the location, but following you fixed that, and you did the hard part for me."

I scowled at him. "Do you or do you not want to get skewered?"

Davin laughed. "There'll be no skewering today. You aren't getting through this diamond without my knowledge, which means you won't be able to complete your mission for Erebus. I wonder, what would that cost you?"

Oh, you're good. You're very good.

"Let me kill him, Finch," Garrett snarled. "Let me kill him the way he killed me."

Rock, meet hard place. On the one hand, I would've liked nothing more than to see the Avenging Angel slice through Davin like butter. On the other hand, Davin had a point. I doubted Erebus would accept this as a completed task.

Oh yeah, I found the location of the Fountain. It's exactly where Ponce said it was. Oh, but there's this whopping great layer of diamond in the way. I hope that won't be a problem. Cheers. Can I have my freedom now? That would go over like a granny on a frosty morning. He'd made a point of saying I needed to be able to access the Fount.

"Ponce screwed us over," I said slowly, trying to buy my thoughts some time. "And if I go back to Erebus with this, he's not going to be happy."

"I should've drilled him harder." Saskia cast me an apologetic look. "If I had, we'd have found a way to break through. All his words were flowing out so effortlessly that I didn't realize he was being deceptive."

"You did what you could," I reassured her.

"Tick tock, tick tock." Davin tapped his finger against his Rolex.

"Listen up, Captain Hook, we'll give you an answer when we're good and ready," I fired back. "Stop the 'tick tock' business, or you might find a Garrett-shaped crocodile coming to bite you in the ass."

Come on, think! I was running out of time. Either Garrett would snap and go into berserker mode, or Davin would do something snaky and underhanded. I had to get my head in order.

Davin wanted to break through the diamond and drink the water. We were standing in his way, so he wanted to give us intel in exchange for backing the hell off. I wanted to hit Erebus where it hurt, but not at the risk of pissing him off so badly he revoked his promise to free me. And not if it meant risking the lives of everyone I cared about. I could live with the regret of not getting a morsel of vengeance if everyone went home happy.

The trouble was, I didn't want Davin going home happy. I wanted him dead. Yeah, this was going to be tricky to navigate. But maybe it didn't have to end with Davin getting away scot-free. If I summoned Erebus the moment Davin broke through the diamond, then maybe I could kill three birds with one stone. My freedom would be intact, my task would be complete, and Erebus would take Davin out of the picture.

At the very least, I could try to distract Davin long enough, post-diamond-smashing, for Garrett to take him on and find the immortality object. That would be a crazy-narrow window of opportunity, but we'd had worse odds.

All these thoughts raced through my head in seconds while Garrett continued to bristle with pure rage.

"I don't get it, Davin," I said. "We're pretty much your only obstacles. Why barter instead of trying to kill us? You've got to be annoyed about us decapitating you and stealing the Trap. Where's the poop, Doncaster? I smell it, but I don't see it."

"How delightfully crass." Davin laughed. "But the truth is, I don't really want to kill you. You haven't caught me in a murderous mood. I have to say, I rather admire you. Well, 'admire' may be too strong a word for you, Finch—I suppose I pity you."

"Charming," I said flatly.

"Allow me to elucidate. You were forced into servitude by your mother, and you have been forced into it again by Erebus. I, on the other hand, only served Katherine because it suited me at the time.

I choose my sides, always, but I am past all that unpleasantness. I had no interest in cults then, and I have no interest in them now. Why do you think I refused to pledge my allegiance?"

"Because you're a coward," Garrett spat.

Davin shrugged. "One man's coward is another man's savant. At present, all I desire is immortality. I would prefer not to kill for it, especially as that will only bring your little chums after me, and I tire of their pursuit."

"Who's to say *you* aren't working for Erebus?" I asked.

He tutted. "You really must pay attention. I choose whom I work for. I would never willingly follow an unworthy Child, like Erebus. It has served me well to keep myself cloaked from him. There are so many wonderful, rare artifacts in this world geared toward avoiding Children of Chaos. Curious, is it not? I suppose it must be a remnant from when they lorded it over mankind. You may rest assured, I am working entirely under my own command." He glanced between the three of us, taking his time with his speech. "I want immortality, but I do not want to continue being mutilated. Just because I do not die, in the absolute sense, doesn't mean getting beheaded or stabbed or magicked to death isn't a painful nuisance. If it should happen to peeve Erebus along the way, even better."

"Don't do it," Garrett warned. "Don't listen to him."

"I agree with Garrett on this one," Saskia added.

I sighed. *Then cover your ears, because you're not going to like this.* "I don't trust you, Davin. I don't trust anything about you, but if you can get us through this layer, then… I can live with that."

"Are you insane?" Garrett snapped.

"What else do you want me to do?" I looked at Garrett with desperate eyes. "We need to get through this layer, and we have no other way. Unless you've been keeping a solution to yourself?"

Garrett dropped his gaze. "No, but—"

"Then this is the only chance we've got." I turned back to Davin. "You have your truce. We let you dig through and have your little drink, and nobody gets hurt."

But it's only going to be temporary. The truce just needed to stand long enough for Davin to get through the diamond floor and come to an abrupt halt right before he lapped up his immortality juice. Now, how to convey that to Garrett and Saskia without Davin realizing? Some nudge-nudge, wink-winks, maybe? That was going to be the hard part.

THIRTY-SIX

Garrett

I had to go and stand against the wall. If I stayed near that sleazy bonehead, I was going to end up running him through with the Avenging Angel while his back was turned.

I couldn't believe he was still breathing. I couldn't believe we just had to stand around and let him get on with his plan as if he were one of us. I understood where Finch was coming from, but anger at his choice broiled in my guts. It felt even worse because Davin had come in with all the answers, and we'd been stumped.

Davin crouched on the diamond floor, preparing the spell that would let him through. At least, that seemed to be the intention. I wasn't convinced he wouldn't try and screw us over at the last moment, but that was why I still had the Avenging Angel out and ready.

Finch and Saskia appeared to have the same idea. Both of them stood with their weapons drawn.

"What are you doing?" Saskia asked.

"I need absolute quiet," Davin retorted. "Not a word, do you understand?"

Saskia pursed her lips. "You haven't even started yet."

"Not. A. Word!" Davin narrowed his eyes at her, which prompted her to take a step back. Evidently, she was having similar violent feelings. She came to join me at the wall, leaning against it.

As Finch paced behind Davin, the evil dirtbag got into the flow of his spell. Opening his palms, he crafted a glowing purple dagger out of nothing. A shudder ran up my spine. This was the same kind of dagger he'd thrown at me in Elysium. I could still feel the icy blade thudding between my shoulder blades. My body tensed, as if expecting a repeat.

Instead, Davin carved a line across his forearm. Blood sprang up. With a swipe of his hand, he made the dagger disappear and dabbed his finger into the trickling blood. He dragged it across the diamond floor, drawing strange symbols over the sleek surface. As he did, he began to whisper.

"*Hic est lapis, et petra. Audi spirituum. Ego sum vocant. Mihi opus tuum tremoribus. Frange est. Et conteret interitus. Ordinem perturbare. Turn ad cinerem. Turn ut pulvis. Ventilabis adversus bellum. Sic fiet nihil.*"

His veins pulsed, some turning black, others violet. The spell lit up the ground, that purple glow reflected by the diamond and the water below it. The liquid thrashed against the covering like it wanted to fight against what was being said.

The symbols solidified. The blood turned silver and hardened on the floor.

Davin used more blood to draw smaller symbols. I realized the outer symbols represented the five points of a pentagram, and these smaller ones were being written inside. He repeated the spell a second time.

"*Hic est lapis, et petra. Audi spirituum. Ego sum vocant. Mihi opus tuum tremoribus. Frange est. Et conteret interitus. Ordinem perturbare.*"

Turn ad cinerem. Turn ut pulvis. Ventilabis adversus bellum. Sic fiet nihil."

As before, the symbols turned silver and hardened. All the while, Davin glowed brighter. I caught a glimpse of his eyes when he raised his head and found that they glowed, too. His power poured out. I felt it in the air around me as the atmosphere thickened.

At least he's got the skills to back up his arrogance.

Goosebumps covered my skin from the ripples of his magic. Beside me, Saskia stared in a mixture of awe and fear.

It bugged me when I encountered people like Davin, who had both immense talent and a crooked moral compass. They could do so much good if they stopped thinking about themselves and considered how they could help others. If he had joined our side instead of Katherine's, who knew what might've happened? But that wasn't Davin's way. He was as self-centered as he was cocky. And that would never change.

He repeated the spell a third time, drawing another set of symbols even smaller than before. Each symbol was different, and I wondered what they all meant. This was beyond my level of magical expertise, and judging from Saskia's face, it was beyond hers, too.

"Iactata fatiscit in pulverem deducat. Perdere et iterum corruptae. Nunc ea facere."

The spell changed as he uttered new and ancient words. He lifted his palms, and they shone with blinding light, forcing me to cover my eyes. I tried to peek through my fingers, not wanting to miss anything in case this was an elaborate diversion tactic. Davin slammed his palms on the diamond floor, and the entire surface began to crack and crumble under him.

He shuffled back to safety as the splinters spread and the diamond disintegrated into the water below.

Aside from the bright blue hue of the water, the pool itself was underwhelming—just a six-foot hole in the ground. But I couldn't see the bottom, which suggested it was deeper than it looked.

Davin edged toward the rim of the pool, each tiny movement noticeably a struggle. Whatever that spell was, it had taken a lot out of him. But it had also narrowed his focus. He was intent on the pool, giving me the chance to creep after him. He leaned over, his hands cupped and ready. I raised my palms, ready to unleash Air.

Before either of us could act, he went flying so fast it made my head spin. My eyes darted to Finch, who held his palms up, a faint thrum showing the tendrils of Telekinesis coiling out of his hands.

"Did you really think I was going to let you do that?"

Finch's tone held a dark, menacing edge. I nearly laughed. I couldn't believe I'd doubted him, that I'd actually thought Finch would allow Davin to get his way. Now, I realized Finch had never intended to keep his word. He'd been playing that tool for all he was worth. It seemed there was still a shred of cold-hearted villain inside Finch, after all.

Davin scrambled to his feet and shot a dangerous look at Finch. "Did you really think I was going to let you leave alive? I just wanted a sip of water first to make sure the odds were in my favor."

He didn't waste another moment chatting. As he twirled his hands through the air, two daggers appeared. He hurled the first at Finch's head, but Finch ducked. The magical blade whizzed over him and hit the wall, exploding in a fountain of purple shards.

I shoved Saskia aside as the second dagger hurtled toward her. It skimmed past her shoulder and landed in the Fountain of Youth, claimed by the water. Angry bubbles rose to the surface as the magical water dismantled the weapon. Then the surface lay flat again.

"Your days of playing with death are over," I snapped at him.

"You didn't fare too well the last time I killed *you*. And if it hadn't been for your human friend, you'd have died again in Daggerston's study." Davin launched two more daggers at Saskia and me, but we managed to evade them.

To my left, Finch surged with his white-handled dagger and poison-tipped Esprit, the lighter transforming into a second blade. Taking his lead, I lifted the Avenging Angel and sprinted for Davin, with Saskia bringing up the rear, twirling her shashka like the badass Ice Queen she was. There wasn't a lot of solid ground to stand on, and Davin was already backed against the wall.

Davin crafted two more daggers and held them in a defensive stance. "I guess I will kill you first and taste my immortality later."

"The only thing you'll be tasting is this blade," I shouted.

THIRTY-SEVEN

Finch

My daggers collided with Davin's. A sharp jolt blasted through my arms on impact, the dark magic of his blades slithering under my skin. I retreated from the clash, only to get smacked in the chest by a barrage of Telekinesis. I arced backward and hit the cavern wall, collapsing in a less-than-graceful heap on the floor.

Ahead, Saskia spun her shashka so fast I could hardly see it while Garrett bore down on Davin like an unleashed, pissed-off gorilla. Davin crafted another dagger and raised it to meet Garrett's sword. I heard the screech of metal on magic as violet sparks flew.

With his free hand, Davin flung another bolt of Telekinesis that wrapped around Saskia's legs. He tugged on the strands, jerking her to the ground and flinging her across the cavern.

Not very gentlemanly, Davin.

I leapt up and hurtled back into the fray. I skidded to my knees and sailed across the smooth floor, my daggers raised for an overdue slicing.

I managed to drag Carnwennan across Davin's thigh before he slashed another purple blade right at my face. I bent all the way down to the ground as if I were in *The Matrix*, and the blade hissed by the tip of my nose.

"You're starting to get on my last nerve, Finch. Any pity I felt for you has gone right out the window," Davin rasped as blood oozed from his wound. All the while, his intact dagger screamed against Garrett's blade. Garrett was putting all his energy into trying to bring his sword closer to Davin, but the small knife wouldn't budge.

"Yeah? Well, I never pitied you. You made your own bed; now you can lie in it. Preferably dead."

I popped up and struck again, but he was too quick. He used his Telekinesis to grab a stalactite that dangled from the center of the cavern, then hoisted himself out of danger and landed on the other side of the pool.

Oh, so we're swinging away now, are we? What are you, a monkey?

The three of us sprinted to the edge of the pool. On the other side, Davin sank to his knees, ready to sip the good stuff. I wondered why he didn't just drag some of it up magically, but this wasn't any old water. If that had been an option, Davin would have tried it.

Not a chance. Lashing out with Telekinesis, I grabbed him around the waist and tugged him back over the pool. Feeling the tension in my muscles, I slammed him as hard as possible into the rockface. Anything to knock this sucker out. But unfortunately, he was back up and raring to go within moments.

"You'll have to try harder than that." Davin leered, wiping a smear of blood from his lip.

"Lucky for you, there's plenty more in the tank." An idea burst into my mind. Not a nice one, but one that would definitely take him by surprise. I turned to the other two and lowered my voice. "Be ready. Oh, and try not to scream."

They looked at me in confusion. I balled my hands into fists and closed my eyes, letting my Mimicry run through my body. I felt the familiar shift of cells as they changed into the image I wanted to create. Sort of like static electricity, but it ran much deeper, right through my veins.

A moment later, the trio of gasps told me the transformation was complete.

"Davin. I wish I could say I was surprised, but you were always a smarmy, self-serving little paramecium."

The voice leaving my mouth didn't belong to me, and I had to fight not to shudder at that oh-so-familiar tone. Arrogant, disdainful, and the root of all my childhood trauma. *Mama's home, Davin.* "Did you miss me, darling? Did you think I would just forget all the promises you made?"

I opened my eyes to find Davin staring at me, his face a picture of doubt and bewilderment. I wished I could've taken a snapshot so I'd have something to laugh at when he was six feet under.

"Nice try. I know you're not her." Even so, Davin hesitated, like he wasn't entirely sure.

"Oh, but I am, darling. Like I always said, even my backup plans have backup plans." I gave him one of Katherine's signature cat-that-got-the-cream smiles. "You didn't think I'd let Finch get away with that martyr shtick, did you? Erebus was no match for me, though he provided a much-needed distraction to slip into my son's form. I tricked them all, and I'm here to attain immortality in a human body, at long last."

I took a step toward Davin, and a flicker of confusion crossed his face.

"That's not possible. You died! I saw you die!"

I knew I didn't have much time. I gave a discreet nod to Saskia and Garrett. *This is the moment, lads and ladettes!* They branched off at either side of me.

"You had your chances, Davin." While he panicked, I unleashed a strand of Telekinesis and wrapped it around his throat. I squeezed until his eyes bulged.

At that, Davin snapped out of it. He lifted his palms and sent out tendrils of his own, the edges tinged purple. They snaked up my strands, freeing his neck from my grip. Before I could counter-attack, Garrett bore down on Davin with his sword.

Davin met the Avenging Angel with two crossed daggers, and the clang echoed around the cavern. Debris tumbled from the gaping void above us, rocks skittering across the floor and falling into the pool. Bubbles rose and devoured the chunks, melting the stone on impact. *What the hell happens if a person goes in there?* I couldn't think about it now, but I made a mental note not to topple into the weird water.

From the other side, Saskia lunged with her shashka and sank it into Davin's shoulder. He cried out and sent a pulse of purple light through his palms, into his daggers. Garrett reeled back in agony, sinking to the ground as black veins spiderwebbed across his hands and up his forearms. Davin twisted, wrenching the embedded shashka out of Saskia's hand, leaving her with nothing.

He pushed a blast of Telekinesis into Saskia, sending her halfway across the cavern. I held my breath, frozen. She was too close to the pool, and I'd just seen what it did to the rocks—evaporating them. This water was supposed to bring everlasting life, sure, but perhaps that was only in small doses. If someone submerged, maybe the pool had a less pleasant outcome. I released my Telekinesis and grasped her out of the air, bringing her away from the pool and setting her on the ground. She lay there, limp, but there was no time to check whether she was all right. She was down, and Garrett was down, which left little old me. I switched back to my normal form, not wanting to waste unnecessary energy.

"Your mother would have been proud of that one," Davin hissed. "Where did you learn to do that? I've never witnessed that before. It was as if she was right here. Your voice, your mannerisms... it was her."

"A lot has changed while you've been under your rock, Davin."

I dug deep for another wave of Telekinesis. It hit him hard and constricted around him. He fought against it, but I lifted him and bashed him against the rock again and again. I was about to smack him into it once more, when something fell from his pocket and clattered on the ground.

It was an amber amulet in the shape of an ankh; its facets glinted in the low light. Davin's eyes darted toward it. He'd gone pale, and it had nothing to do with me hammering his head into solid stone for a good minute.

With renewed strength, he powered his Telekinesis into his palms and broke apart the strands that held him. He dropped to the ground like a sack of spuds, and I could've sworn I heard something crunch, but he didn't seem to notice. He scrabbled toward the amulet. His hand had almost reached it when I whipped it away with another dose of Telekinesis.

It's got to be the thing that resurrects him. I wasn't one-hundred percent sure, but the only way to find out was to keep it the hell away from Davin. Davin released a stream of dark purple energy at me.

It moved in a smoky wave and followed me wherever I went. The smoke forced its way down my throat and into my nostrils. It stank of acrid metal and gasoline, choking me as I struggled for clean air.

"Since you like Shapeshifting so much," Davin snarled.

What? I looked down as my skin prickled. It felt like Shifting, but not quite, as if something had gone wrong.

Thick, dark hairs protruded from my arms. It was fur of some kind, spreading quickly across my body. My lungs burned and my ribs ached. I howled as one of my ribs cracked, and it felt like a force within me was pushing my entire ribcage apart.

Saskia's voice cut through the cavern.

"*Dukhi etogo mesta, poslushay menya. Osvobodi etogo cheloveka ot proklyatiya. Uberite yego. Osvobodi yego. Uberite yego. Sdelay eto seychas.*"

The wrenching sensation ebbed. Whatever she'd done counteracted Davin's curse. I couldn't have been more grateful. Changing into someone, or something, else was an ability I liked to have control over. I didn't want to be a werewolf, or a cat, or anything fluffy, without my say-so.

Up ahead, Garrett raced toward Davin with his sword raised. Davin was so focused on snatching up the amulet that he didn't seem to notice. I held my breath.

Davin twisted around and shot both barrels of Telekinesis at Garrett, who flew through the air and landed on the steps above, writhing in pain. Saskia was on her feet, but she was in bad shape. Blood trickled from her ear and nose. And she was swaying like a daisy in a storm.

"Is that the object?" Saskia staggered toward me. "That amulet?"

I nodded. "We need it. Are you okay?"

"I'm fine. Not a damsel, remember?"

"Right." No matter what she said, I worried. She looked like death warmed over.

"I've got a trick up my sleeve. Do whatever you've got to do to get that amulet off him while I keep him busy. Understand?" she wheezed.

"Affirmative." I put my hand on her shoulder. "Just don't do anything stupid."

She smiled woozily. "Like... this?"

Pure white light exploded through her body and out of her eyes. The force of it tilted her head up, her arms going with it. As the light pulsated out into the cavern, shapes emerged, hazy at first but getting clearer by the second. Saskia was calling on the spirits of this place to help her out, and, boy, were they coming out in force. At least twenty figures answered her, their faces gaunt and macabre. I guessed they must've been miners or something, but it was hard to tell. Hollow eyes stared at her, awaiting instruction. Even Davin stopped, his face twisted in alarm.

Saskia brought her arms down and pounded her hands into her chest. All the light she'd created snapped right back into her, bringing the spirits with it. Each one disappeared into her until she was a mass of raw light and spiritual energy.

Hovering over the ground like something out of a horror movie, she swept toward Davin. He raised his hands to retaliate, but Saskia unleashed every ounce of raw power she had. It pummeled Davin in a never-ending torrent, giving him zero chance to get up and fight back.

I didn't wait, knowing this might be the only shot we had at getting Davin out of the way—and separating him from his amulet. It was time to call in the big boys. Or, rather, the big boy. I didn't want to, but we couldn't keep fighting Davin on our own. Not if we wanted him truly dead.

I ran to the edge of the Fountain of Youth and covered the portal ring that usually sent me to Tartarus. The funny thing was, it also worked the other way. I'd just never had a reason, or desire, to use it for that.

Pressing my palm against the ruby, I closed my eyes and called for Erebus.

"*Veni ad me. Audi, audite me. Te requiro. Et vocavi te. Age nunc. Commotae Erebi veni nunc!*" I cried, sending my message into the ether. It beat going through all the mega-wordy spells that I was forced to use before I became Erebus's slave. And, hopefully, it meant he'd get his ass here that much quicker.

"NO!" Davin howled from the midst of his pummeling.

Saskia hit him harder. Even in her glowing mega-zoid form, she wasn't getting too close to him. Sensible, considering he could still kill her. He might've been taking a thrashing, but cornered enemies were the most dangerous.

I looked over to Garrett. He was still writhing on the steps.

Where are you, Erebus? Come on! I didn't know how long we had until Davin found a way to fight back. The entire mine shook. Rocks and stones and chunks of step hit the floor, exploding into shards. Garrett managed to pull himself to safety.

A huge hunk of rock plummeted down, narrowly missing Saskia. The glow evaporated from her body as the rock's landing thundered around the cavern. She couldn't keep attacking Davin and protect herself from the falling rocks at the same time. Davin detonated a curse in her face, and the purple smoke disappeared inside her. She collapsed, blood trickling from her mouth.

I was torn between running to Saskia by way of a Fountain detour, to carry her some of the water in my hands, and dealing with Davin. After watching Davin try to drink, I was pretty sure a mouthful was safe. And, right now, she looked like she needed it. But Davin was already back on his feet, making the decision for me. Only Erebus could get us out of this, and I couldn't stop until he was here. He was already on his way. I could feel him hurtling through time and space to answer my summons.

Davin ran toward me but halted abruptly. At first, I didn't understand. Then, I turned to face the pool. A smoky figure formed above the water, twisting out of nothingness. A moment later, the smoky figure sank down into the water itself, and Erebus's wispy fronds spread across the surface.

I guess you won't be drinking it now, Doncaster. But I didn't understand why Erebus was messing around in the water when he was supposed to be answering my call. Namely, to kill Davin before he weaseled his way out of here.

"You fool," Davin whispered. "You absolute fool."

"You bitter you can't have your sip?" I retorted, but he wasn't listening to me anymore. His wild eyes were fixed on the smoky presence in the pool.

"You did it, you despicable wretch. That is why you wanted the Fountain... you found a way."

Dread twisted my stomach. "A way to do what, Davin?"

Davin didn't answer me. Still staring at the pool, he scrambled across the cavern and half-ran, half-fell up the first few steps of the staircase. With shaky hands, he took out an Ephemera and closed his palms around it. *So, that's how he's been jumping around after us so quickly.* Under Katherine's reign, he'd had the ability to portal without an Ephemera, but Gaia had taken that away when she'd restored the balance of Chaos. I guessed he'd had to follow us down here on foot for the same reason we hadn't been able to chalk-door into the cavern, but getting out was easier than getting in.

I wanted to go after him, but my legs wouldn't budge. I tried, but they were frozen stiff, as if I'd been superglued to the cavern floor.

What the—?

Erebus's laughter echoed through the cavern. I tried to back away from the pool, but I was still stuck. My mouth opened in a cry of pain as energy jolted through my feet and shot up my legs. It jangled my every cell, sapping me of my strength. Like quicksand, the more I fought, the tighter the ground seemed to hold me.

All I could do was watch as black smoke swelled through the glowing water until there was no blue left. And feel overwhelming regret as Davin disappeared in a vortex of bright red light like a scared little rat diving from a sinking ship.

I'll get you in the end. I'll find you, and I'll kill you. But right now, I had a massive, Erebus-sized problem to deal with.

Just as I thought the energy would never end, an almighty pulse burst out of the water. The force that bound me to the ground shattered, letting the explosion take me right off my feet. It hurled me backward, and I careened into the cavern wall so hard my teeth rattled, my head crashing into the rock with a painful thud.

A dark mist drifted over my eyes, my brain filling with a cold, strange sensation. I was losing consciousness. I'd been knocked out enough times to know the feeling. Before unconsciousness claimed me, I glanced back at the pool. There, rising from the water, was a figure. Not smoky or misty, but solid. And made of darkness.

I tried to get a better look, but it was too late. The darkness inside my head had come to claim me. And I had no strength left to fight it.

THIRTY-EIGHT

Finch

My eyes snapped open. My brain must have decided it was time for a reboot. I wished I'd kept them closed.

A figure stood at the edge of the Fountain of Youth—well, what was left of it. There was no water anymore, just a gaping hole where it should've been. And the one who'd sucked it dry was this man, with a pair of creepy black eyes that stared into my damned soul. And he was completely nude. Everything on show, literally everything. I didn't know whether to laugh or knock myself unconscious again, just to get that vision out of my head.

He definitely wasn't human. His skin was as black as his eyes. Not a natural melanin, but an almost impossible pigment of darkest-night's-sky black.

"What the—!" Garrett rasped. No spiderwebbing veins shot up his arms, and he didn't look like he was rapping on death's door anymore.

"Where… did… he come from? Who is he?" Saskia came to, blinking slowly.

I didn't know if the pool blast had hit them too, or if they'd just been dealing with their previous inflictions. Either way, they were as shocked and horrified as I was.

He found a way... Davin's words replayed in my head.

"Erebus?" The word barely squeaked from my throat.

He laughed coldly. "What do you think?"

"Uh... average? It's hard to tell." My head felt fluffy.

"Try again." Erebus glared at me. Clearly not the answer he'd been looking for.

"Sorry, I don't know what I'm looking at. What's going on here? You're supposed to be a wispy smoke creature, so this is a little... weird." I shook my head, as if that would dislodge the fluff.

He chuckled. "I have acquired a body for myself. What do you make of me in my solid form?"

I had to lean against the back wall to catch my breath. Terror spiked through my chest like a red-hot poker. What was I supposed to say to that? Children of Chaos weren't supposed to have solid forms! They were supposed to stay in their neat little otherworlds where they could only cause so much damage, sticking to the constraints they'd been forced into, way back when they'd gotten too overlordy with the human world. We'd already been through this with Katherine. And I wasn't a fan of déjà vu.

Did Mother Dearest give you this idea? The timing was suspicious at best, calculated at worst.

"Honestly, I think I preferred you before," I finally said. This was bad. Very bad. And that was possibly the understatement of the century.

Erebus smirked. "Always making jokes. That's what I admire about you, Finch. Even in the most perilous circumstances, you retain your sense of humor." He swiped his hand, and a cluster of Ephemeras appeared out of nowhere. I recognized each and every one of them.

"Why do you have those?" My voice trembled. Those

Ephemeras had been the end-goal of my first few missions for Erebus. Seven total, each infused with the Chaos of some very old and powerful, not to mention dangerous, acolytes of Erebus from back in the days when they were still worshipped as Greek gods.

I'd gone to Greece, Italy, Jordan, Syria, Egypt, Tunisia, and Morocco for those Ephemeras. And I'd almost died each time, for various reasons: monsters, magicals, booby traps, feisty spirits, and the more human risks of being caught in a warzone.

Erebus smiled. "My abilities as a Child of Chaos are somewhat diminished in this form. They are still there, but far less diverse. These Ephemeras, which you so kindly collected, will give me what I need to make myself formidable in this body."

"You know they're only temporary though, right?" Garrett cut in. He was breathing heavily.

Erebus threw his head back. "For you mortals, perhaps. For me, they will remain for a long while, simply supplementing what I already possess—continuing for many months, at the very least. Just long enough to allow me to find a more permanent solution."

He closed his palms around the bronze ball, and the Chaos flooded his body. Green light pulsed along his arm, standing out against that pitch-black skin. He moved on to the next, and the next, all of them visibly coursing through his veins in various shades, until the Ephemeras lay empty at his feet.

He dropped each empty ball to the floor like a piece of trash.

I felt like I should stop him somehow, but what did one do against a humanoid supernatural being who'd just poured a load of hyper-powerful magic into himself? Trying any kind of attack was a surefire way to get killed.

"How does this even work?" I glanced at the empty pool. "How is this even possible?"

"You made it possible, my dear Finch." Erebus leered. "Gaia forbade me from finding this place, knowing my intentions. She put up all manner of charms and blockades to prevent me from sensing it. Even if I'd discovered this location, I would never have been able to penetrate the diamond that was used to coat this pool."

Erebus smiled to himself, clearly having the best day of his immortal life. "There is ancient magic in diamonds, for they refract light and they refract Light. Both kinds—the actual and the magical. They have often been used to ward against creatures of Darkness, and it would have prevented my access. I believe that is why Ponce de León constructed it in the first place, under Gaia's persuasion. He may not have realized she was manipulating him, but such a barrier reeks of her influence. She will undoubtedly know, by now, that I have broken through, but the rules of Chaos prevent her from stopping me. A Child can't interfere with another Child's actions, as you well understand."

Come on, brain, think! Fear had silenced my neurons. I struggled to turn the gears, and no brilliant, or even obvious, solutions presented themselves.

I'd always wondered about the purpose of my missions, since they were always as clear as mud, with hardly any explanation or instruction. At the time, Ephemeras hadn't seemed too concerning. I'd never have thought that he could actually use them for his own benefit. I'd gone along with the assumption that, being a wispy smoke Child, he had no flesh to access the Ephemeras. But I'd opened up the Fountain, and now he had it all—body, magic, the works.

"I can tell this has come as quite a shock to you," Erebus said. "But don't worry, my intentions aren't what you likely suspect. You did an exemplary job, and I only had to give you a couple of nudges here and there. And I can tell some of you are more impressed by the result than others." He laughed, nodding to Saskia.

Saskia hadn't said a word. She just gaped at Erebus, equal parts scared and drooling. He didn't look half bad in human form, to be fair. I could understand why folks had worshipped these Children, once upon a time. He resembled the kind of honed, chiseled Greek god you saw on old vases. If only he didn't have those creepy-as-hell eyes. Glinting symbols of his Darkness.

"I'm just trying to wrap my head around all this." *And I'm kicking myself for not seeing it sooner.*

Garrett seemed equally transfixed. No, he was terrified, a fact indicated by his eyes bugging out of his head. He understood what this meant a whole lot better than Saskia did. Garrett had been there in Elysium, and he knew what a human-Child could mean for the wider world.

"At least you hung around, unlike Davin. A perpetual coward, that one." Erebus laughed again. "I suppose I have to thank him for removing the diamond layer for me. If he hadn't, I would have had to give you another sharp nudge, maybe killed a few of your friends out of frustration. Once again, you came here woefully underprepared. You should have known about the diamond layer and made preparations to remove it, seeing as I told you that you must make sure the Fount is *accessible*. But what's done is done, and everything worked out in the end, so I can't complain."

I shot him a dirty look. "It wasn't as if you were forthcoming, Erebus. If you'd wanted me to know the diamond layer was here, you should've told me yourself."

Not that any of that mattered now. Erebus had claimed his victory, all the serendipitous pieces floating into place.

"I confess, I didn't know of the diamond layer, but Davin has dealt with that inconvenience regardless. So, let's not argue now, on this glorious occasion," Erebus said. "I'd hate to have to hurt someone you care about after you've done such good work, just because you spoke to me in a tone I didn't like."

This was a mess. A bigger mess, maybe, than the one my mother had tried to create. Erebus had managed to get a body without giving away a single hint that he was up to something so colossally awful. And I'd done his bidding, thinking the rules applied to him, having no clue about this loophole.

I was reeling from the shock. It didn't feel real yet. But I had one huge, horrifying question, singeing the tip of my tongue. A question I wasn't sure I wanted answered. Nevertheless, I asked it.

"But... what *are* your intentions? What are you going to do with a body?"

THIRTY-NINE

Garrett

_____

"If you're worried about me becoming Katherine part two, you needn't be," Erebus replied calmly. "My reason for doing this is much more personal, and I have no desire to upset the balance of the universe or enslave mankind for the sake of an inflated ego. No, there is something that I want, something I can only find in this world. And I want to claim it myself, which requires this form."

He stretched out his limbs and admired his new appendages. He seemed to like what he saw, turning his arms to catch the faint light of the cavern.

I didn't know where to look or what to think. To be honest, I wasn't entirely sure what was standing in front of us. We knew it was possible for a Child of Chaos to take human form, but it hadn't worked out this well for Katherine.

Yet, here Erebus was, proving that it could be done efficiently, with no cracks to speak of.

He turned his gaze on me, and my blood froze in my veins. "I mustn't neglect your part in this, Garrett, or yours, Saskia." His coal eyes briefly met her wide, frightened ones.

"Finch is very capable and has proven his worth in gaining the artifacts I've asked of him, but he couldn't have completed this mission alone. Not without it taking much longer than I was willing to wait. So, with that in mind, I'd like to thank you both for your assistance. It is the sole reason I'm not going to kill you, so count yourselves lucky that you succeeded."

I was about to respond when Erebus clicked his fingers. The cavern rushed around me as my body disintegrated. I barely had time to understand what was going on before I landed with a heavy thud on solid ground.

Sunlight stung my eyes. A cold wind nipped my cheeks, and my lungs sighed as fresh air rushed into them. I sat up, a searing headache throbbing between my temples. I didn't know if it was the bright daylight or what Erebus had done, but it hurt.

Blinking to try and acclimate my eyesight, I realized I was sitting on the barren earth at the top of the Jubilee mine.

A groan beside me made me turn. Saskia lay on the ground, holding her hand to her head.

"Are you okay?" I hurried to help her as the two of us staggered to our feet.

"I think so," she replied, her voice a bit unsteady. "Hard to say, with someone beating war drums in my skull."

I smiled, about to commend her for keeping her sense of humor, when the earth rumbled violently, shaking our knees as we tried to stay upright. I glanced at the edge of the gaping hole ahead of us and wished I hadn't. The edges were crumbling away, and vast cracks split the ground, breaking through soil and rock like lightning bolts.

One huge crack splintered past us and expanded. Everything in its path toppled into the abyss. I grabbed Saskia's hand and sprinted for the metal fence, both of us stumbling as the volatile shocks grew worse, the roar of the collapsing mine drowning out every other sound.

"Garrett! Saskia!" A faint voice cut through the din. Tatyana was running toward us, a panicked look on her face.

"Tatyana?" I yelled back, struggling over the mayhem behind us.

"What happened?! My charm lit up, and I came as fast as I could!" she bellowed. "Where's Finch?"

I glanced back over my shoulder and realized he was nowhere to be seen. I'd gotten so distracted helping Saskia that I hadn't even noticed. Utter, ice-cold dread punched me in the stomach.

Where is he? Why would Erebus have flung Saskia and me out of the cavern, but not him? I hesitated, torn between running back to the cavern before the mine imploded and getting to safety.

The cracks were multiplying by the second, the mine moments away from complete destruction.

"Tell me later!" Tatyana seemed to realize the severity of the situation.

Together, we sprinted for the metal fence. The gates were open, the guards already fleeing for their lives. We burst through and kept going. The thunder of the crumbling mine followed our every footstep. There was no way of knowing how far the destruction would reach, and we couldn't take any chances.

Racing until my lungs were about to explode, we tore across the flat terrain of Sakha. The roar began to taper off—we were just far enough away that the sound wasn't so intense. Even so, we kept running for another five minutes before I halted.

Tatyana and Saskia stopped with me, all of us bent double to catch our breaths. I used the brief respite to look back. The perimeters of the huge void had changed. The edges had fallen into the basin, and the new lip advanced right past where the metal fences used to stand. The guard towers were gone. Many of the houses of the neighboring town had also vanished into the abyss.

Beneath the steady growl of the falling mine, I heard another sound. Faint and haunting. It was the sound of screaming. My heart clenched in a vise. There had to be miners down there in the subterranean depths. And there had to have been families in town, going about their daily business when the rim started to collapse.

"Oh my…" Tatyana trailed off as she witnessed the catastrophic damage.

Saskia leaned into her sister. "Can you feel them?"

Tatyana frowned. "No. Can you?"

"Feel what?" I gasped, my breathing returning to normal.

"Spirits… people must have died in the mine. We can't sense them," Tatyana replied in confusion.

As if in answer, a crowd of people materialized on the flat terrain, looking around as if they didn't quite understand what had just happened. Miners, families, all sorts.

Saskia gaped. "Did Erebus… save them?"

That didn't seem like Erebus, but perhaps he'd made an exception. Perhaps Finch had said something, or done something, to make Erebus rescue these people. *Speaking of which…*

"Is Finch there?" I asked in desperation.

Tatyana frowned. "I… I don't know. He may be too deep." She glanced at me. "What happened? I came as soon as the medallions told me you were in danger, but when I got here, the mine was already starting to cave in."

I dug my nails into my palm and tried not to think of Finch, possibly dead in that cavern with Erebus, or worse. But if Erebus had gone to the trouble of saving those other people, surely he would have saved Finch too?

"Yeah… we've got a lot to talk about."

FORTY

Finch

———

I ducked and covered my head, fairly sure I was about to get brained by a falling rock. The mine had started to cave in after Erebus sent Saskia and Garrett spinning out of the chamber to safety—at least, I hoped he had.

I also guessed destroying the mine was entirely down to him. After all, he didn't want anyone else finding the Fountain's location, did he? That was his dirty secret. If other Children found out what he'd done, maybe they'd be jealous and give him trouble for it, and he couldn't have that.

Though I wasn't sure why he couldn't have been satisfied with simply draining the pool, to make sure nobody could copy him or receive its gifts. This was beyond dramatic.

I squeezed my eyes shut and waited for death. All I could think about were the innocent miners who were going to die because of Erebus's selfishness. But that was cosmic deities for you. Smiting and destroying and killing whatever, and whomever, they liked.

I'm sorry... I'm sorry I helped him do this. It wasn't enough. An apology would never be enough, but it was all I had right now.

I kept waiting, expecting that final blow to come. But it didn't. Hesitantly, I cracked one eye open. Sunlight ravaged my retinas, taking no optical prisoners.

Huh? Somehow, I wasn't in the mine anymore. Everything had happened so quickly that I hadn't even realized the air had changed, that there wasn't any gloom surrounding me. Instead, there was glorious sunshine and a clear blue sky.

A harsh wind whipped up as I opened my second eye and absorbed this abrupt new setting. I stood on the edge of a cliff. I craned my neck as I looked up at the ancient, enormous structure ahead of me. It reminded me of a monastery, or a cathedral—something ecclesiastical. Grand and eerie, with gaping-mouthed statues of saints and virgins covered in lichen and dirt.

Below me, a frothing sea crashed against the cliff, sending jarring thuds through the ground beneath my feet. Like the drums of war and just as frightening. Beyond the vast building, however, there didn't seem to be anything. It sat in isolation on this clifftop, nothing but swaying green grass and rolling hills as far as the eye could see. The end of the earth or the middle of nowhere. It was hard to tell.

Erebus stood beside me, glistening in the sunlight. If he wanted to blend in, even slightly, he was really going to have to put clothes on. I decided to just not look at the offending articles. Then again, everything about Erebus offended me right now.

He turned to me with a smirk. "Are you ready for the next stage of your mission? There is much work left to do, and we can't waste a minute. I say 'we,' but I really mean you."

Rage spiked my blood. *Of course the scumbag would betray me like this!* "No, no, no, no, don't you dare. You said this was the end. You said that once I'd found the Fountain, you'd give me what I desired most in the world. That means my freedom—so don't go backpedaling now!"

"I said that once you have completed the mission and discovered the Fountain's location, I would give you what you desired most," he replied. "But your mission isn't over yet. It has only just begun."

A stark dose of reality, and another ten points on the "How stupid can you be, Finch?" leaderboard. Erebus had never intended to free me after finding the Fountain. Why release a good, obedient little slave when there was so much more I could do for him?

Now I understood why he'd wrapped his promise up in vague phrasings. Truthfully, part of me had always understood; I just hadn't wanted to accept it. I'd wanted to hope instead of being battered with doubts. But Erebus was a born trickster. Of course this was the way it had gone down. Man, I could've slapped myself for even contemplating freedom.

"Of course it has," I bit out. "I bet you've done something with Garrett and Saskia, too, so you can hold them over my head?"

Erebus smiled. "Don't worry, your friends are safe. I made sure they were far enough from the mine to avoid certain death, though they'll be doing a fair bit of running."

"Are they safe or not?" I snapped.

"They aren't dead, so relax. I don't work well with disgruntled servants, which is why I did you the courtesy of rescuing them." He gazed up at the strange building, with its spires, cloisters, and graying walls. "Their part is definitively over."

"What about my part?" I pressed.

I didn't want to be in Erebus's service anymore. In fact, I'd have happily shoved him over the cliff if I'd thought it would make a difference. Did the Fountain just give him a human body, or had it made his body fully immortal, too? I toyed with the idea of experimenting, then remembered the powerful, ancient Ephemeras he'd sucked up.

No, maybe not.

Erebus laughed. "All will become clear."

"Wow, so helpful." I folded my arms across my chest and tried to swallow my rising rage.

"You really have been a good servant, Finch, and I'm pleased that our business is not yet over. I've come to rely on you, in a curious way."

I snorted. "Am I supposed to be grateful? Are you going to pin a medal on me, or maybe give me a personalized mug with 'Number One Slave' written on it?"

"Always amusing." He snickered, though his eyes didn't move from the building. I followed his gaze, wondering if I was missing something. The structure was incredible, sure, but it wasn't anything I hadn't seen before. I'd been to many a temple and castle on my errands for Erebus.

Scanning the wall, I noticed a woman sitting on a stone bench, half cast in the building's shadow. She was old, with gray hair in a neat bun, and seemed to be waiting for someone. But she hadn't seen us.

I doubt your bus is coming this way, love. There were no roads or paths to speak of.

I turned back to Erebus. "You're in the human world now, you slimy mudskipper. You might as well start acting like it, or at least cloak yourself before someone sees you in all your... glory. I suggest beginning with boxers."

Erebus grinned eerily. "She can't see me, fear not. Your work begins today, Finch. I have other urgent tasks to attend to. Don't return to me until you've learned how to do it properly."

"Do what properly?"

He didn't bother to answer. Instead, he just vanished with a snap of his fingers, leaving me alone on the edge of a cliff.

Yeah, I really should've shoved you over the edge, you evil prick. Next time I saw him, I wanted my freedom. If I didn't get it after whatever this task was, there'd be hell to pay. Even if it meant going against Ponce's warning and involving the other Children of Chaos, I'd get myself out of this. They might not have been able to interfere directly, but I bet Lux had more leeway than the others. If he screwed me again, I was going to bring in the big guns.

Angry and frustrated beyond belief, I walked to the only person who might be able to help me, trying not to get blown off the freaking cliff by a blast of chill wind. The poor woman didn't even look at me as I approached.

"Excuse me? Sorry to bother you, but can you tell me where I am?" I put on my softest voice, in case she thought I was an escaped lunatic or something.

She eyed me. "You mean, you don't know?" Her voice carried a thick, Southern brogue that was oddly comforting and made me desperate for a proper iced tea. "I tell you, that do surprise me mightily, since you're already here. No soul comes here 'less they know what this place is."

"You're looking at the living embodiment of an exception, ma'am." I'd never called anyone ma'am in my life, but it felt appropriate with her. "Now, please, can you tell me where the hell I am?"

She frowned. "Don't be blaspheming, son. That ain't the way to get the answers you're wanting."

"Sorry, I'm under a *lot* of stress right now," I replied. "Please, tell me where I am?"

"Why, you're at the Mapmakers' Monastery."

"Pardon?"

She smiled slightly. *Yay for manners!* "This place has been here for eons, son. They ain't gonna let just anyone in, so I hope you're patient, and I hope you can withstand this here wind. If they do let you in, it'll be the greatest honor of your life. I been out here almost a month, just gaspin' to be let in. Or, rather, to be taught."

"Taught?"

"Oh yes, taught." She didn't seem eager to give too much more away.

What in the world is a Mapmakers' Monastery? Obviously it had something to do with mapmaking, unless that was some crazy false advertising. But why had Erebus brought me here?

I looked up at the monastery. Huge jewels glinted in the spires, catching the sunlight and sending shards of color bouncing between each gem. They seemed to glow as the refraction hit, and created a faint sound, like a chorus singing softly. Beneath the whipping wind, magic thrummed toward me, as if sensing my presence. I hadn't had the presence of mind to notice it before, but the energy surrounding this place was something else. It was in every particle that twisted around me, mingling with the salty breeze. If the building held this much power, there was no telling what sort of valuable secrets lay within.

Understanding came to me in a rush. Erebus had said he wanted a human form so he could find something in this world. And what did you need in order to find things? A map. And, presumably, if this was a place of learning, I would be the one to get that map for him... even if it meant creating it myself.

But if this woman had been waiting a month for the honor, how long would I have to wait to be let in?

Ready for the next part of the journey?

Dear Reader,

Thank you for joining me on this new adventure! I hope you enjoyed this book!

The next book, Harley Merlin 11: **Finch Merlin and the Lost Map**, releases **August 28th, 2019**.

Visit **www.bellaforrest.net** for details.

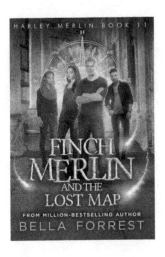

I'll see you there…

Love,

Bella x

P.S. Sign up to my VIP email list and you'll be the first to know when my next book releases: **www.morebellaforrest.com**

(Your email will be kept 100% private and you can unsubscribe at any time.)

P.P.S. Feel free to come say hi on **Twitter** @ashadeofvampire; **Facebook** www.facebook.com/BellaForrestAuthor; or **Instagram** @ashadeofvampire

Read more by Bella Forrest

HARLEY MERLIN

Harley Merlin and the Secret Coven (Book 1)

Harley Merlin and the Mystery Twins (Book 2)

Harley Merlin and the Stolen Magicals (Book 3)

Harley Merlin and the First Ritual (Book 4)

Harley Merlin and the Broken Spell (Book 5)

Harley Merlin and the Cult of Eris (Book 6)

Harley Merlin and the Detector Fix (Book 7)

Harley Merlin and the Challenge of Chaos (Book 8)

Harley Merlin and the Mortal Pact (Book 9)

Finch Merlin and the Fount of Youth (Book 10)

Finch Merlin and the Lost Map (Book 11)

THE GENDER GAME

(Action-adventure/romance. Completed series.)

The Gender Game (Book 1)

The Gender Secret (Book 2)

The Gender Lie (Book 3)

The Gender War (Book 4)

The Gender Fall (Book 5)

The Gender Plan (Book 6)

The Gender End (Book 7)

THE GIRL WHO DARED TO THINK

(Action-adventure/romance. Completed series.)

The Girl Who Dared to Think (Book 1)

The Girl Who Dared to Stand (Book 2)

The Girl Who Dared to Descend (Book 3)

The Girl Who Dared to Rise (Book 4)

The Girl Who Dared to Lead (Book 5)

The Girl Who Dared to Endure (Book 6)

The Girl Who Dared to Fight (Book 7)

THE CHILD THIEF

(Action-adventure/romance. Completed series.)

The Child Thief (Book 1)

Deep Shadows (Book 2)

Thin Lines (Book 3)

Little Lies (Book 4)

Ghost Towns (Book 5)

Zero Hour (Book 6)

HOTBLOODS

(Supernatural adventure/romance. Completed series.)

Hotbloods (Book 1)

Coldbloods (Book 2)

Renegades (Book 3)

Venturers (Book 4)

Traitors (Book 5)

Allies (Book 6)

Invaders (Book 7)

Stargazers (Book 8)

A SHADE OF VAMPIRE SERIES
(Supernatural romance/adventure)

Series 1: Derek & Sofia's story

A Shade of Vampire (Book 1)

A Shade of Blood (Book 2)

A Castle of Sand (Book 3)

A Shadow of Light (Book 4)

A Blaze of Sun (Book 5)

A Gate of Night (Book 6)

A Break of Day (Book 7)

Series 2: Rose & Caleb's story

A Shade of Novak (Book 8)

A Bond of Blood (Book 9)

A Spell of Time (Book 10)

A Chase of Prey (Book 11)

A Shade of Doubt (Book 12)

A Turn of Tides (Book 13)

A Dawn of Strength (Book 14)

A Fall of Secrets (Book 15)

An End of Night (Book 16)

Series 3: The Shade continues with a new hero...

A Wind of Change (Book 17)

A Trail of Echoes (Book 18)

A Soldier of Shadows (Book 19)

A Hero of Realms (Book 20)

A Birth of Fire (Book 69)

A Breed of Elements (Book 70)

A Sacrifice of Flames (Book 71)

A Conspiracy of Realms (Book 72)

A Search for Death (Book 73)

A Piece of Scythe (Book 74)

A Blade of Thieron (Book 75)

A Phantom of Truth (Book 76)

A Fate of Time (Book 77)

Season 10: An Origin of Vampires

An Origin of Vampires (Book 78)

A Game of Death (Book 79)

A SHADE OF DRAGON TRILOGY

A Shade of Dragon 1

A Shade of Dragon 2

A Shade of Dragon 3

A SHADE OF KIEV TRILOGY

A Shade of Kiev 1

A Shade of Kiev 2

A Shade of Kiev 3

A LOVE THAT ENDURES TRILOGY

(Contemporary romance)

A Love that Endures

A Love that Endures 2

A Love that Endures 3

THE SECRET OF SPELLSHADOW MANOR

(Supernatural/Magic YA. Completed series)

The Secret of Spellshadow Manor (Book 1)

The Breaker (Book 2)

The Chain (Book 3)

The Keep (Book 4)

The Test (Book 5)

The Spell (Book 6)

BEAUTIFUL MONSTER DUOLOGY

(Supernatural romance)

Beautiful Monster 1

Beautiful Monster 2

DETECTIVE ERIN BOND

(Adult thriller/mystery)

Lights, Camera, GONE

Write, Edit, KILL

For an updated list of Bella's books, please visit her website: www.
bellaforrest.net

Join Bella's VIP email list and you'll be the first to know when her next
book releases. Visit to sign up: www.morebellaforrest.com